LEARNING TO LOVE

"I didn't mean to scare you, Maddie. I wouldn't hurt you, not ever." He reached for her. "Come here. Let me show you." His arms moved with infinite care to encircle her, and she sat as in a dream, unable to move away.

His lips descended just as slowly; still she gave no thought to turning aside. Her only thought, as his lips claimed hers, was *at last*. At last she was in his arms again.

Then his kiss took her thoughts away, and with them, her breath. Before she knew what she had done, her hands had reached out, touched him. When she tried to move away, he caught her and, without releasing her lips, pulled her hands up his chest and fastened them around his neck.

Goldie's advice sang through her senses. *Enjoy him. Let him teach you* . . . Dare she? Oh, my, how she wanted to . . .

NO PLACE
FOR A LADY

VIVIAN VAUGHN

ZEBRA BOOKS
KENSINGTON PUBLISHING CORP.

ZEBRA BOOKS are published by

Kensington Publishing Corp.
850 Third Avenue
New York, NY 10022

First Printing: June, 1996
10 9 8 7 6 5 4 3 2 1

Printed in the United States of America

To *Arnette Lamb*
A gifted writer
A true and generous friend

One

Eagerness swelled Madolyn Sinclair's properly confined bosom. Unfamiliar as the feeling was, she recognized it. Accompanied by something soft and wonderful, it bubbled to life deep inside her and mushroomed into an impossible-to-subdue sense of anticipation.

She pressed her nose against the window of the slowing passenger car. In wonder, she peered out at the weathered depot, at the similarly weathered people, who blended with the grays and tans of the adobe buildings, the hues of dirt and dust. This was a land of no color. Even the sky seemed to have been sucked clean by the relentless wind, leaving in place of the familiar blue, an eye-piercing dome of white light.

She recognized none of the half-dozen or so booted, Stetsoned men who clustered around one end of the platform, waiting for the train to come to a halt. But then she would not recognize him right off. She knew that. She wondered whether he would recognize her.

When Madolyn realized what she was doing, she pulled her face from the window and sat properly erect in her seat. But the thrill, the joy, of finally arriving in Buckhorn, Texas, would not be restrained.

She was about to see Morley. For the first time in twenty years, she was about to see her brother.

Memories, which had augmented her anxiety on the long trip from Boston, had changed in nature. No longer were they unpleasant. As quickly as rainwater evaporated in the dry heat of this arid land, the bad times she experienced after Morley left home without so much as a word of explanation vanished beneath her tremulous sense of anticipation.

Madolyn poked a wayward curl beneath her black straw bonnet and gripped her parasol in a tight fist. She was about to see Morley, and the eagerness that flowed like a tonic through her veins was impossible to contain, even for one as strictly controlled as she. The moment the coach came to a halt, she sprang from her seat and was the first person down the aisle.

"Wonderin' 'bout that little filly yonder?"

Tyler Grant glared across the railroad tracks to the opposite depot, a mirror-image of the one from which he had watched the unloading of a fancy-stepping, honey-colored two-year-old filly named 'Pache Prancer.

The high-pitched voice of Ol' Cryer shot through his anger, as though to reinforce it. The only thing Tyler wanted to know about 'Pache Prancer was why the hell she hadn't been unloaded on his side of the tracks. But, of course, he already knew the answer to that. Absently, he pitched a quarter to the wiry little man.

Ol' Cryer hooked a thumb in each suspender. "She's Morley's sister."

A joke from Ol' Cryer? The habitually down-and-out loafer hung around the Buck side of the tracks selling news gleaned from the Horn side of town. Generally he didn't resort to charging for sarcasm; Tyler wouldn't have supposed the old codger knew what it was.

"You call that news? Everyone on both sides of the tracks knows Morley Sinclair's a horse's ass."

Ol' Cryer snorted; his shaggy white eyebrows pinched together over a wrinkled face, giving one the impression of a caterpillar that couldn't make up its mind which way to crawl. "You've been spendin' too much time with your cows, Grant. I'm talkin' 'bout that little lady standin' direc'ly in front of you yonder."

Still smarting from his betrayal by his erstwhile partner, Morley Sinclair, Tyler turned his attention to a woman who, indeed, stood directly in front of him, separated by a pair of railroad tracks. Morley's sister? Could be. Even from the rear and at the distance, he could make out a family resemblance—height and weight, leastways.

She was tall for a woman, and skinny. Definitely of waspish temperament, he decided, noting her ramrod carriage and the way one foot tapped out an impatient staccato. Another trait of Morley Sinclair's—cantankerousness.

"What burr's she got under her saddleblanket?" Even as he asked, Tyler's attention shifted from the growing mound of baggage the roustabouts continued to stack around Morley's obviously agitated sister. He turned to the original object of his consternation, the root of his petulance, the reason he had ridden into Buck today.

He watched Jed, Morley's foreman, lead 'Pache Prancer down Horn's dusty main street. The redheaded foreman and the honey-colored horse collected a crowd. Tyler pulled out a pristine white handkerchief, removed his Stetson, and mopped his damp forehead. Absently, still watching the horse and its admirers, he dried the inside band of his hat before stationing it back on his head.

It wasn't hot, yet. A month from now it would be. Today was cool. A spring breeze blew down from the Chisos. It stirred dust between the railroad ties and kicked up a dust devil here and there in the wake of the retreating horse.

Tyler was hot, but not from the weather. His agitation

was caused by his irascible partner. Morley Sinclair, damn his hide, had stolen that filly right out from under Tyler's nose. And Tyler didn't intend to stand still and let him get away with it. Morley had taken enough from him already. Although the exact method by which he could right the situation evaded Tyler for the moment, he knew there was a way to get even. He just had to come up with it.

"Morley wouldn't even meet the train," Ol' Cryer was saying. "Jed there brung her word."

"What're you mumblin' about?" Tyler's attention was trained on one thing: his partner's latest offense. He had put up with Morley's low-down, nasty behavior for close to twenty years; he had drunk and caroused with him like a brother. But all that was over. Finished. *Terminado.*

In the last six months, their relationship had deteriorated to that of enemies. If they were brothers now, it was in the vein of Cain and Abel. Tyler wasn't out to kill Morley, he admitted reluctantly, but he sure had a hankerin'—if not for murder, at least for revenge.

"Jed there brung her word," Cryer repeated.

"What word?"

"That she weren't welcome. Morley sent word by Jed for her to climb aboard that train and head on back to Boston. Said, 'Buckhorn, Texas, ain't no place for a lady.' "

"That's for sure." Tyler scrutinized Miss Sinclair, if that's what she was—a miss. He grinned. The woman standing before him was undoubtedly a spinster. No man in his right mind would have shackled himself to a toe-tapper like that. Even viewed from the rear, she gave no hint of softness. Those clothes—somber black, unrelieved by any sort of decoration he could see; hair in a tight black bun, topped by a no-nonsense black hat; parasol hoisted rigidly above her head, as though she expected it to aid her escape.

Tyler grunted. A broomstick would likely be a more fitting mode of travel for a lady with that much starch in her spine.

But the severe cut of her dress nipped her waist to a nice turn, he acknowledged. Like from the neck of an hourglass, her skirt flared gracefully into a modest bustle.

"Maddie," he mused. Yes, that was her name. Morley had spoken of her often, the little sister he left behind in Boston. She'd been what . . . ten? That would make her thirty. Definitely a spinster.

Tyler pushed his hat back on his head. The term old maid probably would fit her better. "What's she waitin' for?"

"She ain't goin'."

Tyler squinted as if to get a better look. "Not goin'?"

"Tole Jed to tell Morley she come all the way from Boston to see him, and she'll do it 'fore she leaves this godforsaken land, even if she has to walk out to his place."

"Walk?" Tyler chuckled at the idea. "I suppose she aims to carry that heap o' baggage on her stiff spine." The mound of trunks, bandboxes, hatboxes, valises and other traveling paraphernalia continued to grow as the roustabouts stacked one piece of baggage after another around toe-tapping Maddie Sinclair. Pretty soon, she wouldn't be able to see the road she appeared to be staring down so intently.

The same road Tyler had been staring down. He returned his attention to the street where Jed had led 'Pache Prancer off toward Morley's side of the ranch. The horse and foreman were nowhere to be seen. Damn Morley Sinclair!

Fury seethed inside Tyler. He had coveted 'Pache Prancer for better than a year. But try as he had to convince Morley of the wisdom of such an investment, Morley had decried the notion of raising thoroughbred racehorses on their Texas range.

At the time, Tyler had been in no position to take the horse across the river into Old Mexico. Then six months back, when the Mexican government began in earnest to run Tyler off the partners' land south of the border, Morley refused to allow him to move a single head of their livestock

to the Texas range. That was the first volley fired in the
war between the partners.

The next skirmish followed soon after, when Tyler arrived
in Buckhorn one day to find the town divided into two
parts. Separated by the rails, Horn belonged to Morley and
his supporters; Buck was left for Tyler. He was mad enough
to eat railroad ties at that.

But mad wasn't the word when Raúl Ybarra, Tyler's tophand, brought word the day before yesterday that Morley
had purchased 'Pache Prancer and that the now two-year-
old filly was due to arrive on the train today.

Like the proverbial straw, Morley's purchase of 'Pache
Prancer purged Tyler of every last trace of remorse over
their lost friendship, steeling him for revenge.

Revenge. He would get that damned horse if he had to
go out there and steal it right out from under Morley's nose.

He would—

Inspiration struck like a bolt of lightning. Digging into
his pocket, Tyler produced another quarter, which he offered
Ol' Cryer. "Tell me all you know about this sister of Morley's."

Ol' Cryer snapped a suspender against his frail, gray-
shirted chest, a gesture that always caused Tyler to cringe.
One day the bony old man was going to crack a rib doing
that. "Ain't much to it," Cryer was saying. "Nothin' more'n
I said. Minute she stepped off the train, Jed give her the
word from Morley—to go back where she come from."

"What's she doing out here?"

"Didn't say. Figured to visit her kin, I reckon."

Tyler surveyed the heap of baggage that threatened to
rival El Capitán's eight-thousand-foot elevation any minute
now. From the look of things, waspish Maddie Sinclair had
come for more than a visit, unless it was an extended one.

Tyler strove to keep from laughing out loud. He could
see Morley's reaction now! He could see it, feel it, taste it.
Who said revenge wasn't sweet? He dug into his pocket

once again. This time he tossed two quarters to the astonished Ol' Cryer.

"You and Rolly get together. Tell Miss Sinclair she's found a ride out to the ranch."

"No kiddin'?"

"No kiddin'."

"You can't take yourself out there, Grant. Those kids of Morley's have orders to shoot you on sight."

"Hell, Cryer, those kids won't shoot me. I'm a damned sight better to 'em than Morley is. Besides, I'll be transportin' their auntie. Right neighborly of me, under the circumstances."

"Right stupid of you under the circumstances." But Ol' Cryer accepted payment in advance. Shuffling to the middle of the railroad tracks, he stopped and called to a round little man of equally advanced years.

"Hey, Rolly, git yerself over here. You ain't gonna believe this."

Madolyn stood on the platform, swamped by a sickening haze of disappointment and indecision. *What to do? What to do?* The relentless, buffeting wind only added to her distress, to her sense of betrayal and abandonment. As with human fingers, it continued to strip curls from her tight bun; when a gust threatened to lift her parasol to the high heavens, she slid it closed and tucked it under her arm. Groping inside her reticule, she withdrew a gold pocket watch, which she snapped open with a practiced motion of her fingers.

Three o'clock. The train had arrived in Buckhorn two hours behind schedule, although she was beginning to suspect that might be considered punctual in this backward part of the world. Especially when one was required to reset one's timepiece at every depot. The train was due to depart for civilization after taking on a load of cattle, in a couple more hours, if she could believe the stationmaster. Two hours. With luck she could secure Morley's signature by then and be on her way home.

She flipped the watch closed and replaced it in her reticule, swiping unruly curls off her face. The pocket watch had belonged to her father. She carried it for a practical reason: She needed a timepiece. She carried it for a less practical, but infinitely more important reason, as well: to remind her that men were no damned good.

Her brother's startling response to her arrival in this godforsaken land testified to that dismal fact.

She ran a forefinger inside her high, wedding-ring collar, separating it from her irritated skin. In the heat, layers of dirt and perspiration had reacted with heavy starch to blister a ring around her neck. And they claimed the worst was yet to come. Three different people on the train had said virtually the same thing.

"If you think May's hot, wait till July."

She had worried about that, briefly. Until Morley sent word for her to return to Boston. For some reason she doubted the approaching summer had anything to do with his decision to send her home, sight unseen.

She had known he might not be overjoyed to receive the telegram announcing her arrival. He had contacted the family but once in twenty years—she took that to mean he had created a new life for himself. Which was all well and good.

Madolyn wanted a new life for herself, too, but in order to have one, she needed Morley's help. Desperation clawed its way up her chest and lodged in her throat. It took gritty control to suppress tears, but she did. Madolyn prided herself on being the kind of woman who never gave in to hysteria.

"A woman must dig deep to find the strength to survive in this man's world," Miss Abigail taught. Madolyn peered down the long, dusty road. She considered the walk ahead.

She could use a good dose of that strength right now, physical and mental.

She had no idea how far it was to Morley's. Whatever the distance, though, it was too far on feet that were so swollen they threatened to pop the laces on her sensible walking shoes.

"Ma'am?"

Madolyn started when someone tapped her shoulder. Turning, she looked her assailant squarely in the eye. Before she could berate the pudgy-faced old man who gazed up at her with the disquieting manner of a mole squinting at the sight of daylight, he removed his floppy-brimmed brown hat and held it respectfully over his heart. His bare dome rose above a fringe of untrimmed gray hair.

"Yes, Mr.—"

"Call me Rolly, ma'am. Guess you could consider me a messenger." Returning his hat to his head, Rolly swiped the back of a hand across his lips. "That gentleman yonder says he'll drive you out to Morley's."

Madolyn eyed the plump little messenger.

"Turn around, ma'am. You'll see."

Inured to things never being what they were touted, Madolyn nevertheless followed Rolly's pointing arm to a depot on the opposite side of the railroad tracks, where the imposing figure of a man lounged indolently against a post. He blended into the weathered wood and adobe as though he were part and parcel with the depot. Indeed, with one leg bent at the knee and his booted foot propped against the post, he looked for all the world as if he were trying to hold up the building. And he was certainly large enough. She had never seen a man so large.

When she caught his eye, he tipped his Stetson, nodded a silent greeting, and grinned. Embarrassed to be caught staring, Madolyn swirled away.

"Don't'cha want his help, ma'am?"

"It's miss, and no, I do not want his help."

"Then what'd you aim to do?"

"I shall find a way. Kindly direct me to the livery."

"Livery's on the other side of town, miss."

Madolyn frowned, wondering what difference that could possibly make. Everything else out here was spaced miles apart. Why should the livery be an exception? With her reticule swinging from her arm by drawn cords, she slid open her parasol, hoisted her skirts in a mitted hand, and started to walk away.

"Miss Sinclair?"

She stopped, again eyeing the round little man sharply.

"That there feller yonder's Tyler Grant, your brother's business partner."

Business partner? Madolyn turned back. This time she allowed herself a better look. He wasn't quite as large as she had thought, probably no more than a head taller than she. It was his shoulders; or maybe the vest he wore broadened his shoulders, lending him a presence that was at first glance disconcerting.

Morley's business partner? The idea fluttered like a trapped bird in her stomach. On further consideration the man didn't have the appearance of one given to sloth. At least, he looked well-kempt. His clothes were of a sort she had seen before, as one cowboy after another boarded the train: brown duck britches tucked into knee-high black boots, leather vest, Stetson. But unlike the others, Mr. Grant looked almost like he belonged in a suit and tie, not that he could buy one at the local haberdashery, were there a local haberdashery. It would take an expert tailor to fit those shoulders.

Lord in heaven! What was she thinking? Brushing a curl off her wind-stung face, she dragged her gaze away from the man, but not before one last glance revealed a shirt that actually looked white and rather crisp, like it had come fresh from a laundry.

She cast her gaze from side to side. As if anyone this far

from civilization knew what a laundry was. When she looked back, Mr. Grant had pushed off the wall, an action that elevated him to well over six feet. He was smiling again. A gasp stuck in her throat; twice he had caught her staring. How utterly coarse of her! She turned abruptly away.

"What kind of business?" she questioned through tight lips.

"What kinda business?" Rolly squinted from his round face. "Don't'cha know your brother's a rancher?"

A rancher? She wanted to say she hadn't known anything about her brother since he left Boston at sixteen years of age. At that time she doubted Morley had known any more about the ranching business than she knew at this very moment. But one could learn a lot in twenty years.

Such as the danger posed by arrogant, prepossessing men. She gathered wits that seemed suddenly scattered by the relentless wind. The devil, that's what each and every one of them must be considered. The devil in britches.

As if reading her mind, the pudgy little man continued to press Tyler Grant's case. "He's a proper gentleman, miss. Any lady on either side of the tracks'll vouch for that."

I'll just bet, she thought.

"Don't know of an unmarried lady in either town who'd turn down an offer to ride out into the country with Grant. He's far an' away the best catch aroun' these parts."

That did it! She couldn't go. Not with a known philanderer. Fortunately, she had learned in time. "Point me to the livery, Mr. Rolly."

"I can't point you to the livery, miss, on account of it's on the other side of the tracks. I already explained that."

As far as Madolyn was concerned, Rolly had explained nothing, except that she would put her reputation on the line, and possibly more, should she be foolish enough to venture into the country with Tyler Grant. She squinted toward him again, careful to avoid eye contact.

"Besides that—" Rolly's words were effectively cut short, when Madolyn gathered her skirts and stormed off the platform. "Miss Sinclair?" he called.

Indecision was not one of Madolyn's shortcomings. With a couple of hours, no more, to secure the signature she had come all the way from Boston to obtain, she would not allow one surly brother and his cowpoke partner to stand in her way.

It wasn't as if the town were deserted. Low-roofed adobe stores ran perpendicular to the depots along both sides of the road that crossed the tracks not twenty rods away. Although she didn't see a lot of activity up and down the street—not a single woman was in sight—a number of men milled on both sides of the tracks. But to a man of them, everyone in Buckhorn ignored her. Everyone, that is, except this Rolly fellow and Tyler Grant.

Well, devil or not, she didn't appear to have a choice. She wasn't getting anywhere with Rolly, and certainly, she had tangled with worse rogues than a rangy cowpoke who was her brother's business partner. She tried to take solace in the claim of an elderly gentleman on the train.

"Don't go to worryin' about your safety, Miss Sinclair, you bein' alone an' all. Womenfolk are held in high regard in the West. Penalty for accostin' a lady is death by hangin', same as for stealin' a horse."

Tyler watched from the opposite depot with growing concern. Rolly must not be doing a very good job of explaining things, for Maddie didn't appear inclined to accept his offer. Not that she was likely to receive a better one.

His first sight of her knocked him for a loop. He was expecting features worthy of a persimmon, but when she turned his way, it was to reveal fair, smooth skin and lips that looked soft and full, before they tightened in a grimace at his tipped hat. Following which, she executed an about-face that would have done General Lee proud.

He was on the verge of losing patience when she turned around and gave him another once-over. Obviously, Rolly continued to press the matter, although Tyler had issued specific instructions to Cryer not to mention the difficulty between himself and Morley.

Then of a sudden her mood seemed to change. *Just like a woman!* She stomped off the platform, skirts hiked to her shoe tops, headed directly for him, and he saw nothing for it, but to meet her halfway.

Stepping off on his side, he intercepted her at the edge of the rails. His sudden approach took her aback, he could see that in a glance. He also saw that she was much prettier than he had thought from the distance. She didn't smile—from the starch in her carriage, he doubted she knew how—but her black eyebrows had a lovely arch to them and her lips were naturally rosy and full.

He figured she had intended to bypass him and his approach caught her off guard. She stopped abruptly at the rails. They surveyed each other from the expanse of mere feet. What he saw was not what he had expected. Morley's little sister had grown up. Lordy, had she ever! *A full head of black ringlets,* he recalled Morley's description.

Loosened by the wind and what had no doubt been a harrowing journey, straggling black curls blew enticingly around Maddie's oval face. Few in number, they incited a man's interest in the rest of that thick black hair, which was secured in a tight bun at her nape. When it became clear that she wasn't going to speak first, he removed his hat and introduced himself.

"Miss Sinclair, I'm Tyler Grant, your brother's ranchin' partner."

"I've been told." Her clipped tones gave no hint of softness.

"I'm here to drive you out to Morley's." That got her attention.

"He sent you?" She cast a wild glance back over her shoulder. "Then who was that dreadful man who told me . . ."

Tyler heard the hysteria in her voice. Likely the truth was just now setting in, the truth—that she had come all this way and her brother refused to see her.

"That was Jed, Morley's foreman." He softened his tone, conscious now of not causing her more pain. "His business in town was to pick up 'Pache Prancer."

" 'Pache Prancer? Oh, the horse?"

Tyler nodded, trying to capture her gaze. Her eyes were green, like Morley's, but infinitely more appealing. Unshed tears glazed their surface, but their core was hard as emeralds, bespeaking determination and grit. Or plain old stubbornness.

"Oh," she was saying. "You mean Morley sent that Jed fellow for the horse, and you for—" She ducked her head before finishing. "—for me."

"In a manner of speakin'." He motioned over his shoulder. "I've called Raúl to bring the wagon. We'll load your belongin's and be on our way."

Relief vied with terror. Madolyn's heart raced. Up close there was no denying Tyler Grant's size. She had to look up to him, which said it all in a nutshell; she rarely encountered men she had to look up to. *Or around.* When she tried to look beyond him, his shoulders blocked her view of the opposite depot.

Her gaze darted across his face. He wasn't exactly handsome she saw now, but his features were strong and bold. Small lines etched the corners of his mouth and eyes. He looked rugged, like the country; like he had been born in this land of wide open spaces and towering mountains and was a part of it. He emanated strength and a sense of masculinity that was at once comforting and unsettling. Dragging her eyes away, she glanced up the tracks, to where a man had backed a wagon up to the railroad.

"Rolly an' Ol' Cryer will help Raúl load your trunks," Tyler drawled in a calm, matter-of-fact tone that should have put her at ease but didn't.

When she glanced back at him, she was again unable to meet his gaze directly. That appalled her. Few were the men she could not intimidate with a cold, unwavering stare. Along with her parasol and an imperious tone of voice, learned from Miss Abigail, Madolyn's direct gaze was a valued weapon against members of the opposite sex.

But this man was different. Although she had seen handsomer, it had been a city-sort of handsome and could not compare with the rugged, raw appeal of this Western man. She had never been comfortable around ladies' men. Philanderers they were, each and every one of them. Oh, he sounded harmless, to be sure, friendly even, but Madolyn knew from experience that gentlemanly behavior could be feigned.

On the other hand, he was Morley's partner. Morley wouldn't take a partner who wasn't a gentleman. Surely.

"How long have you and my brother been partners?" She chanced another peek at him as she spoke. A shock of thick dark hair fell over his broad forehead and he smelled of baywood, as though he had come straight from the barber.

Tyler studied her, contemplated his response. She was as skittish as a fawn, he could see that. One wrong word would scare her off. "A while. We've been friends for twenty years." Her countenance brightened; rather, the frown that creased her brow like a piece of corduroy relaxed.

"Best o' friends," he added, truthfully, if one omitted the last six months.

Best of friends. Memories rushed to the fore of Madolyn's brain, taking her back twenty years to when Morley was at home. Unlike a lot of older brothers, Morley had never objected to her tagging along with him and his friends. She smiled, remembering Morley, how he had made her life bearable. How she cried when he disappeared, mourned him when their father told her he died at sea. *Morley.*

She remembered her joy and confusion when, only one month ago, she discovered he was alive and living in Texas. Questions assailed her, overriding enough of her trepidation that she was able to peruse Tyler Grant a bit closer. Morley's best friend. Did Morley dress in boots and tight-fitting britches? Did he wear a Stetson? Were his shirts crisply laundered?

But this wasn't Morley. This man was a stranger. Her trepidation returned. "I'd thought to hire a carriage and drive myself to Morley's."

"It's a piece, Maddie."

Maddie? Her head jerked up. Her eyes alighted on Tyler's. They were warm and brown, she noticed for the first time. Her heart thrashed wildly. *Maddie?* She glanced from side to side, disconcerted. Here in the middle of a railroad track that ran from civilization to nowhere, this stranger had called her by a name she hadn't heard in twenty years.

Yes, he must be Morley's friend. His very best friend.

"You're surely tired from your journey," Tyler was saying.

His soft drawl flowed over her like spilled honey. Tired? She was that. Exhausted. In the misunderstanding with Morley's foreman, she had forgotten how tired she really was. And how dirty. She wiped her brow with a mitted hand, but resisted running a finger beneath her sticky collar.

Tyler watched her consider. When she wiped her brow, she left a smudge of black coal dust, like a streak of war paint, above one eyebrow. He lifted a hand to brush it off, caught himself midway to her face. What the hell? She was skittish enough already. If he touched her, she would bolt, for sure.

And she probably should. Already he was questioning his intentions to use her as a pawn in his quest for revenge against her stinkin' brother. What he would rather do—

Tyler's brain skidded to a halt when he realized that he was standing here in the middle of this damned divided town, thinking seriously about kissing Morley Sinclair's sister.

"Tell you what." His tone was more brusque than he intended, but he forged ahead. "I'll drive you over to the, uh, hotel. You can rest up, get a good night's sleep. We'll head out for Morley's first thing in the mornin'."

"The morning? Oh, no. I—"

"It's a long drive, Maddie. If we start at daybreak, we can make it there by dinnertime. That way we'll be able to return to Buck before supper."

Madolyn considered reminding this overly friendly stranger that she had not given him permission to address her by a familiar name. Then again, he was Morley's best friend. "I don't plan to return to Buckhorn, *Mr. Grant.* I've come to visit my brother."

Tyler didn't miss the chill in her tone. Her emphasis on *Mr. Grant* left no doubt how she felt about him calling her Maddie. But by damn, he gave up formalities—and a lot of other conventions society deemed necessary—twenty years ago when he fled to this land of the free, and he didn't intend to pick them up again, certainly not to please Morley Damn-his-hide's sister. He watched Raúl and the roustabouts, directed by Rolly and Ol' Cryer, load the last of Maddie's baggage onto the wagon bed.

When he reached for her arm, her gaze darted to his, then away, like a water bug skittering across a clear green pond. But Tyler didn't relent. He grasped her elbow in a firm grip, only to be startled when his hand grew suddenly warm, even through the heavy fabric of her sleeve. Ol' Cryer must be right; he'd been spending too much time with his cows. Hell, he couldn't recall the last time he escorted a lady, across the tracks or anywhere.

At Tyler's touch Madolyn flinched. She tried to jerk free,

but he held fast. *He's Morley's best friend,* she repeated. *Morley's very best—*

"We'd best get off the tracks, Maddie. Train's fixin' to move on around the bend to the loadin' pens."

Drawing her wits together, she glanced down the tracks. Sure enough, the porter had lifted the steps and climbed aboard. As if on cue, the engineer blew his whistle. Propelled by the force of it, she scrambled across. Tyler steadied her, but the moment she gained her balance, she pulled free. Her skin still prickled from his touch—and his use of her childhood name. She couldn't for the life of her decide why.

She was lonely for her brother, true, but she had learned to live with that long ago. On the other hand, she hadn't been this close to seeing Morley in twenty years. With his foreman's garbled message corrected, her earlier eagerness returned. She was on her way to see Morley. She could have skipped down the street from the sheer joy of it.

But she didn't. Madolyn Sinclair never skipped. She squashed the fleeting reminder that *Maddie* did, or had. Twenty years ago.

Tyler crammed his Stetson on his head and ushered Maddie briskly toward the wagon, careful to keep his distance. It wasn't as if he wanted to touch her. Hell, she was Morley's sister. He started to tell her as much, but he couldn't tip his hand before he used her to get back at Morley. First, he would settle her into snug accommodations on his side of town. The fact that the only hotel in Buckhorn was on the Horn side of the tracks—Morley's side—didn't make any difference. Tyler knew just the place to take the starch out of straight-laced Maddie Sinclair.

By the time they reached the wagon, she had regained her equilibrium. She shrugged off his helping hand again, gathered her skirts, and climbed up on the wagon seat unassisted. She didn't need a man's help. Never had; never would. Especially not that of a hulk of a man whose brown eyes were far too warm, whose touch peppered her insides with fiery sparks, and whose use of her familiar name brought an unwelcome longing to her lonely heart.

When she jerked away, refusing his help as though he had a plague of some sort, Tyler's patience snapped. "I'll be glad to furnish references."

"References?"

"Character references. It's obvious you think I crawled out of a hole in the ground somewhere."

His claim startled Madolyn, until she realized that was exactly how she had been treating him. And would continue to do so. She dared not relax her guard. Not with a man like Tyler Grant. Something inside her argued against judging him too quickly. He was, after all, Morley's partner. Surely she could trust him. Morley had sent him; Morley wouldn't have sent an untrustworthy man to drive her to the ranch.

Pragmatic to a fault, Madolyn admitted that, regardless of whether Tyler was a gentleman or not, if she wanted to see her brother, she had no choice but to trust him to deliver her safely to Morley's front door. She wasn't being run down by offers to help. And, regardless of her earlier boast, she could not strike out on her own, for she had absolutely no idea which way to go. From the sound of things, Morley's ranch was a bit farther than the outskirts of town.

No, her only recourse would be to follow Jed's dictum and return to Boston without seeing Morley. Which she had no intention of doing. Until Morley secured her inheritance, she had nothing to return to. The moment he did, she would leave this godforsaken land with pleasure.

"I shan't require references, Mr. Grant." She strove to sound in control of her senses, but her voice shook and she knew it. Tyler Grant was right, she was dead tired. And he was an extraordinarily distracting man. It was his size, she decided. He filled the space around her. "My brother wouldn't send anyone other than a gentleman to fetch me."

Of course, she couldn't be certain of that after twenty years, but saying it out loud bolstered her confidence. In Madolyn's experience, one method that never failed to put a man in his place was to create an image for him to live up to. If she believed him a gentleman and told him so, he would be more likely to behave like one. She took consolation in the fact that she had only to ride to Morley's in his company.

"Morley's ranch?" she questioned after Tyler climbed up on the wagon beside her. "How far is it?" His broad shoulders took up more than half the seat and she gave it to him. Moving to the far edge of her side, she readjusted her parasol and held it aloft in a silent declaration of her own space.

"Ranch house is a good half-day's ride from here."

"Then we can drive there this afternoon."

"We could make it out there before it gets good and dark," Tyler admitted. "But we couldn't return tonight. That road's not safe to travel after dark, leastways not for a lady."

His slow, almost lazy, drawl, mesmerized Madolyn. To counter its effect, she drew herself up, stiffened her spine, and called forth her most imperious tone. "I shan't be returning to town, Mr. Grant. Not right away."

Tyler cast a backward glance at her baggage, which rose shoulder-high behind them. "I don't know how else to say this, Maddie." He paused, savoring her reaction to his use of her pet name. She had the damnedest way of blanching he had ever seen. Those green eyes looked downright sultry. Not that she was likely to know what that meant. But he could— "Morley's lifestyle isn't, well, it's . . . What I'm trying to say—"

"Yes, Mr. Grant? I'm listening. What is wrong with my brother's lifestyle?"

"Nothing, accordin' to him. But, well, his house is a mite small for all this paraphernalia. I mean, we'd be puttin' everyone else out to pasture, if we were to carry all these trunks and valises and bandboxes and—"

"I take your meaning, sir."

They rode in silence.

"Your recommendation?" she questioned abruptly.

"That you put up here in Buck at the, uh, the hotel. You'll have comfortable rooms with plenty of space to stretch out. You can go and come to the ranch as you please."

Madolyn thought about it. Absently, she readjusted her reticule cords on her arm. It was a sound idea, no doubt about it. "Was that Morley's idea? Or yours?"

Tyler hit a pothole head on. "Mine, for the most part." He stared pointedly at the reticule and wondered whether it was empty or just naturally flat. "If you're short on funds, I'm sure Morley'll take care of your room and board for a few days."

"A few days?"

"For the duration of your visit," he amended. "You didn't say how long that would be."

"And you didn't ask. I told you, you were a gentleman, Mr. Grant."

"I never doubted it, Maddie. Never doubted it." He winked at her. "But you surely did."

Two

One of the few truly feminine indulgences Madolyn allowed herself was a steaming, soaking, scented bath. It was a habit rooted in childhood. To soothe her fears and anxieties, her mother would fill a tub with tepid water, pour in violet-scented salts, and set a tense, crying Madolyn into it. In a matter of minutes the scented water had combined with her mother's gentle hands and soft, rhythmic crooning to set Madolyn's world aright.

It wasn't until much later that she realized her mother's songs had more nearly resembled dirges than nursery rhymes, and that she herself had not caused her mother's tears by her terrified screams.

No one knew about Madolyn's secret passion for scented baths, which made them all the more enticing. Certainly, she had never mentioned such a shortcoming to Miss Abigail or to any of her co-workers in the Boston Woman Suffrage Society. Anything as sensual as a scented bath would be frowned upon as submitting to one's baser nature. With the plight of women in today's world, one's baser nature must be submerged at all costs.

In her heart, however, Madolyn looked upon the baths as therapeutic; they relaxed her body and soul and revived her mind for the difficult and important work she performed.

For that reason, and for a multitude of other reasons that tantalized her from the fringes of her subconscious, Madolyn had been instantly seduced, rather than offended, by Tyler's suggestion of a hot bath. And he hadn't been speaking idly, she discovered, when no sooner had the last of her baggage been deposited in the luxurious, rose-red draped parlor of her two-room suite, than a freckle-faced young man entered, lugging a sitz bath. He was followed by a short but plump maid who looked much too old and grandmotherly to be carrying two buckets of steaming water. But she managed them without spilling a drop. Finished, she rested a round fist on one hip and smiled up at Madolyn with such an affectionate expression, Madolyn half-expected a hug.

"I'm Lucky, Miss Maddie. Sure is a pleasure to have you here."

Madolyn tensed at the use of her childhood name; Tyler had been quick to spread the news. *Just like a man.* "Lucky at what?" she had asked, refusing to fret over that man. She prided herself on being able to shut out unwanted thoughts at will. She'd had enough practice, Lord only knew.

The maid laughed, setting two round cheeks to bobbling. Pink scalp peeked through thin strands of white hair that stretched up the round head to form a sparse topknot. "Lucky's my name, honey, but truth be known, I ain't been lucky at nothin' all my life. Miss Goldie, she give me the name, but it ain't changed the course of history, not so's I've recognized it." While she spoke, Lucky traipsed back and forth carrying additional bath water from a container in the hallway.

Madolyn surveyed the elaborately appointed parlor. It was so littered with baggage that one could hardly squeeze between the trunks and valises, certainly not before removing one's bustle. Her eyes strayed to the steaming water.

Lucky set a stack of flannel bathing towels on top of a trunk. "I'll be back direc'ly, Miss Maddie. You sink into that water while it's pipin' hot." She offered to help Madolyn undress, which Madolyn declined; offered to bring her a fresh gown, which Madolyn also declined.

Lucky eyed the assortment of baggage. "I could run a flatiron over a dress of your own, if you could find one." Although her tone indicated the assessment of such a search as futile, Madolyn went straight to the trunk that held her dresses and pulled out a two-pieced black faille creation, devoid of lace or decoration, and handed it to the surprised maid.

"Soak yourself, honey. When I git back, I'll make your bed so you can climb in an' take yourself a nap."

Madolyn glanced up from a valise, where she searched for bathing paraphernalia—flannel bathing cap, a long-handled back scrubber, a bar of rose-perfumed soap, and a vial of bath salts. "I never waste daylight hours in bed, Lucky." Or in a scented bath, she thought, already feeling guilty for indulging herself, when she needed to straighten up the parlor. If Tyler proved right about the size of Morley's house, she would have to arrange to store some of her belongings in town.

"I have too much to do to rest," she added. "Besides, I'm anxious to meet Mrs. Nugget." From another valise she took her silver comb set and from yet another, a complete change of underclothing.

"You mean Miss Goldie?"

"Oh, I'm sorry. It's *Miss* Nugget?"

"Yes, indeed."

"She owns a fine home."

"She surely does that, honey. Runs the place, too."

"Well, tell her I'm anxious to meet her. I'm a staunch advocate of women's rights, you see. I feel ever so much safer boarding in a private home than I would in a hotel that caters to drummers and cowboys."

This time Lucky's laughter rattled the lamp globes. *Little you know,* Madolyn thought. If women in Buckhorn had ceased to worry about their safety, the lot of women must have advanced with the westering frontier. Perhaps the gentleman on the train had been right about hanging being an effective deterrent against accosting women.

Left alone, Madolyn quickly undressed and slipped as far into the sitz bath as she could. Even by doubling up her legs, she was cramped. That was far from unusual. With her long legs, she rarely found a mattress long enough or a tub with enough room to stretch out. But that did not lessen her pleasure as the soft warm wetness slipped up her body. It soothed her swollen feet and stung her blistered neck. Unconstricted by whalebone and laces, her body relaxed.

Her mind turned to Tyler Grant. With his size he surely never found— My, oh, my! She pulled her wits together. She had never been attracted to a man, thank heavens. Until today she had never been alone with a man, even in broad open daylight. Fortunately, Tyler had proved himself a gentleman, if the most direct person she had ever met. He and Miss Abigail would make a pair.

The idea was ludicrous! But her estimate of him had risen dramatically after he brought her to this respectable boarding house. Even so, she had been taken aback that he expected her to enter by a rear staircase.

The back door! She snuggled deeper into the soothing water; its warmth and familiar rose scent calmed her. She smiled, recalling Tyler's reaction when she hesitated to obey his command.

"Just do it, Maddie," he had retorted.

Actually, if she recalled correctly, they hadn't arrived at the boarding house in too good a humor, neither of them.

She had ridden the distance from the depot pressed against the side rail of the wagon seat, and Tyler had driven the team like a man with a purpose—his jaw set, his eyes focused on the road ahead.

As though he were racing the devil, she remembered thinking, he allowed the team to barrel down the center of the road, neither steering the horses around potholes, nor slowing for corners.

Terrified, Madolyn had feared for life and limb. She clutched the seat with one hand and gripped her parasol tighter with the other, holding it aloft as if it could keep the wagon upright and its occupants seated.

When her bath water began to cool, Madolyn hurried. Her mind, however, wasn't on removing grime or relieving the aches and pains induced by her two-week trip in cramped railcars and hours spent sitting on hard benches at depots, awaiting connecting trains. Her mind was filled with Tyler Grant.

Lathering her body absently, she recalled how the wagon had hit one pothole after another, the last with such force she bounced on her bustle. It was a Langtry bustle, constructed to fold when one sat, and to spring out again when its wearer released it by standing. A comfortable invention, designed strictly for horsehair sofas, Madolyn learned, for she had bounced up and down on the hard wagon seat that had little or no padding.

"Sorry," Tyler mumbled, after hitting a pothole that more nearly resembled a meteor crater she had seen once.

"I'll just bet."

"I'm not used to drivin' draft horses, Maddie." He bit off the words with a curtness that further infuriated her.

"What do you usually drive, Mr. Grant? The four horses of the Apocalypse?"

He had chuckled at that, then surprised her by saying, "You're definitely Morley's kin." Her body flushed, recalling his soft drawl and the inspection he had given her person. " 'Course the old reprobate's not anywhere near as comely."

"Spoken like a true man." To cover her discomfiture, Madolyn had flounced on the seat, then studiously rearranged her skirts. But the battle had gone her way, for Tyler guided the team around the next pothole and slowed at subsequent corners.

To Madolyn's relief, he seemed disinclined to conversation, which suited her just fine, for she had never been one for idle prattle, especially not with a member of the opposite sex.

She used the respite to peruse the town. The train had passed through several places similar to Buckhorn, but having never ridden down their dusty streets or among their weathered buildings, she was unprepared for the harshness, the downright ugliness.

Most of the houses were small square buildings constructed from a substance called adobe, which was no more than dirt and water, if she understood correctly. Obviously she had, for Buckhorn's houses looked exactly like the earth on which they sat. They had flat roofs and deep-set windows and were surrounded by earthen yards, some swept, others unkempt.

She glanced at her driver, wondering quite without design whether his yard would be swept or overgrown with scrawny weeds. Swept, she decided, since his shirt was ironed and his britches creased. To her dismay, Tyler caught her staring at him.

His brown eyes danced over her face with a playfulness that took her aback. He looked like an overgrown child with a secret he was fairly bursting to share. For a moment her mind played with what that secret might be.

But coquetry wasn't in Madolyn's repertoire. The prospect that she might be engaging in some sort of intimate exchange further discomfited her. Redirecting her gaze to the rutted road, she scooted away, or attempted to, an action that wedged her hip into the seat bracket. She willed her heart to still.

What was the matter with her? Miss Abigail would be mortified! Why, she had almost flirted with the man, for heaven's sake. She, secretary of the Boston Woman Suffrage

Society. She, Madolyn Sinclair, who everyone agreed would someday follow Miss Abigail Blackstone as president of what was widely held to be the most active suffrage group in the country.

That is if she didn't end up in the poorhouse first.

Shouts from the left drew her attention. She watched Tyler lift a hand in greeting. Aghast, she turned quickly away from the cluster of rowdy men gathered around a— *A saloon!* Her opinion of Tyler plummeted lower than the bottomless pit of some of Buckhorn's potholes when he returned their whoops with an ear-splitting greeting of his own.

But he must be a gentleman, she insisted, striving valiantly to regain her composure. He was, after all, Morley's partner. The disconcerting truth, however, would not be suppressed. She had not seen Morley in twenty years. When he left home at sixteen, he had been her best friend. If he remained true to his upbringing, he would now be thirty-six and . . .

Not a gentleman. If Morley took after their father, he was certainly no gentleman. But he couldn't have taken after their father. Not Morley; not her beloved brother, her childhood idol.

Two blocks later, rowdy whoops again startled Madolyn. This time she felt compelled to express her disgust. "Another block, another saloon." Tyler only grinned.

"What are you, Maddie? A teetotaler or something?"

"Or *something,* Mr. Grant. I am secretary of the Boston Woman Suffrage Society."

"No sh—, uh, kiddin'!"

She stiffened her spine, savoring the satisfaction that flowed through her like a soothing cup of Earl Gray tea.

"Son of a gun! Woman suffrage has arrived in Buck, Texas."

Not long afterward, the wagon rolled to a stop beside a magnificent frame structure, diverting Madolyn's attention from her victory over the arrogant Tyler Grant. Momentarily stunned by the lovely building—three-story, freshly white-washed, cheery red shutters—she belatedly realized that he had stopped at the rear. A narrow staircase led directly from the ground to the third floor. A premonition nudged Madolyn's always-wary consciousness.

"What is this place?"

Tyler jumped to the ground. For a man his size, he was unusually agile—to her untrained eye, of course. The man called Raúl stepped from beneath the shade of a mesquite tree. He was a lanky man and wore earth-toned clothing and a large-brimmed felt hat. Several similarly-clad men followed him. Tyler executed a sweeping bow. "Buck's only hotel, ma'am."

The premonition nudged a bit harder. "I would rather go straight to Morley's." As though she hadn't spoken, Tyler motioned Raúl and the men to the baggage stacked on the wagon bed. *Just like a man!*

"Tell you what, Maddie. Let us move you in here. Get some rest, and bright an' early tomorrow mornin' I'll drive you out to Morley's. If you still want to stay out there after seein' the, uh, place, I'll come back to town and haul every last stick of this stuff out there for you."

Lost in thought, she ran a finger inside her collar, reliev-ing a bit of the sting. "You're certain Morley's house isn't suitable—"

"As certain as I am that your eyes are green, Maddie Sinclair."

Madolyn slumped against the sitz bath, faint even now, recalling the rush of heat that had swept through her. She scrubbed her face with the rose-perfumed soap she had or-dered from an advertisement in *Godey's,* attempting to re-move all traces of the uncharacteristic blush she feared had blossomed again, just thinking about the intimacy.

Tyler hadn't seemed to notice the hornet's nest he'd stirred up inside her. He rounded the wagon, offered her a hand, and Lord in heaven, if she hadn't placed her hand in his.

She, Madolyn Sinclair, who had vowed never to rely on a man for help in her life. Well, not after she prevailed upon Morley to claim their inheritance, of course.

Fortunately, she had the presence of mind to jerk free the moment both feet were planted on solid ground. Perusing the whitewashed house with its red shutters, she knew she should be relieved that Tyler hadn't taken her to some rat-infested shack. And she was. The only frame house in town, he claimed. It looked comfortable and respectable—except for the fact that they were gathered around the rear staircase like a band of thieves.

"Isn't there a front door?"

"Sure, there's a front door."

"Then I shall find it, Mr. Grant." She hadn't taken more than a couple of steps, however, when Tyler caught her elbow and pulled her around.

He nodded toward the stairs, drawling, "Easiest way to transport your baggage."

"Perhaps, sir, but I do not require transporting." Even as she spoke, her swollen ankles and aching feet protested the possibility that they might be required to climb such a steep flight of stairs.

"Quickest way to a hot bath and soft bed," he coaxed.

Tired as Madolyn was, dirty as she was, those words went right to the heart of her. She knew instantly that she desired nothing else in the world, at least not for the moment.

"As soon as I register, Mr. Grant—"

"For heaven's sake, Maddie, stop ditherin'; you'll work up a sweat. I'll send Goldie upstairs to take your money."

"Goldie who?"

"Uh, Nugget, I guess." He bobbed his head at the house. "This is her house."

"Her house? You mean . . . ?" Suddenly Madolyn felt

like an imbecile. A private home. Of course. No wonder it was so well kept. A private home, with the top floor for boarders. "You mean paying customers aren't allowed to use the front door?"

Tyler's brown eyes practically popped from his head at that. He laughed out loud. A full, rich, bass-toned, straight-from-the-belly laugh.

Leaning her head back against the tub, Madolyn closed her eyes and let the remembered sound trill down her spine. It was a rare sound, a good, soothing sound. It had invited her to laugh, too. But of course she hadn't. With a strange sense of loss, Madolyn realized she couldn't recall the last time she had laughed.

"Boarders use these stairs," Tyler had agreed, after he stopped laughing. Even then, however, the corners of his mouth twitched and his eyes danced with that conspiratorial expression she had noticed earlier.

She had gone willingly, then, with thoughts of a hot bath soothing her tired body. Her aching feet slipped only once on the staircase, and Tyler had been right behind her. He caught her with a firm hand to her waist. And Lord help her, if she hadn't gained strength from it. Briefly she allowed him to support her.

Briefly. She hadn't needed his support. But afterwards, the climb seemed somehow easier, with his strength rising as a buttress behind her. Before she knew it, she was standing in the middle of this elegantly appointed suite. Both rooms were draped and carpeted in rose-red. The furniture was of fine-quality walnut, and the brass chandelier sported burgundy glass globes.

The luxury was a surprise; the plump-mattressed bed beckoned. Shortly afterward, young Clements and Lucky arrived with the tub and hot water, and Tyler took his leave.

He paused, hat in hand. His bulk filled the doorway. "Listen, Maddie, I, uh . . . Don't be nervous here. My rooms are across the hall, an' I'll . . ." His words drifted off. His gaze alighted on the sitz bath, then darted to a trunk. "I'll be going. See you in the mornin'."

"Fine."

He didn't leave, however, but stood in the doorway, looking again like that overgrown child with a secret to tell; this time it was a worried child. "Sure you're all right?"

"Yes. Thank you, Mr. Grant."

His warm eyes held hers, and she allowed it, unable for some reason to look away. At length, he nodded curtly, turned to leave, paused again. "Remember to use the back stairs."

His discomfiture concerned her. When he was gone, she stood momentarily stunned, by what she couldn't guess. The steaming water beckoned her tired muscles; her feet fairly cried to be out of her heavy, sensible shoes. As soon as Lucky left her alone, she disrobed and slipped into the piping water of the first real bath she had taken in two weeks. And an hour later, she secretly admitted it had been every bit as refreshing as she had known it would be. Not only had she cleansed her body, but her peace of mind had been restored.

After drying with the flannel bathing towel, she rubbed cream into her skin from hairline to the bottoms of her feet, paying careful attention to the blistered ring around her neck.

Next she rubbed ample cream into each elbow, recalling her mother's admonition not to let her elbows get rusty. As a child, Madolyn had worried about that. Were rusted elbows like rusted hinges? Would they squawk when moved? Or refuse to move altogether? Later, learning the meaning of the term, she wondered why it mattered whether one's elbows were rusty. No one ever saw them. Now, she knew that the sensuousness of caring for her body somehow restored her sense of well-being. Not that she would ever admit as much to a single living soul.

Wrapped in a soft flannel robe, she knelt on the floor

beside the tub and began to scrub her hair. How good it felt! At a knock on the door, she started.

"Miss Maddie?"

Lucky.

"I've brought more hot water. If you want, I'll help wash your hair."

What luxurious treatment guests received here! Dare she indulge? "Oh, yes, Lucky, that would be wonderful. Come in."

By the time Lucky finished scrubbing Madolyn's scalp with hands that were both strong and gentle, the remaining traces of tension had vanished and Madolyn felt ready to tackle the world, as Miss Abigail would have said.

"Wrap your head in this towel, honey, and let me look at that neck of yours."

"My neck?"

"Mr. Tyler said your neck is plumb blistered."

"Mr. Grant?" Abashed at the notion that a man, Tyler Grant, no less, had taken such intimate note of her person, Madolyn felt her face grow warm again. Another blush? From one who never blushed? Until today, it seemed.

"Yes'm, Mr. Grant, honey. He told me to smear some of this on your blistered neck. Skinned it hisself, he did, with that Bowie knife o' his."

"Skinned it?" Madolyn grimaced at the slimy, green mass Lucky held toward her. She couldn't recall any slimy green creatures crawling around, but she certainly hadn't seen everything this strange country had to offer, not by half. "Is it . . . was it . . . alive?"

Lucky guffawed. "Don't you go to worryin' 'bout that, Miss Maddie. This here's a cactus plant called *aloe vera*. Miss Goldie grows it outside the back door for medicinal purposes."

Slimy though it was, the sticky substance soothed Madolyn's stinging skin. While Lucky busied herself making the bed, Madolyn retired behind a floral dressing screen, where she pulled on soft clean pantaloons, chemise, and stockings, and began lacing her corset. "Thanks for the bath," she called over the screen. "I feel human again."

"Don't go gittin' used to baths on a reg'lar basis, honey. Water's scarce as hen's teeth in these parts. Generally we don't take baths 'cept of a Saturday, an' then ever'one shares the same water. Draws straws to see who goes first."

Never far from the surface, Madolyn's guilty conscience blossomed. "Oh, my." She hesitated a moment, then offered, "If another lady would like to use this water, please invite her in."

"You sure it wouldn't put you out none?"

"Indeed not."

With that permission, Lucky left, only to return a few minutes later, accompanied by a petite young woman clad in the most outlandish costume Madolyn had ever seen— wide-legged green satin trousers that ended at the girl's white calves, topped by a matching kimono. Her hair was tied in a towel, turban-style.

Madolyn stood in the doorway between her bedroom and parlor, holding her own properly tasteful black skirt. She must have been gaping, she thought later, for the girl turned big, kohl-outlined eyes to her.

"Hi, Miss Maddie. I'm Annie, but you can call me Penny-Ante. Ever'body does." Speaking, the young woman flung wide the lapels of her green kimono and, before Madolyn knew what was happening, dropped the garment in a puddle at her feet, exposing two extra-large, softly-rounded, bare white breasts.

Madolyn spun away.

Annie giggled. "Don't worry about modesty. We ain't a bashful bunch of— OUCH!"

At the girl's scream, Madolyn turned back to see Lucky with a fistful of Annie's copper-colored hair. The turban was nowhere in sight, and Annie's naked body was thankfully submerged in Madolyn's dirty bath water.

"Shut your mouth, Penny-Ante," Lucky was ordering. "Git your bath and git outta Miss Maddie's parlor so's she can have some peace an' quiet."

Madolyn hastily completed her toilette, her brain astir. She donned her bodice, pinned on her brooch, and twisted her thick wet curls into a tight bun at her nape. She adjusted her proper black bonnet, picked up her reticule, and entered the parlor, her eyes carefully averted from the immodest bather.

"I'll swan but don't you look like an angel, honey."

"Thank you, Lucky. Could you kindly direct me to Miss Nugget—"

"You gonna work for—"

"ANNIE!" Lucky bellowed. "I told you onct an' I don't aim to tell you agin. Hush your mouth. Git your business finished and git outta Miss Maddie's parlor."

Outside in the hallway, Madolyn attempted to organize her flustered thoughts. Annie must be a maid, or perhaps another boarder. But her outlandish costume looked more like . . .

With grim determination, Madolyn pulled her thoughts away from the impossible. When she headed for the back staircase, however, her feet refused to oblige. What a ridiculous rule. Why should she be required to traipse down two flights of steep stairs, round the house on the outside, and knock on the front door? Even with her laces loosened at the top, her ankles were beginning to swell again.

Surely she would not disturb anyone's sense of propriety by using the central staircase. Of course, she wouldn't. If Madolyn's mother had taught her anything, it was proper etiquette, and nothing she ever heard instructed a lady to use the back entrance of a private home. Obviously Mr. Grant's education in such matters was lacking.

The carpeted stairs wound from the third-story to the foyer below in a sweep of elaborately carved walnut newels.

Madolyn felt rather grand taking them, even on wobbly ankles.

"Evenin', Miss Maddie."

She stepped onto the second floor landing to the greeting of another young woman, this one clad in a floral satin dressing gown. Caught in the midst of dressing for dinner, Madolyn assumed. "Good evening." She resisted fanning to clear the air of some exotic, but potent fragrance.

"I'm Dolly." The woman brushed slender fingers across the chest of her shimmering, silver-colored garment. "Folks call me Silver-Dollar."

"How nice to meet you, uh, Dolly." Madolyn glanced around. The second floor hallway looked exactly like the one on the third floor, except the carpet was a bit more worn. Threadbare down the center, for that matter. No doubt this was a large and active family.

"I'm looking for Miss Nugget."

"Goldie? She's downstairs. Call out when you reach the bottom. She'll come a-runnin'."

Madolyn smiled hesitantly. She couldn't quite see herself stepping into the foyer and shouting for her hostess.

Dolly hurried to her rescue. "Where're my manners, Miss Maddie? Come on, I'll show you to Goldie."

On the way to the stairs, two more ladies joined them—Daphne, who claimed the improbable nickname of Gold-Dust; and Bertie, called, incredibly, Two-Bit. Each wore a separate fragrance, applied with equally heavy hands.

Surrounded by a growing entourage of scantily clad ladies and a cloud of their mixed scents, Madolyn continued to the foyer. Then suddenly, midway down the staircase, the disconcerting truth struck her with the velocity of a winter storm. Without warning, it screeched through her brain and left her cold with dread that her premonition could be—might be—true. She halted on the staircase; turning, she scrutinized the ladies who followed behind her like a flock of doves.

Surely not. But . . . Madolyn scanned their billowing masses of hair—Dolly's was black, Daphne's the color of mahogany, Bertie's was blond, and upstairs Annie was washing her copper-colored mane in Madolyn's dirty bath water. Although Madolyn had never to her knowledge set eyes on artificially colored hair, something told her these colors were not the natural shades given the women at birth.

Her gaze darted from the flocked wallpaper in the stairwell to the brass, burgundy-globed light fixtures. Suddenly everything seemed garish instead of luxurious. She thought of the threadbare carpet and in her mind heard boots tramping up and down the hall and raps on doors and . . .

Tyler Grant's rugged face rose like a giant specter through the fog in her brain. Fury vied with revulsion. Panic rose in billows, blinding her. Turning swiftly, she raced down the stairs. In her haste to escape, she forgot to hold her skirts. She tripped. Caught her balance.

The next thing she knew, her right foot had slipped out from under her. She reached for the banister, but the carpet was slick, and her ankles were weak in her loosely laced shoes. With effort she managed to land on her bottom a couple of stairs down. Her bustle collapsed.

A hand reached for her from behind, but when Madolyn began to slide, she brought the helping hand, and its attendant body, along with her. Lord in heaven! She wanted to crawl under the carpet and die. Miss Abigail would be mortified!

Then all thoughts of Boston and Miss Abigail and woman suffrage fled before the most basic of human needs—survival. A body landed on Madolyn's shoulders, flipped over her head, and tumbled to the foyer floor, which was by now only three or four stairs distant. She heard a shriek. Surely it hadn't come from her own lips.

She felt another bump; a second body thudded into her from behind. Voices, shrill with panic, shrieked all around. "Miss Goldie!"

"Help!"

"Miss Goldie!"

"Come quick!"

With a kaleidoscope of satin colors blurring her vision, Madolyn tumbled into the body sprawled before her on the foyer floor; two others landed on top of her. Everything fell silent. No one moved. Mixed scents of heavy perfumes clogged the air.

She struggled to unearth herself from the layers of bodies. But she was effectively scotched in place, with a knee to her stomach, a foot to her back; someone's buttocks pressed against her inner leg, and Lord in heaven, if the perfume didn't choke her, the bosom mashed against her face surely would.

Had she died and gone to hell, to find, not fire and brimstone, but tangled masses of reeking, half-clothed bodies? *Miss Abigail would be mortified!*

A robust voice boomed through the melee. "Bertie! Daphne! What on earth is going on? Get up from there."

The ladies on top of Madolyn scrambled to untangle their satin clothes and bare limbs.

The moment she was free to sit, Madolyn struggled upright.

"Here, Miss Maddie, let me help."

That voice. The fall had cleared Madolyn's brain of the panic that precipitated it, but Annie's voice brought the situation back in a rush of nausea.

"I'm Penny-Ante."

"I remember." Madolyn accepted the offered hand of the girl who had used her dirty bath water.

Gaining her feet, she forced a tremulous smile, thanked Annie, straightened her skirts, and swept back a loose curl. When she reached to right her bonnet, which had shifted to the neighborhood of her left ear, Madolyn's gaze rested on the woman who stood eye to eye with her, fists on ample hips.

Billowing henna-tinted hair drifted around the painted face like storm clouds. Although older than the others, and larger, this woman, too, was garbed in a kimono, hers a brassy gold silk. Her air of command clearly put her in charge.

Madolyn clasped her arms with opposite hands to still the trembling that rumbled from deep within her. What on earth was she doing in this place?

The woman raised eyebrows, which, even to Madolyn's untrained eyes, looked artificially arched and colored. "I'm Goldie, Miss Sinclair. We're mighty pleased to have you with us. Believe it or not, we aren't in the habit of tacklin' our guests."

"Unless they come upstairs wearin' spurs," one of the girls quipped, to the accompaniment of a chorus of giggles.

Madolyn stared aghast. She understood the ribald tone, even if the exact meaning of the statement escaped her. She glanced from one grinning girl to the next. What was she doing in this place?

An oppressive weight descended on her lungs, forcing her breath out in a heavy, ragged gush. When she tried to inhale, the mixture of thick sweet fragrances choked her. Her gaze darted to the front door, which stood open. Its screen was decorated with elaborate wooden scrolls and cutouts of cupids and hearts and, heaven forbid, dollar signs.

Around her the girls continued to giggle.

Through the screen, Madolyn glimpsed a swept yard, a shade tree, the open sky. With no thought except to draw a breath of fresh air, she fled. Bursting through the screen, she crossed the porch, only to be brought up abruptly on the top step by a blinding flare of light.

Everything around her turned black. Inside her head brightly colored circles spun dizzily out of control. It was the voices that brought her back to the real world. Voices of the girls.

"Tyler!"

"When'd you get to town, big boy?"

"Welcome home, stranger."

"Long time, no see, honey bun."

Madolyn opened her eyes to clear vision and muddled thoughts. A black-draped tripod stood in the front yard, the kind used by photographers. She watched a small man disentangle himself from the heavy drape. He peered out at her with a wide grin, made even wider by the broadest blond handlebar mustache Madolyn had ever seen. A black derby topped his head, and in his hand he held a flash.

"Miss Sinclair," he called. "Welcome to Buck, Texas." Before she could think what to do, the flash went off again. Again, she blinked. Again, she heard giggles, this time from either side.

When her vision cleared, she saw them, settled on the porch railings around her—Bertie, Annie, Dolly, Daphne, and the soiled dove in charge of the flock, Goldie Nugget, who stood shoulder to shoulder with her, Madolyn Sinclair, secretary of the Boston Woman Suffrage Society.

Fleeting thoughts of Miss Abigail's reaction to such a travesty left Madolyn physically ill. Lifting her skirts to ankle height—she had no intention of precipitating another debacle like the one that occurred inside—Madolyn stormed off the porch and down the steps.

She marched straight toward the photographer, wagging a forefinger in his direction. "I don't know what you think you're doing!" Advancing upon the startled man, she vented her rage. "I did not give you permission to—" A form behind the photographer caught her eye.

As if she had been struck by lightning, Madolyn stopped in her tracks. Tyler Grant, looking ten feet tall and every inch of it menacing, leaned against the trunk of a mesquite tree, chewing on a twig. He watched her from beneath hooded brows, which she now realized gave him the appearance of wearing a perpetual frown. An erroneous impression, for his eyes fairly danced with mischief. The devil, she thought. Tyler Grant was indeed the devil garbed in britches and boots.

The photographer forgotten, Madolyn changed course and headed for Tyler. "You are just the man I want to see, sir."

"Now, Maddie, I can explain—"

"I don't recall giving you permission to address me as if I were your . . . your . . ." Madolyn twisted her neck to glare back at the soiled doves who watched as if with single vision from the porch. Then she saw the sign. It hung from the eaves—a white sign, painted with red and gold letters: HOUSE OF NEGOTIABLE LOVE. Her heart pounded against her stays. Her knees turned to jelly. No wonder he had taken her to the back door. Miss Abigail would . . . Perish the thought!

When she turned back to him, Tyler had shoved his hat back on his head and removed the twig from his lips. His eyes still danced. "As if you were my what, Maddie?"

"You insolent, despicable . . ." Furiously, she clamped her jaws together. "You are exactly like every other man I have ever known. You get your thrills at the expense of innocent women. Well, I, for one, will not stand for such treatment, sir, not from you, not from any man." She gathered her skirts. "How dare you bring me to a . . . to a . . ." She shot a glance toward the photographer who stroked his mustache and watched her without flinching. Indeed, instead of retiring beneath her scrutiny, he stepped forward.

"Price Donnell, Miss Sinclair. Editor of the *Buckhorn News.*"

The newspaper! Lord in heaven! No doubt, not only the photograph of her standing on the porch of the House of Negotiable Love surrounded by the town's soiled doves would appear in the *Buckhorn News,* but an account of the tongue-lashing she had given Tyler Grant, as well.

What would Morley think? Suddenly the feeling of betrayal struck home. If Morley had come to fetch her, none of this would have happened. But he hadn't. Now she realized he probably had not sent Tyler Grant. Whatever reason Tyler had for lying—

Before she lost all will to do so, Madolyn turned on Tyler. If Mr. Donnell wanted a story, she would oblige him. She had stood up for other women in her day, why not for herself?

"You are even more wicked than I guessed, Mr. Grant. It takes a devious mind to move a lady into such a place, then call the local newspaperman to publish her presence there."

"Now, Maddie, I didn't know you were—"

"Never address me by that name again, sir."

Turning swiftly, she stomped out of the yard, stormed into the street, and marched defiantly away from the House of Negotiable Love, unmindful of the direction she took, heedless of her destination. All she knew was that she had to get away, as far away as possible, as quickly as possible.

Embarrassment and fury whirred inside her, blinding and deafening her to anything else, until at length the train whistle pierced her wall of anguish. In the distance she spied the railroad tracks. *The train.*

Morley sent word for her to return to Boston. Well, that's exactly what she would do. She might starve after she got there, but at the moment starvation was definitely the lesser evil.

She picked up speed. When her brain cleared a bit more, she realized that she had only a pittance in her reticule. Certainly not enough money to get her home. Probably not enough to purchase passage back to Abilene.

Perhaps she could persuade the conductor to wait until she sent someone to that wretched house for her belongings. That's what she would do. Surely she could persuade—

"Maddie!"

Tyler's voice struck her like an arrow fired by a savage.

Even though her ankles wobbled painfully in her loosely laced shoes, she charged ahead.

The train whistle blasted again. She fought to clear her mind, to think. The train had headed west of town to load cattle; the stationmaster said it would leave for points east at five o'clock. Or thereabouts. She had no idea what time it was. It seemed like an eternity since she arrived in this godforsaken land. She dared not stop to check her timepiece.

Then she heard Tyler's boots, stomping up behind her. Running boots. Coming fast. Gaining.

She ran as fast as she could with loosened laces and swollen ankles. Her gait was uneven, hobbling, but she reached the railroad tracks. Tyler was close behind, shouting at her.

"Damnit, Maddie, stop."

She leaped to get across the tracks. For some reason, she felt certain her safety depended on her reaching the other side. Once there, she could hail the train. Once there—

Her shoe slipped on the steel rail. Her heel lodged between the fishplate and tie bar. She yanked. Her ankle twisted. She winced.

"Maddie!"

Wriggling her foot, she tried to slip it out of her shoe, but only the top was loose; the bottom laces held her foot firmly in place. Tyler caught her by the shoulders.

"I can explain, Maddie."

"Get your hands off me." Struggling, she refused to look at him. His grip tightened. A sense of futility swept over her; her eyes glazed with moisture.

Tears? From her? Madolyn Sinclair? Absolutely not. Fiercely she struggled to free herself. She bent forward; he bent over her. His bulk encompassed her. In her despair, she forgot her foot and concentrated on freeing herself from this wretched man.

The train whistle blared. Stricken, she glanced up. The

sound had come from around the bend. The engine wasn't in sight—yet.

"We've gotta get off the tracks, Maddie." Tyler grabbed her around the waist and tried to pull her onto the grading. But her heel wouldn't budge.

"Damnit, Maddie, come on."

"Get away from me. Let me—"

"Come on—"

"Get out of my way." Wishing for her parasol, she tried to fend him off by jabbing her elbows into his solid midsection. "Turn me loose. My shoe's caught. I can't get my foot—"

Tyler held her so close, she felt him gasp. In an instant, he released her. She watched him glance toward the bend in the tracks, even as he knelt to free her foot. "How the hell did you get caught like this?" He fumbled with the laces.

"It's your fault," she accused, wriggling her foot.

"Be still, will you?" The train whistle blasted again.

She looked up the tracks, then regretted it, for at that moment the front guard, the cow-catcher, folks called it, rounded the corner. Like a monster out of the Middle Ages, the engine hurtled toward them belching smoke. The whistle blared in a succession of quick, sharp blasts. The conductor leaned out the side. He shouted at them. His words were obscured, but his meaning was clear. Wheels screeched against rails in an obvious attempt to stop the advancing train. She looked down at her foot.

"Hurry, please." Her words were no more than a whisper. Tyler couldn't have heard her, she knew that, but his warm hand tightened around her ankle.

He glanced up. "Hold on, Maddie. I'll get you out of here." His brown eyes spoke of confidence, and somewhere deep inside she trusted him.

While she watched, almost as stunned by her reaction to this man as by the difficulty she found herself in, he withdrew a long-bladed knife, dipped the point into the center of her shoelaces, and sliced them apart from toe to top. Of an instant, he had sheathed the knife, scooped her in his sinewy arms, and rolled the two of them off the tracks and down the grading. The train screeched to a halt within inches of where she had stood. She felt the life drain out of her. Relief began to seep into the void. Relief and disbelief.

She couldn't recall the last time she had fallen to the ground, lain there in a heap of tangled arms and legs. Certainly not since she reached adulthood. Yet, in less than an hour, she had found herself in just such a position, not once, but twice. She didn't know whether to laugh or cry.

Neither of which she was in the habit of doing. But she had never been almost run over by a train before, either. Her fear was real, palpable.

Tyler's expansive shoulders and strong arms sheltered her, and for the moment, she was content to lie there, shoulder to the ground, face buried in his solid chest, effectively shutting out thoughts of anyone who might be gawking at her unseemly behavior. Indeed, when she felt his arms loosen, she glanced up, tensed against the trembling that overtook her.

"It's all right, Maddie. You're safe now."

His soft drawl stroked some unknown chord deep within her. His tone carried an undercurrent of teasing. She realized suddenly that everything he said was voiced in such a tone. When she tried to bury her face in his chest again, he nudged it up with his chin to her forehead.

She saw concern in his brown eyes, a touch of worry, and questions. His embrace formed a sheltering barrier between her and reality. His burly arms protected her; his large hands gathered her to him, making her feel small, delicate, and secure, none of which she had ever felt in such abundance.

"You all right?"

She nodded, but the tenderness in both his tone and his expression were too much. Tears rushed to her eyes.

"You're safe, Maddie." Taking her by complete surprise, his face dipped, his lips brushed hers. It was the briefest of contact. But, oh, my! What earth-shattering sensations! *A kiss!* It was a kiss, wasn't it? She had never been kissed before. Not in all her thirty years.

A shiver sped down her spine. She saw in his eyes that he felt it. He winked. Then before she could dredge up one single, coherent thought, his lips descended again.

Suddenly she came to her senses. She remembered where she was, who she was. Madolyn Sinclair. Secretary of the Boston Woman Suffrage Society. Miss Abigail would . . .

Moving swiftly, she dodged his lips, extricated herself from his arms, and jumped to her feet. Daring to look neither left nor right, she attempted to flee. But his hand closed around her arm. In one deft motion he halted her escape and brought her around to face him.

His warm gaze bore into hers, intense now, serious. "I didn't send Donnell to take your photograph, Maddie."

"I'll just bet."

"I didn't."

"Well, you certainly took me to that . . . that house."

"Hell, it's the only place in town, thanks to your brother. I mean, the only place to board. Goldie uses the top floor for boarders."

"And for what else?"

Storm clouds gathered in his brown eyes, turning them as cold as a harsh winter day. His Stetson had fallen off in the melee, and a shock of dark hair fell over one brow. At length, he grinned wickedly. "You really want to know?"

Incensed, she yanked to free herself, but he held her by two hands now. "You are despicable, sir."

"Didn't I warn you to use the back staircase?"

"Men! I should have known not to trust you." Even be-

ore she finished speaking, his broad brow had begun to
arrow. "You're despicable," she charged. "A beast, a—"

"In that case . . ." He jerked her to him. This time he
idn't stop with a soft brush of his lips; this time his mouth
round against hers, warm and wet and harsh.

She struggled to free herself, but he held her in a fierce
grip. When she tried to kick him, he moved his legs out of
he way. Just when she thought he intended to set her free,
applause erupted from both sides of the tracks. His kiss
took on urgency.

Embarrassment flushed Madolyn with the heat of a wild-
fire. Yet, suddenly she felt tired and weak and curiously
safe here in the shelter of Tyler's encompassing embrace.

Tyler's embrace? She wasn't sure when he had taken her
in his arms. But here she was, leaning against his sturdy
chest, feeling his heart race, his arms on her back. The spot
where each of his fingers made contact left a little heated
circle on her skin, even through her clothing.

When at length he lifted his lips, his gaze delved into
hers with mute questions. Without speaking he rested his
forehead against hers, while they stood, breathing heavily,
both of them.

Finally he set her aside. "Think you can hobble back to
the house, or should I carry you?"

Carry her? Were she the swooning type, Madolyn felt
sure she would have succumbed to vapors at such a suggestion, uttered, she doubted not for the benefit of the gawking townsfolk.

Miss Abigail would be mortified!

"If you think I'm going back to that—"

Her words came to an abrupt halt when Tyler scooped
her in his brawny arms and strode off down the street. Disconcerted, she debated whether to set up a ruckus by kicking and exposing her pantaloons and petticoats to the
barbaric populace of this town or to wait until he set her
down to vent her wrath.

A spectator to her disgrace dashed out of the crowd and slapped Tyler's Stetson on his head.

"Thanks, Buster."

He didn't break stride. "I'll expect you to thank me for this later, Maddie," he told her in that half-jesting drawl of his. "Cowboys don't take to walkin' any better'n we take to drivin' a wagon."

Three

By morning Tyler Grant filled her life. Throughout the sleepless night, his memory permeated her mind with the same nauseating effect of the bad perfume that suffused his house. In the harsh light of day she blamed him for all the wrongs that had been visited upon her in the past twenty-four hours.

He was, after all, Morley's best friend. And brother or not, Morley had let her down.

Tired as she was, she hadn't slept a wink. Daylight found her exhausted from tossing and turning, from trying to exorcise Tyler Grant from her mind, and from worrying about her future. For one solid month she had yearned for a hot bath and a soft bed with clean-smelling sheets and enough legroom to stretch out her knees. And what good had either done her?

Relieved to learn that Morley hadn't intended for her to return to Boston sight unseen, she had enjoyed the bath. But everything after that had gone downhill at the pace of a runaway team. By morning she had reached an inescapable conclusion: She had made a grave error in judgment by coming to this barbaric land. Her actions had been rooted in emotion, and emotion, as Miss Abigail steadfastly maintained, had led to the downfall of many a well-bred lady.

Penniless in Boston was looking better by the minute. But she wasn't in Boston—she was in Buckhorn, Texas, which she suspected must surely be the last stop before the gates of hell.

A loud knock at her parlor door was followed by Lucky's call. " 'Mornin', Miss Maddie. I've brung your breakfast."

Tears, which Madolyn had fought all night, threatened again. She pressed the heels of her hands into her eyes and let the ensuing black circles soothe her. *What to do? What to do?*

"I'll bring it back later, if you ain't ready."

"No." Madolyn jumped from the bed. "Come in, Lucky." She shrugged into a batiste wrapper and struggled to find her common sense. Common sense, which she desperately needed to see her through this day and at least one more. After that, surely she would have gained Morley's signature on the papers she brought for him to sign. As soon as she secured that signature, she would board the next train for Boston.

In the meantime, the immediate present, she must decide how to comport herself around a houseful of soiled doves and an outrageous man who obviously planned to turn her into one.

She opened the door to Lucky's cheery smile. "Mornin', honey. Hope you slept well."

Madolyn cast a hasty glance across the hall to Tyler's closed door. "Well enough, thank you." How could she admit the heinous truth, that squeals of laughter and cries of delight from the second floor had jarred her awake every time she drifted off?

More disgraceful yet, that each and every time she awakened, her first thought had been to wonder whether Tyler was a participant in the debauchery. How could she face the man this morning?

"Fried you a hen egg to go along with the steak an' gravy an' biscuits," Lucky was saying. "Miss Goldie insisted. Said no tellin' what you're liable to find out at your brother's."

She watched Lucky pour tea from a porcelain teapot into

a matching cup. "It doesn't matter what I find. I am well beyond hoping for anything more than his signature."

"Some of Miss Goldie's store tea. She uses it for a quick pickup."

"Tea?"

"Reckon store tea seems too civilized for a wide spot in the road like this. Sassafras or even—"

"Oh, no," Madolyn broke in, eager to avert a repeat of the scene the evening before when she arrived back at the House of Negotiable Love.

After her attempted escape and the disastrous turn of events at the railroad tracks, she had had little stomach for facing the soiled doves again. But she endured Tyler's march back to the House, biding her time until they were out of earshot of the crowd at the depot before she would revile him for intruding in her life. Her efforts, however, ended like everything else she had attempted since her arrival, dismally.

"I'll thank you to put me down," she had spat at him the moment they were alone.

Tyler hadn't broken stride, but carried her as effortlessly as if she were a feather—she, Madolyn Sinclair, who had never been anything but gawky.

"Now, Maddie," he had drawled, "you should be thankin' me for savin' your life, not beratin'—"

Somewhere along the way, she had lost her bonnet and most of her hairpins. Her hair hung in thick waves, embarrassing her further. No one had ever seen her hair down, not since she gained adulthood. "I could have saved my own life."

"Sure. With your heel wedged in the fishplate and your laces tied in knots."

"My laces were not tied in knots, sir."

"I beg to differ."

"Differ all you like."

"Your laces were tied in knots and the train was barrelin' down and—"

"I could have saved myself if you hadn't—"

Without slowing his determined pace, Tyler had grinned—actually grinned. "I know what's got you riled, Maddie. It's that kiss."

Madolyn's heart raced at his suggestion—or reminder. "Oh, is that what it was?" Her boldness startled her. Almost as much as it did him.

He stopped in his tracks. His expression turned serious and she realized with a start that his patience was thinning. "You know damned well, it was."

For a moment she couldn't speak, for quite literally, her heart had jumped to her throat. Seeking to return to a safer and to her mind a more pressing subject, she warned him, "I shan't return to that despicable house, Mr. Grant."

His waning patience snapped. She could see it in his brown eyes, which were suddenly neither warm nor teasing. "Another thing, Miss Madolyn Morley's-sister Sinclair. You're to treat Goldie and her girls with respect."

"How dare you—"

"No, how dare you? An advocate of woman suffrage, by your own admission, a champion of women's rights, passin' judgment on the way other women are forced to make their livin'."

Madolyn stared at him, wide-eyed. Fury pounded in her heart and throbbed in her throat. She looked away from his assessing stare, not liking the verdict she saw there. "There is always another way to make a living."

"Reserve judgment, at least till you're out from under their roof." He bounced her in his arms, drawing her attention back to him. Before she could berate him further, he added, "Promise me that, or I'll leave you to sleep in the street."

She glared at him.

"Trust me on this, Maddie. I'll leave you right here. And good riddance."

Embarrassment battled with anger. "How dare you dress me down in such a . . ." She cast her eyes wildly from side to side, slightly relieved to find that they were still alone. But that didn't make him any less right. Or her any less wrong.

"Promise?"

Madolyn gritted her teeth. "I can't be gone from this place soon enough."

"Is that a yes or a no?"

"I shall keep my mouth shut about what I think of . . . of . . ." Nothing she could say fitted into the realm of topics suitable for a decent woman to discuss. Surely he got the idea.

"That's a start," he said good-naturedly. "But I'll require more before I carry you up those two flights of stairs."

"The back way," she instructed.

"Any way you cut it, Maddie, it's two flights."

"The back way, sir, or I shall not go."

Abruptly Tyler set her on her feet in the middle of the road and started off toward the House of Negotiable Love. Tears stung her eyes. "You are a beast, sir. Every man out here is a beast."

Tyler turned, studied her, finally tipping his hat. "Then Morley Damn-his-hide is right, this is no place for a lady."

She watched him stride confidently toward the house. Gathering her skirts, she hobbled after, one shoe on, one shoe off. Her twisted ankle throbbed unmercifully, but she made it back to the house and up the steep back staircase.

Entering her room, she found a welcome surprise— Lucky and a tub of warm water.

"Mr. Tyler tole us 'bout your mishap, honey. Take off that stockin' an' sit down right here. Soak your ankle in these salts while I fetch you a tray of supper."

While Lucky was gone, Tyler poked his head in the door. His ominous presence filled the doorway. She glared at him.

"Still not ready to thank me, huh?"

"Get out of here, Mr. Grant, before you have me shrieking like a shrew."

He grinned, glanced around at the stacks of baggage, then settled his brown gaze on her naked foot. She flushed in spite of herself.

"I suppose it's safe to assume you brought along another pair of shoes."

"Of course, I brought another pair of shoes."

"Well, search 'em out, Maddie. We'll leave for Morley's first thing in the mornin'."

"I shall find another way, thank you."

"What is it with you? You keep thankin' me for things I haven't done. Somebody ought to teach you gratitude, Maddie." He winked. "Maybe I'll have a go at it myself."

It was a confusing statement, one Madolyn pondered off and on all night. Now, with the clear light of day, she sipped Miss Goldie Nugget's store tea and chastised herself.

"Hope that ankle's not swollen on you this mornin', Miss Maddie," Lucky called from the bedchamber where Madolyn could see her making the bed. *What luxury!* And at what a price! Her pride, her dignity, and if that wretched Tyler Grant had his way, her immortal soul.

"It's fine, thank you." Madolyn shook out the crisply laundered white napkin. It reminded her of Tyler's shirt. She paused, lost in thought. Where did he have his shirts laundered? She examined the napkin absently. Here? Who? How—

"Miss Goldie sends her apologies, honey." Lucky tucked a pillow beneath her chin and tugged on a freshly ironed pillow case. "Said you're not to worry 'bout runnin' into her or the girls. They'll keep their distance while you're with us."

Guilt, which Tyler had successfully pricked the night be-

fore, reared its ugly head again. "Oh, Lucky, I didn't intend
to offend her or any of you."

"We know that. Mr. Tyler should have tole you what
kinda place he was bringin' you to, 'fore he moved you in
lock, stock, an' barrel."

"That's water under the bridge." She sipped the tepid tea.

Lucky laughed. "Now there's a sayin' we don't hear much
of out here."

"And it's no excuse for rudeness. Would you tell Miss
Nugget that the accommodations are most comfortable. I'm
sure they shall be the most pleasant part of my stay in Buckhorn. I appreciate her hospitality. And yours, Lucky. I'm
sorry for—"

"No need apologizin'. You didn't offend no one. The girls
got a good laugh out of it. And Miss Goldie, too. Now you
eat up 'fore your breakfast gets cold. Mr. Tyler'll be waitin'
to drive you out to your brother's."

"Oh, no. I shall find someone else."

"Mr. Tyler says he's agonna do it."

"But surely . . . I mean, he must have a lot to do at the
ranch. Surely there's someone I could hire to drive me to
Morley's."

"If Mr. Tyler says he's agonna do it, he's agonna do it.
This here's Mr. Tyler's town, and what he says goes."

Madolyn hadn't realized she was so hungry. She stuffed
the last bite of biscuit in her mouth and stared at her empty
plate. "His town?"

"Yes'm, his town."

"That sounds like feudalism."

"Nope, honey, sounds like jes' what it is. Two men ownin'
all the country aroun' here. Mr. Tyler an' your brother. But
don't you fret none. Ain't a finer gentleman aroun' than
Mr. Tyler."

"Then Buckhorn is certainly hard up for gentlemen!" But
she whispered the response, mindful not to offend this
kindly woman again.

* * *

It had been a bitch of a night. Generally Tyler enjoyed the nights he spent in town. He would drink a while in the parlor, then come upstairs and climb into his soft bed, pull up sunshine-fresh sheets, and let himself be lulled to sleep by the tinkling of Elmo's piano, which was faint as fairy-music by the time it drifted up two flights of stairs. Only rarely did he accommodate himself with a trip to the second floor of the House of Negotiable Love. That was never the reason he came to town.

At a knock on his door, he pulled on his duckins, ran fingers through his hair, and opened the door.

"Brought your things, Tyler."

"Thanks, Annie."

"An' your breakfast."

Tyler watched the slight, copper-haired girl peek into his room. "Thanks," he said again. "Here, let me take these things." He examined the two crisply laundered shirts. "Beautiful, as usual." When he reached for the breakfast tray with his other hand, Penny-Ante Annie held on.

He could tell by the way she wrinkled her nose that his peculiar behavior confused her. Generally, he invited her in, flirted a little, and that was the end of it. He glanced to Maddie's door, relieved to see it closed. Damnation, had that stiff-spined woman gotten under his skin? While his thoughts were distracted, Penny-Ante slipped past him. Jittery as a June bug, he watched her set the tray on his tea table.

Still he stood in the open door, as though his feet were fastened to the floorboards. He held the laundered shirts in one hand, unmindful of his bare chest, his bare feet, or of the top two buttons on his fly, which were undone.

Annie uncovered his plate and poured his coffee.

"Don't bother with that," he said. "I'll take care of it."

She looked up, a coquettish grin on her rosy lips. "Missed you downstairs last night, Tyler."

"Yeah, well . . ." Voices came from beyond Maddie's door. Must be Lucky, bringing Maddie's breakfast. "Listen, Annie, uh, you'll have to excuse me. I'm facin' a bitch of a day."

She sidled up to him, twirled an index finger playfully in his exposed navel. "Too bad, Tyler."

At that moment, Maddie's door opened. Tyler started. Penny-Ante giggled. "What kinda day was that you said, Tyler? Doin' what? Or should I say with—"

"Mornin', Mr. Tyler."

Tyler stood, unable to move, his attention focused on Maddie's door. "Mornin', Lucky."

But the maid had already shuffled down the hallway, and standing in the open door was none other than Miss Maddie Sinclair, herself. She was draped from chin to toe in white batiste; her green eyes were soft with astonishment. He watched her take in his half-clothed body. He took her in, too, as though drinking his fill of some exotic concoction from the bar downstairs. Not too sour, not too sweet—but highly intoxicating.

Black hair flowed in abundant waves around her shoulders. Disheveled waves, that indicated she hadn't brushed it since she arose from bed. His groin tightened at the sight of her, looking every bit as though she had just climbed out of bed. He was hard-pressed to keep from wishing it had been his.

He barely heard Penny-Ante's coos. "Well, Tyler, reckon you'd better get started on that *promisin'* day." She scooted off down the hall, leaving him to gape at Maddie.

Suddenly he realized he was standing there half-dressed. He glanced down at his bare feet. Not even half-dressed. When he looked back at Maddie, he could almost read her thoughts.

"It isn't what you think." He turned to the staircase where

Penny-Ante had disappeared, all except a few wayward strands of copper-colored hair. "She didn't sl . . ." He cleared his throat. "I mean . . . she just brought . . ." Damnation, what had this woman done to him? Why did he care what she thought? His love life—or lack thereof—was his own business and certainly none of Miss Madolyn Morley's-sister Sinclair's.

"Daylight's wastin', Maddie. Get dressed and meet me downstairs in an hour."

"I'll find another—"

"Damnation, don't you ever let up?" He ran fingers through his own disheveled hair. "I had a bitch of a night, so don't rile me. Just get yourself dressed."

Convinced that she had no choice, short of leaving town without setting eyes on Morley, Madolyn allowed Tyler to drive her. Not until she took her place on the wagon seat beside him, however, did she allow herself to admit how frightened she was. Her stomach tumbled and she felt rather faint—unusual, for she had been blessed with a sturdy constitution. But, of course, she was about to see her brother for the first time in twenty years, a brother who hadn't even bothered to meet her train. Miss Abigail herself would likely have stomach flutters on such an occasion, delightful, though it would surely turn out to be.

With no more than an arched eyebrow Tyler had taken the valise she packed. He even inquired about her ankle.

"Fine." She refrained from thanking him for his inquiry.

They skirted the towns and headed north, following a double-rutted wagon road that grew ever fainter the farther they traveled from town. Tyler guided the wagon along the slope of a mountain. Although up close the terrain looked less barren than it had from the train window, it was still a desolate land.

Again she thought how devoid of color the landscape

was—grayish brown tufts of grass, with here and there a touch of green; strange-shaped trees and cacti with stranger-sounding names, some of which she had heard on the train—foreign names, like cholla and agave and Spanish dagger. Made the more exotic by the occasional vivid blossom—a pure, waxy white or magenta, or oranges and yellows so brilliant they must have come from the sun itself. The rare splotches of color formed delightful oases for the sight in the midst of an otherwise colorless desert.

A desert populated by no humans, she surmised, for they neither met nor passed anyone for hours. At length the isolation encroached around her, surrounding the wagon as with an invisible barrier. She wished the rails ran through here, then she wouldn't feel so alone. With a man.

A man like Tyler Grant, who smelled fresh and clean, with just a hint, a satisfying hint, of baywood; a man who filled the wagon seat as he had filled her night, making it impossible not to bump his shoulder or, heaven forbid, his knee. As before, she staked her space with a lofted parasol.

Tyler's contradictory personalities confused her. He could be kind, gentle even, like when he arranged for her to have a hot bath or to soak her injured ankle. But he could be harsh, cruel almost, like when he left her standing in the road.

He was decisive, no doubt about that. He took charge of matters in a way that lent her a sense of security she rarely felt with anyone, especially with a member of the opposite sex. Of course, some of his decisions were opposite to what she would have chosen. But that didn't seem to faze him.

And he was passionate. Lord in heaven, she felt weak recalling the way her baser nature had responded to his passionate attack. Still wanted to, truth known. But as Miss Abigail taught, one's baser nature must be suppressed at all costs.

Deliberately, Madolyn tucked the edge of her skirt beneath her leg, removing the fabric from contact with Tyler's britches. She gripped her parasol tighter and tried to do the same with her emotions. She had been in dangerous situations before, many of which, unlike her present difficulty, had been foisted upon her unawares. This time she had been amply forewarned. Dismally she recalled Mr. Rolly's words:

Don't know of an unmarried lady in either town who'd turn down an offer to ride out into the country with Tyler Grant. Madolyn's palms grew wet; her fingers stuck to her cotton gloves and her gloves in turn slipped on the handle of her parasol.

"Damnation, Maddie, put that thing down before you poke out my eye."

Disconcerted, she jerked her parasol upright. "If you had hired a carriage, sir, I wouldn't have need of a parasol."

"A carriage? Where the hell would I have found a carriage? Consider yourself lucky I didn't make you ride a horse."

Madolyn huffed, discomfited by his proclivity for treating her as though she had no sense at all. But of course she had been treated like that before. By every man she had ever known. Every man except Morley. Even when she was only ten, Morley had treated her as an equal.

"I'll thank you not to swear in my presence, Mr. Grant."

"There you go again. Thankin' me for the impossible."

She eyed him furiously.

Flicking the reins over the draft horses' rumps, Tyler winked at her, turning her already-squeamish insides into a writhing mass of anxiety. She tried to think of a retort, but her brain seemed made of the same queasy mush as her stomach.

Tyler stared down the road, aggravated that he had broken his self-imposed aloofness. If he bickered with Maddie all the way to the ranch, he wouldn't be prepared to confront Morley. Throughout the night he had tried to plan his strategy for approaching Morley about 'Pache Prancer, but every time he attempted to call forth an image of that honey-colored horse, he saw instead green-eyed Maddie Sinclair. By morning he had relived every image his brain had stored away of her, every word they had exchanged, every touch, every taste . . .

"Tell me about Morley, Mr. Grant."

Tyler glanced around at the softening in her tone. Her eyes held his briefly, then skittered back to the road, where her gaze remained fixed on the dim trail. He studied her profile a moment, examined the parasol—rather, her grip on it.

He had figured it was the wind whipping the thing around, but now he saw differently. Maddie was shaking, trembling to be more exact. Damnation, was she afraid of him? What the hell had he done this time? Even handing her onto the wagon seat, he had taken care not to touch her in a familiar way. And he certainly hadn't threatened her since they set out.

"Morley?" he repeated. "What about him?"

"He was sixteen the last time I saw him. He must have changed since then."

Tyler grunted. "Count on it."

"In what way?"

"Wait an' see, Maddie," he hedged. "Don't let me ruin your surprise." Then they rounded a curve, and Tyler figured Maddie's surprises were about to commence.

Madolyn's heart flew to her throat at sight of the slight figure who stepped into the roadway from out of nowhere. She gripped the seat with her free hand and gaped at the sight.

A barefooted creature, he wore baggy britches, topped by what looked like a brightly striped blanket. When he removed the oversized hat, she saw a tousle-haired boy of no more than fifteen. But the shotgun he held in his hand was aimed at them.

To be accurate, it was aimed at Tyler.

"Alto, tío. No puede pas—"

Madolyn's mouth was as dry as the landscape looked. She stared from the boy to Tyler, who sat with no more than a bemused look on his face. Using a congenial tone she considered inappropriate for such desperate circumstances, he spit out a stream of words in Spanish. Madolyn checked to see how the boy took that, and was doubly alarmed to find him staring at her with an expression of unabashed curiosity.

After another exchange in Spanish, the boy stepped aside. Tyler clucked to the team.

"Adiós, Jorge."

"Adiós, Tío Tyler."

Mesmerized by the shotgun-wielding child, Madolyn kept the boy in her sights as they passed him by. "Who was that? What did he want? Why—"

"Don't work yourself into a dither, Maddie. The kid's name is Jorge; that's Spanish for George, George Washington, to be exact. He's guardin' Morley's livestock."

"Livestock?"

"Cattle."

But Madolyn wasn't listening. She had seen the boy's black wavy hair, his vivid green eyes. "Who is he?"

Tyler shrugged. "Just a kid."

"He's Morley's son."

Tyler turned wide eyes to her.

"He looks just like Morley did when he was young." She watched Tyler's Adam's apple bob. "Morley's complexion wasn't as dark," she conceded, "but his hair was like that. And his eyes. Those green eyes."

Tyler stared a moment into her own green eyes, but she couldn't read his expression.

"Stop," she instructed him. "Stop this wagon."

"Now, Maddie . . ."

"Don't *now, Maddie* me, Mr. Grant. Stop this wagon. Turn around. I shall speak with the boy." Anticipation fluttered impatiently inside her. "He's my nephew."

Tyler sighed, exasperated.

"Isn't he?"

"Suppose so," he mumbled, refusing to meet her eye. By this time he had stopped the wagon, but instead of turning it around, he called to the boy, who came running. After a rapid-fire exchange, the boy doffed his hat to Madolyn.

"Hola, Tía Maddie. Bienvenida."

"What did he say?"

"Hello, Aunt Maddie. Welcome," Tyler translated.

Madolyn's breast swelled against her corseted ribs. *Aunt Maddie.* "How do you do, George Washington Sinclair. I am most delighted to make your acquaintance."

The boy grinned.

"Doesn't he speak English?"

"Not much," Tyler responded.

"Not much?" Madolyn perused the boy again. Bare feet, in a land where every plant had thorns. And a shotgun. Threatening people with a shotgun! Whatever had become of Morley to allow his son to run around unattended this way?

"Climb in," she told Jorge. When he didn't budge, she motioned to the wagon bed. "Tell him to climb in, Mr. Grant."

"Now, Maddie . . ."

"Just do it, Mr. Grant."

Tyler shoved his hat back. "What are you up to?"

"I'm . . ." Madolyn stared from the boy's quizzical expression to the treacherous landscape. When her gaze alighted on Tyler, her mind was made up. "We shall take him home, where hopefully he has a pair of shoes."

"Now, Maddie, I wouldn't—"

"And I shall replace that shotgun in his hand with a schoolbook."

"Maddie—" When she tried to interrupt, Tyler held up his hand. "This is none of your business."

"None of my business? The boy is my nephew."

"Not necessarily."

"You said he's Morley's son." She smiled at Jorge. "Even if you hadn't, I would have known. He's near the age Morley was the last time I saw him. And the spitting image, except for—"

"Be that as it may, Jorge has a job to do, and he's out here doin' it. You'll play hell meddlin' in Morley's business." He frowned at her. "Likely I know Morley better'n you do, and I'll be frank. He won't cotton to a stranger meddlin'—"

"I am no stranger, sir."

"An unfamiliar relative, then. Meddlin's meddlin', Maddie, any way you cut it."

"If this is how Morley treats his son, it's high time someone meddled in his affairs."

Tyler watched Jorge study Maddie from beneath the brim of his sombrero. The boy seemed to be wavering between curiosity and downright confusion. If he could understand one half of what his auntie had planned for him, he would likely hightail it into the brush. Tyler grinned.

The moment he spied Maddie tapping that toe at the depot, he had known she was an old maid of the first order. Now she was proving it. She was about to wreak havoc on Morley Damn-his-hide Sinclair.

"Tell you what, Maddie," he drawled. "Leave Jorge to his chores an' you can take it up with Morley when we get there."

Madolyn gazed longingly at the boy. How she would love to climb down off the wagon and hug him close. But she didn't, she couldn't. She didn't even know how to do something so bold.

Standing before her was her nephew, her own flesh and blood, as near as she would ever come to having a son of her own. Not her business? This child was most definitely her business. "I suppose you're right," she relented. Still craving contact with the boy, she extended a mitted hand.

After prompting from Tyler, Jorge took it. Madolyn couldn't tell how he felt about her. Obviously he wasn't as captivated by this unexpected turn of events as she was. But he wasn't as old as she was, either. He hadn't lived through the hell she had lived through after Morley left; he hadn't grown to adulthood and faced the terrible, sad and lonely fact that she had—that she would never have anybody to call her own, neither a husband, nor a child. Morley was all the family she had or ever would have.

At least she had thought so. Until this moment.

She closed her hand over Jorge's dirty one, then held it a moment longer when he attempted to pull away. "George Washington Sinclair. How lovely. How utterly lovely. It proves your father hasn't entirely lost sight of his heritage, naming you after the founder of our country."

They proceeded along the dim road. Mountains ringed the horizon in the distance. The land that ran up to them was flat, the vegetation sparse, with a few straggly shrubs and even fewer trees. But suddenly, Madolyn felt much less isolated and lonely than an hour before, than a year before. Than for the last twenty years.

She ran a finger between her collar and skin. Heat built quickly in this country. Already her collar was damp, and her skin had begun to prickle. No matter. Nothing could dim her joy. Regardless of how this journey turned out now, she would never regret it. Not for one moment. She had gained a nephew.

Tyler whipped up the horses. By damn, but this little endeavor was turning out better than he had hoped. Miss Maddie was fixin' to turn that no-good brother of hers every way but loose, and Tyler intended to sit back and enjoy the fireworks. Morley Damn-his-hide was in for the floggin' of his life and he deserved every lash of her viperous tongue.

A mile or so down the road they rounded another curve and encountered another child. Dressed identically to Jorge, the boy stepped out to bar their passage with a similar shot-gun. "Whoa, Tomás," Tyler called. *"Es Tyler, tu tio."*

The child flipped the sombrero back from his head. Mad-die gasped; her parasol fell from her hand and lay unat-tended on the wagon bed at her feet.

"Another one?"

"Maddie, meet Thomas Madison. Tomás, for short."

She squirmed on the seat. Extending her hand, she greeted the bewildered child with more exuberance than Tyler had seen her display yet in their brief association. The smile she turned to Tyler confirmed his worst suspicions— Maddie Sinclair was not only a handsome woman, she was a woman with a very human and possibly even a warm heart, regardless of the cold front she erected for the world to see.

He could tell she fairly itched to get down and grab hold of the boy. Such a move would likely surprise Tomás as much as it would her. Somewhere deep inside, Tyler wished she could work up the gumption. She deserved a little pleas-ure, before meeting up with that surly brother of hers. As before, she repeated the boy's name in hushed tones.

"Thomas Madison Sinclair. My, oh, my."

"How old are they?" she asked when they rode off, headed, once more, for the ranch house Morley Damn-his-hide had stolen from Tyler, along with their Texas range and 'Pache Prancer.

"The boys? Let's see . . . Jorge would be fourteen, if I'm countin' right. He was born the same year we settled here. And Tomás is two years younger."

"Fourteen and twelve. My nephews are fourteen and twelve." She turned a beaming face to him. With a start he saw that warm heart glow in her earnest green eyes.

"Certainly of an age where education is important," she mused. "Most important." Then they rounded a curve and encountered the third of Morley's sons.

"Hola Abe," Tyler hailed. "Abraham Lincoln," he informed Maddie.

A mitted hand flew to her breast. "Abraham Lincoln Sinclair."

"¿Ouantos años, Abe?" Tyler inquired.

The boy shrugged. Tyler repeated in Spanish the tale he told the other boys: Morley's sister had arrived from Boston for a visit and he was transporting her to the ranch. No need for alarm. He wasn't about to start a shootin' match with their auntie in the wagon. He wasn't sure they understood the concept of aunt. Other than to call him *tio,* or uncle, they had never known any relatives. But his explanation seemed to work, for Abe, like his brothers before him, lowered his gun.

Or was it the effervescent reception they received from Maddie? She startled them, intrigued them, delighted them. He could tell that. And by damn if she wasn't beginning to have the same unsettling effect to him.

"I figure Abe is ten or goin' on it," Tyler explained when they were once more on their way.

"Fourteen, twelve, ten," she mused. "Jorge, Tomás, Abe. Three little nephews. And I didn't even know they existed."

Tyler thought how her surprises were just beginning.

"Since they don't speak English," she began, "I shall—"

"Damnation, Maddie. Stop your—"

"I shall have to learn Spanish," she finished with a supercilious tone that ordinarily would have set his teeth on edge. That it didn't was cause for worry.

A few bends in the road later, Tyler drew rein in front of the smallest child yet. This boy, like his brothers before him, held a shotgun steady, barring their progress.

"Little Jefferson Davis is eight." Tyler said. "I know that, for a fact."

Astonishment took its toll, silencing Maddie, another fact Tyler felt inspired to investigate one of these days.

Little Jeff was more inquisitive than his brothers had

been. *"¿Tía?"* he repeated after Tyler explained who Maddie was. Tyler nodded.

The little boy's eyes danced from Tyler to Maddie, then back again. *"¿Tía y tío. Tío y tía?"* He sang the phrase backwards and forwards, startling Tyler with such an association.

"What is he saying?" Maddie questioned.

Unwilling to explain and feeling the fool for it, Tyler shrugged and headed for the ranch house, which lay just around the next corner.

"Jefferson Davis?" Maddie inquired. "However did Morley settle on that name? He didn't marry a Rebel, did he?"

Tyler chuckled. "Little Jeff's named for me." The insipid expression Maddie turned on him reinforced Tyler's notion that four nephews in one morning had taken a bit of the starch out of her.

"My ties to the South," he explained. "I hail from Georgia, ma'am. Atlanta, Georgia."

"A Rebel?"

"Johnny Reb, himself." He winked, experiencing an alarming sense of light-headedness in the presence of this spinster. "But the war's over, Maddie."

Then they arrived at the ranch house—if the two-room adobe hut could be called by such a highfalutin name—and Morley made a liar out of him. This war wasn't over, not by a long shot.

Tyler drew rein under a mesquite tree, where he had hitched the reins over a low limb and stepped around to assist Maddie down from the seat before Morley saw them. One thing was clear as rainwater: In the month since Tyler had last seen him, Morley Sinclair had lost none of his belligerence.

"How the hell'd you get out here, Grant?" Morley stomped toward them, bellowing. "Those harebrained kids let you through? I'll blister ever'one of 'em." When Tyler didn't respond, he continued to bluster. "You ain't gettin' your hands on that filly."

Tyler's hands tightened on Maddie's waist. He lowered her to the ground, then turned her to face Morley. "Thought maybe we could work out a trade, Morley."

Beside him Maddie straightened her waistcoat, then her skirt. Tyler didn't miss her trembling hands; hell, he could practically feel her nervousness. That is, if he hadn't been so busy feeling like a first-class heel, he would have. When she reached for her parasol, he stopped her.

"I'll fetch it, Maddie. Go ahead and greet the ol' sonofabitch."

Morley's belligerence evaporated like a puffball on a hot summer's wind. "What the hell . . . Maddie?"

Four

Morley. Madolyn gaped at the stranger, stupefied. He bore little resemblance to her brother, not nearly as much as did his sons. He was older than when she last saw him, of course; she had expected that. He was larger, too, much larger. Although he could still pass for lean, he had filled out and looked solid now—his shoulders, his girth. He and Tyler were similarly built. But Morley had a paunch.

Like Papa.

Weakness swept over her at the comparison. She forced herself to search for some sign of her beloved brother in the man who stood defiantly before her. Her assumption about his attire had been right: He wore duck britches stuffed into knee-high boots, vest, chambray shirt, and Stetson hat. Like Tyler.

Unlike Tyler, she corrected. For there was nothing well-kempt about Morley. Indeed, he could more accurately be described as slovenly. His hat was sweat-stained and grimy. His shirt had probably never seen starch or a flatiron.

About the only familiar feature on the man was his eyes, green eyes that took her in even as she stood before him. His assessing gaze left no doubt that he found changes in her, too.

He removed his hat, revealing wavy black hair, now streaked with gray. Morley, her brother, gray-headed.

"What're you doin' here, Maddie? Didn't Jed tell you to go back to Boston?"

"Jed?" She turned to Tyler, who glanced away too quickly. "Yes, he did, but Mr. Grant explained—"

"Well, you should have done it. What'd you mean, gettin' this sonofabitch to drive you out here?"

Madolyn steeled herself against the disappointment she had expected. After all, she was here uninvited. And although she had longed to see Morley, obviously he had not been all that anxious to see her. "Mr. Grant was the only person who offered."

"Well, you shouldn't have let him. You shouldn't have got off that train on the wrong side of the tracks."

"The wrong side . . . ?"

"Hold on a cockeyed minute, Morley. No need to take it out on Maddie. She didn't start this fight between you and me. Truth is, she doesn't even know about it."

As her nephews had done earlier, Madolyn struggled to comprehend the conversation taking place around her.

"You shouldn't have come, Maddie," Morley was saying. "This ain't no place for a lady."

She glanced around. From what she had seen so far, she tended to agree with him. The house—could that hut be considered a ranch house?—was small, no more than one room, with an even smaller addition made of some sort of dried pickets or stalks. The roofs on both sections were thatched, both sagged.

The barn, or what she supposed was a barn, was adobe, also, and a little larger than the house. It was surrounded by a picket fence that probably formed a corral.

The buildings sat in the middle of nowhere. The land surrounding them stretched to infinity, which shrunk them even further in one's perception. A distant ridge of blue mountains ringed the western horizon. Two trees were in sight, only two: the mesquite Tyler hitched the team to, and another one out beside the barn. Indeed, from every angle, this was a hostile, barren land.

Returning her attention to the man before her, she

squinted through the harsh midday sunshine, trying to see her brother in this stranger, who was every bit as hostile as the landscape.

But stranger or not, he was still her brother. A deep sense of sadness suffused her. Not ten yards away stood the brother she had cried for and mourned; the brother she had longed impatiently to see. Envisioned as a reunion with the prodigal son, their meeting was nothing like she had expected—or hoped.

Angrily, she fought tears. Hope had never come easy for her, but, after believing Morley dead for twenty years, upon learning that he was alive and living in Texas, she had been unable to suppress a swelling of hope. Now once again hope had let her down. When Tyler touched her shoulder, she started.

"Go ahead, Maddie. He might sound rough around the edges, but he won't bite. You were brave enough to come all the way from Boston; surely you can stand up to one reprobate of a brother."

Madolyn drew a shaky breath. Tyler was right about it taking courage to have made the journey. But that was nothing compared to standing here now, facing a brother who was sorry to see her—and beside a man who had obviously used her for his own gain. Whatever the trouble between Tyler and Morley, she wanted no part of it. "I need to talk to you, Morley. To tell you—"

"That the old man died?" Morley spat a stream of brown chewing tobacco juice off to the side. "You wasted good money to come out here an' tell me that filthy old man died?"

"Papa left—"

"I don't care what he left, Maddie. I don't want a damned red cent from him. Go on back to Boston where you belong. You can have it all."

She glared at the hostile stranger who shouted at her like she hadn't been shouted at for three blessed years—not since Papa lost his mind. What peace she had enjoyed then. Even at the cost of a guilty conscience, the peace had been a welcome respite. Now, it seemed, she was faced with another battle.

She squared her shoulders, straightened her spine, and stepped toward him. "Not without your help."

"I ain't interested." Morley turned, dismissing them.

"Morley, please," she called. "Let me explain. I need your help . . ." Pausing, she glanced toward Tyler who wore a pained expression. Pity? Well, she didn't need his pity. He had done enough already. Perhaps if she had come alone . . .

"Papa didn't leave anything to you," she told Morley. "But I can't have it either, not without your help."

"That's no concern of mine."

"It is." One glance at this run-down operation revealed that Morley needed Papa's money almost as badly as she did. "I'll gladly share the inheritance, if you will help me get it."

"I told you. I don't want one red cent—"

Of a sudden, Tyler stepped around Madolyn, grasped Morley's arm, and swung him around.

Morley shook him off. "Get your goddam hands off me."

Tyler grabbed another handful; this time he held on. "Hear her out, Morley. I don't know what this is all about, but I do know that Maddie is one spunky female. If she says she needs your help, by damn, she needs it."

"What's it to you, Grant?" Freeing himself, Morley quickly went on the attack. "Don't go lookin' toward my corral. That filly's mine. M-I-N-E."

"This isn't about a horse, Morley. It's about your sister."

"Then take her back to town and see her off to Boston."

The air was suddenly rent by the ear-splitting sound of metal clanging against metal that reminded Madolyn of the train that had barreled down on them the day before. Tyler reached toward her, touched her shoulder, a brief, reassuring gesture, no more. But she relaxed, feeling secure in his presence. She had never known anyone so acutely attuned to another's feelings.

"Carlita!" Tyler called.

Following his gaze toward the house, she saw a woman clad in black, who lifted a hand in response to Tyler's greeting.

Tyler nudged Madolyn again, this time toward the hut. "Looks like we're in luck, Maddie. You haven't lived until you've eaten Carlita's cooking."

"No, you don't!" Morley bellowed after them, but Tyler was already halfway across the swept yard. With a hand to the small of her back, he ushered Madolyn toward the squatty little woman.

It was an intimate gesture, one that fired her deep within. She should object, of course, but with the disappointment of Morley's rejection, she couldn't dredge up even one ounce of outrage. Indeed, she welcomed warmth from another human being.

What was she doing so far from civilization? Why on earth had she thought she could traipse halfway across the country and find ladies and gentlemen like in Boston?

Rather, she had found ruffians and barbarians—

Like in Boston!

They stopped at what Madolyn took for the back door of the hut, although it was the only door she saw. She realized immediately that Tyler had been right. She couldn't move her baggage into this place. If indeed, it was Morley's home, which didn't seem possible. It wasn't large enough for a family with four growing boys. Nor sturdy enough. The wind that continually whipped this country clean must surely blow through chinks in the walls. Why, the inside must—

"Carlita," Tyler was saying, "meet Maddie, Morley's sister."

Stooped from hard labor, Carlita looked ancient until she

met Madolyn's gaze, at which Madolyn realized the woman could be no older than she, if that old. The subservient manner in which she dipped her head, dispelled Madolyn's initial impression that she was meeting Morley's wife. Until Tyler spoke again.

"Mother of your nephews."

Morley's wife? She didn't look old enough to be the mother of a fourteen-year-old son. Neither did she look anywhere nearly as belligerent as Morley.

"They're wonderful boys," Madolyn offered. "I didn't know . . . I mean, I'm delighted to be an aunt, Mrs., uh, Carlita. I may call you Carlita—"

"Room for two more?" Tyler interrupted.

Carlita wrung her hands on the massive apron, while casting a troubled glance beyond Tyler. "He won't like it."

"Morley? Does that ol' bear ever like anything?"

Carlita looked sad and worn out and sounded even more so. "*Sí,* Tyler. There is always room for you. If he agrees." With downcast eyes, she opened the back door and ushered them into the dimly lit interior which smelled of exotic spices and peppers.

Morley reached them. "No, you don't, Grant."

Ignoring him, Tyler steered Madolyn into the house with a firm hand to her waist. He stood close behind her; his head just skimmed the low ceiling. "While we're eatin', Morley, you can listen to Maddie's request. Sounds like it wouldn't be hard to take care of."

"Not at all," Madolyn hurried to say. "A signature. That's all. I have the papers with me."

The room was dark, sparsely furnished and had an earthen floor. Rolled blankets were piled in one corner; in another stood a table that looked sturdy enough, but there were only two chairs that Madolyn could see. The fireplace, on which Carlita obviously prepared meals, heated the already-warm room.

Carlita pulled out one of the two chairs.

Madolyn glanced around, unsure what to do.

"Sit, Maddie," Tyler instructed.

"But there isn't—"

"There's plenty of room. She's holding your chair. Sit."

Reluctant to intrude, Madolyn started to refuse, but she recalled the repercussions when she defied Tyler about using the back staircase at the house. This country obviously operated by its own rules of etiquette, most of which made no sense. Not that she would be around long enough to worry about it.

While she was taking her seat, a small girl entered from the lean-to, carrying a stool, which Tyler accepted. All thoughts of etiquette fled when Madolyn looked into the little girl's green eyes. Her mouth fell open.

Tyler caught the child around her waist and pulled her onto his lap. His big arms engulfed her, leaving only dangling legs and arms, which she quickly threw around his neck. She burrowed her head up under his chin in a show of affection that left Madolyn's limbs weak. "How long since I've seen you, little one?"

"A coon's age," she responded so quickly that Madolyn realized the exchange was a ritual of some sort.

Meanwhile, Morley straddled the chair opposite Madolyn. He glared at Tyler. "No one invited you to barge in here."

Tyler ignored him. "Clara, meet your *Tía Maddie.*"

The little girl scrutinized Madolyn with a frown, an open assessment, neither belligerent nor hostile, simply the natural reaction of a child. Madolyn's heart fluttered. She quickly found her voice.

"Clara, my dear, let me guess your name. Clara Barton Sinclair."

The little girl nodded eagerly.

"Where's Betsy?" Tyler asked Clara. Before she could answer, another girl, older than Clara, stepped hesitantly into the room from the lean-to.

"Betsy?" Madolyn watched as the girl shyly bobbed her head. "Betsy Ross Sinclair. I declare, what wonderful names, Morley."

Morley ignored her. "Betsy, *café.*" While Morley glared at Tyler, Betsy brought coffee. Little Clara, who could be no more than six or seven, set an earthenware bowl in front of each of the three diners, which Carlita filled with a rich-looking stew.

"*Carne guisado,*" Tyler explained. Although in actuality no one had explained anything.

Madolyn glanced around nervously. "Where will you sit, Carlita?" She started to rise.

Tyler grasped her wrist and pulled her back to her chair. "Sit down, Maddie. Carlita'll eat later."

"Later?" Madolyn's eyes flew to her brother, who had already begun to spoon heaping spoonfuls of stew into his mouth. The excess dripped back into the bowl. She shuddered.

"And the girls?" When she tried to rise again, Tyler grabbed her wrist and held on.

"Sit down." He tugged her back in place. "You didn't come out here to meddle. You came to see Morley. So here he is. Talk to him."

She glared from Tyler to Morley then to the submissive Carlita, who watched wide-eyed while another woman championed her cause, or tried to. No, Madolyn thought, not another woman. Carlita was her sister-in-law, a sister-in-law who resembled her own submissive mother too much for comfort.

Far too much for comfort. And Carlita was obviously rearing her daughters in the same fashion. Her daughters; Madolyn's nieces. Madolyn's ire rose. She clasped her hands together in her lap.

"Clara, bring three more bowls, please," Madolyn instructed. "Betsy, I'm sure you can find three more stools.

Boxes will do. Anything to sit on." *Until I find some furniture.*

When she glanced at Tyler it was to see a bemused grin. Even as she watched, he shoveled a heaping spoonful of stew into his mouth, tore off a piece of tortilla, and stuffed it in, too. She glanced at her brother, who was still busy eating. When he wiped his lips with the back of his hand, she turned away.

Barbaric! After their mother's strict adherence to the rules of etiquette. Their mother, who was surely turning over in her grave this very minute.

And Miss Abigail! Madolyn realized with a start that this was one of the few times today she had even thought about Miss Abigail. All the better, she knew, because Miss Abigail would not approve of a thing she had done lately. Madolyn gripped her hands in tighter fists. But all that was fixing to change. Plans stirred in her brain.

If she did nothing else before leaving this barbaric land, she must rescue these precious girls from a future of servitude. How she could accomplish such a formidable task remained to be seen. At her request, they had vanished into the lean-to and had yet to reappear. Whether they understood her was debatable. But one thing was certain, Madolyn did not intend to eat one bite with her hostess—her sister-in-law—standing meekly by.

Submissive. Madolyn shuddered. Submissive, like her mother. Like Morley's mother. Conventional wisdom held that a man married his mother. But Madolyn held with Miss Abigail's interpretation—that a man turned the woman he married into a facsimile of his mother.

When Morley suddenly scraped back his chair and rose from the table, Tyler chastised her.

"Looks like you missed your opportunity, Maddie. 'Less all you came out here to do was meddle."

Madolyn tipped her chin, but held her tongue, for Tyler

was right. She had let the opportunity slip past. "Morley," she called. "I really must speak with you."

He leveled indifferent eyes on her. "So who'd the old man leave his money to?"

Madolyn took a deep breath and wished Tyler Grant weren't sitting there taking in every word. "The Gentleman's Select Smoking Club of Boston."

Tyler laughed. Madolyn cast him a withering look. He wiped his mouth and started to rise.

"Good riddance." Morley crammed his Stetson on his head.

Madolyn's heart lurched. "All of it," she added lamely. "Even the house."

Morley ran practiced hands along the creased brim, as though to reinforce what time, neglect, and the weather had likely rendered as hard as saddle leather. "So?"

"I have no place to live." Feeling Tyler's eyes on her, she hissed, "I don't want your sympathy, sir."

He held up his hands in defense. "Don't mind me, Maddie, I'm just a fly on the wall."

She glared at him, feeling abandoned, betrayed, and beneath all that, confused. Resolutely she approached her brother. Her face grew warm when she explained, "Unless I give up my work and marry within a year of the reading of the will, everything goes to the Gentlemen's Select Smoking Club of Boston, even the roof over my head. One month has already passed."

"Your work?" Morley barked.

Madolyn lifted her chin. "I am secretary of the Boston Woman Suffrage Society."

Morley actually laughed. And, finally, she recognized him. He had laughed a lot back when they were youngsters. He taught her to laugh.

"Learn to laugh at life, little girl," he instructed. "That's the only way to get through some of it."

"Woman suffrage!" He whooped the words to the low-hung ceiling. "No wonder the old man had a conniption."

Madolyn refused to be sidetracked. "This is my plan, Morley. You, as Papa's legal heir, can break his will."

Morley's smile faded. Madolyn hurried on. "A lawyer drew up papers for you to sign. The money can be divided. I don't need much. With what's left, I had planned to start a Center for Women's Rights." She cast a glance toward Carlita, who huddled near the fireplace. "That was before I knew about . . . I mean, before I met the children. I didn't know you had children, Morley. The inheritance belongs to them, too."

"How many ways do I have to say it? I don't want nothin' from that ol' man." Morley's eyes had gone dark; his face turned red. "Go back to Boston, Maddie." He glanced to Carlita, then back to Madolyn. "Take your woman suffrage and women's rights with you. They don't fit our way of livin' out here."

Tyler snatched his hat off the back of his hide-bound chair. "Hear her out, Morley." He pushed his former partner aside, opened the door, then turned back with, *"Gracias, Carlita."*

Courage drained from Madolyn's spine. "Mr. Grant? Where are you going?"

Tyler tipped his hat. "To find me a stolen horse."

"Like hell!" Morley took out after Tyler. Madolyn heard them bicker even while they stomped away from the adobe hut.

"Hear her out, Morley."

"She's done. So am I. And so are you."

Twenty years. For twenty years she had pined for her lost brother. Now it looked as if the brother in her fantasy had never existed. Heavy-hearted, Madolyn repeated her litany: *Men are no damned good.* When she turned back for her reticule, the two little girls had returned to the room and stood beside their mother. All three stared at Madolyn with doleful, uncomprehending expressions.

"Don't you worry about a thing, Carlita. I'm here now, and I intend to help you straighten him out. Morley will not turn out like his father. I guarantee you that."

Carlita remained silent, her eyes downcast. Poor thing. Poor submissive thing. Well, she had learned one thing today, Madolyn thought: Women in the West were not as liberated as she had believed from her brief association with Miss Goldie Nugget.

On the other hand, women of the ilk of those who ran the House of Negotiable Love had always been liberated. Prostitutes had always had more control over their lives than wives. A wicked thought.

"I'm here now, Carlita. Everything will work out." Kneeling before the smallest girl, she took both the child's little hands. "How old are you, Clara?"

The little girl shrugged, her green eyes alight with curiosity.

"*Siete,*" Carlita responded in Spanish, then added in hesitant English, "Clara is seven; Betsy is eleven."

"Clara Barton," Madolyn declared. "And Betsy Ross. He can't have gone *all* bad." She wanted to hug little Clara to her, like Tyler had done earlier, but she couldn't quite bring herself to act so freely. Instead, she squeezed the child's hands. "I'm very glad to have found you. I didn't know I had a niece." She turned to Betsy and took one of her hands, although the girl tried to pull away.

Somehow rejection from a shy child wasn't the same as being rejected by a brother who had been her best friend twenty years before.

What had happened? Why had Morley grown hostile? She had a good idea why he left home, but that had been twenty years ago. Now he had a lovely family. Although his home was in obvious need of major improvements—

The thought returned. Money. The children were barefoot,

the house was small and inadequate by anyone's standards for a family of eight.

Eight! A few hours ago she had believed Morley to be the only relation she possessed in this world. Within the space of half a day she had discovered seven more relatives. Seven. A sister-in-law, four nephews, and two adorable little nieces!

And they obviously were in dire financial straits. Yes, things did happen for a reason. She had come here to seek her brother in her hour of need, and what had she found? A brother who needed her even more than she needed him.

Money. And guidance. Shoes for the children. Clothing. A table with eight chairs. And that was only a beginning. Morley might act like he didn't want her around, but he needed her. In no time she would show him how much.

Standing, she gripped Carlita's hands. "Thank you for a lovely meal, Carlita." She spoke to the woman's downcast head. "Let me fetch my valise. I won't be a burden, you'll see. I can help out. I shall sleep with the girls."

Suddenly, in place of the despair that had been her constant companion for so long she couldn't recall when it actually began, joy and expectation swelled her bosom. *A family.*

She had found a family. She hadn't known how much she needed one. And they needed her, too. Oh, the joy of it!

She would fetch her valise, then she would find Tyler and tell him to go back to town without her.

Tyler folded his arms over the corral fence and watched the honey-colored thoroughbred romp around the enclosure, which, like the lean-to, was made from stalks of the sotol plant.

He had coveted that horse for over a year, and now, Morley Damn-his-hide had bought her out of spite. Which wasn't all that surprising, given the state of their friendship.

But look what the bastard was doing to his sister. For twenty years Tyler had known the man possessed a mean streak. But if he hadn't witnessed firsthand the sonofabitch's treatment of Maddie, Tyler knew he would never have believed it. And damned if he hadn't set her up for the fall.

"You played hell this time, Grant."

Tyler didn't turn. Truth known, he was afraid to face Morley, lest he lose control of his itchin' fist. "Never knew you were such a bastard, Morley. Always suspected it, but until today, I never knew it for fact."

"We didn't have the money for that horse when you wanted it. We were investin' our money in cattle, if you recall."

"Help her, Morley."

"Stay out of it, Grant. It ain't none of your business."

"Help her. It's the quickest way to get rid of her."

"That woman don't need my help or anyone else's."

"You heard her. She doesn't have a roof over her head."

"You bet. Jed told me how it took nigh onto two baggage cars to haul all her stuff to Horn."

"Give her your damned signature, Morley."

Morley stood beside Tyler, his arms crossed over the fence, staring at the same honey-colored horse. "Not that it's any of your damned business, Grant, but that signature wouldn't be the end of it. It'd open a can of worms better left sealed. Before we were done, I'd have to go back to Boston, get involved in a situation I vowed never to have any part of again."

"Help her."

"Damnit, Grant, I never knew you for one to stick your nose in other folks' affairs."

"Me? You don't know half about meddlin' till you see your sister at work. Help her, Morley. That's the only way to get her out of your hair."

"I have a better idea. You brought her out here; you take her back to town. See her off on the train."

"Morley." Madolyn's voice startled the two bickering men.

Tyler turned to see her standing in the barn door, valise in hand. Morley's face took on the hue of the sky at sunset.

"You're not running me off, Morley. I'm staying right here until you sign those papers."

"Like hell!"

"Mr. Grant, you promised to retrieve my baggage after I had a chance to look things over."

Morley exploded. "You what?"

"You'll be more comfortable in town, Maddie," Tyler advised.

"I'll be more comfortable right here with my family."

Morley turned wild eyes on Tyler. "This is your doin', so you fix it. Take her to town an' send her back to Boston. An' stay the hell away from here, yourself. If those boys won't shoot you next time, I'll hire men who will."

Tyler cocked his head, studied his combative partner— *former* partner. He lowered his voice. "Tell you what, Morley. I might be willin' to work out a trade. Sign Maddie's papers, and, in exchange for that little filly in the pen yonder, I'll get this one out of your hair."

Five

"You used me, Mr. Grant!" Madolyn gripped the wagon seat with both hands. Her parasol lay in the back along with her valise, where Tyler pitched them, just before he grabbed her around the waist and tossed her to the wooden seat, as though she were a sack of feed. Following which, he whipped up the team and drove away from Morley's in his usual bat-out-of-hell manner.

"I brought you out here, didn't I?"

"For your own gain."

"What gain's that, Maddie?"

"I don't know. One would think from the way he acted, Morley was angrier to see you than he was to see me."

"That's possible."

"You claimed to be his partner."

"I am." When Tyler flicked the reins, his shoulder bumped Madolyn. "Was."

She scooted away. "I knew it. You didn't tell me the truth, Mr. Grant."

"Maddie. Maddie."

At his conciliatory tone, she grew wary. Even so, his next suggestion surprised her.

"Why don't you drop that Mr. Grant nonsense?"

"It isn't your name?"

"Of course, it's my name, but—"

"Then I shan't drop it."

"You might as well call me Tyler, that's my name, too."

"I know your name, Mr. Grant. But I shan't drop the formality. Who knows, one of these days my good manners might rub off on you." She focused on a magenta blossom in the distance, the only bright spot in sight—either in the country or in her life. "Or on someone."

"If you're talkin' about Morley, don't hold your breath."

"Morley was reared to be a gentleman, Mr. Grant. My mother—"

"This has nothing to do with your mother, Maddie. Morley's behavior is no reflection on his fine, upstandin' family."

Madolyn's stiff spine relaxed a bit. Perhaps Tyler didn't know as much about her as she had feared, not if he called her family fine and upstanding. Obviously, Morley hadn't revealed all the family secrets to this friend of twenty years. If she could believe Tyler on that, either.

"It's the country," Tyler was saying.

"The country?"

"This country's hard on a man. Harder, yet on a woman. Every livin' thing either has thorns that stick you or poison that kills you. Summertime, it's hot as Hades; winter, you'd swear you were at the North Pole. There's never enough water, not until a flash flood hits the mountains, then the run-off strips the land of what little topsoil there was. It's a hard country, Maddie. Too hard for a man to give much thought to manners and the like."

"Then why are you here?"

Tyler shifted the reins to his outside hand and propped his other hand on his knee. Madolyn studied it, fascinated. A tingling sensation reminded her how that hand had felt at the small of her back, sturdy, secure. She had never seen a hand so large, or one that looked so strong. His fingernails were clipped and clean, but his fingers were scarred, the skin so dry tiny little cracks ran around the edges of them like miniature trails in the sand. Proof that work strengthened a person, she decided. When Tyler didn't respond, she repeated her question.

He grinned. "Speakin' of manners, in this part of the country, it's considered downright rude to make personal inquiries."

She gasped.

"But considerin' all we've been through together, if you'll agree to call me by name, I'll consider tellin' you all about my sordid past."

She fidgeted self-consciously on the seat, but he only grinned. He was teasing. He must be teasing. But she couldn't be certain; she had little experience with jovial people. She declined the offer by glancing off.

"Be that as it may, Mr. Grant, I feel obliged to help Morley's family while he comes to terms with helping me."

Tyler frowned at her from beneath his deep-set eyes. "What kind of help?"

"To begin with, the children need shoes."

"Boots."

"Boots, then. I won't quibble over footgear."

"Hallelujah!" His warm brown gaze zoomed in on her. "We've found our first area of common ground, Maddie. There's hope for us yet."

Taken aback, she sat up a bit straighter, dodging contact with his shoulder. "I wasn't aware we were searching for common ground."

He laughed, that deep-throated, straight-from-the-belly laugh. Contagious, that's what it was, and she couldn't help but smile, hearing it. People should laugh. No matter what Miss Abigail said about frivolity being a woman's downfall—third behind promiscuity and sloth—Madolyn had long suspected that laughter was good for the soul. She had never been able to let herself go to that extent, but, hearing Tyler, she longed to.

"Boots," he prompted. "What other kind of help are you offerin' Morley?"

"They need so many things, I don't know where to be-gin—material things like furniture and clothing and even a larger house."

"A house?"

She ignored his skeptical tone. "And things for the soul and the mind, like education and—" Her train of thought ran out when she realized she had been about to discuss Morley's personal life. "Of course, that works in my favor."

"Your favor? How's that?"

"Morley will have to file suit to break Papa's will. He needs the money."

"You mean because of the way they live?"

"The things they lack," she amended.

"Morley Sinclair doesn't need that money, Maddie. Not one half as bad as you need it yourself."

Madolyn sat a little straighter. She had never discussed personal matters with a stranger. Of course, Tyler had taken it upon himself to become more than a stranger, no matter that he and her brother were scarcely on speaking terms.

"If he has money, he certainly doesn't spend it."

"Trust me, Maddie. Ol' Morley spends plenty. He just laid down five hundred dollars for that thoroughbred horse."

" 'Pache Prancer?"

"Uh-huh."

"Five hundred dollars for a horse, when his sons and daughters are barefoot and his wife—"

"There's something else you should know before you jump into tryin' to change things out there."

His tone forewarned her. At least, she thought it had, until he spoke again.

"Carlita isn't . . . what I mean to say is . . . Morley and Carlita aren't . . ." Breaking eye contact, he turned to stare straight ahead. She watched veins pop up on the backs of his hands, a sure sign of tension.

She gripped the edge of the seat a little tighter. Although

he had slowed down during their discussion, she had re-
tained her death-grip on the wagon seat, lest he drive
straight across one of those gravel beds he called gulleys.

"Morley and Carlita are not married." His statement took
her by complete surprise.

"Not married?"

"That's right."

"Oh, no, Mr. Grant. That's *wrong*. What about the children? How could Morley rear his children in a home where
their mother and father—"

"Truth known, it isn't, well, it isn't what you'd call a
normal household."

Normal? "Whatever do you mean?"

"Well, they're not really Morley's kids, they're Carlita's
kids, and Carlita—"

"Not Morley's children! You can't expect me to believe
that."

"Well, I mean, he fathered 'em, all right."

Madolyn wished suddenly that she were the swooning
type, for short of passing out, she saw no recourse other
than to continue this delicate conversation—convention and
personal comfort aside. She pressed on. "Then they are
Morley's children, Mr. Grant."

"Technically, yes. Truth is, Carlita's just his maid. I mean,
Morley doesn't claim those kids, not as heirs or anything
like that."

Madolyn slumped forward. Never had she heard of anything so barbaric. Never had she imagined a member of her
own family . . . But there was Papa. She could almost hear
Miss Abigail hiss, Like father, like son.

"You mean, she cooks his meals, but he doesn't allow
her to eat at the table?"

"I've never known her to eat at the table with him. By
the same token, I've never heard her complain."

"Spoken like a true man, Mr. Grant. You think a woman

takes such punishment because she likes it? Not on your life."

"I've known women who had it worse."

"Perhaps, but this is my brother." Suddenly the dreariness of the desolate landscape engulfed her. "They must have been . . . uh, together a long time. I mean, the children . . . George Washington is fourteen you said."

"Thereabouts."

"Fourteen years. And he . . ." Madolyn struggled to hold her emotions in check. She could not cry in front of this man; she simply could not. "I mean, there are six children."

"Yep."

"How unspeakably wicked. Those poor dear children." Suddenly overcome by the afternoon heat, and by the wind that tore at her bun and buffeted her straw bonnet, Madolyn laid her parasol at her feet and dug into her reticule, producing a linen handkerchief with which to mop her brow and wipe her neck inside her high collar. Tyler Grant and her brother were right about one thing—this barbaric land was no place for a lady.

Watching Maddie's starch wilt hit Tyler where he lived. He could tell she was near tears, and it was all his fault. Well, most of it. If she had gone back to Boston when Morley sent word . . . If she hadn't come out here in the first place . . . If he hadn't . . . He owed her an explanation, damnit. Suddenly, on the other side of Aguja Creek, he halted the team in the shade of a madrone tree. She came instantly alert.

"What are you doing?"

"Calm down, Maddie. I just want to talk to you a minute."

"You seemed perfectly capable of talking and driving at the same time."

He chuckled. "You say the damnedest things."

"And you swear more than any human I have ever known."

"That's possible." He considered. "You comin' from Boston and bein' involved with woman suffrage, I'd have thought you might know something about swearin'."

"The two have nothing in common."

"From what I understand, you people don't intend to stop with gettin' the vote for women. Aren't you aimin' at other rights now held primarily by men?"

She nodded warily.

"What about swearin'?"

"What about it?"

"Don't women want the right to swear, too?" That touched a nerve! He blanched at her eager response. Damned if he hadn't been right. With her dander up, Maddie Sinclair was one hell of a fighter. And an attractive one, to boot.

"That is exactly the sort of backward mentality we are fighting, Mr. Grant. Chauvinism. We intend to better the world, yes. Bettering the world means that a lot of conventions enjoyed by men will not only *not* be appropriated by women, but will be disenfranchised altogether."

"Appropriated? Disenfranchised? Sounds like you're serious."

"Make sport, if you will, but yes, we are serious." A loose curl blew around the vicinity of her left ear. Tyler lifted a hand to tuck it back, then froze at the terror in her eyes.

"I'm sure you didn't stop here in the middle of the desert to discuss woman suffrage," she accused.

"Town's just around the next bend, Maddie. You're perfectly safe with me."

"Safe?" He could tell she was discomfited; likely she hadn't expected him to recognize the source of her discomfort.

"Give me a minute," he said. "I want to explain something . . . to, uh, apologize."

"Apologize?"

"For using you."

Her green eyes opened wide. She directed her gaze to the slick, almost barkless branches of the madrone.

"Like I said earlier," he explained, "Morley and I have been friends for twenty years. We were partners for better than fourteen of those years. We own a bit of land, here in Texas and across the Rio Grande in Mexico."

"Mexico?"

He nodded. "Six months ago the Mexican government confiscated our property over there—the ranch and all the livestock on it."

"Whatever had you done?"

"Nothin'. It had nothin' to do with breakin' the law. One government gave us the land, for service in their fight against Maximilian—"

That caught her attention. He watched her eyes grow round, as for the first time, she seemed to concentrate on his tale, rather than on him, a man to be feared. Unguarded, her expression relaxed, her features softened. Her lips parted. She ran her tongue around them. Inviting.

Unconscious of it, he knew. But he wasn't unconscious of it. Surprised, maybe, but he was definitely aware of the woman and her stunning effect on him.

"Anyway," he continued, "the present Mexican government decided to take it all back. By longstandin' agreement I ran the ranch in Mexico and Morley ran our spread here." He paused, glanced around, taking in the Texas land he had never given thought to losing until Morley Damn-his-hide interfered. "When Mexico kicked us out, Morley refused to allow me to bring our Mexican cattle over here."

"Refused? Why would he do that?"

"Several reasons. He's afraid of infectin' our Texas herd with hoof-and-mouth disease. A legitimate concern, but I found a solution for it. Then, too, he didn't want to risk the Mexican government crossin' the river and takin' back not only our Mexican cattle but all the others."

"That doesn't sound like much of a feud if you ask me."

"I agree." His eyes danced over her face. "That makes two things we agree on."

Quickly she turned away, but not before he glimpsed the splotches of color on her cheeks.

"Boots for the boys," he coaxed, "and Morley's cantankerousness."

When she refused to respond, he continued. "Look, Maddie, I'm sorry. I apologize." He watched her purse her lips and stare straight ahead. "I should've played it straight with you."

Her chin tipped up a degree or so.

"I shouldn't have taken you to Goldie's."

Her pursed lips tightened into a tight wad. Her knee started bouncing, and he knew she was tapping that impatient toe of hers against the wagon bed.

"Damnit, Maddie. I'm sorry."

Another lengthy moment passed before she said, "What about that newspaperman?"

"Donnell? Hell, I explained about him."

Again, he caught her attention. She turned on him, her green eyes fighting. "You explained nothing. You set me up—"

"I did it for the good of the town."

"The good of the town? How is my descent into disgrace good for Buckhorn?"

"It wasn't meant to be that way. As a matter of fact, there is no Buckhorn."

"No Buckhorn? You talk in riddles, sir." When he opened his mouth to continue, she interrupted. "I am not interested in your lies, Mr. Grant."

That did it. Tyler reached out, grabbed her pointed little

chin, and pulled it around. She refused to meet his eye, but that didn't stop him.

"Your brother, damn his hide, divided the town into his part, Horn, and my part, Buck."

"Why would he do such a stupid thing?"

"That's three, Maddie." He was able to hold her gaze for one brief instant, before she lowered her eyes. "To answer your question, he's low-down, mean-spirited—"

"He's my brother, Mr. Grant."

"Take it from one who's had experience, Maddie, loyalty will get you nowhere with that scoundrel. Not long after he refused to allow me to move our Mexican cattle over here, I rode into Buckhorn one day to find that he had divided the town straight down the middle of the railroad tracks."

"The railroad tracks?"

"North side's Horn—Morley's territory; south side's Buck, mine."

"That's what he meant. And Mr. Rolly?"

"I don't know what Rolly told you, but by tacit agreement, no one crosses the tracks."

"What did you do about such foolishness? Surely you didn't just go along."

"Hell, no, I didn't just go along. Give me more credit than that."

"What did you do to rectify the matter, Mr. Grant?"

"I went across the tracks and tried to talk sense to several men. They would have none of it."

"I can't believe this."

"Neither could I. You see, by the time I learned about it, the businessmen had drawn their own battle lines. Those who remained loyal to Morley moved to Horn; those who were loyal to me, stayed in or moved to Buck. There wasn't much I could do at that point."

"How do they do business?"

"They . . . we don't do business. Except for what comes

in and goes out on the rails. Rolly and Ol' Cryer make rum money by scuttlin' gossip back and forth. That's about the extent of it."

He tried again to win her understanding, for what purpose, he wasn't sure. "I took you to Goldie's, because there's no hotel in Buck. I contacted Donnell, thinkin' a story about a fine, upstandin' citizen, a champion of woman suffrage, no less, bein' forced to put up in the local . . . uh, at Goldie's, well, that might draw attention to the fact that we need a hotel in Buck."

"I must have looked like a fine upstanding citizen. Tumbled up from falling down the stairs, surrounded by the town's . . . I'll never forgive you for such a travesty."

"Damnation, Maddie. How was I to know you would come barrelin' out that door followed by every whore in town?"

She turned an instant, flaming red at his coarse language.

"Sorry. I got carried away. Sorry."

She tilted her head, stared out at the mountains. "There's a hotel in Horn?"

He nodded.

"But you didn't *think* to tell me?"

"I thought about it."

"You decided to lie instead."

"I didn't lie. Not about that. And wasn't I the only person who offered to drive you out to Morley's? Wasn't I?"

"We don't know for certain that would have been the case, do we, Mr. Grant? If I had gone to the hotel in Horn, perhaps some true gentleman—"

"There aren't any true gentlemen in Horn, Maddie. No one over there would have driven you out to Morley's."

"How do you know?"

"Jed told them not to."

She confronted him at that. Tears glistened in her eyes. Tears, from this starch-backed, tight-laced . . . Before he thought, he had reached for her. For the moment it took him to pull her into his arms, she didn't resist.

"Maddie, I'm sorry." She went stiff as a dead tree branch and felt about the same with her corseted frame and sharp elbows jabbing him in the ribs. But he held her in place, cradling her face in the lee of his shoulder.

"I didn't mean to hurt you, Maddie."

"I'll just bet," she mumbled into his shirt. He felt her breath, through his clothing, warm and moist.

"I didn't," he repeated, and at that moment he meant it more than he had ever meant anything in his life. Tugging her face back with both hands, he tried to look in her eyes, but they were tightly closed.

"I didn't mean to hurt you." The last was mumbled against her skin, because he couldn't resist kissing her.

Her pursed lips were soft, unschooled. He knew she was wary after the way he'd treated her at the depot. At the thought, a gentleness that was at once strangely foreign and bewitchingly erotic took hold of him.

She surprised him by not pulling away, but she sat stiff as a pillar, even when he folded his arms around her and pulled her close and deepened the kiss.

Then of a sudden she seemed to relax. Her lips became pliable and her tight fists loosened against his chest.

Sweet, fiery passion consumed him. It had been simmering inside him all day. Hell, ever since the day before when she charged across the railroad tracks and he saw something in her green eyes that no man had ever seen before.

That must be the case, else Maddie Sinclair wouldn't be a spinster. And if she weren't a spinster, she wouldn't be sitting on this wagon seat, wrapped in his arms. He tightened his hold, deepened his kiss. When her fingers inched up his chest, his body responded as though he had just come through a twenty-year drouth.

Madolyn had never experienced anything so sensual. Tyler's lips were as soft as the air itself; his arms encircled her like the mountains that embraced this barbaric land, and were every bit as strong and protective. She snuggled against him the way a child would snuggle into her pillow, seeking solace, seeking protection.

Her hands opened against his chest. She felt his heart beat beneath his crisp white shirt. In her mind's eye she saw him as he had been that morning, filling his doorway with broad, muscular shoulders and bare chest sprinkled with a dusting of silky brown hair. She saw his trim waist, the open placket of his duckins. Inside, she began to glow, as though her veins ran with molten honey. She saw Penny-Ante—

Reality returned in a heartbeat; sanity cleared her brain. She pulled herself free, then scooted as far away as the short wagon seat allowed. Her ire rose. Of all the wicked, barbaric . . .

"How dare you!" she shrieked. Not knowing what to do with her hands she was suddenly conscious of them flying about in the air. "How dare you!" Gaining direction, she slapped him hard on the cheek. The sound echoed through the stillness; surprise registered in his eyes.

"You might have put me up in a house of ill repute, sir, but I am not that kind of girl." Something inside her denied the claim. Whatever *that* kind of girl was, something inside Madolyn had enjoyed every sweet, sensuous moment of being in Tyler's embrace, of having his arms pull her close and closer, of feeling his lips, of tasting him, of kissing him back. *Kissing him back!*

He fingered the place on his cheek where she slapped him. "I know the kind of girl you are, Maddie. And I explained about Goldie's. There was no other place."

His words barely registered in her unsettled brain. *She had kissed him!* Miss Abigail would be mortified! She had let down her guard, and look where it got her.

For one as proper as she, the last two days had been filled with anything but decorum. In two days' time, she,

Madolyn Sinclair, secretary of the Boston Woman Suffrage Society had exchanged intimate glances with this . . . this devil in britches. But had she stopped there?

No, ma'am, she had not. She had flirted, she knew that, for she had felt light-headed and dizzy numerous times, just from looking at the man. Her blood pounded through her veins anytime she was near him.

Lifting a hand she placed it over her heart. Lord in heaven, her heart had fluttered itself silly the last two days, and that kiss hadn't helped at all. Not one whit.

But that wasn't the half of it. She had kissed the man. First, she allowed him to kiss her in front of the uncouth citizens of this divided town. She tried to convince herself she had no choice in the matter.

And she might have believed that—until today. Until this moment. Madolyn stared forlornly into the dense whiteness of Tyler's rumpled shirt, realizing that it was she who had rumpled it; she who had lain her head against it, and worse, she even rubbed her breasts into it. Lord in heaven, if the thought didn't do unbelievable things to her even now.

She had to get out of here, that's what she had to do. She glanced to the ground, then up, off toward where town must surely lie. But how far?

She should walk. That's what she should do. But could she? As if he read her mind, Tyler caught her arm.

"You can't walk to town, Maddie. Not in this heat."

"Unhand me!"

He tightened his hold. "For Pete's sake, Maddie, it was just a kiss."

Just a kiss? "To one as experienced as you, I'm sure, sir."

"Damnation! Get off your high horse. You enjoyed it, too."

She gritted her teeth, ready to deny the charge, unable to do so. For, heaven help her, she had enjoyed it. *Enjoyed it!* Lord in heaven! Morley wasn't the only one to inherit their father's depravity.

"Unhand me," she ordered again.

"I ought to. I ought to let you find out just how hot it is out there."

She jerked to free herself, but still he held on. His eyes bore into hers. He was angry. And that frightened her.

"I intended to find you a more respectable place to stay," he was saying, "but on second thought, maybe you have a little more to learn about life."

"Such as?"

He grinned, a wicked grin, befitting a devil. A wicked grin that set her heart to pounding in her throat, even as it chilled her blood.

"Take me back to town, Mr. Grant."

"I'm considerin' it." He appeared to mull over the situation, while his eyes roamed her. They lingered on her lips and she was unable to draw her gaze away from him. Her heart pounded loudly, like thunder.

"Tell you what," he drawled. "I'll make you a trade." He released her arm.

She rubbed the spot where he had held. "You're big on making trades."

"I'll take you back to town, when you call me Tyler."

Her mouth dropped open. The nerve of him. The everlasting nerve of him. She turned away. Stared out at the mountains. The sun was low on the horizon; soon it would be setting. The sky was turning pink. The wind had died down to a breeze.

Crossing her arms, she gripped them with tight fists. Why had she come to this barbaric land? Her brother didn't want her. It would take every ounce of perseverance she could muster to persuade him to sign those papers.

And Tyler was propositioning her. Oh, she realized it wasn't a real proposition. But that's the way her heart heard it—making more of that kiss than she should. More of his touch, his piercing looks.

But, Lord in heaven, she was lonely. *So lonely.* And she had been for such a long, long time.

"Come on, Maddie," he pressed. "It's just a word. There's no harm in it."

"No harm? What would you know about harm? You, who . . . who . . ." She inhaled trying to think of one wicked thing to single out from among all his wickedness. "You can wear clean shirts every day of the week and Sunday, too, Mr. Grant, but it won't make you a gentleman."

"I never claimed to be a gentleman, damnit. All I'm askin' is . . . one simple word."

"It isn't simple," she shouted. Embarrassed, she gripped her emotions, turned back to stare at the mountains. Tears threatened, as they had so often the last two days. This time she feared they might win. She fought harder.

"Come on, Maddie."

"Please don't," she whispered into the wind. "Please, don't do this to me."

He didn't press her further, but released the brake and headed the team for town. The wind in her face cooled her; she strove to regain her composure before they reached the House of Negotiable Love, where she would be forced to deal with yet another of life's sordid aspects.

Madolyn was used to tackling her emotions. She prided herself on being able to suppress tears, smiles, to control her anger, her disappointments, yes, even her loneliness, so that no one ever suspected the little weaknesses that nettled at her strength like a dog nipping at one's heels.

Under Miss Abigail's tutelage, she had learned to subjugate personal concerns to those of other women. Now she called forth every lesson she had ever learned. To begin with she had to get her mind off this devil sitting beside her. And how better, than to concentrate on her other problems?

Such as convincing Morley to sign those papers. Such as helping his family. First thing tomorrow she would send off an order for shoes—boots, rather—for the children. Then she would engage the aid of some mother in Buckhorn—surely she could find one decent family in the town. With a mother's aid, she could make a list of everything the children needed.

Morley might not claim them, but she certainly did. They were her nephews and nieces and she intended to do everything in her power to see that they were reared properly and educated to meet the future. And the first order of business was to straighten out the disgusting situation between their parents.

"Under the circumstances, I suppose it should be simple . . ."

"What's that?" Tyler inquired.

Unaware that she had spoken out loud, she started at his question. But thinking on it, perhaps it was just as well. Tyler had to learn her plans sooner or later. Why not discuss them now, while she had a chance?

"A simple ceremony," she repeated. "Morley and Carlita's wedding."

Tyler jerked back on the reins, bouncing both of them on the wagon seat. "Wedding?"

"They have to get married."

He stared, gaped would be a better word, she decided.

"I shall speak with the preacher. You do have a preacher in . . . uh, which is your town?"

"Buck."

"You do have a preacher in Buck, don't you, Mr. Grant?"

His features were unreadable. "Now, Maddie, that's not such a good idea."

"Never mind. Lucky can direct me." She paused, thinking. "Do you suppose he will hold it against me for boarding at the . . . uh, the house?"

Tyler shook his head, as though she were the strangest

creature in the whole world. "You beat all, Maddie Sinclair. Damned if you don't beat all."

Although she knew he was berating her, his tone didn't sound hostile, rather, he grinned when he said it, and, Lord in heaven, if her heart didn't pump a little faster. She forged ahead, trying to ignore this man's unwelcome, yet potent, effect on her.

"When the plans are firm," she told him, "such as the date the preacher can go with us to the ranch, I shall inform you."

"Whoa, now, Maddie. This is your shindig. Don't count on me. You're in way over my head already."

"But you must participate. By your own admission, you are Morley's best friend."

Tyler glared. "You're the meddlin'est woman I've run across in all my life. Do you know that? You take the prize and leave the competition in distant second."

"I've been called worse." She smiled, pleased to have regained her composure. "Believe me, Mr. Grant, my skin is tough. And this is part of my work. Sometimes only a woman can straighten out the messes you men make of our lives." She smiled again. "Morley will expect you to stand up as his best man."

"Best man!"

"You are his best friend."

"Hell, Maddie, I don't believe what I'm hearin'." He shoved his hat back and wiped his brow with his sleeve. "Let me put it this way. If Morley Sinclair and a Comanche brave decked out in war paint were both caught in a bog, I'd sooner save the Comanche."

Madolyn shrugged. "Then it's high time the two of you made up. Friendships shouldn't—"

"Never in a million years. Look at me when I say this, Maddie. Never in a million years."

"You must serve my brother as best man, Mr. Grant. There is no other way. It's for a good cause."

Tyler didn't respond; she knew he didn't dare. Wasn't it true that the first person to speak after an ultimatum had been issued, lost? This was one issue Madolyn did not intend to lose.

Shortly, then, and in silence, they arrived back at the House of Negotiable Love. No sooner had Tyler drawn rein at the back staircase, than Lucky hurried down the steps to meet them.

"Miss Goldie asks would you have a word with her an' the girls right away, Miss Maddie. They're in a tight place."

"A tight place?" Without thinking, Madolyn stepped off the wagon into Tyler's hands. His touch went straight to the heart of her, and for a moment she was tempted to look in his eyes. She resisted, striving to focus on Lucky's explanation.

"I'll see what Goldie wants," Tyler was saying.

"She sent for *me.*"

"I'll handle it, Maddie. No tellin' what she's up to." He nudged her toward the back stairs with a hand to the small of her back. That sturdy hand, that intimate gesture. The glow spread like honey inside her again.

Deliberately, she moved away. For some reason, she was able to think straighter without him near. "Goldie sent for me, Mr. Grant. When a woman calls, I answer. It is part of my work."

Six

"This is no place for a lady, Maddie." Tyler caught up with Madolyn before she reached the front door of the House of Negotiable Love.

"Spoken like a true man." Gaining the porch, she glared back over her shoulder at him. "Are you not the person who brought me here?"

"To the back entrance."

"I shan't use the back entrance, sir. Regardless of what you think of me, I am a lady."

"Miss Maddie!" Goldie stuck her head out the gaudy screen door and peered anxiously up and down the deserted street. "You needn't come in by the front."

"You called for my help, Miss Nugget. Lucky said you've found yourself in a tight place." When Madolyn reached for the screen, Tyler jerked it out of her grasp.

"Hold on a cockeyed minute, Maddie." He tried to bar her entrance.

"Excuse me, sir." As though to prove to herself she could face him without faltering, she held his defiant stare. *Hold fast,* Miss Abigail taught. Set your sights, and allow no one to turn you aside.

"What is it with you?" he barked. "Yesterday you hobbled to this house on a wrenched ankle because you thought I might carry you in the front way. Now, you charge in on your own two feet in broad open daylight—"

Madolyn cast a withering glance at the sky. "In Boston we call this dusk. And yesterday I was wrong."

"Hot damn! Madam secretary of the Boston Woman Suffrage Society can be wrong about something."

"Certainly." She stiffened her spine. "You should try such an admission sometime, Mr. Grant. It's good for the constitution. Miss Abigail says so."

"Who the hell is Miss Abigail?"

Incensed, Madolyn sashayed through the door.

"What about my apology?" Tyler followed her into the foyer. "Isn't an apology the same as admittin' one's mistakes? Huh? Isn't it?"

"Tyler, hon." Goldie placed a restraining hand on Tyler's arm, squeezing his biceps. The blatantly sensual act did queasy things to Madolyn's stomach.

"Miss Maddie'll be all right in our enclave of misfits," Goldie was saying. "We don't intend to boil her for dinner. Or even sign her up to work for us."

The outlandish suggestion was so startling, Madolyn didn't think to turn away. She watched Goldie wink at Tyler.

"But if we do, big boy, you'll be the first to know."

Mortification mobilized Madolyn. She scurried into the parlor, pretending—or trying to—that she hadn't overheard the ribald remark. She wasn't exactly certain what Goldie had in mind, but Tyler must have known, for she heard him growl a reply under his breath. Indistinct though his words were, she had no doubt he had uttered one of his frequent oaths.

"Come on in, Tyler," Goldie invited. "You might as well join us, since we're fixin' to discuss your town."

"My town? What about my town?"

The heavy mixture of fragrances in the parlor almost overwhelmed Madolyn. Lavender and roses and violets and geranium. Somehow they were never so stifling mixed in a garden. In this room, applied with the heavy hands of Goldie's girls, one was left with no doubt as to the sort of establishment this was. The soiled doves perched on velvet-covered settees, chairs, and cushions.

What had she gotten herself into, coming into this parlor? But she was here, and she saw no recourse but to hear these women out. The sooner they got down to business, the sooner she could escape the presence of the soiled doves and Tyler Grant alike. Calling upon her years of training, she charged ahead.

"We should take our seats, Mr. Grant. Obviously, we have interrupted a meeting in progress. Where should we sit, Miss Nugget?"

"Over here, Tyler," Annie invited.

"There's room beside me, honey bun," Two-Bit called.

Madolyn's skin prickled at the lurid invitations. She took a seat on the edge of a gaudy gold-brocade sofa. These women needed her help, she argued silently. She must not treat them with less respect than she would any other downtrodden woman who called upon her. But even that little lecture failed to still the cold trepidation that tightened inside her chest.

She sat rigidly on the edge of the sofa, knees pressed together; when her ankles began to knock, she pressed them together, too. Lord in heaven, she hoped their request was simple . . . and decent. She wondered fleetingly whether she would understand their problem.

Tyler did not take his seat, at her direction. In fact, he stood staring at the vacant place on the sofa in an indecisive manner that was quite foreign to his usual nature, which was to attack a situation head-on. At length, he crossed to stand at the window beside the sofa.

Goldie, garbed as before in a brassy gold kimono, henna-tinted hair flying about her painted face, began the meeting by addressing Madolyn from the center of the gaudy carpet.

"Price Donnell told us about your work with the suffrage movement, Miss Maddie. We're hopin' . . ." She indicated the girls who sat in an arc behind her. "To be quiet frank, honey, we need your help."

Madolyn eyed the garish gathering, careful to avoid eye contact with either the madam or the soiled doves. With great effort, she was able to suppress her desire to jump up and run from the room. "If I can help, Miss Nugget, I certainly shall. I have dedicated my life to improving the lot of women in this cruel world."

"Has Tyler told you about our divided town?"

"Yes."

"Some of it," Tyler corrected. "What's that got to do—"

"Some of it," Goldie interrupted. "What he didn't mention, I'd venture, is the havoc it's playin' on our business."

Madolyn felt certain her heart would beat itself out this time. "Well . . ." She paused to clear her throat. Her mouth had never been so dry. ". . . I'm not sure what I could do about that."

"For starters, maybe you could talk some sense into your brother."

"My brother?"

"Morley. It's all his fault. Mostly, anyhow. If you could persuade him to sit down with Tyler and work out a way to reunite the town—"

"Hold on a cockeyed minute, Goldie," Tyler barked. "I'm not so sure I want this town reunited."

"Spoken like a true man."

Madolyn did a double take. "I second that, Miss Nugget."

"What I mean is," he explained, "reunitin' the town under Morley's conditions will come near to ruinin' me."

"In case you haven't noticed"—Goldie's tone was icy— "it is already ruinin' everyone else."

Madolyn took heart. "Your establishment isn't the only business hurt by the division?"

"Not by a long shot."

Her enthusiasm mounted. "Then I suggest you get together with the other townsfolk and work this out." She glanced to Tyler. "Mr. Grant and my brother are only two among many. This is a democracy. Or it was, last I heard."

Her final remarks were directed to Tyler, and she was pleased to see him grimace.

"It isn't that simple, honey," Goldie moaned.

"Most of the men don't give a rat's ass about this town." Goldie frowned at Daphne.

"Well, they don't," Annie retorted. "An' you know it, Goldie."

"That's why we turned to you, Miss Maddie." Daphne flung her mane of yellow hair, which must have prompted the moniker Gold-Dust; or perhaps it was the other way around, Madolyn mused.

"The minute Donnell told us you were workin' for women's rights, we knew you could help us out," Annie added.

"It's like you've been sent to us from heaven above, Miss Maddie," Two-Bit chimed in.

Heaven above? Madolyn glanced inadvertently toward the pressed-tin ceiling. Heaven above? Realizing the object of her attention, she felt a heated flush race up her neck. Heaven above! The business of this house was conducted just beyond that fancy ceiling. She recalled the threadbare carpet. If business was bad . . .

Lord in heaven! How had she gotten herself into such a situation? She ducked her head—or attempted to. But instead, without knowing how or why, she found herself gazing into Tyler's amused brown eyes.

It was all she could do not to clasp her hands to her face. But even that would not have retarded the glow that flushed her from the inside out. The roots of her hair felt singed. Her lips trembled, and Lord help her, but the feel of Tyler's lips sprang suddenly to mind. She pursed hers and in that instant, she knew he was thinking the same thing. Lord in heaven, how had she ever gotten herself into such a predicament?

Swiveling her head with a haughtiness designed to put an offender in his place, she returned her attention to Miss Nugget and the girls. "I'm not sure that the Lord had much of a hand in this, Bertie, nor what I can do to help, for that matter. This is not the sort of situation I regularly deal with."

"That's right, Goldie—"

"We've already heard your objections, Tyler. It's time for us women to get to work. Daphne was right, the men in this town don't give two spits in a rainstorm what happens around here. When they divided the town—"

"Morley divided the town," Tyler snarled.

"And you sat by and let him," Annie accused.

"When they divided the town," Goldie repeated, "the men gave no thought to services needed to run a home or household. The school is on this side of the tracks, which means only the children in Buck have use of it."

"They have the mercantile," Daphne explained.

"We have the livery."

"They have the hotel."

"We have the church."

"They have the bank."

"And we have the newspaper," Madolyn added, "which will certainly work in our favor."

"*Our* favor?" Tyler exploded. "You're not gettin' involved in this, Maddie."

Before she thought not to, she looked the man straight in the eye. His brown eyes were serious now. Pained, might be a better word. His mouth was grim-set, giving his chin a bluntness she had not seen before. The brown lock that fell over his brow softened the effect somehow, reminding her again of an overgrown child fighting for his toys. But Tyler Grant was no child; she had learned that lesson today. And this town would be no one's play toy.

"I will involve myself in whatever causes I deem important, Mr. Grant."

"Now, Maddie—"

"The women in Horn don't get the paper," Goldie broke in.

Madolyn returned to the problem with new enthusiasm, as the looming fight overrode her hesitancy to align herself with the sort of women who reclined around the room, their posture and costumes leaving no doubt as to their trade. Not that any of them seemed inclined to deny it.

"Why can't Mr. Rolly and Mr. Cryer deliver the newspapers?" she inquired.

"Now hold on a cockeyed minute. This little tea party has gone far enough."

Goldie glared at Tyler. "It'd probably be fine with Donnell, Maddie, but the Horn merchants might stop them."

"There is a way. There has to be." Madolyn was in her element. Her brain began to function, as though Tyler Grant had never turned it to mush. "We shall find a way." She jumped to her feet, paced to the window, parted the lace curtains, and peered out into the swept yard. "Yes, that will be our first step. We shall place a notice in the *Buckhorn News.*"

Lost in thought, she hadn't realized how close she stood to Tyler. When he grabbed her arm, he startled her.

"There's no need for you to involve yourself in this little difficulty," he drawled in that soft voice that washed over her.

She inhaled a deep breath to steady her senses, and breathed in, not the heavy perfumes of Goldie's girls, but Tyler's heady scent, the faintest hint of baywood, a strong bouquet of masculinity. He hovered over her, filling her senses again. Heat swirled up her spine. Passion such as she hadn't felt for a cause in a long time coursed through her.

"Oh, my, but there is, Mr. Grant. For several very good reasons—my brother divided this town, and you brought me to these ladies. Perhaps Bertie is right. Perhaps I was sent here for this very reason."

"Maddie, for God's sake, listen to me. You have enough trouble with Morley as it is. You'll play hell gettin' his help if you don't stop your meddlin'. A lady shouldn't—"

"A lady shouldn't what? Stand up for her sisters? She wouldn't be a very fine lady if she hid her head in the sand when called upon. Like Miss Abigail says, we cannot pick and choose our causes, men have already chosen them for us."

"Who the hell is Miss Abigail?"

Before Madolyn could respond, Goldie interrupted. "A vaquero's here to see you, Tyler."

Tyler glared at Madolyn. Finally, Goldie's words seemed to register. He glanced toward the door. *"Sánchez? ¿Qué pasa?"*

Madolyn followed Tyler's gaze. A swarthy-complected cowboy with a drooping black mustache stood awkwardly in the foyer. He twisted a very large, stiff-brimmed hat in his hands. His chaps were dirty but elaborately decorated with tooled engravings and silver medallions.

"Rurales, *jefe,*" the man responded. "They're comin'."

"Damn." Tyler's eyes found Madolyn's. She was ready.

"Miss Abigail is founder and president—"

"Save it, Maddie." He searched her face with silent questions, but for the life of her she didn't know what he was asking. "Come here." Without releasing his grip on her arm, he pulled her across the room, shouldered past the man called Sánchez, and drew her out the screen door to the front porch.

"Who is he?"

"A vaquero who works for me. I've gotta go with him."

She returned his heated gaze, unable for some unfathomable reason to look away. His nearness engulfed her, heating her as never before. His voice, like his bold features, was stiff.

"That'll mean leavin' you here for a while."

A dozen different retorts came to mind, but none of them

seemed appropriate at the moment. Actually, she couldn't think of a thing that was appropriate, so she asked a question that was doomed to show her ignorance. "What are Rurales?"

"Mexican soldiers. Accordin' to Sánchez, they're crossin' the river."

"For your cattle?"

"Sounds like it."

She smiled. "Then you have troubles of your own, Mr. Grant. Don't worry about me. Your town will be perfectly safe in my hands."

"Like hell it will." But his tone wasn't gruff. Indeed, he smiled when he said it; his features relaxed; his eyes danced. Before Madolyn knew it was happening, he had drawn her to him and covered her lips with his own.

Ah, such a blessed sweet tenderness swept over her. Caught unaware, by the time she thought to object, his mouth was moving over hers, wet and hot. Although she knew her actions—and his—were the height of indecorum, she was powerless to object, for never had she imagined anything as sweet and tender.

When he lifted his face, his eyes mesmerized her further with their sultry, heated perusal, as though he were delving into the very soul of her. He kissed the tip of her nose. "If this Miss Abigail of yours claims a lady wasn't meant to be kissed, stand forewarned, Maddie, I'm out to prove her wrong."

Then Lord help her, before she could grip her senses, he kissed her again. "Another thing, Maddie, when I get back to town, we're gonna do something about that 'Mr. Grant' nonsense."

Your town will be perfectly safe in my hands. Like hell! Buck, Texas, would be safer in the hands of Morley Sinclair than in the clutches of his sister—a woman with a cause.

The difficulty worried Tyler for the better part of the following week. He couldn't keep his mind off it.

Rather, he couldn't keep his mind off *her*. And he came to fear that even his town was safer in the hands of militant Maddie Sinclair than was his life—his future, leastways.

He had so much trouble concentrating on business, that once a Rurales' bullet whizzed past his shoulder, leaving a tear in his shirt and powder burns on his arm, before he realized he was in enemy territory.

"¡Chingaba, jefe!" Sánchez cursed. "You aimin' to get us all kilt."

"Hell, Sánchez," Raúl returned. "The chief ain't interested in those heifers out yonder. It's that little one in town's got his attention."

"Cut the bullshit," Tyler barked. "Give away our position, and we'll be drawin' black beans down in some Mex jail."

For the past four days and three nights, they had skirmished with the Rurales, reclaiming some of the cattle, losing others. But the Rurales managed to work their stolen herd ever closer to the Rio Grande—and safety. Now Tyler lay on his stomach between Raúl and Sánchez on a bluff overlooking a dry gulley that ran down to the river a hundred yards farther west.

"There's still six of 'em," Sánchez whispered. "Reckon that shot of mine must've hit a mesquite tree instead of the man sittin' underneath it."

They hadn't gone in shooting, not that first day. Tyler insisted on trying to talk to the Rurales; he wanted to explain that the cattle they were 'confiscating' had been born and bred on Texas soil. But the Mexicans would have nothing of it.

"I could've told you they wouldn't palaver," Raúl complained, after the trio was forced to hightail it under a barrage of rifle fire. "What the hell were you thinkin', anyhow?"

"Thinkin'?" Sánchez questioned, "Hell, he left his brain

back at that whorehouse, along with the rest of his vitals."
He laughed at his own joke. "It figures. *El jefe* falls for
the only woman in the house who don't charge for her services."

The suggestive remark fired Tyler as even the fight with
the Rurales hadn't done. "That woman's a lady, and both
of you had better remember it." He glared from one man
to the other. "She means nothin' to me. She's Morley
Damn-his-hide's sister."

Tyler studied the scene below them; he tried to concentrate on the six Rurales who were at this moment herding
his cattle down the ravine to a clearing just this side of the
river. From all indications they intended to bunch the herd
for a night drive across the river. Tyler recognized the tactic;
hell, he invented it; that was his method for moving cattle
from Mexico to Texas, spiriting them across the river in the
dead of night. Trouble was, this looked to be a moonlit
night.

"It's already late in the day," Tyler commented. "Let's let
them do our work; once they bunch 'em, we'll ride in from
three directions. Maybe if we make enough racket, they'll
think we've come up with reinforcements."

"Shoot to kill?" Sánchez questioned.

"Not unless you want both governments on our tail. Try
not to wound them, just scare the hell out of 'em."

"Nothin' we've come up with so far has scared the
sonsabitches," Raúl reminded his boss.

Tyler swatted a bee that droned above his head. Sweat
trickled down his neck and seeped beneath his shirt collar.
Indications of things to come. Of summer.

Would Maddie be gone by summer?

Damnation! If he didn't get his mind off that woman and
on the business at hand, he would be the one not around
come summer. The situation was unexpected, unwelcome,
and unexplainable. Why, after all this time, had he started
thinking about a woman? A woman wasn't in his plans,

hadn't been for twenty years. Hadn't he vowed never to shackle himself to another woman? After Susan?

Susan, his wife. She had been pretty as a picture and they married in a shower of youthful bliss. For a moment her springy blond curls and pert little nose danced in his vision. A pretty picture, but one he hadn't so much as thought of in twenty years. No, even before her death, Susan's curls had ceased to spring, her lips to smile.

The war. Sherman's army. No one in Georgia escaped unscathed. Most lost everything. The lucky ones got out with their lives—and their sanity.

Gone were the palatial homes and fashionable clothes. Gone, the balls and fox hunts and youth and innocence. Along with her youth and innocence, Susan had lost her mind.

And Tyler had sworn on her grave never to shackle himself to another female as long as he lived.

As long as he lived. Whether the end came this very night in a fight over a couple hundred head of cattle, or forty years from now on the deathbed of an old man, Tyler had vowed never to shackle himself to another woman.

And he had damned well better get to remembering that pledge. Digging in his pocket he withdrew a watch that had belonged to his father.

"Ahora, Raúl," he whispered. "Time to get movin'. You first."

Raúl scooted back from the cliff, standing only when he was beyond sight of those in the gulley. Tyler watched the minutes tick off. When he had given Raúl time to get in place, he signaled Sánchez.

"Ahora."

Sánchez followed the path Raúl had taken to his horse, which was tethered out of range in a thicket. Again, Tyler concentrated on his watch.

The moon was up now, a ball of white at about eight o'clock in the night sky. He quietly made his way to his

horse, tightened the cinch, and mounted. He hoped Raúl
and Sánchez were listening for his whistle, instead of
dreaming over black-eyed señoritas.

What a thing for him to think! What he really hoped was
that Raúl and Sánchez never found out he had entertained
such an idea! Not after the way his mind had roamed the
last few days.

Suddenly he was moving. He hooted in his best imitation
of an owl, then galloped hell-bent-for-leather into the clearing. They didn't frighten the Rurales, but they took them
by surprise.

"Buenas noches, señores," Tyler greeted the two men who
stood guard at the north end of the clearing. They were
dismounted and had squatted on the ground, smoking and
swapping stories. Tyler wagged his pistol at them. "Throw
down your guns and get movin'."

One man lifted his rifle, and Tyler fired. The man dodged,
and Tyler cringed, hoping he hadn't dodged the wrong way.
Tho bullet thudded into the crown of the lawman's sombrero, knocking the heavy braided hat to the ground.

When the man reached for it, Tyler stopped him. "Leave
it; you can buy another when you get home." When they
tried to step in their saddles, Tyler stopped them again. "Not
this time, amigos. Tonight you travel on foot."

A sudden shot from across the way drew their attention.
Sánchez rode up. "Any trouble?"

"Not yet. These fellers aren't too keen on swimmin'—"
Animals splashed into the river.

"By damn, if that's my cattle—" Tyler began.

"It's horses." Sánchez motioned to the two Rurales. "If
you two hombres want to catch a ride back to headquarters
you better get a move on. Don't look like your compadres
are waitin' for you."

Raúl rode up cursing the two that got away. After that,
it didn't take the remaining Rurales long to head for the

river. Tyler and his vaqueros watched them swim into the black current.

"They'll be back," Sánchez commented.

"Bank on it," Raúl agreed. "The Mex government ain't gonna give up this easy."

"That's why we have to move these cattle away from the river tonight," Tyler informed them. "After all the trouble we've gone to, I'd hate to lose them."

With a whoop, they started the cattle back up the ravine. Tyler glanced at the night sky, which was black by now and glittered with stars. He wondered whether Maddie had seen the sky out here. By damn, he'd like to show it to her. If she was still around.

"Think we can make that free range before dawn?" Raúl asked.

"We're takin' 'em to Buck." The idea had come suddenly, and he liked it. "We'll ship 'em off to market before the Rurales or Morley Sinclair can get their sticky hands on 'em."

"Looks like you an' me are fixin' to be out of a job, Raúl," Sánchez told the tophand.

"No way," Tyler replied. "Once we get these critters off to market, we'll swim the river and bring back another herd."

The week had been a disaster for Madolyn. She couldn't keep her mind off that man. No matter what she did, Tyler Grant was on her mind; no matter to whom she talked, she thought about him.

It was that last kiss that had done it. If only he hadn't kissed her like that—so tender and sweet a deep longing burrowed its way inside her, thinking about it.

And think about it she did—morning, noon, and night. She tried to dispel his image, to force him out of her mind, by diving head first into the town's difficulty. But every day that passed, she missed him more, rather than less.

It made absolutely no sense. But for once, she had no control over her own mind. Miss Abigail's dictums were the first to go. In desperation Madolyn turned to the system of survival she had learned as a child.

She set limits: She would not think about Tyler until after she met with Loretta James, the schoolmarm. She would not think about him until after she talked with Price Donnell about printing extra copies of the *Buckhorn News* to distribute across the tracks in Horn.

She had so much trouble concentrating on the Spanish lessons she engaged Loretta to give her, that she considered dropping them, lest Loretta think her an imbecile. She didn't drop them, though, for her two most private and precious goals concerned her newfound family: Before she left for Boston, she would hug each of her nephews and nieces and she would communicate with them in their own language.

Her turmoil over Tyler had not been well hidden, however, she discovered one morning when Goldie approached her. Early in the week Madolyn learned that Nugget wasn't the woman's surname. In fact, it wasn't part of her name at all.

"My mama named me Mable, honey. Mable Thorndecker. You can imagine what customers did with a name like that!"

Truthfully, Madolyn couldn't begin to imagine what customers would do with a name like that, but she silently agreed that Goldie fit the woman's lifestyle better than Mable. So she obliged the madam by calling her Goldie. And Goldie turned out to be quite an observer of human nature, Madolyn learned.

"It's my business, honey." Goldie settled into the rose-red settee in Madolyn's parlor. "Woman in my business has to be able to spot trouble between a man and a woman."

"Trouble?" This was Goldie's first visit to the third floor

since Madolyn arrived. Shocked to find her landlady at the door, Madolyn must have shown her uneasiness, for Goldie had exclaimed, "Just a little visit, honey. Thought you might be lonely." Although the direction of Goldie's conversation evaded Madolyn, the madam seemed to know exactly where she was headed.

"Love," Goldie explained.

"Love?" Madolyn's wariness increased.

"Why, honey, you say that word like it's new to the world. Let me tell you a thing or two. It ain't."

"I don't know what you're talking about, Goldie."

"About you and Tyler, that's what?"

"Me and Mr. Grant?"

"Whatever you call him, you can't hide the fact that you're head over heels."

"Head over heels?"

Goldie tossed her mane of henna-tinted hair. "I'm good at spottin' the trouble. Have to be, in my line of work. Anytime a girl of mine falls for a customer, she's out the door."

The conversation was not only bizarre, but disconcerting. Was Goldie kicking her out? "There's nothing for you to be concerned about, Goldie. I'm not . . ." She shrugged. ". . . head over heels—or anything else. Mr. Grant is just . . ." She sighed, wondering what on earth Tyler Grant was to her.

"He's always on your mind, that's what he is, honey. It's plain as mold on day-old bread."

"Oh, no—" Madolyn regrouped, attempting to put on a stern face, as Miss Abigail instructed. "I mean, I can change. I shall stop thinking about him. I shall. Don't worry about it."

"Worry about it? Honey, I'm tickled pink."

"But you said—"

"I said any of *my* girls. That's a different horse, all together. One of my girls falls for a customer, her work falls off; she doesn't want to accommodate anyone but him; times, she'll even stop chargin' him."

Madolyn clasped hands to heated cheeks. "My goodness. Well, I never . . ." Were she the fainting sort, Madolyn knew without a doubt she would be lying on her rose-red carpet this very moment. What a conversation!

Miss Abigail would be mortified!

But Miss Abigail, drat her, had already let Madolyn down. Her dictums were well and good for life in Boston, where one was protected by the support of like-minded sisters. Madolyn observed the woman who sat before her. Out West more things than the landscape were different. She couldn't imagine herself sitting, no living, in a house of ill repute in Boston. But here she was, discussing something sordid, yet not so sordid, either, with the madam of the House of Negotiable Love. No, out here things were different. Out here—

She had met Tyler Grant, and heaven help her, but her heart raced every time she thought about him. Bracing herself against the pain of it, she explained to Goldie.

"I am not a candidate for love, Goldie. Nor for marriage. I have pledged my life to the women's movement."

Goldie cocked her artificially colored head, pursed her tinted lips, and arched her painted eyebrows. "Is that so? I'm here to tell you, Maddie, when the love bug bites, there ain't nothin' you can do about it."

"Well, I can do something about it. I mean, I could, if it were necessary. You're worrying needlessly, Goldie. I couldn't be in love with Tyler Grant. I'm not going to fall in love with anyone."

One of Goldie's painted eyebrows arched. "Well, then, that's a different story. You can rest your mind, honey. You have nothing to fear from ol' Tyler. He, too, has pledged to remain single for the rest of his life."

"He has?" Madolyn's heart clattered against her ribs.

"For a fact. He was married at an early age to a young

thing back in Georgia. She died before the war was over, and Tyler vowed never to harness himself to another female again in this lifetime—those are his words, not mine."

"Oh." *He was married.* Questions popped instantly to Madolyn's mind. What had the woman been like? What was her name? Was she beautiful? Had he been in love with her? Was he still? She dared not ask Goldie. She couldn't reveal the extent of her curiosity, even though confiding in one so learned in such matters was definitely tempting.

"Way I see it," Goldie continued, "you and Tyler are cut out for each other."

"I told you—"

"I know, honey. That's what makes it perfect. You can enjoy each other's *company* without worrin' about makin' a commitment."

Madolyn wondered exactly what Goldie meant by company. The emphasis she put on the word brought Tyler's kisses to mind, rather than their limited conversations, conversations better described as confrontations.

"Maddie, honey, quit your blushin'. Kissin' and cuddlin' are downright healthy. Courtin's good for the constitution."

"I already have a good constitution."

"But you're lackin' something, honey. I can see it in you. An' Tyler is just the man to give you that little extra bit o' life. Can't blame you for not wantin' to marry. Matrimony's a different proposition altogether. Trust me, Maddie. There's no reason for you to deny yourself some of the more pleasurable lessons in life when Tyler Grant is here to teach 'em to you. Especially since he won't expect a commitment."

Seven

Madolyn tugged on her black gloves and glanced up the circular staircase. No sight of Goldie. Taking her father's pocket watch from her reticule, she consulted it. Daphne sashayed down the stairs at that moment, tails of her red satin kimono flying around her knees.

"Where's Goldie?" Madolyn asked. "Isn't she ready?"

"Says she ain't goin'. For you to go on ahead without her."

Madolyn stiffened her spine. With a practiced flip of her wrist, she closed the watch and dropped it back into her reticule. "Then I shan't go, either, Daphne. Please relay that message to Goldie."

Daphne started up the stairs, but stopped midway to the second-floor landing. "Miss Goldie!" she bellowed, in a manner that would have appalled Madolyn a week ago.

A lady never raised her voice, not even in the privacy of her own home. Madolyn hadn't needed Miss Abigail to teach her that, her mother had done it quite well. Now, after a week in Texas, the teachings of a lifetime were vanishing like so many soap bubbles.

With each passing day Tyler was being proved more and more right. And Morley. The West was no place for a lady. She might as well have traveled to the moon, so different was almost every facet of life out here.

But in another sense, life in this isolated corner of the world was invigorating, empowering in a way she had never experienced in Boston. Why, just this morning, she had despaired of girding up in a corset and tight-fitting basque. She had done it, of course. Oh, my, yes, she had done it.

But that didn't mean she hadn't been changed by her week in Buckhorn. One week. Seven days ago if anyone had suggested she would find herself living in a house of ill repute, not only living there, but actively battling to save the women's business, she would have accused them of tippling at the local pub.

Now she felt—actually felt comfortable in the presence of women whose modesty was limited, whose conversations were often incomprehensible, and whose occupation was not only objectionable but highly degrading to the plight of women in general.

Daphne continued to shout up the stairs. "Miss Maddie says she ain't goin' without you, Go—" Her voice stopped suddenly, when Goldie appeared on the landing.

"Oh!" the chorus raised. Madolyn stood speechless. She had never seen any of the women attired in street clothes. She had actually feared Goldie might wear her brassy gold kimono to the meeting. Indeed, she had braced herself against such a possibility, after Goldie rebuffed her suggestion to hold the first meeting of the Buck-Horn Reunited Society here at the House of Negotiable Love.

"I thought you would be more comfortable in your own surroundings," Madolyn had argued.

"What about the other women? Ever last one of 'em would be glancin' up the stairs, tryin' to take a gander at the girls, wonderin' which one accommodates her man, which one—"

"All right," Madolyn interrupted. Along with not to raise her voice, she had been taught not to interrupt people. But lately, she discovered her best line of defense against ribald conversations was to interrupt the speaker in midsentence. "We shall hold the first meeting at the schoolhouse. Tuesday. As soon as the children are excused—three o'clock sharp."

Three o'clock sharp had almost arrived. Madolyn tapped her toe. With the five-minute walk, they would have trouble making the meeting on time, even now.

But above her stood the madam of this house attired in a day dress of uncommon beauty, if a trifle on the flashy side. The tone on tone striped satin was a shade of rose-red Madolyn had been taught belonged on flowers in the garden. Although the bodice was high-necked—a relief—its tight fit stretched across Goldie's voluptuous bosom, giving one cause to wonder how strong the thread was and to hope for the best.

Goldie even wore a hat. The same rose-red as the dress, broad brimmed, with a spray of matching ostrich feathers that must have cost the poor bird its entire tail.

With her henna-tinted hair, fuchsia gown, and enough fragrance to eclipse the entire rose garden at the Boston Botanical Gardens, the madam presented a spirited front, to be sure. As it turned out, that's all it was—a front.

"I can't go," Goldie called down.

Madolyn stared at the woman who ran her home and business with such authority. "Of course, you can go."

"I can't. I would only hurt the cause."

"Nonsense."

"It isn't nonsense. It's fact. One look at me and the society would fall apart."

"You're the driving force."

"I'm the local madam."

"This was your idea, Goldie. You stated your case with enough conviction to persuade me to join you."

"You're the one to fight for us, Maddie. You have the experience, and the respectability."

"Respectability! What does that have to do with anything?"

"Everything!"

"Nothing."

"Everything," Goldie insisted. "Every woman at that meeting will be castin' sideways glances at me, those who don't turn tail and run the minute I step through the door."

"Speaking of which, we shall be late if we don't set out immediately."

"I can't go."

"And I shan't go without you."

"You must, Maddie."

"Must I? This isn't my fight."

"You've dedicated your life to betterin' the lot of women. You said so, yourself."

"How am I bettering your lot by doing your dirty work while you hide behind your painted shutters and wallow in self-pity?"

"Self-pity? Me? I do not wallow in self-pity."

Madolyn examined herself in the hall looking glass. She tucked a loose black curl beneath her black bonnet with black-gloved fingers. Seeing Goldie's reflection behind hers, she was struck by the disparity. She and the madam made a startling pair. But maybe that was what the world needed, beginning with Buck and Horn. If she and the madam could come to terms, could work together for the betterment of all, surely others would join their ranks.

She extended her hand. "Come, Goldie. Since I'm in charge, I shouldn't be late. The meeting can't begin until we arrive." Madolyn held her breath, and realized that those around her were doing the same.

"We need you, Goldie," she encouraged. "To stand the slightest chance of succeeding in this world, we women must stand together, united, one for all and all for one."

"You won't go without me?"

Madolyn shook her head. "Not one step."

Goldie inhaled, a deep, tremulous breath that tested every stitch in her rose-red bodice. "All right," she huffed. "All right." She glanced around, her gaze alighting on one of her girls after the other, taking them all in, coming at length to Madolyn. "If it's absolutely necessary."

"It is." Madolyn reached again. This time Goldie took her hand, placing a rose-red crocheted mitt into the fine black leather of Madolyn's glove. Madolyn led her out the door. Together they stood on the porch.

Madolyn took a step, tugged, and Goldie followed. When they crossed the swept yard, the soiled doves began to clap. The applause brought a sense of satisfaction to Madolyn, but Goldie wasn't convinced. At the edge of the yard, she dug in her heels.

"I should have had Clements drive us over in the carriage."

Madolyn tugged Goldie into the road. "The exercise will be good for us. Miss Abigail always says walking clears the mind."

"If that's true," Goldie conceded, "by the time you get to the schoolhouse, you will have recognized the error of your thinkin'."

"Goldie!"

"This Miss Abigail of yours?" Goldie asked after a while. "What would she say about me? About us . . . teamin' up?"

Madolyn considered the question. "I don't know," she responded, forthrightly, as was her nature. Nothing was to be gained by beating around the bush, she had learned. "But it really doesn't matter. In the past week, I've learned that some things that are right in the city, lack substance here in the West. Mr. Grant was right, this is indeed a harsh world for women. I don't see that it's much easier on men, though, judging from the depths to which Morley has sunk."

Madolyn set a brisk pace, with the excuse that they would be late to the meeting if they didn't hurry. In truth, she was reluctant to be seen walking across town in the company of the local madam.

Reluctant and ashamed of the fact. Goldie had treated

her with nothing but respect, and regardless of the woman's occupation, she was a woman in need. Madolyn had pledged her life to helping women in need. Then they passed the first saloon, and several men called greetings.

"Afternoon, Goldie!"

"Afternoon, Miz Sinclair."

Madolyn trained her gaze on the road ahead, as though she were both deaf and blind. Goldie, however, waved between bouts of moping her forehead with a damp handkerchief.

"Maybe I should've agreed to hold the meetin' at the house," she wheezed, breathing hard.

"The schoolhouse is quite a distance off," Madolyn acknowledged. To which Goldie harrumphed.

"Far side of town. Farthest buildin' away from my place."

"Farthest?"

"By design. Separatin' whores and schoolchildren ranks high priority even in a town this size."

"Perhaps we should have held the first meeting in between, then. There's the church . . ."

"I'll take the schoolhouse, Maddie. You have a lot to learn about this ol' world."

Madolyn smiled. A feeling of satisfaction suffused her, when she recalled the week just past and all the things she had learned. "I'd say I've gotten off to a pretty good start."

A short time later, she realized that the ground was rumbling, had been for some time. "Is that the train?" Her breath came short, but not from the walk, now. "Oh, my, I forgot all about the train." A curious sort of gloom settled over her.

"That rumblin' you feel ain't no train, honey."

"What is it?"

They approached the main road, which had run down the center of Buckhorn before the town was divided. It crossed the railroad tracks near the depots and headed out of town in a north-south direction.

At the intersection, Goldie stopped, directed her attention south. "That's cattle. A whole herd of 'em."

Madolyn followed Goldie's gaze. A hundred yards or so to the south, the road made a sharp turn west. A vaquero with a bandanna secured over the lower part of his face sat his horse at the apex of the bend. Madolyn stood immobile, mesmerized in turn by the vaquero's courage and seeming stupidity, for he whooped and waved his sombrero at the herd of stampeding cattle. At the last possible moment before running down both man and horse, the cattle turned. In no time, the roadway was filled with them, and the air with dust and noise—thundering hooves, clattering horns, whoops and shouts from the vaquero.

She had never seen so many cows in her life—and in town, for heaven's sake. Two more vaqueros emerged in the melee of cattle, their hats pulled low; bandannas covered their faces.

Incomprehensible as it seemed, bandits and cattle now filled the roadway. "What are they doing?" She gripped her parasol, knowing without being told that open or closed, it offered no protection against such a disaster.

"Come on, Maddie. Get out of the road." Shouting as she went, Goldie dashed to safety.

Madolyn turned to see the herd headed straight for her. With no more time lost to hesitation, she leaped for the closest barrier she could see, a graduated adobe fence. Attaining the lower section, she scrambled higher.

Cattle crowded the roadway now, brushing the low yard fences on either side. Then suddenly, before she could jump to the relative safety of the yard beyond, an arm grabbed her from behind and hauled her up against the flanks of a horse. Terror pounded in her head, in concert with the thundering hooves. Horse and rider bounded past the fence and came to a jarring halt in the side road.

"What the hell are you doin', runnin' into a herd of cattle? Haven't you ever seen cows before?"

Tyler's voice was gruff. He held her up against his hip as if she were no more than a sack of potatoes or something. She took a moment to savor the glow that spread through her fright.

"That herd of cattle ran into me," she retorted. "And yes, I have seen cows before." Although she had to admit never so many at one time. "Where I come from cows don't band together and charge down the street, running everyone down like they—"

While the herd thundered past, Tyler managed to shift Madolyn across the saddle in front of him. "Is that so?"

At the change in his tone, she stopped talking and looked him in the face. Using the hand in which he held the reins, he tugged the bandanna off his mouth, exposing clean skin, in contrast to the dust that caked his upper face and the portion of his forehead uncovered by his Stetson. He looked sinister now, with his mask of dirt.

He's going to kiss me, she thought. Right here in the middle of this dusty street, with cattle and vaqueros rushing past. To avoid such a catastrophe, she started talking. "Those are the cows? You got them back from the Rurales?"

He nodded, grinning. "But they didn't just band together. Took a lot of help from the boys an' me."

His warm eyes focused on her lips. She struggled to free herself because it was the thing to do, not because she wanted be set free. "I have to go, really. I'll be late."

"Late?"

Something foreign mixed with the dust and Goldie's rose fragrance; it clogged her throat.

"Late for what?"

"I, uh . . ." An innate sense of self-preservation tied her tongue. The pressure of his hand increased on her back; his face dipped.

"Really," she said hastily, attempting to wriggle off the horse. "I'm late already."

He hauled her closer. "Late for what, Maddie?"

She glanced across the street in time to see the last of the cattle clear the crossroads. A couple of vaqueros tagged along behind, quietly now, no whooping or waving of hats.

Dust began to settle. Goldie watched from the other side with an amused expression. *Oh, my,* Madolyn thought, recalling the madam's advice.

"Goldie, wait. I'm coming." She struggled in earnest. "Set me down, sir."

"Not until you tell me what you're late for."

Calling forth willpower she wasn't sure she possessed, she met him eye to eye. Then with glee, she informed him, "The first meeting of the Buck-Horn Reunited Society."

"The what?"

She smiled. "It's our organizational meeting, Mr. Grant. They can't start without me. Kindly set me down."

"Damnation!"

Madolyn scooted to the ground, skirted in front of him, and joined Goldie in the crossroads. The madam let go an ear-splitting whoop.

"Welcome home, Tyler, hon!"

Tyler pushed his hat back and wiped his forehead with his sleeve. His eyes widened in mock astonishment. "That you, Goldie? Hell, I didn't recognize you wearin' all those, uh, feathers."

Watching the exchange, Madolyn thought again about Goldie's advice and heat rushed up her neck. Her cheeks burned. She took Goldie by the arm, turned the madam away from the gawking Mr. Grant, and fairly pulled her down the street.

"Where's the meetin'?" Tyler called after them.

"Ignore him," Madolyn ordered. But *she* couldn't ignore him. His presence followed her down the road like a soft cloud.

"Schoolhouse," Goldie tossed back over her shoulder.

"Soon's I bed these critters down in the railroad trap, I'll join you."

Madolyn turned in her tracks. "Don't you dare."

"Why, Maddie, how could you, a fair-minded woman, exclude me? I own the town, case you forgot."

"As if anyone could forget after that show of power."

"Show of power? What . . . ?" But Madolyn was already leading the madam down the street.

Loretta James met them at the schoolhouse door. Five years younger than Madolyn's thirty, Loretta had become good friends with Madolyn during the past week while they planned the new society's organization, and Loretta tutored Madolyn in Spanish.

From Saint Louis, Loretta had been forthright about her reasons for coming west to teach school. "To catch a husband. Oh, I don't mean to sound unscrupulous about it. But isn't that the reason every woman comes west, to tame a cowboy?"

Madolyn had not been as forthright with the schoolmarm. "I've come to tame a wayward brother," she hedged, sidestepping the issue in a manner that was unlike her.

She needed Loretta's help, she rationalized, and Loretta had already balked at including the town madam in their plans. How would she feel about an avowed spinster?

"I was getting worried," Loretta whispered now, casting her unusually large black eyes toward Goldie.

"We ran into a little trouble. But we are here and ready to roll up our sleeves. Loretta, meet Goldie."

Madolyn had argued for using Goldie's real name, Mable Thorndecker, but Goldie wouldn't hear of it.

"This is business. I'll use my business name. Ain't gonna change any of those women's minds about me, no-how."

To Madolyn's relief, Loretta extended her hand, shook

Goldie's rose-red mitt, then drew the two of them into the room.

A crowd had already gathered.

Goldie balked at the door. "They've come to see me."

"No, they haven't," Madolyn whispered. "They're here for the same reason you are—to save this town."

"Easy for you to say."

"Come on." Madolyn prodded Goldie through the crowd like a mother with a recalcitrant child. She didn't stop until they reached the front of the room, where Loretta had saved two front-row seats for them.

The silent room seemed to hum with energy. Madolyn was in her element. Her pulse pounded. She was good at organizing people to fight for causes, and she knew it. She thrived on such work. But on this day when she rose to face the crowd, she was momentarily taken aback. Beside every woman sat a man—her husband.

Parson Willard Arndt had accompanied his wife Francis; Owen Jasper, mercantile owner, sat beside his wife, Hattie; saloonkeeper Victor Crane, had come with his Camilla; not even Price Donnell's bookkeeper, Inez Bradford, had been able to escape her husband, Bill.

Every pine bench in the schoolhouse was filled, and a good half those in attendance were men—the men of this community who supported Tyler and opposed reunification.

She inhaled a deep breath and tried to think it was for the best. After all, the businessmen were the ones suffering, whether they admitted it or not. "I apologize for being late," she told the group. "The owner of this fair city chose this particular day to drive his cattle through the center of town." She brushed off a patch of dirt. "Goldie and I seem to be the worst for it."

Price Donnell had set up his tripod front and center, from a position where he could get shots of both the gathering and of the speaker. Madolyn blushed to think she might be headline news for two weeks running. Oh, well, if it was good for the cause.

The paper the week before hadn't been nearly the disaster she had feared. For one thing, the photograph was so grainy the lettering on Goldie's sign wasn't legible. Then, too, Mr. Donnell's camera obviously wasn't equipped to handle both sunlight and shadows, for the faces of those gathered on the porch were obliterated by the deep black shadows of the porch.

Not that anyone who saw the picture would doubt for one moment where the photograph had been taken or who the subjects were. And in case one happened to forget that the House of Negotiable Love was the only three-story frame house in all of Buck, Texas, the caption named the house and each individual in the photograph—prostitute, madam, and spinster, alike.

"Since this is an organizational meeting," she began, "our first order of business should be to elect officers."

"Reckon you'll have to be the president, Miss Sinclair, since none of the rest of us've given thought to reconnectin' the towns." The speaker sat in the rear, a man she didn't recognize.

Madolyn perused him, while trying to decide how best to continue. Hecklers were not new to her. Far from it. But the men in this room not only had businesses to consider, they held control over their wives. She could not openly offend them and hope to meet the society's objective. On the off chance that she could gain their support, she addressed the heckler.

"Many of you are more qualified than I, from the standpoint of being familiar with the town, its history, and its needs."

"I say we put off votin', till we decide whether we can pull this thing off, sayin' we want to do it a'tall." The suggestion came from a man she had never met, but knew by sight, Victor Crane, saloonkeeper. Before she could respond, Owen Jasper, mercantile owner, spoke up.

"Victor's right. Even if we wanted to do what you're askin', I don't see how we could be successful, short of shootin' both the principals in this little fight."

Every man in the room laughed. Madolyn blanched. Shoot Morley and Tyler? At this point, she might offer to pull the trigger.

"I assure you, such drastic measures will not be necessary, Mr. Crane." Another man, unfamiliar to her, pursued the topic.

"What I'm wonderin', is how you figure on reunitin' the town, long as them two heathens continue to fight like two coons in a sack?"

"You have a point, of course, Mr., uh . . ."

"Melrose, ma'am. Pete Melrose, hostler."

Mr. Melrose obviously had no wife, or else he had left her home to tend house. Madolyn reached deep inside and drew forth courage. As long as she stood at the front of the room, she remained in control.

"We have several avenues open to us, Mr. Melrose. I have spoken with Mr. Donnell about printing extra editions of the newspaper to distribute in Horn."

"Who you figure on gettin' to do your deliverin'?"

"Mr. Cryer and Mr. Rolly."

A buzz spread through the room. What it meant, she had no idea.

"What good'll gettin' the newspaper out do?" questioned another male voice.

Obviously the men intended to do nothing but nettle her. Since she had little to lose, Madolyn decided to address the women directly, but when she attempted to catch a female eye or two, one by one the women dropped their heads. Despair threatened. She fought for control.

"The newspaper is our method of communicating with one another and with those on the other side of the tracks," she explained. "Anyone who is so inclined will be allowed to write articles, calling on all citizens to unite in this effort. We shall espouse the benefits of reunification; print personal accounts of what the division has cost citizens on both sides; delineate the process by which we will attain our lofty goal; and create a general air of camaraderie that will be impossible for my brother and Mr. Grant to ignore. As I said earlier, they are but two among many. Both towns belong to the United States of America; America is still free; a democracy. If worse comes to worst, we shall call in the federal authorities. Buckhorn was formally organized as a single unit; I have already checked on that. No matter what Morley or Mr. Grant did, their action did not revoke the charter."

"You'd call in the troops?" an unidentified male challenged.

"Not I," she retorted. "This is a community effort. I was asked to organize an endeavor from which the whole town will benefit. I, sir, shan't be around to reap the rewards. But to answer your question, hopefully, it will not come down to calling in federal troops."

Madolyn glanced over the gathering, taking in the belligerent male eyes and the bowed heads of their wives. "Since most of you ladies must get home in time to prepare supper, shall we continue with our business?" Madolyn spread her notes on Loretta's desk. "The officers we must elect today are president, vice-president, secretary, treasurer—"

"Treasurer?" the parson inquired. "What do we need with a treasurer? We haven't got any money."

"True," Madolyn acknowledged. "But we should keep track of the cost of things, regardless of who foots the bills."

"Bills?" echoed a chorus of male voices.

"There won't be many expenses," she stressed. "Things like paper and paint for signs . . ."

"Forget about a treasurer," Owen Jasper directed. "Whatever we need, we'll donate ourselves."

"If that's the way you want it," Madolyn succumbed. "No

treasurer. But we will need committees. A committee to fold and distribute newspapers on both sides of the town; a committee to keep the citizens informed of changes or marches or meetings . . ."

"Meetings? Where would we meet? I mean both sides together? Folks don't cross back and forth."

Madolyn perused the crowd. That was one question she had come prepared to answer. She had the solution, the only solution. But she had not planned to speak her mind to a roomful of men. She eyed Goldie. "What about your place?"

"My place?"

"You said it's the only place on either side of the tracks where . . . I mean . . ."

"HOLD IT!" came a shout from the rear.

Madolyn turned her attention to the speaker, who stood up, fiddling with his hat brim. "With all due respect, Miss Sinclair, I don't rightly see how exposin' the gentlemen who frequent Miss Goldie's will be for the good of the town."

Madolyn's eyes popped. She pressed her lips together. When she dared, she scanned the crowd. Men were red-faced; a few of the women had raised their faces, only to reveal pinched lips and mottled cheeks. Oh, my, what had she done?

"I didn't intend to expose anybody, sir. What I meant was . . . well, the third floor . . ."

Price Donnell took over. "Look at it this way, Miss Sinclair. We can't end one war by startin' a lot of smaller ones."

Miss Abigail's dictum held the opposite view, that if one were to win a war, one must be willing to engage in the battles. "Does anyone have a better solution?"

Every man eyed his neighbor.

"A different solution?" she reworded.

Still no one spoke up. One look at Goldie revealed a flush beneath the face paint and a grim set to her red lips. Goldie embarrassed? Madolyn's ire rose another notch. The nerve of these sanctimonious men!

"When you divided this town," she said tersely, addressing the men as a group for the first time today, "perhaps you should have taken care to provide a few necessities— such as a hotel." To the man of them, they stared at her, uncomprehending.

"Do not insult me by pretending not to know that I live on the top floor of Goldie's establishment."

Every eye sought a different mark.

"Rather than diminish my respectability," she continued, "the experience has hopefully awakened my regard for all my fellow . . ." Madolyn's words trailed off, as something akin to a heat flash prickled her skin. Her gaze flew to the door. Sure enough, there he stood. Tyler Grant.

He lounged in the doorway, filling it with his broad shoulders and arrogant presence. She had seen that stance before, that insolent expression before. Her dander rose even as her body began to glow.

"Mr. Grant. To what do we owe the honor of your presence?"

Lazily he removed a twig from his mouth. He didn't stand up straight, but continued to lounge against the door. She realized that, unlike when she had seen him earlier, he was clean. His face was scrubbed and shaven, his boots were polished, his duckins creased, and his shirt starched. She recalled Penny-Ante, the scene she had opened her door to one day last week, Penny-Ante twirling her finger in Tyler's nude navel.

Madolyn's knees went weak. She grasped the edge of the table, her mind far away, at the house, in her room . . .

"Whenever you're finished organizin' the destruction of my town, Maddie, I'd like a chance to *talk* some sense into you."

Eight

Applause erupted in the crowded schoolroom. Maddie's face turned the shade of a West Texas sunset in late autumn. And Tyler knew he was in deep trouble.

But damnation, she was fun to tease—so serious, so holier-than-thou. Yet, somehow he had to stop her from ruining his business, which is what he figured reuniting Buckhorn would amount to.

"Quiet," Madolyn called over the ruckus. "Quiet. Ladies, we must finish our business before we adjourn." But the men were already on their feet. She watched helplessly, while they congregated around Tyler, shaking his hand and clapping him on the shoulder as if he owned the town—which, of course, he did.

"We must elect a president before we adjourn." Madolyn scanned the room. Only a few of the women sat now, all except Goldie with downcast eyes. Whipped, that's what they were, whipped into submission by men who felt themselves superior; men, whom some had begun to term chauvinistic. Men like her brother.

Like Tyler Grant.

"Ladies . . ." she called again.

"Save your breath, Miss Sinclair." Price Donnell stood at her elbow. "The job'll fall to you, anyhow. Might as well accept that fact and get on with things."

"I hadn't realized there was so much work to be done here."

"No different from any other place," Donnell allowed.

"Except that my brother is responsible for the plight of these people."

"You are not your brother's keeper."

"If not I, sir, then who?" She watched the women rise and join their husbands, not as equals, side by side, but standing back, yielding their rights as human beings. It filled Madolyn with sadness—and with anger. "If I don't try to mend things, Mr. Donnell, who will?"

Even as she spoke, Tyler began to wend his way toward her. He worked the crowd like a politician—grinning, shaking hands, slapping men on the shoulders.

The men looked sheepish; the women hung their heads. Unhappy that he caught them plotting against him, Madolyn knew. When he came within earshot, she learned to what depths this man would stoop to defeat her, as he greeted citizen after citizen in much the same manner.

"Good to see you out, Miz Crane. How's that gout?"

"Better, Mr. Grant, since I've been usin' that ointment you sent by."

"Glad to hear it. Glad to hear it." Tyler moved through the crowd.

"Miz Jasper, how's that leg of little Huey's?"

"Mendin', Mr. Grant. Thank you kindly."

"We should have a doctor arrivin' on the next train or two. I sent word off to several of the state's newspapers— *Austin Statesman, San Antonio Light,* and a couple of others."

"Bless you, Mr. Grant."

"Don't bless me for doin' my job, Miz Jasper. It's my town, my responsibility." By the time he moved on, Hattie Jasper was practically drooling in his wake. Tyler stopped at the next man.

"Jedediah, Morley ever let you use that bull of ours? No? Tell you what, I've got one over in the railroad trap you might want to take a look at. See what you think. If you like what you see, take him on out to your place. I can hold off sellin' him till next time."

Jedediah pumped Tyler's hand; gratitude oozed from his pores. Madolyn felt sick. Then Tyler was beside her. But after no more than a skimming glance, his attention was diverted to the schoolmarm.

"Miss Loretta, you receive that new set of *Britannicas?*"

"Yes, Mr. Grant. Thank you so much. The children are already benefiting."

Madolyn watched, dumbfounded, while Tyler withdrew a roll of bills from his pocket and began to count them off.

"Summer's comin' up fast," he told Loretta. "Might as well settle up now so you can have travel money. Didn't I hear somethin' about you spendin' the summer with your folks in St. Louis?"

"That's right." Loretta folded the money without counting it and stuffed it inside her black reticule. "Thank you, Mr. Grant, you're always so thoughtful."

Tyler favored Madolyn with a satisfied smile, then turned back to the schoolmarm with a concerned expression. "Just be sure you come back to us, Miss Loretta. Buck's children need you."

Madolyn's indignation rose to new heights. Leave it to a man to play politics with every important issue. Anxious to escape, she glanced down the aisle to see Goldie sashay out the door. Even Goldie was defecting! Retrieving her parasol, Madolyn followed. The meeting had been a dismal failure, dismal. And, as usual, men were to blame. Their plan was as clear as a bright summer day. They had accompanied their wives with the express purpose of running the show themselves, and they succeeded.

But as she made her way toward the door, Madolyn's systematic brain began to work. Plans took form. She must get the women alone. The lesson learned today was that they must meet in secrecy or under false pretenses, in order to prevent the men from interfering.

Madolyn had always hated that part of working for women's rights. In order to accomplish the smallest gain, she was often required to lie, or as she preferred to think of it, fabricate, to use all the creative powers she had been born with and a few she dredged up from who knew where. Miss Abigail had complimented her more than once on her inventiveness.

"Necessity is the mother of invention," Miss Abigail would say, and although the saying wasn't original with the suffragette, it fitted the occasion.

Nevertheless, from time to time Madolyn had been afflicted by pangs of remorse for having lied to her fellow man. At such times, however, she only had to visualize how dismal the women's lives would have been had she stuck to the literal truth. The guileful performance she had witnessed from Tyler Grant today proved that no lie would be too harsh, no fabrication too original.

Price Donnell stood in the doorway when she approached. His derby was tipped back on his head, and he stroked his blond mustache in a contemplative manner. Reaching him, she strove to control the rage that caterwauled inside her.

There was work to be done in Buckhorn, Texas. She had known that when she agreed to organize this meeting. Although she had known from the outset not to expect smooth sailing, she hadn't expected the men to interfere so openly, or Tyler to mount such a blatant counterattack. Neither should have come as a surprise. Certainly not as a disappointment.

That they did, fired her determination.

"Doesn't look like things got off to too good a start, Miss Sinclair," Donnell asserted.

Let the lies commence, she thought. "On the contrary, Mr. Donnell. I am very pleased with our first meeting. Organizational meetings never run smoothly. I'm not certain how many articles we can count on for our first edition, though. Other than my own, of course, which I shall deliver to you first thing in the morning."

The newspaper editor looked bemused, but she deliberately tried to think the best of him. He was, after all, a willing ally. "What topic have you chosen?" he wanted to know.

"I haven't decided. Rest assured, it will stir the souls of those in this divided town who would hinder progress."

Donnell grinned. "I look forward to reading it then, Miss Sinclair, I certainly—" The newspaperman's reply was cut short when Tyler approached and took his hand.

"Donnell! What you doin' alignin' yourself with these rabble-rousers?"

Tyler's tone was jocular, but his words sped to the heart of Madolyn's anger. Grabbing her skirts in both hands, she stomped down the steps and across the swept yard, only to be brought up short before she reached the road.

"Maddie, wait up."

"I'll thank you to unhand me, Mr. Grant."

"We need to have a little talk. Once I explain my side—"

"Once you talk some sense into me?"

Tyler held fast.

"Rabble-rouser, my eye!" Madolyn was so mad she didn't realize he was leading her toward a wagon hitched at the pole rail until he attempted to lift her up to the seat. The nerve of him! Glancing about for help, she spied Goldie, who was already a block down the street.

"Goldie!" she called. "Wait for me."

The madam stopped just as Tyler grabbed Madolyn around the waist and swung her onto the wagon seat.

"Stay," he ordered, when she started to scramble down. "Stay right there, Maddie."

Madolyn stayed, although she didn't look on it as obeying Tyler's command. She had no desire to create more of a scene.

"Goldie," she called again. "We'll pick you up."

But they didn't. Reaching the crossroads, Tyler turned away from the house. "You don't mind, do you, Goldie?"

Goldie waved a rose-red mitted hand and grinned broadly. "No way, Tyler."

"Men!" Flouncing as far away from his broad shoulders as she could on the short wagon seat, Madolyn thrust open her parasol. Tyler ducked to keep from being jabbed by the ribs.

"What's that supposed to mean?"

"Everything!"

"Everythin'?"

"Everything bad, negative, hateful—"

"Whoa, now, Maddie. I can see where you might have your dander up at me, but condemnin' the whole human race—"

"Male race."

"Male race, then. I don't know what men ever did to you—"

"You saw them in there. Bullying their wives."

"Now, be fair about it. I didn't see one man bully his wife an' neither did you."

"Perhaps not physically, but those poor women know their places. They didn't dare speak up. Their husbands came along to speak for them. How many years of marriage does it take for a woman to learn her place, Mr. Grant?"

"I wouldn't know."

"And you played right into their hands. Don't deny it."

"I don't deny it. You started this shootin' match; am I not allowed to defend myself?"

"Defend yourself?"

"And my town."

"Your town?"

"Thanks to your brother, yes, Buck, Texas, is my town."

"I see. That's why you were so solicitous back there. Bringing in a doctor? Providing encyclopedias for the school, paying the teacher, providing a bull for . . . for—"

Madolyn stopped short when she realized the direction she was headed.

"For what, Maddie?"

Stiffening her spine, Madolyn gripped the edge of the seat with her free hand. How did she always manage to put herself at a disadvantage with this man?

"What were you sayin', Maddie?"

"The topics of conversation in this barbaric land are . . . are . . ." Madolyn's words drifted off when she realized they had left the town behind.

The road they followed wound up the side of a hill, ever higher. When she peered from beneath her parasol, she had to look straight up to see the top. Rolly's words came back. *Don't know of an unmarried lady in either town who'd turn down an offer to ride out into the country with Tyler Grant.* Out into the country?

"Where are you taking me?"

"To see my town."

She cast a worried glance back the way they had come. "We've left it behind."

"There's a place up here where you can get a better view, especially at sunset."

"Sunset?"

"Put that parasol away and you'll see. There's no sun left to defend against, Maddie. And I'm not much of a menace."

She wasn't convinced of that, not by a long shot, but she slammed her parasol closed. The moment it was secured, Tyler took it and tossed it to the wagon bed behind them.

He winked. "Just to be on the safe side."

Madolyn glanced around, wary, her nervousness increasing now that they were alone. When Tyler pulled the team off the road, she froze. And when he rounded the wagon and offered his hand, she balked.

"Come on," he encouraged. "There's a great spot over yonder where you can look out over the town while I explain my position."

"I know your position in this town, thank you. You own t." Emotions warred inside her. She was angry with him, urious. But heaven help her, if, halfway up the mountain Goldie's advice hadn't come back in a rush. That slow heat had begun to glow inside her much earlier—the moment she saw him standing in the schoolhouse door. By now it had now increased in intensity until she felt like she might melt. The throb of her heart echoed up and down her spine. For the life of her she couldn't stop it, no more than she could stop the hum in her ears. She shouldn't get out of the wagon. She shouldn't . . .

In spite of her best intentions, she placed a gloved hand in his offered one and allowed him to assist her. Once on the ground, she had the presence of mind to withdraw her hand promptly, though she dared not look him in the eye, least he read her perfidious thoughts.

Why was it, she reasoned, that when Goldie suggested such a thing as enjoying Tyler's *company,* Madolyn hadn't been offended or even taken aback—well, not after thinking it over? It had actually seemed like a sound idea. But now, alone with him, all she wanted to do was run down the hillside.

Not that Goldie's suggestion didn't still hold a curious sort of appeal. Unfortunately it did. Similarly, she supposed, one of criminal predilection was drawn to robbing banks or holding up stagecoaches. However, the allure of the dastardly pursuit notwithstanding, she certainly intended to hold her wicked self in check. Especially after the episode at the schoolhouse, where Tyler had shown his true stripes.

To that end, holding her wicked self in check, the moment Tyler's hand touched the small of her back, she scurried away. Of course, she did so without meditation, therefore, she wasn't careful where she planted her feet, and as a result one foot skidded off a rock and the other flew out from under her.

"Whoa, now, Maddie." Tyler's drawl was infuriatingly

mirthful, but his hands were firm when he caught her around the waist, lifted her in the air, and set her down on a stone slab.

He even ignored her little mishap, which surprised her. Generally, he jumped at every chance to make fun of her. Instead, he hunkered down beside her, balancing on the balls of his feet, arms crossed over duck-clad knees. Not touching her, but close, so close she could hear his breath rise and fall; so close she inhaled his scent—fresh, clean, baywood, and something else, something she couldn't put a name to, something peculiar only to him, in her experience, anyway. It set her heart to pounding as nothing ever had.

"Look down there, Maddie," he encouraged. "Tell me that town is barbaric, uncivilized."

They sat halfway up the side of an almost-barren hill on a gray limestone slab that had fallen from the cliff in ages past. Here and there gray-green tufted plants sprouted through the rocks; a few of the tufts sported towering spikes that were topped by clusters of waxy white blossoms. The white stood in stark relief against the weathered landscape.

She willed her emotions to steady, her brain to clear. She tried to focus on the anger she felt for this man, anger that to her horror steadily ebbed. Tyler sat quietly by her side.

Below them the town was enveloped in a fiery scene that looked like it could have come straight out of Dante's *Inferno*. The setting sun streaked the adobe buildings a dozen different shades of red. Black shadows slithered out of alleys and across broad expanses of unpaved roads. One, the main artery down which Tyler had driven his cattle, connected the two towns north and south; the railroad ran east and west through the middle of the scene, separating the towns—or joining them. It all depended on one's point of view.

"It looks like a Degas painting," she commented.

"Humm," he agreed. "I never cared much for his vivid colors, though. His pastels now, those I appreciate."

Madolyn shifted. Her shoulders grazed his arm. Her comment had been spontaneous; she hadn't intended to launch a discussion of French impressionism here in the barbaric West. Her surprise must have showed, for Tyler chuckled, a warm, friendly sound that spilled over her like rays from the setting sun.

"I haven't always lived this far from civilization." His eyes danced over her face. "Atlanta is . . . was . . . a city filled with culture. Of course, it started out like all places, a little rough around the edges. Takes people to add refinement, a lady's touch."

Pulling her gaze away from his, she focused on the scene that stretched before them, but was far more conscious of the man beside her than of the spectacular view. His fresh, soap-scented masculinity filled her nostrils; his presence filled her mind. She heard his breath rise and fall, no steadier than her own. Something strange and curious seemed to be taking place here on this hillside. She wasn't sure what it was, but she had begun to feel light-headed. She thought perhaps she should try to stop it.

"From here they look like one town," she said, in an attempt to still the silent dialogue she imagined traveling between them.

"They're not, and for good reason."

"You said you were angry when Morley divided the town."

"I was. But after thinkin' it over, I came to the conclusion that I'm better off for it."

Just like a man! "Be that as it may, Mr. Grant, you heard Goldie. Everyone else is suffering."

"Not anymore than other folks who come West to make a new life. I told you, Maddie. This is a harsh country. Only the strong and most determined survive."

"If that's true, those people certainly don't need the added misfortune of being pawns in a contest of egos."

She felt his shoulders bunch, could almost hear his teeth grind. After a while he spoke, quietly. "Those are my people, down there. I help them. You saw it. I'll do anything I can to make their lives easier. But reunitin' the town would ruin my business; if my business fails, the town dies."

"Precisely the attitude I mean, sir. An inflated ego—"

"Ego has nothin' to do with it," he drawled. "At least not mine. I hate to bring this up, but Morley Sinclair is no saint."

"You are?"

"No." The silence stretched in measured heartbeats between them. "No, I'm not a saint." She felt his eyes on her. "Neither are you, buttin' into everyone else's business."

Even though his voice held no censure, his accusation stung, and Madolyn had learned early that when stung to sting back. "I was invited to organize the women for the purpose of reuniting the town. Reuniting the town is for the purpose of straightening out the mess you and Morley made when you divided it."

"I didn't divide it."

"Then why are you fighting me?"

"I told you why. Morley Sinclair would ruin me if the town were reunited."

"How could Morley ruin you?"

"You don't know him, Maddie. He's mean as an ol' mossy horn that's been caught in a bog all summer. If you reunite those towns, Morley Damn-his-hide will refuse to let me ship cattle."

"How could he? You're as big as he is. Or as . . ."

"As mean?" he challenged.

"Not mean." Lulled by the constantly varying hues of sunlight that played across the valley below them, and by the light-headedness that seemed to increase moment by moment, Madolyn's guard slipped. "Dangerous, I think."

"Dangerous? Me?"

"Yes." She made the mistake of looking at him, and found him staring at her. Her breath caught. "I mean, you appear capable of standing up for yourself. If Morley tried to keep you from shipping cattle, I doubt you would sit by and allow it."

His brown gaze was warm, his expression one of bemusement. "You're suggestin' Morley and I start a war?"

She couldn't look away. "A war? Certainly not. Must you exaggerate everything, sir?"

His eyebrows raised a notch in an expression that instantly confirmed her description of him. *Dangerous.*

"That's what it would be, Maddie. An all-out war. Hell, it's already off to a good start. You saw how he had those kids guardin' the pastures."

"They wouldn't have shot you."

"No, they wouldn't have. But if push came to shove, Morley wouldn't blink an eye at hirin' someone who would."

"Shoot you?"

"No. Try to. I'd damned sure defend myself."

"Oh."

"Yes, Maddie, *oh* . . . . oh, what a mess that would be. A full-scale range war would be worse for every man, woman, and child in that town below than anythin' they have to endure right now. Fact is, they've learned to manage well enough. You saw what they think of me. They wouldn't be that supportive if their livelihoods were threatened as much as Goldie makes out."

"Are you suggesting Goldie and the girls are lying, sir?"

He moved quickly. Taking her off guard, he caught her chin in a firm grip and turned her face to his. Though intense, for some reason his expression did not frighten her. Then he spoke.

"If you call me *sir* one more time, I might just turn you over my knee and teach you a lesson."

A red haze of terror blinded her. She froze, everything except her skittering heart. When she was able to move, she jerked free and turned to stare at the scene below, seeing nothing but red, a glowing, threatening red. The only reason she didn't jump up and run down the hill was the certainty that he would catch her.

Catch her and . . . what? Anger forced its way through the mire of chaos that muddled her brain.

"This is the most barbaric, uncouth land I have ever seen. It drags everyone down—"

"It's no place for a lady." Tyler's voice was calm again, as if he had never uttered a threat in his life. "Ladies see the world through different eyes. Ladies need refinement and education and the arts."

And safety. And protection. "The ladies of Buckhorn will see to that, once their town is reunited."

"Will they? Weren't you just complainin' about how little control they have over their lives?"

"I didn't intend to imply that Buckhorn is different from any other place on earth," she insisted. "The female of our species is taught from the cradle to be submissive to the male."

"History tends to back up that attitude."

"True, but the wickedness fostered by such antiquated behavior suggests that it's past time for a change."

Tyler didn't miss a beat. "Not in my town, Maddie. I won't have you stirrin' up a hornet's nest in Buck. Do you hear me?"

"I hear you, Mr. Grant. If you're so eager to get rid of me, convince Morley to secure my inheritance."

"That's the damnedest suggestion you've come up with yet!"

At his astonished tone, she turned to find his face nearer than she had thought. His eyes were for her alone, and even if he had never touched her, never kissed her, she would have known what was on his mind. When he moved toward her, she flinched.

He paused. "What's the matter?"

She ducked her head, but with two fingers, he lifted her face to his.

"Look at me, Maddie."

For some reason, she complied, but her eyes darted away after only a glance. She knew what he was thinking, what he wanted. Lord in heaven, she wanted it, too. When her lips trembled, she pressed them together.

"What are you afraid of?" he asked gently.

She swallowed, unable to reply, unwilling to pique his anger again.

"Come on, Maddie, out with it."

When she remained silent, his pressure on her chin tightened. "Maddie . . ." he warned. At least that was what she heard in his voice, a warning.

She didn't want to believe it, not of him, but the proof was sitting here before her. Gritting her teeth to still her trembling, she jerked her chin free. "Or what? You'll turn me over your knee?"

"What?"

"Like you threatened—"

"Damnation! I didn't mean that. I was frustrated. Hell, I've never struck a woman in my life."

"Not even your wife?"

"My wife? Who told you about Susan?"

Susan. Her name was Susan. A beautiful name. Much prettier than Madolyn or Maddie. "Goldie."

"I should have known." Absently, he took Madolyn's hands in his. His soft drawl was earnest. "No, Maddie, I never struck my wife. I was taught to respect women."

"Even when you're angry? When they displease you?"

"All the time." His tone held her mesmerized, and his eyes, his warm, sincere brown eyes. The silence lengthened, her heart fluttered. His claim permeated the very air, suffused it with his earnestness. Or with her desire to believe him earnest? With infinite slowness, as though unaware of his actions, he began to tug off her black gloves, finger by finger. When at length he spoke, his tone was light, soft.

"I didn't mean to scare you, Maddie. I wouldn't hurt you, not ever." He cast her gloves aside, then reached for her. "Come here. Let me show you." His arms moved with infinite care to encircle her, and she sat as in a dream, unable to move away.

His lips descended just as slowly; still she gave no thought to turning aside. Her only thought, as his lips claimed hers in a long, wet, mind-boggling kiss, was *at last*. At last she was in his arms again. His tender, gentle, protective arms. At least, they were protective at this moment. She wouldn't be here long enough for them to turn violent.

Then his kiss took her thoughts away, and with them, her breath. Her mind soared to the heavens; her body glowed as with the fiery magenta rays of the setting sun. His lips became the wind playing through new leaves; a sonnet written by a poet, a song sung by an angel. He caught her bottom lip between his and tugged; he tilted her head back in a probing kiss that speared glorious tingles down her spine. Before she knew what she had done, her hands had reached out, touched him. When she tried to move away, he caught her and, without releasing her lips, pulled her hands up his chest and fastened them around his neck.

Goldie's advice sang through her senses. *Enjoy him. Let him teach you* . . . Dare she? Oh, my, how she wanted to.

His dark hair felt soft between her fingers, clean and silky. His shoulders were much broader than she had realized. Her arms couldn't span them, one to the other. When she ran her hands across them, his muscles flexed; he pulled her closer and her breasts sprang to life against his crisp white shirt.

He must have felt them, too, for he moved around her

sides until the heels of his hands rested against the curve of her breasts. Her heart thrashed; she knew he could feel it. What did he think? What should she do?

Move. Run. Flee this man!

But the essence of him was overpowering, startling in its simplicity—clean, fresh, mysteriously masculine, with that slight hint of baywood; not heavily applied, like fragrances at the House of Negotiable Love, but pleasingly faint, like the whiff of a cactus blossom or an occasional sage in bloom.

Then he renewed his attack with his lips, and her brain went numb. Goldie was right! Intense pleasure swelled inside her, dispelling for the moment her anger and disappointment and even her fear. She had never known such gentleness, such tenderness, such exquisite pleasure.

His palms moved over her breasts; tingles sped down her spine, low down, to the most intimate reaches of her body, the most inner and private places in her soul. Then his rhythm changed; he rolled her nipples between his fingers and, even separated by several layers of clothing, she felt the heat, the pleasure, the need. She had never imagined such—

Through the haze, a vision appeared . . . Annie dropping her kimono; Annie with breasts twice the size of Madolyn's; Annie, twirling her finger in Tyler's navel.

"Oh, my . . ." Of a sudden Madolyn's depravity hit home. She pulled back, searched his face, his eyes.

"What's the matter?" His tone was husky, his words slurred.

"No . . ."

"No, what?" His hands continued to move over her breasts, while his gaze sent shattering repercussions throughout her system.

Her breath came short. She cast her eyes down, to where his hands cupped her breasts. It felt so good, so bad, so . . . She tried to move away, but found herself powerless. "No, please."

Tyler's hands stilled, but he didn't remove them. Indeed, he held her in a proprietary way that made her feel strangely secure, yet deeply frightened. "No . . ." She found his eyes; they echoed her feelings, those deep inside her.

"You don't like it?"

"I, uh, no." But that was a lie, and she saw instantly that he recognized it as such. She did like it. Heaven help her, she did like it. "I'm afraid," she admitted in a quiet voice, ducking her head again.

He released one breast, took her chin between the same two fingers, and lifted her face. "So am I, Maddie. So am I."

Well, that made no sense at all. While she tried to sort out his meaning, for she was quite certain Tyler Grant had never been afraid of anything in his adult life, he drew her to his chest. The side of her face rested against his heart and she felt its erratic cadence.

Everything has a lesson, Miss Abigail taught. But Miss Abigail also taught that a woman must never, not under any circumstances, submit to a man's passion. Weapons of the heart, she called them. It was beginning to look more and more like Miss Abigail's teachings needed a bit of revision. But that certainly did not give Madolyn a mandate to change them herself.

Struggling free, she lifted trembling arms and began to tuck her hair beneath her straw bonnet, which now hung crookedly from the back of her head. Her cheeks burned. Maybe he would think it was from the sunset. Before she could stick the last hatpin through the straw, he reached suddenly and pulled the entire bonnet, ribbons and all, from her head, and tossed it in the direction of her gloves.

Her embarrassment doubled. Finally she reached for the bonnet, expecting a scuffle. "I'm sorry to have behaved so boldly." She picked it up. He took it from her hand.

"Don't apologize, Maddie."

"Oh, but I must. I mean . . ." When she reached for her bonnet again, he tossed it further away.

"If anyone was out of line, it was me." He tipped her face with two fingers. "I'm sorry I embarrassed you, but I'm not sorry it happened. Not by a long shot."

It was all she could do to meet his gaze directly. She wasn't sorry it had happened, either, but if she had learned anything from the adventure, it was that Goldie's advice would be impossible to follow.

"No," she insisted, "it was my fault. I tried to follow Goldie's advice." She watched surprise light his eyes.

"Goldie's advice?"

"Goldie said I should . . . I mean . . . She said it would be all right for us to—"

Tyler's silent, amused perusal stopped her.

She drew a deep, quivering breath. "I see she was wrong."

Nine

Tyler couldn't believe his ears. "You're takin' courtin' lessons from a . . . from GOLDIE?!"

"Who better?"

"Who better? You, a suffragette of the first order, takin' courtin' lessons from the town whore?"

"Watch your language, sir—" Her sentence stopped abruptly. Tyler saw her blanch. He kept perfectly still. Hell, Morley never mentioned being reared by a stern disciplinarian, but that must have been the case. She recovered quickly.

"I shan't have you disparage Goldie or her girls."

Her seriousness captivated him. "Me, disparage Goldie? Far be it—"

"In this man's world a woman cannot be held responsible for the way she is forced to make a living. Weren't those your words?"

"Close."

"You were right. How could I throw stones at Goldie for the despicable job she's required to do to put food on the table?"

"Despicable?" Tyler cocked his head. "Is that what you think about . . . *kissin'?*"

She turned away, scanned the scene below them, silent.

"I expect the truth," he prompted. "The truth and nothin' but. Did you find kissin' me despicable?"

She pursed her lips. Below them the town was no more

than a black hole now, having been swallowed up in shadow. He watched tiny yellow lights pop out of the night like fireflies, as one citizen after another lighted lanterns.

"Did you find kissin' me despicable?" he asked again.

She sighed. "Truthfully, I . . . No I didn't, Tyler."

"What?!"

She turned, her eyes round. "I didn't find your, uh . . . Kissing you was not despicable. Quite the contrary."

"No you didn't . . . what?" he repeated, while his heart beat in a new and erratic pattern.

"I didn't find kissing you . . ."

"That isn't what I'm askin', Maddie. I want you to say it again, exactly like the first time."

Madolyn frowned. She had no idea what he meant, which wasn't surprising under the circumstances. She had known she was out of her depth, never having so much as kissed a man on the lips before she arrived in this barbaric land. To be honest with herself, she had never seen a man and woman touch each other except in anger. Except for a mother touching a child or a concerned friend touching a friend's arm, she had never known contact between two people could be so soft and gentle, so pleasurable.

"Say it like the first time, Maddie," Tyler was urging. "Say, No I didn't . . . what?"

"Find kissing—"

"Damnation, Maddie. Say my name."

"Your name?"

"Hell, you didn't even know you said it."

"Said what?"

"TYLER!"

"Tyler?"

He shook his head. "You didn't even know you said it."

She heard disappointment in his voice, and something inside her leaped for joy. In a manner quite foreign to her serious nature, she quipped, "I didn't realize it was so important."

"Damnation!" he swore again, but his eyes caressed her face in a most unsettling manner. "A man'd think you had no more sense than a fence post."

She bowed her neck at that. "Spoken like a true man."

" 'Less of course he had witnessed the little charade at the schoolhouse today."

"Charade? My performance couldn't hold a candle to yours, Tyler Grant. If you think it was no more than a parlor game—"

Moving suddenly, he took her face in his palms. In the gentlest gesture she had felt from him yet, he kissed her in midsentence, with her mouth open. "Let's not get into that right now, Maddie. I'm not near through kissin' you."

And Lord in heaven, did he ever prove that. Before he was finished, her arms were around his neck again, although she had no idea whether he placed them there like before, or whether she had been bold enough to move them herself.

Her concerns and fears were soon swamped by a tidal wave of passion such as she had never imagined existed. Kissing involved much more than lips touching lips, she was surprised—and delighted—to discover. Before she knew what was happening, he was kissing her neck, through her proper wedding-ring collar.

She felt her pulse pound against the fabric; she imagined it against his skin. The very thought impelled her to tighten her hold on him, for it sent heated flushes chasing heated flushes through her body.

Again, he caressed her breasts through the fabric of her bodice and undergarments, and again thoughts of his lips on her skin sent heat racing after heat.

Where such thoughts came from she had no idea, for she had never heard it spoken, or even insinuated, that a man would touch a woman in such intimate ways, nor that a woman could suddenly imagine things she had no knowledge of ever having happened.

It must be an innate sense of moral depravity on her part,

but even so, she was unable to resist, either Tyler's advances or the thoughts that his hands and lips evoked from her own brain. Her lightheadedness increased, and she began to feel sensual, similar to the way she felt in a scented bath, only magnified many times over.

After his hands moved away, she marveled that her breasts seemed to probe of their own accord into the crispness of his shirt. Once again, her mind envisioned them nude, skin to skin, and the thrill of it was almost too much to bear.

Then, of a sudden, she felt his hands on her back. Not through the fabric this time, but on her skin. For a moment she allowed it, no, she more than allowed it; she enjoyed it—his warm work-hardened hands on skin that had never felt such a sensation; she soaked up the pleasurable emotions, entranced, as though to store them away against a famine she knew beforehand she would experience the moment he removed his hands.

Or the moment she forced him to, she thought, regaining a measure of her wits. She sat back, dislodging his lips, then his hands, which came to rest at her waist in a gesture that filled her with more sweet longing.

"Goldie said you were a gentleman," she accused softly.

"I am."

"You unbuttoned my dress."

"You allowed it."

"No. I mean, I didn't know . . . I wasn't aware . . ."

"That proves the point, Maddie." Speaking, he moved one hand around, found the opening he had made in her dress, and slipped beneath the fabric.

When his skin touched hers, she flinched, but she didn't shake him off.

"Does it hurt?"

"No."

His fingers moved over her back in a gentle circular motion. "What does it feel like?"

"I don't know." She felt five little circles of heat from the pads of his fingers. "Like fire."

"Fire, umm. I feel it, too."

"You do?"

"Of course. But that doesn't make me less a gentleman or you less a lady. This is what we do together, ladies and gentlemen."

"No."

"No?" Pressure from his flattened hand drew her to his chest. She felt his lips against her forehead. She wanted to cling to him, but resisted, suddenly aware of her ignorance in such things. How was she supposed to act? What was expected?

"What else did Goldie tell you? Did she mention anythin' besides kissin'?"

"Just kissing and . . . and cuddling." She spoke into his shirt, and even as she did, she wondered what his bare skin would feel like against her face.

"Like this?" Cradling her in both arms, he rocked them gently from side to side. "Put your arms around me, Maddie. I like to be cuddled, too."

"You do?"

"Sure."

After a while, she obliged, albeit hesitantly. They rocked for a time. Her anxieties settled down. He must have sensed it, she thought later, for he began to talk again.

"I'm curious about somethin'," he drawled.

"What?"

"How you and Goldie came to have this little discussion?"

"Well, I . . . I mean after the last time, you know, when you stopped on the way back from Morley's?"

"I remember."

"I was confused after that, so I talked to Goldie."

"Confused about what?"

She heaved a sigh. "I've never talked about personal

things before, I mean, not before I discussed them with Goldie."

"You were that troubled?"

"Troubled isn't the word. I . . . It's hard to talk to you about this, but it shouldn't be, since you're the one responsible."

"Responsible for what?"

"It was the way you kissed me on the way back from Morley's. I couldn't get it out of my mind."

He didn't respond for the longest time. Finally, he said, "So, Goldie told you it was safe to kiss me, because I'm a gentleman. I wouldn't take advantage of you."

"That, too, but I wasn't too concerned with that. I can take care of myself."

Tyler glanced to the wagon beyond. "You and your trusty parasol."

She grinned. "I'll use whatever is handy, sir—" Instantly, she tensed and pulled away.

"Maddie, hold on a cockeyed minute." His hands dropped to her waist again. "Let's get somethin' straight." He peered earnestly into her eyes. "You aren't a child." His eyes caressed her face, dropped to her body. "You're a woman. A . . . a most desirable woman. What I said earlier about takin' you over my knee, well, that's just a way of ventin' frustrations."

She bit her lip and looked away into the twilight. "It certainly is."

"Sayin' it, Maddie. The expression. I would never, ever strike you or any woman. I made that idle claim out of frustration. Damnation! I don't like for you to call me *sir.* It's worse than Mr. Grant, although they're both bad enough for a . . . I mean, it sounds like you're sittin' up there on your high horse lookin' down."

She grinned, hesitantly.

"Or worse," he continued, "it sounds like you're talkin' to your father."

The idea jolted her.

"I don't want to be your father, Maddie. I'm sure he was a fine man, but I don't want to be like him."

She stared, gripped by horror. *Tyler like Papa?* Oh, no. Pray God he wasn't.

"How 'bout I show you," he offered.

"Show me what?"

He cradled her face in his hands and kissed her lips tenderly. "That I think you were made to be kissed and cuddled."

"You do?"

"Sure do. What say we engage in a little more?"

"If you wouldn't mind."

"Mind?" When the surprise left his eyes, he continued with, "I think it's safe to say I'm enjoyin' myself every bit as much as you are."

"Oh, I doubt it."

"Then how 'bout I show you?"

Again her inexperience came into play, for while she concentrated on the way his lips caressed hers, he unbuttoned her bodice all the way to her waist in the back. By the time he slipped it over her shoulders and down on her arms, panic had begun to set in.

She held perfectly still while he bent his head. When his lips touched her bare neck, the sensations rocked her. How magnificent! She had imagined it, and it had come true, but even better than she imagined.

He grinned into her upturned face, winked, then returned his lips to her neck, where her pulse beat in rapid consent. She knew he could feel it; she thought she should be embarrassed by the fact; but she was too busy enjoying it—the feel, the heady sensations, the hunger that grew inside her like a flood.

While she tried to dredge up enough compunction to protest, he slipped a hand beneath her corset in the back. Then suddenly, with her concentrating on the hand he slipped beneath her corset in the back, he kissed her chest. Her breasts reacted with a feeling that, had it been sound would have been an agonized cry for more. *More!*

And as if he heard, he gave her more. More than she had ever, could ever, would ever have imagined. She sat in a state of pure enchantment. Then he lifted a breast out of her corset, cupped it in his palm, and—Lord in heaven, she thought she might faint from the sheer pleasure of it!—he took her breast in his mouth. In his mouth. Of all the strange and wondrous . . .

"Oh, Mr. Grant, I—"

"Tyler," he mumbled against her skin.

She tried to pull back, away from his touch, but her body was practically useless by now. Finally she gripped his head in both hands and forced it up. His eyes were glazed.

"Tyler," she mumbled into his passion-besotted face. When he tried to duck back to her breast, she renewed her hold on his head.

"Remember you're a gentleman."

"A gentleman in dire need."

She wasn't sure she took his meaning. Her body seemed to, for it hummed with a cry for fulfillment she didn't understand, one which her brain rejected as ultimately wanton.

"I might have come west to this barbaric land of yours, Tyler Grant, but you will not turn me into a wanton."

That broke the spell. She could tell it in an instant.

"Me turn you into a wanton? You're the one takin' courtin' lessons."

"And an apt teacher you turned out to be, I'll have to admit. But enough is enough."

"You've had enough?"

Enough? She ducked her head. No, she hadn't had enough. Her body cried for more.

"Be truthful, Maddie. Say you've had enough and I'll never touch you again."

"Truthful?" Her voice trembled, she heard it. "Truthfully, I'm not sure I could ever get enough. But I must remain in control of my wits, Tyler. I seem to have lost them for a while."

"Nothing like a dose of candor to douse a fire."

"I don't understand."

"Don't worry your pretty head about it." He readjusted her dress. At the last minute, though, before he covered her chest, he dipped his head and kissed her breast once more. "Ah, so sweet."

She inhaled a deep satisfied breath that pushed her chest against his lips. "I think so, too."

A sly grin tipped his beautiful lips and he winked. He didn't speak, he didn't have to. But she felt a sense of communion with him that made words unnecessary. It filled her with joy, and she could tell he felt that way, too.

Still without speaking, he tugged her dress back up and rebuttoned it. After a while, he guided her back to the wagon with a wrist draped across her shoulders, and he lifted her up to the seat, then retrieved her bonnet and gloves. But when she tried to put the bonnet on, he stopped her.

"Leave it off."

She questioned him with her eyes.

In response, he lifted a strand of her black hair, then turned it loose to sift slowly through the evening breeze. He lifted another and watched with wonder in his eyes. "I've never seen such thick, beautiful hair. Makes a man want to curl up and bury his face in it."

Compliments were rare to nonexistent in Madolyn's life. She sat stupefied as his words spirited her off on a flight of fancy. Then he dropped her hair, smacked her on the lips, and rounded the wagon. Before starting up the team, he reached in the back and handed her the parasol.

"If you weren't worried about protectin' yourself against a wolf like me," he drawled, settling his bulky form on the seat beside her. She resisted the urge to snuggle closer. "What was your concern? What else did Goldie tell you?"

"She said you wouldn't expect a commitment."

He turned so abruptly, she knew she had startled him. "She's right, but what difference does that make? To you?"

"I, too, am unable to make a commitment. Like you, I have vowed to remain single." Madolyn smiled to herself. "And you know, Goldie was right. I thought I was destined to go through life without experiencing things like—" She stopped suddenly, unable to continue.

"Kissin' and cuddlin'?" he prompted.

His matter-of-fact tone eased her discomfort. After all they had just done together, it was silly not to allow oneself to discuss it. Aided by the growing dusk, she admitted, "I thought I would go through life without ever knowing how it felt. Now I won't. Thanks to you and Goldie."

The wagon bounced its way down the hill, but Madolyn hardly noticed. A feeling of contentment suffused her. Loose curls whipped around her face. She tucked them behind her ears and enjoyed the wind on her face. How good it felt to ride through the hazy light of dusk, sitting beside a man. A handsome man, like Tyler Grant. A man who made her feel young and alive and, yes, even sensual.

Tyler broke into her reverie. "So, what'd you think about my town, now?"

"You were right. It's beautiful at sunset."

"Will you give up your crusade to ruin me?"

"I'm not trying to ruin you."

"Reunitin' the town will do it."

"Not if you and Morley make up."

"Morley and I are enemies, sworn to the death, Maddie. So stop meddlin'."

It was pitch dark by the time he drew rein at the back of the house. Lucky stuck her head out the kitchen door.

"That you, Miss Maddie?"

"It's me, Lucky."

"And me," Tyler added. "Send Clements out here to take this wagon and team back to the livery, would you, Lucky?"

"Sure 'nuf, Mr. Tyler." Then she added, "I'll send Penny-Ante up with a supper tray, Miss Maddie."

Madolyn froze at the suggestion. She must look a fright. Besides, she had no desire to provide Annie with an extra opportunity to see Tyler. "Don't bother with that. I'll come downstairs."

Tyler rounded the wagon and helped her down. His warm hand lingered at her waist, until she moved away. By silent consent they walked together toward the outside stairs. She started up the steep flight, felt his presence behind her, longed to feel his hand on her back, his arms around her. But what else did she want from this man? How much could she take and still remain in control of herself? How much was he prepared to give and still walk away?

All the way to town she had tried to sort out her feelings. Despite Goldie's claim that kissing and cuddling with Tyler would be harmless, Madolyn felt a strange sense of foreboding about the whole affair.

The mention of Penny-Ante only magnified her dismal spirits. Annie, who laundered Tyler's shirts and what else? Did he kiss Annie like he kissed her? Did he touch her so intimately? Take her breasts into his mouth . . .

Madolyn shuddered at the thought.

"Are you cold?" Tyler hovered behind her, close, yet not close enough. She stopped on the stairs and felt him stop, too.

With her back to him, she said, "Tyler, I . . ."

He came to the step beside her. "What, Maddie?"

Turning, she reached to touch his cheek, which was about all she could make out in the pale moonlight. But no sooner had she moved, than he moved, too.

In one fluid motion he gathered her in his arms and fell back against the side of the building. Sensuous lips covered hers, caressing hands roamed her back. She pressed against him, shamelessly wanting more, yet not fully aware of what *more* meant.

The mention of Annie had again called to mind the scene she witnessed from her doorway that first morning—Tyler's enticingly bare chest, his unbuttoned duckins, bare feet. And Annie's finger twirling in his navel. The sight had disturbed her; now the memory of it disturbed her even more. Recalling the scene fired some inner drive, setting her on a quest to discover more. But what? What could a woman pledged to spinsterhood hope to discover about the more sordid aspects of life? What did it say about her that she longed—no, craved to experience such things?

"Goldie was right," she whispered when they paused for breath. "This is most pleasurable."

He grinned against her skin. She felt his labored breathing, and her own. "I couldn't agree more, Maddie. But I don't think this is all Goldie had in mind."

"No? It's nice."

Of a sudden, he scooped her in his arms and carried her the rest of the way up the stairs. Without releasing her he opened the door and stepped into the upstairs hallway, which was lit by a series of wall fixtures down its length.

"Put me down," she whispered.

He tightened his hold.

"Someone might see us, Tyler. Put me down."

By this time he had made it to her parlor door. He held her a minute longer, then set her on her feet. But instead of releasing her, he bracketed her legs with his and pressed her back against the door. "Would it matter?"

Shadows from the fixtures played across the planes of his face. His dark hair was disheveled, enticingly so. She knew hers was, too. "Yes."

He kissed her once, then lifted his face enough to make eye contact, nose to nose. "Why?"

"It isn't proper."

"I thought you said it was nice."

"It is."

"Uh-huh." Encircling her small waist he drew her up,

held her tight, while one hand flattened against her spine, running its length, fitting her body to his.

She had no choice but to throw her arms around his neck and hold on. Struggling was out of the question. Not because of his greater strength. She was certain he would turn her loose if she asked. But asking for such a thing didn't enter her mind. She basked in the fiery heat that coursed through her, at the wet persistence of his lips on hers. "This could become addictive."

"Uh-huh."

"One could come to crave it."

"One does."

"Like rutabaga pie."

"Rutabaga pie?!"

"You don't like rutabaga pie?"

"I know something I like a whole hell of a lot more."

"What?" she asked, a bit hesitantly, for she had half a notion she should not be engaging in such intimate banter.

He kissed her again, another of those deep, wet, mind-boggling kisses he was so good at. At least, she thought he was good at them. Even with her limited knowledge on the subject, she didn't see how anyone could do it better.

"Kissin' and cuddlin' . . . for starters." His deep voice quivered along her spine. "But there's a whole lot more, Maddie." When he spoke again it was with his lips softly brushing hers, which set off another tremor, which, in turn, caused her body to shudder against his.

Like on the hillside, she entertained the shameful image of their bodies touching, heated skin to heated skin. Finally she succeeded in pushing herself back. "Maybe Goldie's suggestion wasn't such a good idea, after all."

"No?" His expression left no doubt that he could see through her pretense. "I'll bet every cow I own that you think this is the best idea of a lifetime. If you don't kill off my town, when ol' Buster's term is up, I may appoint Goldie mayor."

"Mayor?" Madolyn had never been so charmed by anyone in her life. The strangeness of the situation left her uneasy, but not so much that she wanted the evening to end. He kissed her again, and she decided she wouldn't mind spending the entire night standing here in the hallway being courted by Tyler Grant.

"Hell, yes. Maybe I'll even bake her a rutabaga pie. Have to do something to thank her."

She laughed at that, out loud; then she heard the footsteps.

"Here's your supper, Miss Maddie." Madolyn turned to see Annie standing not three feet away, holding a tray.

Embarrassment flooded her. She lowered her arms and scolded the startled girl with, "I told Lucky I would come downstairs." Awkward now, Madolyn freed herself and fumbled to open her parlor door. Waves of hair cascaded around her face, concealing, she hoped, the flush that felt like a blast from a furnace.

"She didn't want you to go hungry," Annie explained. "We didn't know you were busy entertainin' Tyler."

Tyler exploded. "She was NOT entertainin' me!"

"Well, you couldn't tell from lookin'."

Consternation buzzed so loudly in Madolyn's ears she could hardly make out the words or Annie's defensive tone. She shouldered the door open.

"Set the tray down," Tyler directed. At the same time, his arm shot around Madolyn. He caught the doorframe, preventing her escape. She stiffened in the prison of his arms, faintly conscious of the sounds Annie made setting down the tray, retreating down the hall.

After what seemed like an eternity, Tyler turned Madolyn around. He forced her face up with two fingers to her chin. She felt his breath, soft and warm on her flushed face.

"Guess that puts an end to our kissin' an' cuddlin'," he whispered in tones that spread over her like warm honey. "For tonight."

Ten

"Mornin', Miss Maddie! I've brung your breakfast."

Lucky's call came as a mixed blessing. On one hand Madolyn welcomed an end to her sleepless night. On the other, she dreaded facing the women of this establishment after the scene Penny-Ante interrupted the evening before. Annie had no doubt spread the word throughout the House of Negotiable Love.

Negotiable love. The term carried even more scandalous overtones, since her own episode of indecent behavior with Tyler Grant. Whatever had possessed her to follow the directives of a . . . of a woman of ill repute?

But in the week Madolyn had been in Buck, Goldie and her girls had become much more than women of the night. She knew them now as simply women—compassionate, caring, and possessed of the same human desires and fears as other women.

And that, in itself, was a further botheration. For Madolyn had not only learned a few things about the nature of women in general since coming to Texas, she had learned some unsettling things about herself, as well.

Such as her dismal lack of control over her body. Shameful as her conduct with Tyler had been, she could not dredge up the slightest bit of remorse. Even being caught by Annie hadn't been the embarrassment it should have been.

Would have been a week before. Madolyn grimaced at the realization that one week ago she would not have engaged in such despicable conduct in the first place. And that, in turn, provided even more cause for alarm than her behavior. What if she had *not* talked to Goldie? What if she hadn't followed the madam's advice? Oh, my, what she would have missed!

As with her inability to dredge up remorse for her behavior with Tyler, Madolyn found herself unable to brand her conduct despicable—not even when she knew beyond a shadow of a doubt that Miss Abigail would frown and frown sternly on such behavior.

But my, what a shock it had been—the sweetness of it. For the life of her, she couldn't help but want more.

"Hope you done slept well, Miss Maddie." Lucky paused in the doorway, holding a tray covered with a cup towel.

Madolyn flushed what she knew must be three shades of red when Lucky peered over her shoulder at Tyler's closed door. Quickly, she shooed Lucky inside.

The elderly little maid didn't say more until Madolyn's breakfast was uncovered—the same dishes as every other morning since Madolyn arrived. But today the aroma seemed somehow much more sumptuous. Likely because she hadn't eaten supper. Indeed, she had sent the startled Annie scurrying back down two flights of stairs with the full supper tray.

"Don't reckon Mr. Tyler had time to wait 'roun' and share breakfast with you, honey. But don't you fret none—"

"Share breakfast with me?" Madolyn came out of her reverie. "We never share breakfast. Why should we start now?"

Lucky jerked her head around so sharply her topknot bobbled. "Why, honey, it seems like a right civilized thing to do."

"There is no reason on God's green earth for Tyler Grant and me to share breakfast."

"If you say so, honey. But the good Lord didn't see fit to give us much of His green earth out here. Maybeso that means that other things folks hold with back where you come from ain't all that important, neither."

Madolyn picked up the freshly ironed napkin, quickly drawing her thoughts away from Annie and Tyler, where they had been a good part of the sleepless night.

"One hen egg," Lucky was saying, "one piece of bacon, two sourdough biscuits, an' some of Miss Goldie's store tea."

"Oh, no, I shouldn't." She avoided further eye contact with Lucky, which wasn't easy, since the woman kept turning her head, as though to catch a glimpse of the truth.

"Miss Goldie wants you to have it."

"I wouldn't want to use it all up." But Madolyn wasn't thinking about tea. Her thoughts were on Tyler and they brought a sinking feeling to her stomach. She wasn't sure why thinking about him should do that, or why it was impossible for her to ask the question foremost on her mind— *Where had Tyler gone without waiting for breakfast?*

Or had he eaten breakfast early? Served by Penny-Ante? And what else? Had Annie spent the night in his room, like before? Had they kissed and cuddled, while Madolyn tossed and turned and rued the day she set foot in this barbaric town?

"If the train comes today, I shall replenish Goldie's stock of store tea," she told Lucky, more to get her mind off Tyler and Annie than because she wanted to converse about tea. "Do you think it will?"

"The train? Can't rightly say," came the expected response. "In this country trains run pretty much like the rain falls, whenever they take a notion."

"Well, when it comes, I shall replace Goldie's tea with some of what I ordered from Abilene." Madolyn recalled the other items she ordered from Abilene, and her method for paying for them. She hoped she hadn't borrowed herself a barrel of trouble.

Although she was not the slightest bit hungry, she sat at

the tea table and began to eat, one ear attuned for some indication from Lucky whether Annie had spread the word of her wanton ways.

Lucky, it turned out, was more interested in the meeting the day before, which Madolyn had almost forgotten. She chastised herself and turned her attention to the maid's version of Goldie's report.

"Miss Goldie's mighty glad she went up there yesterday. Said she knew she'd been right about you all along."

"Right about me?"

"You bein' able to hole your own with the men in this town," Lucky explained.

"I'm afraid Goldie exaggerated on that score."

"That ain't the way she tole it."

"She must not have told the whole story, Lucky. I didn't handle the husbands well at all. Since they had no intention of helping reunite the town, they should have stayed home."

"No husbands? How you figure a man's gonna let his wife go off an' make decisions without him goin' along to tell her what to decide?"

"I don't, not anymore." That was the same conclusion she had come to during the long, sleepless night, along with an equally dismal conclusion—the submissiveness of the women at the meeting was no different than the submissiveness she felt in Tyler's arms. For a while last night she would have done anything he wanted, a disquieting notion. Even now, recalling their scandalous behavior, she felt herself grow weak. She wanted him still. Her body ached for his touch. Was this one of the weapons husbands held over their wives?

Never had she considered that a man might use tenderness and sensual, loving acts as weapons. In her parents' house the weapons had been fists and voices—violent, loud, aggressive, physical. She had not known grown men possessed a tender nature until she experienced it in a myriad of ways in Tyler's arms.

Was tenderness his weapon? If so, it could prove as deadly as physical violence. Blatantly aggressive behavior forewarned a woman. But the tender side, that was different. She recalled telling Tyler it could be addictive. Was that the way men caught women? Snared them with kisses and gentle caresses, then dragged them into the lair of marriage, where everything turned ugly? Miss Abigail preached against weapons of the heart. Were these what she meant? Tenderness, gentleness, and sweet fiery passion?

Sipping Goldie's store tea, Madolyn pulled her thoughts from her narrow escape to the difficulty of reuniting Buckhorn.

"We will never succeed with the husbands involved," she worried. "You should have seen how they intimidated their wives. It was disgraceful. Those women are so browbeaten they wouldn't meet my eye, much less participate in the discussion."

"That's the way it is out here, honey."

"That's the way it is everywhere, Lucky. I thought women in the West might have more backbone, but I was wrong. I must have confused strong backs with stiff constitutions."

"They's got that, sure 'nuf. Couldn't survive in this country without mighty stiff constitutions."

"I'm talking about inner strength, Lucky. Somehow I have to tap the inner strength these women use for everyday living and divert it to saving this town." She smeared her last bite of biscuit with agarita-berry jelly, thoughtful. "To do that, I shall have to get them away from the men."

"Humph! That'll take more'n a whippersnapper like you's up to. 'Less, of course, you enlist Mr. Tyler's help."

"Tyler?" Madolyn met Lucky's gaze for the first time this morning. Although she flushed at what the little maid might be thinking, she quickly regained her mental footing. "I'll thank you not to mention that outrageous man to me again, Lucky. Mr. Grant is the root of the evil, not the cure."

Lucky had the audacity to laugh out loud. "Do you say so?"

"Indeed, I do. He and my brother. You should have seen how the men kowtowed when Ty . . . , when Mr. Grant walked into that schoolhouse. And the women, too. Of course, they hadn't much choice. The way he worked the gathering, why you would think he was running for sheriff or something."

"Sure 'nuf? If he did, he'd get my vote."

"If you had one, Lucky, which is what this is all about."

"What's that?"

"Women versus men. Men running roughshod over women and getting away with it."

"Been thataway since the world began, honey. Ain't likely to change for one determined girl."

"Not one, Lucky, a town full."

"You said it yourself. Long's those women's husbands are runnin' the show, there ain't likely to be much you can do to change things."

"What their husbands don't know, they can't spoil."

Lucky peered around the corner from the bedroom. "What bee you got in your bonnet, Miss Maddie?"

"Wait and see, Lucky. But be sure to clean my parlor extra good. I wouldn't want to show off Goldie's establishment except to its best advantage."

"Say what?"

"Wait and see," she repeated. "Miss Abigail claims that the best way to stave off a worried mind is with an active body."

"Just what kinda activity you plannin' for that body of yours, honey?"

Madolyn was mortified! Positively mortified. *Lucky knew.* Of course, she knew. Annie would have rushed downstairs to tell every girl in the House about catching Madolyn in Tyler's arms . . . *kissing.* There had been no way she could pretend to have a speck of dust in her eye; not with the way Annie sneaked up on them.

"Organizing the women, Lucky. Oh, my, I do have a lot to do. And so little time. When the train arrives, I shall take the boots and things out to Morley's. Then maybe he will sign those papers and I can return to Boston."

But it won't be soon enough, she fretted later, while she hurried through her toilette. Pulling her unruly hair into a tight black bun, she slipped into a proper black gabardine frock and sensible shoes. Her haste, she knew, came as much from wanting to escape Tyler Grant—who was Lord knew where—as it did from being anxious to sort out the details of the Buck-Horn Reunited Society.

She didn't recall that she had promised an article to Price Donnell, until she was ready to leave for the schoolhouse, and by that time it was too late. She simply did not have time to sit down and compose a satisfactory piece.

What to do? Searching the trunk in which she had stored her most treasured articles and mementos from the Boston Woman Suffrage Society, she pulled out her favorite piece.

"The Art of Negotiating with the Male of the Species," by Miss Abigail Blackstone. That would do nicely, thank you. As would the preponderance of Miss Abigail's advice Madolyn carried in her head, if she would settle down and put some of it to use.

Her first brilliant idea—at least, she considered it brilliant—had come earlier, while she attempted to evade Lucky's inquiry about Tyler. That was exactly the way Miss Abigail claimed things worked:

"Often, when one's mind is engaged in strenuous battle," her mentor advised, "the subconscious performs one's best work."

And so it proved. The schoolchildren could fold the newspapers. She wouldn't have to worry about convincing the women to help this time.

When Madolyn arrived, Loretta James was engaged in a

spirited game of King of the Mountain with the children. An appropriate game for a school run by Tyler Grant, she fumed.

"Be with you in a minute, Maddie," the teacher called.

Madolyn sat on the steps in the shade of a madrone tree, watching, pensive. What a lovely young teacher Loretta was. Vivacious, interacting so effortlessly with the children. Unrestrained in a way Madolyn would never be. One day Loretta James would marry and have children of her own.

As Madolyn never would.

The image of Loretta gushing to Tyler flitted through Madolyn's mind like a bird in flight. Goldie claimed Tyler was committed to living a single life. But that could change. Loretta had confessed to being in the market for a husband, a cowboy to tame. Well, Tyler needed taming, if anyone ever did. A pretty thing like Loretta might be able to do it. Could she change his mind about remaining single?

Change his mind? Not if he was as committed to the single life as Madolyn was herself.

"I'm glad you've come, Maddie. I didn't get a chance to tell you yesterday, but you did a superb job handling those men."

"I'm afraid they did a better job handling me."

"Don't let them bother you. You're a determined woman, and I have a feeling they're running scared."

"Running scared? Of what?"

"Of you, silly. They think you're going to influence their wives."

"I certainly intend to try, Loretta. I certainly intend to try. Do you think there's a chance of us getting the women together secretly?"

"I don't know how—or where."

"My parlor."

Loretta's expression froze somewhere between approval and alarm. "Goldie's third floor? I'm not sure the women in either town are prepared for that."

"You mean the men aren't prepared for their wives to go there, either alone or in their company?"

"Especially in their company, I should think," Loretta laughed, a soft, tinkling sort of laughter that further worried Madolyn.

She hurried on. "I've also solved the paper-folding quandary for today."

To that, Loretta agreed readily. "I'll bring the children around to the news office an hour before school lets out."

That was when Madolyn entertained her third brilliant idea of the day. "Mr. Grant indicated that you'll be closing the school for the summer."

"Yes, I'm going home to St. Louis for two months."

"What will they do with the schoolhouse?"

"Tyler said he'll see it's kept up."

Tyler? Oh, my, could she be right? "I wonder," Madolyn began, "I mean, don't think I'm after your job, because I'm not; I'll be back in Boston before you return in the fall, but do you suppose I could use the building while I'm here."

"To hold our meetings in?"

"To hold school in. Your students could attend, too. It's just that . . . well, I'm concerned about my brother's children. They need schooling. I thought perhaps if I could get them started before I leave, they would continue when the new term begins in the fall."

"That's an excellent idea, Maddie. All the children would benefit. There's never enough time to teach everything I'd like. We'll talk to Tyler about it."

"You talk to him, would you?"

Loretta gave her a sideways grin. "Is it true, what I heard?"

"What did you hear?" Madolyn asked, wary.

"That you went riding with him . . . up to Lovers' Leap."

Lovers' Leap? Lord in heaven! Her face must positively glow! "We rode somewhere," she admitted. "Mr. Grant is determined to keep us from reuniting the town. He took me up on the hillside so I could see how beautiful the town is at sunset. As if that were the problem!"

Loretta grinned again, unfooled, Madolyn feared. "And to work his wiles on you?" the schoolmarm quizzed.

What do you know about his wiles? Madolyn wanted to know. She tried to steady her voice. "Whatever his intention, Loretta, it didn't work. I remain steadfastly determined to right the wrong wrought by my brother and his partner."

Stopping by the *Buckhorn News* office, Madolyn gave Inez Bradford the article written by Miss Abigail. She watched Ines's thin cheeks take on a rosy hue at sight of her. Inez avoided meeting Madolyn's eye; nor did she mention the meeting. If she regretted bringing her husband, so much the better. Maybe next time she would show more backbone.

Price Donnell met Madolyn on her way out. He didn't try to hide his disappointment that she hadn't written the article herself.

"Miss Abigail is a far better spokeswoman than I," she assured him.

"Folks here don't know her," Donnell argued. "They want to read things about folks they know. After the meeting yesterday, your by-line on a front-page article would double my readership."

She was tempted to retort that improving his business wasn't the object, except in the long run. "Be that as it may, sir, I simply cannot find time today. Perhaps later in the campaign."

He stroked one side of his blond mustache. "You're really serious about this, aren't you?"

"Indeed. And lest you think me remiss, I should thank you for recommending me to Goldie."

Donnell's hand stopped on his mustache. His pale face took on a telltale blush. "Recommending you to Goldie for what?"

"Oh, uh . . . I certainly didn't mean . . . Goldie said you

mentioned my suffrage work. That's how I got involved in Buckhorn's crisis. Goldie asked me."

"You blamin' me?"

"On the contrary, sir. I thanked you. Since it was my brother who wrought the town's ills, I shall consider it my privilege to help these good people restore unity."

Donnell laughed. "After yesterday you should realize that all these *good* people don't want unity, Miss Sinclair. You're facin' an uphill battle, at best."

"I am well aware of that, sir. And I am prepared. If I may say so without sounding presumptuous, sexual battles are my forte." Again, she saw she had taken Price Donnell off guard.

"Being a man of letters yourself," she retorted, "you are certain to take my meaning without further elucidation."

The editor's mouth dropped open, but his response was lost in the whistle of the train. "Oh, my, I must be on my way. Miss James will bring the children around to fold papers. Have you spoken to Mr. Rolly and Mr. Cryer about distributing them?"

Donnell nodded. "Can't say they're excited about it."

"Why ever not?"

"Reuniting the town will put them out of work. They make their living shuttlin' news back and forth across the tracks."

"With their advanced years, sir, they surely enjoyed occupations before the town was divided. They can go back to them. Whatever they were."

"Their occupations, if you want to call them that, were sitting in front of the saloons begging for handouts."

Another blast of the train whistle rent the air, squelching thoughts of beggars or pessimistic newspapermen, or towns that needed reuniting. Excitement grew inside Madolyn, excitement chased by a strange sort of emptiness.

Taking her leave, she fairly skipped along the dusty road to the tune of screeching wheels and a tooting whistle. Her parasol bobbled in her haste. By the time she reached the depot, several large boxes had already been stacked on the platform. She headed for them, eager to see whether they were addressed to her.

"You're up early, *jefe*. Expectin' the train today?"

"More like wishin' for it." Tyler gripped the tin cup in both hands. With one boot propped on the rail fence, he stared into the railroad trap at his cattle. Or, he would be staring at cattle in another thirty minutes or so, after the sun topped the far hill. Right now about all he saw were silhouettes of cattle and trees and scrub oak. He sipped the hot coffee, pensive.

"Heard you took that little señorita up to Lovers' Leap last night."

It was Sánchez asking the questions. Raúl Ybarra, Tyler's tophand, minded his own business. Sánchez, however, liked nothing better than to rib Tyler about everything from Morley Sinclair to Rurales to women, women being his favorite topic.

"What you heard and what happened are two different horses," Tyler retorted. At Sánchez's knowing grin, he added, "What happened up there is for me to know and you to ponder, amigo."

"Sounds like you've been doin' some ponderin', yourself," Sánchez bantered.

"You might say so." Sometime during the sleepless night, the puzzlement Tyler had been pondering became crystal clear.

Once his fervor cooled down, his instinct kicked in, and by the time Goldie's bantam rooster began to crow, he had come to the disturbing conclusion that Goldie hadn't done him such a service, after all. Very likely she'd had something up her sleeve besides a freckled arm when she undertook to counsel Maddie in the fine art of courtship.

It smacked of a matchmakin' scheme of the first order. He saw that now. He had been caught off guard, he had argued into his pillow. He'd been hoodwinked by Maddie's surprising reaction—hell, her passionate reception of his overtures. And by her candor.

He had never known a woman so free to speak her mind, regardless that speaking her mind often meant going against conventional wisdom, as well as exposing her own ignorance. There wasn't a cunning bone in the lady's body, he would bet the ranch on that—if he had a ranch to bet.

He was certain she didn't recognize Goldie's matchmaking scheme for what it was. If she had, being the staunch spinster she claimed, she would have rejected the advice out of hand. He had no reason to doubt her. Maddie Sinclair was a confirmed suffragette and spinster.

But so sweet and innocent a spinster he had never expected to cross his trail. Her tough exterior hid a lack of sophistication in matters of the heart, but that's what she was—unsophisticated, naive to the dangers of love. Beneath the armor, Miss Madolyn Sinclair was about as innocent as a babe and therein lay Tyler's quandary.

Maddie might profess to being committed to a lifetime of spinsterhood, but she obviously knew little about the ways of the human heart. More often than not in matters of the heart, the brain and all its best intentions were just so much gyp water.

Fortunately for him, Tyler had identified the danger in time to evade the noose—if he played his cards right. And he certainly intended to play his cards right. He had vowed never to find himself harnessed double again, and he intended to see that vow fulfilled. Regardless of the challenge.

But what a challenge! He knew the dangers inherent in Morley Damn-his-hide's sister's new favorite pastime, even if she did not. He liked to kiss and cuddle as much as she did, but he surely didn't have a hankerin' for the commitment ladies expected to accompany such pleasurable activities.

By the time the rooster crowed, Tyler was fit to be tied. He had tossed and turned the night away and with the approaching dawn had still not resolved himself to being caught by the tempting female sleeping soundly across the hall. No matter how sweet her lips, how soft her skin, how inviting her body, he had no choice but to keep his distance. Beginning *now*.

He had dressed in haste, escaped down the outside staircase, and rounded the back of the building, where he ran smack-dab into Lucky returning from the privy out back.

"Where you sneakin' off to in such a hurry, Mr. Tyler?"

"Work," Tyler mumbled. "Gotta see to my cattle."

"Cattle, my foot. You runnin' out on that pretty little girl upstairs?"

Tyler shuddered even now, imagining the conversations that must have taken place on the bottom two floors of the House of Negotiable Love, after Annie found Maddie in his arms.

By damn! Her reputation would be ruined. In an effort to nip trouble in the bud, he had eyed Lucky with a grave expression. "There is no pretty little girl sleepin' upstairs, Lucky. Maddie Sinclair is an avowed spinster, and you know it. Nothin' happened between us last night. Listen to me carefully—nothin' happened."

"If you say so, Mr. Tyler."

"I say so, and furthermore, I expect you to tell Goldie and every one of her girls exactly that—nothin' happened between Maddie and me."

"No need to get so het up. I hear you."

"Good." Tyler had relaxed. He liked Lucky; he hated being harsh with her. But, like Maddie said when she ordered him to make up with Morley, it was for a good cause. This time that good cause was Maddie's reputation.

"See you later, Lucky." He took off across the yard, only to have her call after him.

"I hear you, but ain't sayin' I believe a word of it."

The train whistle pierced Tyler's troubled daydreams. A thrill raced through him. The train had arrived, the answer to his prayers. Now he could get out of town—and get her off his mind.

"Find Raúl and start headin' those critters toward the loadin' chutes," he told Sánchez. "I'll run tell the station master we have cattle to load."

By the time he reached the depot a triumphant sense of relief had begun to replace the trapped feeling he had awakened with. He had escaped the noose! Now all he had to do was stay out of town until she headed back to Boston.

Then he reached the depot, and his boots skidded to a halt. He gaped, his gut gripped by a terrifying sense, which he at first—erroneously, as it turned out—took to be disappointment that his little scheme hadn't worked.

For there she stood. Maddie. On the platform, before a passenger car, her parasol wobbling drunkenly, surrounded by a stack of parcels. *A stack of—*

His heart leaped to his throat. By damn! The woman he had sought to escape was escaping him!

Eleven

"Where the hell do you think you're goin'?"

Startled by Tyler's harsh shout, Madolyn watched him stomp across the platform. He was dressed for work, in chaps, vest, and chambray shirt, but his bandanna was tied around his neck instead of over his face like the day before when he'd driven a herd of cattle through the streets of town. His bare face revealed a stubbled, unshaven jaw. For a moment she stood mesmerized; he was somehow even more appealing than all starched and polished.

Or did she mean more threatening? His presence filled the small platform; memories suffused her.

"Where're you headed?" he demanded again.

Around them people ceased work. Silence fell, as those gathered stopped to listen. Madolyn's ire rose. He had made a spectacle of her at this depot once; she had no intention of allowing him to do so a second time. Her neck bowed, she stiffened her spine and looked him directly in the eye. Triumph exhilarated her. Triumph, for she hadn't been at all sure she could ever look him in the eye again without reverting to being that simpering, submissive woman she had been the night before.

"My intentions, *sir,* are none of your business."

"Sir?" He shoved his hat back off his brow. His eyes rolled in their sockets. "Damned, if you're not the most infuriatin' woman I've ever run across in all my born days."

But when he pierced her with those brown eyes again,

they were not the eyes of an enraged man. He was angry, yes, but it was a different sort of anger than she had seen displayed at home, where her father became enraged over her mother's slightest infraction of his many self-serving rules. Tyler sounded almost as if he were the one affronted.

"I'm going out to my brother's," she explained.

His expression changed from perturbed to confused. "To Morley's?"

He frowned at the boxes, then lifted solemn eyes, perusing her from head to foot. "I thought . . ." His words drifted off. He glanced to the left, stared at the passenger car as though it were a dragon he might have been called upon to slay in defense of a maiden in distress.

A maiden in distress? Madolyn was certainly distressed, although at the moment he was the one who looked it. "You thought I was returning to Boston?" Her assessment was right, she saw that, for it stunned him; the way his reaction had stunned her. *He didn't want her to leave.* Joy swept through her. Joy, followed by confusion, followed by discomfiture.

"You're out of luck, Mr. Grant. I have no intention of abandoning my task here."

As though viewing the sunrise, she watched his composure return. Humor danced in his eyes and played around the corners of his mouth.

"You're still bent on destroyin' my town, huh?"

"I'm not bent on destroying anything." She tore her gaze from his grinning, knowing scrutiny. "Freeing women to take responsibility for their own lives only creates better citizens."

Tyler glanced at the packages at her feet. "All those— they aren't your . . ." Again his gaze roamed, this time in the direction of the house. "What are all these packages?"

"Weapons, Mr. Grant."

She could tell that her calling him "Mr. Grant" needled him. Indeed, it sounded a little stilted to her own ears, after

4 FREE BOOKS

These books worth almost $20, are yours without cost or obligation when you fill out and mail this certificate.

(If the certificate is missing below, write to: Zebra Home Subscription Service, Inc., 120 Brighton Road, P.O. Box 5214, Clifton, New Jersey 07015-5214)

Complete and mail this card to receive 4 Free books!

YES! Please send me 4 Zebra Lovegram Historical Romances without cost or obligation. I understand that each month thereafter I will be able to preview 4 new Zebra Lovegram Historical Romances FREE for 10 days. Then if I decide to keep them, I will pay the money-saving preferred publisher's price of just $4.00 each...a total of $16. That's almost $4 less than the regular publisher's price, and there is never any additional charge for shipping and handling. I may return any shipment within 10 days and owe nothing, and I may cancel this subscription at any time. The 4 FREE books will be mine to keep in any case.

Name _____

Address _____ Apt. _____

City _____ State _____ Zip _____

Telephone ( ) _____

Signature _____
(If under 18, parent or guardian must sign.)

LF0696

Terms, offer and prices subject to change without notice. Subscription subject to acceptance by Zebra Home Subscription Service, Inc.. Zebra Home Subscription Service, Inc. reserves the right to reject any order or cancel any subscription.

*A $19.96
value...
absolutely
FREE
with no
obligation to
buy anything,
ever!*

4 BOOKS FREE!

the intimacies they had shared. But that was precisely the reason she must adhere to polite conventions. She must not, would not, allow herself to lose control again.

"Weapons?" His tone warned her he had regained full fighting faculties. "What the hell kind of weapons?"

"I'll thank you not to swear at me in public, Mr. Grant."

"And I'll thank you not to test my patience, *Miss Sinclair.*"

She smiled, delightfully accepting her victory. Something told her this was only the first round, however.

"As to the packages, they contain various and sundry things that we have a shortage of out here." She tapped a box with her parasol. "Store tea and a few other luxuries for Goldie and the girls."

His eyebrows raised a couple of notches.

She tapped a second box. "Literature for our fight to save this town."

"Fight to— Now hold on a cockeyed minute—"

Madolyn tapped a third box, a fourth, and a fifth. "These should hold schoolbooks, piece goods,"—she glanced off before continuing—"unmentionables . . ." Favoring him with a satisfied grin, she finished, "and boots."

"Boots?" Light dawned in his eyes. "For the boys?"

"And shoes for the girls. I ordered sturdy lace-ups, brown, so they won't require so much upkeep. I had so wanted them to have patent leather." She shrugged. "Perhaps next time."

"Next time? Hell, Maddie, you're not exactly . . . I mean, not to bring up such a personal subject as money, but you came to town penniless."

Madolyn felt her cheeks burn. "Perhaps I did. But there are other ways to skin a cat, Mr. Grant."

"To skin a cat?"

"So to speak."

"Exactly how're you plannin' to pay for this stuff?"

She started to tell him that, like the rest of her plans, that was none of his business, but she was far too proud of the idea to keep it secret. "Morley is paying for it. All of it."

"Morley? You'll play hell gettin' one red cent out of that tightwad."

"Watch me."

"What kind of scheme are you cookin' up now?"

She grinned. "You may have realized that Morley and Madolyn begin with the same letter of the alphabet. I signed the drafts M. Sinclair."

"You forged a draft? On what?"

"On Morley's bank, of course. But I forged nothing. As I explained, the letter *M* is my initial, too."

"It sure as hell isn't your bank account." Removing his Stetson, Tyler ran a hand through his hair. She watched him stare into the distance, through the train, toward the Bank of Buckhorn. "Even if you could cross the tracks, Sam Allen wouldn't accept your endorsement."

"I am fully aware of the limitations of living in a divided town, sir. That is one reason I have decided to stay on. The people here need my help."

"Like hell," he muttered. But his gaze held hers reminding her of the day before. His voice softened. "Any other reasons?"

She opened her mouth, then closed it sharply, refusing to stammer and stutter before half the citizens of Buck. Her composure regained, she tipped her chin. "To gain my inheritance, of course."

"Anything else?" His brown eyes bore into hers. She held her ground, difficult as it was. She would not allow this man to intimidate her. Although curiously, intimidating men usually provoked anger, rather than . . .

Rather than what? The situation suddenly became untenable. She felt as though she were in a stage play, where she was required to play out every encounter with the villain before the entire cast of characters. Calling forth her best imitation of the imperious Miss Abigail, she tipped her chin another notch and questioned, "What other reason could there be?"

He didn't flinch at her tone; nor did he respond for a long, silent moment, during which his gaze heated her to the bottom of her feet. "Beats me," he said with a grin.

Suddenly his mood changed. He slapped his hat against his thigh. "Listen, uh, I've got some cattle to load. Soon as we finish, I'll send Raúl and Sánchez to haul this stuff over to the house for you."

"I've already sent for Clements." His expression dimmed, and she experienced a twinge of regret. Obviously, he wasn't used to females taking charge of their own lives. "But thank you," she added, for what reason she could not fathom.

"When do you figure on goin' out to Morley's?" he asked.

"Tomorrow, maybe. I haven't decided. I wasn't sure when the train would arrive."

"I could drive you out there. We're headin' for Mexico for another herd of cattle, soon as these are loaded. But I could—"

"I don't think that's such a good idea."

"Yeah, you're probably right. Well, I'd better get movin'."

She watched him turn aside, unable to speak what was on her mind, uncertain just what it was, anyway. He spoke to the stationmaster. Turning back to her, he tipped his hat with an unusually solemn expression and headed for the bend in the tracks.

Suddenly Madolyn seized the moment, as Miss Abigail was always instructing women to do. "To get ahead in life, we must seize the moment, ladies. That's what men do. And I always say, What's good for the gander is better for the goose."

Although Madolyn wasn't certain how the action she had in mind could be termed "getting ahead in life," she was compelled to act, nonetheless. Instructing the stationmaster to send her parcels along with Clements, she hurried off the platform.

"Mr. Grant," she called.

Tyler turned in his tracks. He scrutinized her with an unreadable expression as she lifted her skirts and ran toward him. By the time she caught up with him, she was out of breath and her head hummed.

Out of earshot of the crowd, who, she was sure, still gawked after them, Tyler greeted her with a wry grin. "I thought we settled that Mr. Grant nonsense last night."

At mention of their intimate interlude, the old glow flushed through her. She wanted to meet him eye to eye, but was unable to work up the gumption. "A lady never addresses a gentleman by his given name in public."

"Well, I suppose that squelches my argument. I may not be much of a gentleman, but you, Miss Sinclair, are one hell of a lady."

A foreign sense of recklessness took hold of her. "Should I thank you for a compliment, sir, or slap you for an affront?"

He laughed out loud, and she grinned in spite of herself. "I'll settle for neither, Maddie. What can I do for you?"

Hold me, she thought. For the first time merely standing beside him wasn't enough. She craved to feel his encompassing presence, not just hovering over her, but surrounding her, claiming her. She gripped her emotions and glanced from side to side before speaking in a hushed voice. "Could I watch you load your cattle?"

"Could you what?"

"Watch you load your cattle?"

His eyes danced, tripping a response deep inside her. "Watch me load my cattle . . . what?"

She held his gaze, even though sanity cautioned her to turn away, to run away, now, quickly, without tarrying one second longer. But for some unknown reason, she ignored every one of the million or so warning bells that sounded in her brain. "May I watch you load your cattle, Tyler?" Instead of feeling submissive for acquiescing to his request, she enjoyed a sense of triumph.

He felt it, too! *Triumph.* Even though his response was a casual, "Don't reckon there's any harm in that," she saw triumph in his warm dancing eyes and in the swaggering way he extended his elbow. She heard it in his voice and felt it in the very fiber of his muscles, when she placed her hand on his blue chambray-clad arm and warmed to the way he squeezed her fingers in the crook of his elbow.

And when he led her around the bend to the railroad trap, a tremor sizzled up her spine, and she wasn't altogether certain she had made a wise decision. If she were triumphant, and he were triumphant, then together . . .

"Mornin' Miss Maddie." Lucky shuffled into the room. "MISS MADDIE! What do you think you're doin'?"

Madolyn leaned over the basin, squeezing her eyes against the sting of soapy water that dripped down the sides of her face. "Could you bring me a pitcher of clear water, Lucky?"

"Ain't nobody ever tole you, you can't wash your hair in a hand basin?"

"A woman does what a woman must," Madolyn responded, quoting Miss Abigail. For the first time in days, she figured Miss Abigail might approve of something she was doing. Cleanliness was naturally next to godliness.

She heard Lucky set down the breakfast tray, felt her pick up the pitcher from the dressing table.

"It'll take a minute, honey. Used the last of the hot water for your tea."

"I don't need hot water. Just dip a pitcher from the container in the hall."

"It'll be cold as field mice's feet."

"So was this."

"I'll swan," Lucky clucked to herself; her words drifted off when she left the room to fill the pitcher. "Here it is, honey, but you're agonna catch your death."

"Not likely in this heat." Madolyn covered her eyes with her hands, while Lucky poured clean, cool water over her head.

"You ain't gonna never get all the soap out this way." The plump little maid grumbled on, while she squeezed soapy water out of Madolyn's hair. "What you want to do this for, anyhow? Saturday's just around the corner."

"I couldn't wait for Saturday. Not after all that dust at the railroad trap."

"Ah, so that's it."

"That, whatever you mean, isn't it at all. I'm going out to my brother's and I want to look my best."

"Can't say's how it's agonna help you out none, not with folks like Morley Sinclair. Now Mr. Tyler, he's another story—"

And one Madolyn did not want to discuss. Not the day after bidding him good-bye. "I think it's rinsed as much as possible under the circumstances, Lucky. When you get downstairs, would you remind Clements he's to drive me out to Morley's today?"

"Sure thing, honey."

"And tell Goldie I'll be back tonight. For her not to cancel the women's quilting session tomorrow."

"Miss Goldie ain't too sure that's agonna work."

"Of course, it will work. The women know to leave home with bags of scraps and a quilting needle. They know to use the outside staircase. Goldie said you could set up a quilting frame in the spare room next to Mr. Grant's."

"That's where Clements stored them trunks o' yours."

"The room next to it," Madolyn explained.

"I don't know, honey. I don't know. Looks to me like you're borrowin' trouble."

"No woman borrows trouble, Lucky. The men in our lives

thrust it upon us. What we make of it is up to us." Again she quoted Miss Abigail. Fleetingly she thanked her lucky stars that she was still able to recall a modicum of her mentor's teachings. She certainly hadn't recalled any the day before, while watching Tyler and his vaqueros load their cattle. Nor afterwards.

Arriving at the railroad trap, Tyler had stationed her off to the side, behind a railed fence.

"Can't have all that paraphernalia of yours spookin' the cattle."

She hadn't been sure how to take that, nor what to make of her own startling request to watch the operation. Although in no time she was glad she had. Not being a horse-woman herself, she appreciated the skill Tyler and his vaqueros exhibited. They rode casually in the midst of a hundred or so head of cattle, the largest animals she had ever seen. Their horns reminded her of Price Donnell's handlebar mustache, only magnified many times over and turned to bone.

The men earned the name cowboys, as they maneuvered their horses with a facility she wouldn't have imagined pos-sible, cutting in and out among the longhorn cattle, driving them, separating some from others, as though they handled no more than so many gentle milch cows. All the while, they whipped coiled ropes against their chaps and shouted words in Spanish, words she had a notion would sizzle her sensibilities if she understood them.

Neither did she understand the curious glances the va-queros cast her from time to time. Later, when she ques-tioned Tyler, he brushed it off.

"They're men, Maddie. You know how men are."

Actually, she had no idea what he was talking about, but from the gleam in his eye, she decided it best not to pursue the matter.

With the last of the cattle loaded in a slat-sided railcar, Tyler huddled briefly with his vaqueros, then sauntered toward her, slapping his hat against his stained leather chaps. Dust flew all around.

"A danged dusty job," he commented, reaching her. "What'd you think about it?"

She grinned. "A danged dusty job."

As though absently, he took her parasol, slid it closed, and tucked it under his arm. He reached for her elbow, then hesitated with a grimace. "I probably smell worse'n the inside of that cattle car."

"Don't mind me," she surprised herself by returning, "I've been smelling it all afternoon."

He cocked his head. His warm brown eyes were just for her. "Sorry you came?"

"No." Her mouth was dry . . . from the dust, of course. "Not a bit." She wasn't sure what he meant by the question, nor what she meant by her answer, but his hand to her elbow showered her with warmth; his presence covered her like a familiar and beloved blanket. He guided her toward the house, as though it were the most natural thing in the world for them to walk through town side by side. And it felt natural. Far too natural.

Before he could complicate things further, she changed the subject or tried to. "You're going to Mexico?"

"Yep."

"Where in Mexico?"

"My ranch. Las Colinas del Rey."

"Las Colinas del Rey? I haven't gotten that far in my lessons."

"Lessons?"

"I told you I was going to learn Spanish."

He stopped, halting her, too. The look in his eyes was familiar. She had seen it before. Now she knew what it meant. He wanted to kiss her. And heaven help her, if she didn't want it, too.

At length he resumed their walk toward the House, explaining, "It means Hills of the King. I didn't name the place, but it's beautiful, Maddie. Fit for a king . . . and queen. Again she sensed an underlying subject, and again she tried to change it.

"When will you go?"

"Soon as I see you back to Goldie's."

Disconcerted by his directness, she glanced behind her to see the vaqueros riding off toward the center of Buck. The man named Raúl led Tyler's horse. "Where are they going?"

"To water the horses and get the stationmaster's voucher for the herd."

"Shouldn't you—"

"Raúl can handle it."

He seemed edgy, suddenly, discomfited. And she certainly was. They walked in silence, yet not in silence, for an aura surrounded them; a humming, as though a hive of bees hovered overhead and advanced with them toward the house. When they crossed the backyard, Madolyn wondered whether anyone was watching and what they thought if they were and what they should be thinking. She didn't even know what she was thinking. Actually, she was so giddy, even her mind was aflutter. Being escorted across town by a man was a totally new experience, new and extremely pleasing.

Tyler drew her to a halt at the foot of the outside staircase. "So, what're your plans for my town while I'm gone?" He smiled when he asked it, and she smiled, responding.

"That depends on how long you'll be gone."

He laughed. "You have short-term and long-term plans? That's interestin'."

"Yes, it is." Suddenly her brain cleared enough for her to recall her plans for the schoolhouse. "There's something I wanted to ask, if Loretta hasn't already—"

Instantly, he sobered. His gaze held hers, serious, intent. "I haven't seen Loretta James since the meetin' at the schoolhouse."

"Oh." Madolyn fidgeted under his scrutiny. "Well, she said it was all right with her if you agreed, that I should ask you, or she would, that you would—" His hands played across the tops of her shoulders disconcerting her. She ducked her head.

"Stop ditherin', Maddie."

Abashed, she glanced up. His warm brown eyes delved into hers, into her brain. Like a schoolgirl's in early spring, her thoughts flew out the window on the wings of a songbird. Why couldn't she retain one whit of sense around him? She hated losing control.

"What about the schoolhouse?" he prompted.

"I want to use it for—" Before she finished, his hands had tightened.

"No."

"No? You don't even know what I want it for, yet you can't wait to refuse."

"I'm not givin' you one inch in your crusade to take my town, Maddie. This is war."

His warm smile went a long way toward alleviating her exasperation. "Well said, sir. But, as usual, you misjudged the situation by a mile. I merely want to use the schoolhouse to instruct my nieces and nephews in Loretta's absence. Any other students who want to attend would be welcome, of course."

"Instruct your nieces and nephews?" His eyes danced. "What'd ol' Morley say about that?"

"He doesn't know . . . yet."

"I suppose you plan to spring it on him the same time you tell him about the bank draft."

"Actually, I hadn't planned to tell him about the bank draft."

He arched an eyebrow. "Wouldn't have taken you for a thief."

"I haven't stolen anything."

"I'm tellin' you, Maddie, I know the ol' sonofabitch better'n you. He's goin' to be . . . well, I don't reckon I can describe what I think his reaction will be, since you asked me not to swear in front of you."

"You wouldn't recognize swearing if it ran you down in the street," she quipped, then added in a lofty tone, "it's an uneducated man who has nothing but swearwords in his vocabulary."

"Straight from the lips of your precious Miss Abigail, I'd wager."

"Then you would lose again. I came up with that one by myself." She bit her bottom lip, in an effort to squelch her urge to grin. "It does fit the situation, don't you think?"

"If you say so. But I'll tell you again, it'll take more than verbal barbs to fend off Morley's fury when he learns about all your meddlin'."

"Must you always return to that? Those children are my family. Regardless of what you think, their education is imperative. If I could start them in school this summer . . ."

While she spoke, he dropped her parasol to the step beside them and backed her against the side of the building. With one booted foot propped on the bottom step, he brought his face to within inches of hers. He was grinning that grin that promised secrets. Her breath caught. Now she knew what those secrets were. She tried to ignore the possibility that her latest pledge was about to be demolished by his lips and that she possessed neither the strength nor the will to resist.

"Use the schoolhouse, Maddie," he was saying.

"You don't care?"

"Not enough to spend our last few minutes arguin' about it." The words brushed against her skin; his lips followed with agonizing slowness.

She didn't struggle. She didn't even consider it. Not with Tyler's lips wringing every last drop of resistance from her mind. Her opposition became acceptance; her fear turned to need, made even more urgent by the knowledge of what would come.

Of what could come. She slipped her shoulders up the wall, dislodging their lips.

"I'll take good care of your town, Tyler."

"Sure you will." But he didn't sound worried, nor even very interested. And his lips, when they reclaimed hers in a wild and sensual game, shattered her sensibilities, leaving her empty and yearning and totally at his mercy. Through the haze she heard horses draw up in the front yard, voices.

"I will," she assured him, breaking lip contact, once more.

"It doesn't matter." His nose nudged hers. His lips pecked at hers. She would never have suspected that grown people could indulge in such playfulness. Or that she, Madolyn Sinclair, could let herself go in such a reckless, wonderful way.

"I don't figure you can do any damage I can't straighten out when I get back." Someone began banging on the front door.

An almost childlike mood pervaded her, except that she didn't feel like a child. She felt more worldly, more empowered than ever in her life. "The *damage* I do won't require straightening out," she promised.

His eyes danced. "Like hell, it won't." And his lips found hers again. Like a runner nearing the end of the race, she was breathless; like a traveler searching for water, she felt anxious and in great need of a consummation she now understood, or thought she did. She tightened her hold around his neck. She didn't want him to leave. She didn't want to be alone. Not now . . . not before . . .

"MIS-TER TY-LER!" Lucky bellowed down the staircase from the third floor.

Still wrapped in Tyler's embrace, Madolyn turned to look up the stairs. Lucky was grinning from ear to ear.

"Them vaqueros of yours is waitin' out front." Lucky winked. "You want they should go ahead without you?"

It wasn't only her face that flushed this time. Madolyn felt her whole body flame at being caught in such a compromising situation. But not once, though embarrassment raced in a heated rush up her neck, not once did she consider removing herself from Tyler's embrace. Already she dreaded him turning her loose.

As if he understood her innermost longings, his arms tightened around her. *As if he felt the same way.*

"No, Lucky," he called up at length. "Thanks, but tell 'em I'm comin'."

The disparity didn't hit Madolyn until later. At the time it seemed like the most natural thing in the world for Tyler to expect Lucky to traipse through the center of the house and down two flights of stairs to relay a message he could have stepped around the corner and delivered for himself. At the time all she could think about was being in his arms.

And of not being in his arms. "How long will you be gone?"

"Want to plan your battles accordin'ly?" Before she could respond, he kissed her again, deeply, possessively. When he lifted his lips, it was mere inches. He rested his forehead against hers. Their breathing labored to the same cadence. "Promise me somethin', Maddie."

She resisted the frightful urge to say, Anything. "What?"

"That you'll be here when I get back."

Madolyn sat on the wagon seat, her back stiff, her parasol held high. Young Clements had eagerly accepted the chore of driving her to her brother's. She felt a twinge of guilt for not preparing him for a less-than-cordial reception.

Truthfully, she wasn't sure what to expect from Morley. But since she had heard nothing in response to the message she sent him earlier, she could envision the scene. It could well be a repeat of last time, even without Tyler along to antagonize him.

Regardless, she could not give up on gaining his help to secure her inheritance or in providing for his children. She could not give up—not for Morley's sake, nor for the children's, nor, for that matter, for her own. Daily she became more and more aware of the scant amount of time left her. With every passing day her year's grace dwindled further.

But more than her inheritance was at stake now. Much more. Somehow, she sensed that were she to remain in this barbaric land much longer, her relationship with Tyler would get out of hand. Already, she feared she was becoming too fond of the man.

And if his parting words were an indication, he was beginning to feel things for her. Goldie's advice had turned out to be fool's gold.

Madolyn ran two fingers inside her high collar, loosening it from her skin. Already the dire weather predictions were proving true, and it wasn't even June. My, what would summer bring?

Higher temperatures and shorter tempers, no doubt.

She turned her attention to the boy beside her. He was what her mother would have called a string bean, lanky to the point of being skinny. Under the hot sun, freckles fairly popped out across his nose and cheeks.

"You should have worn a hat, Clements."

"Naw, Miss Maddie. Sun don't hurt me none."

"Nevertheless, I would hate for you to blister on my account. You were awfully kind to agree to drive me all this way. I shall speak with my brother about your fee."

"You might as well try diggin' for water in them mountains yonder as to try to get money outta ol' Morley."

"Why do you say that?"

"Ever'one knows him for the biggest tightwad this side of the Mississip. Why Goldie won't even let her girls service him no more."

Madolyn gripped the wagon seat with her free hand. Perspiration beaded her forehead, and only half of it from the weather. Would the indignities never cease to shock her? Why, even children in this barbaric land discussed disgraceful matters. A boy Clements's age shouldn't know about . . . about things that even she, at thirty, didn't know.

"How old are you, Clements?"

"Goin' on sixteen, I reckon."

"You don't know?"

"Not rightly."

"Are you, uh, what happened to your parents? If I may ask so bold a question."

"No need to worry 'bout bein' bold. I ain't ashamed of the fact I'm orphaned."

"Orphaned?"

"Yes, ma'am. Left at the depot, I was, back when the town was whole."

"Left? By your parents?"

"Don't rightly know. I was a tyke. Goldie figured me to be no more'n three or four. 'Course, there's always the chanct that I'm overgrown for my age. Then again, I could be undergrown. Don't reckon I'll ever know for certain about my age. Don't reckon it to be a bother, not knowin'."

"Of course not, Clements. So, Goldie's been your . . . uh . . ."

"Goldie's like my ma, I reckon. 'Course I don't rightly know what a ma'd be like."

"I'm sure Goldie has made a fine mother." Notwithstanding the scandalous education he had received, Clements had proved himself an exemplary young man.

"What about education?"

"Education?"

"How far have you gotten in school?"

"A bit here an' there."

"You aren't enrolled in Miss James's class?"

"Miss James is new to town. Fact is, 'fore her, we didn't have no school a'tall."

"No school. You mean there was no school in Buckhorn while you were growing up?"

"No, ma'am. Ol' Morley don't believe in such."

"Well, he certainly had the privilege of an education himself." Until he ran away from home, she thought. "What does Morley have to do with it?"

"He's against spendin' money on a schoolmarm."

"But he will spend five hundred dollars on a horse?"

"What's that?"

"Oh, nothing. I was just thinking about my next order from Abilene. I shall add some things for you, Clements."

"Not for me. I don't want nothin' from Ol' Morley. Not that he's likely to go to payin' for it no-how."

"He owes you, Clements. Do not doubt that. And every other child he has deprived of an education."

So incensed was she, that when Clements drew the team to a halt, she was startled into dropping her parasol. Without thinking, she jumped to the ground to fetch it.

There stood George Washington Sinclair. Although she could tell he recognized her, he still leveled the shotgun on them.

"Hola, Jorge." Madolyn picked up her parasol, swatted at the dust that clung to it, suddenly tongue-tied. *"Ven,"* she tried, motioning to the wagon as she spoke. When Jorge made no move to climb aboard, she wondered whether she had the word right. Or whether, like last time, he chose to obey his father over her. She could hear Tyler now, "Mind your own business, Maddie."

Relentless to a fault, she persisted, but at the end of an exchange that was nowhere near as fluent as when Tyler spoke with the boy, she had understood only one thing.

"No, tía."

Disappointment mounted; still, she forged ahead. Climbing into the wagon, she stepped over the seat and began to rummage through a crate. Presently, she withdrew a pair of black boots, which she extended to Jorge. The boy's green eyes popped. Then she realized she had failed to learn the words for foot or size, or, as it was beginning to seem, for anything really helpful.

"Do you speak Spanish?" she asked Clements.

"Some."

"Well, tell him to hold up his foot."

That met with a measure of success, for in response to the relayed message, Jorge hopped around on a bare foot, waving the other one toward Madolyn. She stared at the callused sole that gave new meaning to her mother's term, "rusty." But this child's calluses were real, a result of running around the rocky, thorn-riddled countryside without protective footgear. Yes, Tyler had been right, boots were a much better choice than shoes.

She watched Jorge sit on the roadside and stuff his foot into the boot she tossed down to him. She prayed it would fit, for she had guessed at the sizes and this was the largest pair.

His foot slipped in nicely. She tossed him the other boot and he stood proud and tall with his ragged duckins tucked into the stove-pipe tops.

She had forgotten socks, but he didn't seem to notice. When he walked, however, she could tell the boots were too large. Oh, my. She rummaged through another parcel, searching for something to stuff in the toe.

"He's got it," Clements called.

When Madolyn looked around, Jorge was busy stuffing handfuls of dried grass into the toes.

Finished, he stood up, stomped his feet, and favored her with a wide grin. *"Gracias."* His sombrero bobbled with his eagerness. *"Gracias, tía."*

Tía. Tears rushed to Madolyn's eyes. *Tía.* Undoubtedly the sweetest word she had learned in this barbaric land.

"How do you say nephew?" she asked Clements. She

would have to go back to Loretta with a list of phrases. Hello, How are you? and What time do you have? were proving as worthless as last year's calendar.

Her young driver shrugged, thought a moment, finally admitting, "I don't know. Say it in English."

"An excellent idea, Clements." Scrambling to the ground, Madolyn took one of Jorge's hands. It felt nearly as callused as his foot had looked, but even through her gloves, touching the boy did wondrous and warm things to her heart. With her free hand, she tapped her chest. "I am *tía*."

Jorge nodded, grinning.

She tapped his chest. "You are nephew."

His eyes widened.

"Ne-phew," she repeated, tapping him again.

"Ne-few," he tried.

"Yes."

"Sí." Jorge tapped Madolyn, then himself, *"Tía y sobrino."*

Madolyn laughed. *"So-bree-no,"* she tried. *"So-bree-no."*

Jorge laughed with her, and for a moment, Madolyn was lost in time and space and in the love that enveloped her in the wary but softening eyes and laughter of this boy, her nephew. Reaching, she straightened the brim of his hat. She fairly itched to hug him.

She didn't. She couldn't. But when she climbed back aboard the wagon and instructed Clements to whip up the team, she departed from her nephew with a swelling of love. It didn't bother her that she couldn't allow herself to hug him today.

Tomorrow. Or one day soon. Before she left.

By the time they reached the second boy, Thomas Madison Sinclair, Madolyn had shaken off the bout of melancholy she experienced at the thought of leaving her nephews.

The boots fit close enough. The boys accepted them eagerly, but each in turn refused her offer for a ride home.

All except Little Jefferson Davis. Madolyn smiled fondly, recalling that he had been named in honor of Tyler.

That said a lot, in her estimation, about the friendship between Tyler and Morley. Such a friendship, one that had flourished for nearly twenty years, could not be allowed to die for lack of care.

Would not be allowed to die, she vowed, adding one more item to her list of things to accomplish before she returned to Boston. My, oh my, but she had better get a move on.

With Little Jeff sitting proudly on the seat between them, his eyes on his shiny new boots and one grubby hand clutched in Madolyn's, Clements drew the wagon to a stop in the shade of the same mesquite tree Tyler had hitched the rig to that day.

Morley saw them coming. He came stomping up from the barn, his same blustering self. "You haven't left yet?"

But his tone was more quarrelsome than hostile. His voice was merely gruff when he frowned at Little Jeff and spat out an order in Spanish.

Little Jeff pointed to his boots.

"What the hell—" Morley transferred his attention to Madolyn, then to the parcels heaped in the wagon bed. "I told you there's no room out here."

"I'm not moving in, Morley." Reaching, she braced herself with a hand to his shoulder, before hopping to the ground. He made no move to assist her. Not that she needed it.

MEN! For the first time in her life, she added her brother to the category defined by that perfidious term. "I've brought things for the children. Surely I'm allowed to bring gifts for my nieces and nephews." Her smile wavered when he eyed her sharply from beneath the brim of his soiled Stetson.

"If Grant's put ideas in your head, I'll—" he accused.

"No one had to put ideas in my head, Morley. Unfortunately, I saw the despicable state of affairs on my first visit."

"They're *my* affairs," he quarreled. "I won't stand for you meddlin' in my business."

"I consider nieces and nephews my business, too." When he started to object, she interrupted with, "even if you don't."

"Well, I damned sure don't. You oughta get yourself back to Boston. How many times do I have to tell you? This ain't no place for a lady."

Taking a tactic from who knew where—Goldie and her girls, most likely—Madolyn twirled her parasol over her head and smiled in an enticing way that surprised her more than it did her brother. "Thank you for the compliment, Morley. I knew you couldn't be all that angry to see me."

She used his stunned reaction to link arms with him. "Clements, would you unload the wagon while I visit with Carlita." So saying, she began to stroll in the direction of the hut. "And be sure to open those crates . . . like we discussed."

Morley dug his heels into the dirt. "No, you don't, Maddie. I don't know what you're up to, but I aim to put a stop to your meddlin'. You ain't agonna sashay in here an' ruin my life."

"Ruin your life? If I were half as clever as you and Tyler make out, I would be president of the United States of America."

"What's Grant got to do with this?"

Ignoring his question, she continued, "And if I were—president, I mean—the first thing I would do is give women the vote. Once we have the vote, Morley, we won't stand for behavior like yours."

"My behavior ain't none of your business." He spat a stream of tobacco juice off to the side.

Madolyn had hoped to save this argument until last, but seeing the boys, one after the other, barefoot and armed, afraid to come to their own home for fear of their father, she simply could not keep her mouth shut.

"It appears to me, Morley, that you are entirely too much like our departed father." Before the words were out of her mouth, Morley had jerked away from her.

"The hell you say!" His eyes were dark and angry.

Madolyn jumped back, her parasol lowered ever so slightly, just in case. The thought of having to defend herself against her own brother's temper appalled her. "Morley, please, I didn't mean to anger you. But if we needed proof, there it is."

"Proof of what?"

"That your children are afraid of you."

"You don't understand this situation, Maddie. Not by half. So stay out of it."

"I understand more than you think. I know you and Carlita aren't married."

"That damned Grant!"

"Tyler told me, yes, but I would have heard it, anyway. You aren't all that well thought of in Buck."

"Buck ain't my town. What'd folks in Horn say?"

"I wouldn't know. I'm not allowed over there."

"That got you bumfuzzled, too? It's a free country."

"What good is it to be free to cross the tracks, when you ordered every single person on that side to ignore me? You don't know the misery you've wrought, Morley. And before you say you don't care, let me tell you that I intend to right it."

"Right what?"

"Everything. Beginning with the divided town. You might as well know, we have formed the Buck-Horn Reunited Society, with the ultimate goal of rejoining Buckhorn."

"No one in either town will go for that."

She smiled. "Wait and see. But listen, if you dare. There's more. I have Tyler's permission to use the school during the summer. I shall be holding classes for the children."

"Bully for you."

"Your children."

"My children? These kids have work to do. I can't afford to run this ranch without their help."

"You'll be able to run it better when they're educated."

"I can't afford—"

"Before you start poormouthing, let me advise you that I know about the five hundred dollars you paid for 'Pache Prancer."

"That sonofabitch Grant! I'll—"

"You might as well stop blaming Tyler, because you and he are about to make up."

"Says who? I'll bet he hasn't agreed to that."

"Not yet. But I can't let either of you destroy a twenty-year-old friendship."

"It ain't your friendship. Who the hell'd you think you are?"

"Your sister, Morley. Your only relation, except these wonderful children, and Carlita, who is soon to be your wife."

"Soon to be my WHAT?"

Madolyn swallowed, cleared her throat, and continued, "I spoke with Pastor Arndt. I know you would prefer an Episcopal priest, but Baptist will have to do. You'll be just as married—"

"And you're just as wrong. I don't aim to alter my life, not one single bit. Not to suit you or anyone else. Do you hear me? Not one single bit."

"Oh, it looks like Clements is finished unloading. Let me sum things up, Morley, lest you failed to catch everything the first time. I shall expect the children in Buck one week from tomorrow for classes. I have arranged for Goldie to rent you the two rooms at the end of the hall—one for the boys, one for the girls. At fifty cents a day including meals, that comes to two dollars and fifty cents a week. Keep track of their chores, so they won't be idle on the weekends. You know how idle time—"

"Those kids ain't goin' in to school, so don't hold your breath."

"My nieces and nephews will be educated, Morley Sinclair. Even if I have to hold school under a mesquite tree at each of their posts."

"Damn that Tyler Grant!"

"I shall speak with Carlita about the wedding date. Traditionally, the bride sets it."

"NO! Do you understand me, Madolyn Sinclair. I said no. No. No. No. Stop meddlin' in my life!"

"Call it meddling if you like; I see it as righting the wrongs of an earlier generation. In this case, Morley, I cannot sit by and allow the sins of the father to be repeated. I will not allow my nieces and nephews to go uneducated, nor will I see them reared in an immoral environment. It's unhealthy, unchristian, and if it isn't illegal, it should be."

"Then when you're elected President, goddamnit, pass a law. Until then stay out of my business. Go back to Boston."

"I will, Morley. Just as soon as I have your signature on these papers." Slipping the handle of her parasol under an armpit, Madolyn rummaged through her reticule. "I have them right here."

Twelve

Until challenged by an obstinate brother, Madolyn hadn't known she possessed such persuasive powers. Not that Morley signed the papers, he didn't. But before she left the ranch, he did show a whisker of his old self, a touch, however slight, of the affection he once felt for her.

What an encouragement that had been! One day she would have Morley back to his old self. She hadn't really believed he was like Papa. She hadn't wanted to believe such a heinous thing. But Morley possessed a temper, no doubt about that. She watched him struggle to control it when she withdrew the papers.

"I told you, goddamnit—"

Carlita came out the back door at that moment, stopping Morley's tirade in midsentence. She wore the same black dress and apron and the same wary expression as on Madolyn's first visit. At sight of Morley, she stopped in her tracks. When her wariness turned to fright, Madolyn's stomach bunched in a knot. Morley couldn't, he just couldn't, have turned out like their father. But of course he could have.

Clements passed Madolyn, carrying an oversized crate on his shoulder. "This here's the last one, Miss Maddie."

"You uncrated and assembled everything?"

"Yes'um."

"What in tarnation's goin' on?" Morley shouted.

Anticipation eased Madolyn's anxieties. Thrusting the pa-

pers she so desperately wanted him to sign into his hands,
she took off after Clements.

Carlita continued to wring her hands on her apron. She
shook her head vigorously when Madolyn approached.
"No, no."

"You don't like it?"

Carlita cast a furtive glance toward the hut. "No, no."

Madolyn's heart sank, but she graciously attempted to
soothe the woman's concern. It was, after all, Carlita's
home. "Then we shall send it back for another, Carlita."
Inside the earthen-floored adobe, the remembered aroma of
peppers and spices welcomed her.

There it stood. Not a fancy dining table, but looking for
all the world like one, here in these primitive surroundings.
With all three leaves in place, the table took up most of the
room. "Perhaps you would like it better without these."
Madolyn grasped one of the leaves, prepared to remove it,
but Carlita stopped her by flattening both work-scarred
hands on the leaf.

"No."

"But you said . . . ?"

"What in tarnation's goin' on?" Morley bellowed from
the doorway. Madolyn's precious papers were fluttering in
his limp hand. His eyes fairly popped from his head. She
ignored him.

"I know it takes up a lot of room," she told Carlita, "but
with ten chairs— I mean, you only need eight unless I or
someone . . . The extra two chairs are for company."

"We don't have company!" Morley bellowed. She tossed
a calm smile his way.

"Then it's time you started."

After what felt like one full minute, every second meant
to intimidate, Morley turned his attention to the crates
stacked on the floor beyond the table. Clements had opened
them, but for some reason, Clara and Betsy stood by, holding them closed.

Madolyn's disappointment evaporated at the expectant expressions in their wide green eyes. "Here, here, let's get these things open, girls."

"You'll do no such thing!" Morley bawled. But she ignored him, again. That was one thing she was good at, one thing she had learned on her own without Miss Abigail's tutelage—how to ignore belligerent men.

Moving Clara aside, Madolyn opened the first box and began emptying the contents onto the new table. "Piece goods," she explained to Carlita. "For dresses and shirts for the boys."

At the bottom of that box were the shoes. When she handed the girls each a pair of brown leather shoes, their reticence vanished. Each little girl sat on the earthen floor and began to stuff her dirty little feet into them.

"Wait, girls."

In unison the girls looked up at her, their eyes round at the prospect of having their prizes taken away.

"I ordered stockings. Let's find the stockings."

"So, you're broke, are you?" Morley accused, still from the doorway. "I told Grant you were an impostor."

Madolyn tensed. She wasn't actually afraid of Morley; at least, she didn't want to be. But good sense prevailed, and she decided to wait for another day to break the news that he, not she, had paid for every item in the room.

Trembling inside, she nevertheless managed to smile sweetly. "The pittance these things cost wouldn't go far in providing me a secure future, Morley."

"Spend your last dime, then. See if I care." He tossed the papers to the new table and turned to leave. "Go back to Boston, Maddie."

"You signed—"

"I ain't signin' nothin'."

Behind her, the girls' whispers tugged at her heart. Morley stomped away from the hut. *Don't sign them,* she thought. *You'll pay for it, Morley Sinclair.* This family needed so many things she didn't know where to start, what to order from Abilene next.

But what they needed most was love and security, patience and compassion. Even after she returned to Buck, Madolyn was plagued by the haunted look on Carlita's face—gratitude that someone was doing something for her children, uneasiness that she was breaking all the rules.

When Morley was out of earshot, Madolyn restated her willingness to exchange the table for one that suited Carlita.

"No, gracias. Está hermosa." She ran callused hands over the leaf. Her smile was wistful. Her eyes anxious, yet proud.

"Beautiful," Madolyn translated quietly, glad that on this day she had understood one positive word spoken by her family.

The girls alternated between running circles around the table in their new shoes and sitting in one, then another of the new chairs.

"It is beautiful, beautiful, beautiful." Carlita's wistful eyes were even more expressive than her chantlike repetition. "But you do not understand," Carlita explained in halting English. "You cannot change our life."

"He's my brother. As badly as I hate to admit it, much of his abominable behavior was learned at home. Not his swearing, mind you. Mother wouldn't have stood for that. But the way he treats you, well, our father treated our mother much the same. Some people claim such dastardly traits are inherited."

"How he treats me?" Carlita quizzed with bowed head, as though to utter a simple question were a breach of conduct.

"You're submissive," Madolyn explained. "The girls, too."

Carlita's head came up. "We are servants."

"Servants?" Madolyn was horrified. "You are the mother of his children. No decent man would treat you like a servant. No decent man would refuse to allow his children to be educated, or deny his family a proper home to live in, when he spends five hundred dollars for a horse."

Carlita shrugged.

"With your help, Carlita, I shall right those wrongs. Before I leave this place your life will be eased and my nieces and nephews will be educated."

Carlita's black eyes begged. "Please, señorita, leave us to our life. Do not give Morley cause to send us away."

"Send you away?"

Carlita clutched her girls to her skirts. "My girls and me, señorita. The boys, he would keep to work the ranch. But my girls and me . . . we have no place to go."

Madolyn struggled to contain her outrage. "Send you away? You are his . . ." Rage swallowed embarrassment. "You're the mother of his children." Her gaze dropped to the girls. "His precious daughters. He couldn't send you away. Not even the son of our father could be so hateful."

Carlita straightened her shoulders a bit. "It is not so hateful, señorita. We are servants . . ."

"You are not servants . . ."

"Sí. It is not to be ashamed of; it is the way things are."

"The way things are! Not to claim one's children? Not to care what happens to them? Not to want them to have better lives?"

Carlita shrugged.

"Why, he has you so frightened you won't even eat at the table with him. Or the girls."

"In my country it is the way."

Madolyn doubted that. A place where women were more downtrodden than in America? Little green eyes peered at her from the girls' precious faces. "You're not my servant, Carlita. Call me Maddie, uh, Madolyn or something. I'm your sister-in-law, or I will be—"

She stopped. Perhaps she should wait a while longer before she tackled their living arrangement. As though he were inside her head, she could hear Tyler accusing her of meddling. Perhaps she was. But it was for a good cause.

The children did not arrive for school one week later. Not that Madolyn had expected them; but she was sorely disappointed. In an effort to right matters, she telegraphed another order to Abilene, this one for beds—one large enough for the boys to share, one for the girls. A second telegram to Lyman Bridges of Chicago requested a price list for their mail-order houses. Morley and Carlita simply had to have a larger house; the size of the dining table proved that. After Tyler explained the reason for so much adobe—lack of trees. for lumber—she realized a mail-order house would fit the bill perfectly—Morley's bill, she thought with a smile, albeit, a short-lived one.

She could not dispel the gloom engendered by Carlita's fear—realistic or not—that Morley could send her and the girls away at the drop of a hat. How utterly inhumane.

During the following weeks, while she worked day and night to get the Buck-Horn Reunited Society off the ground, Madolyn never once lost sight of her vow to see Morley and Carlita legally married before she returned to Boston. Perhaps Carlita's fears would diminish, once she was married.

Then again, perhaps they wouldn't. Madolyn's mother's fears never diminished, not until the day she died. Which proved the point: men were no damned good. And husbands headed the list.

It took three meetings of the Buck-Horn Reunited Society for the women to become comfortable with the idea of keeping secrets from their husbands.

"I have never kept a single thing from Willard in all our twenty years of marriage." Frances Arndt, the parson's wife, voiced her concerns immediately upon setting foot in the third-floor workroom. "I'm sure it goes against the Bible."

"The Bible says to honor thy father and mother, not thy husband," Madolyn returned.

"It's a matter of interpretation," Frances insisted.

Camilla Crane squinted down the bridge of a knobby nose to thread her quilting needle. "It also says not to bear false witness."

"You aren't bearing false witness," Madolyn argued.

In unison the women glanced up from the wedding-ring quilt that stretched on a frame between them. They eyed each other, then turned astonished expressions on Madolyn.

"Didn't you tell them we're making a quilt to raffle off at the fall bake sale?" She tried to concentrate on the quilt, repositioning the needle before she pulled it through the layers of fabric and batting. Although her stitches were not as uniform as Frances Arndt's, who sat beside her, Madolyn had known in advance that to become one with the group, she would have to participate in their activities.

Besides, Loretta James had decided to postpone her vacation until after the demonstration. With school out, she eagerly joined the quilting session. "Independence Day! What a perfect day for the march. I couldn't leave town at such an important time. Why, I would feel like an outsider when I returned."

"Wonderful," Madolyn had replied. "We can use your help." She liked Loretta, she really did, but watching the care the schoolmarm took with every stitch on the wedding ring pattern, Madolyn suspected that more was at stake here than bringing the founding fathers to their knees.

Unless it were one particular founding father, brought to one particular knee. She stabbed her needle through the quilt top, batting, and lining, trying to dispel the sickening image of Loretta and Tyler.

"Aren't we making a quilt to raffle at fall bake sale?" she asked, again rhetorically.

"Yes, but—"

NO PLACE FOR A LADY   223

"Don't you always make a quilt to raffle at the bake sale?"

"Yes, we do, but—"

"What if they ask where we're making it?" Camilla quizzed. Worried glances darted from woman to woman.

"I doubt they will," Madolyn argued. "Since making a quilt is an annual project, they will assume you are quilting in the same place." She paused, needle poised, to consider. "Where is that? In case someone asks."

"At the parsonage," Frances supplied.

"And here we are hiding out at the local house of ill repute." Murmurs spread in a wave around the perimeter of the quilt. Madolyn was glad Goldie had declined to join them.

"No offense, Maddie," Hattie Jasper, wife of the mercantile owner, added. "We know you had no choice."

No choice? Indeed, she hadn't had a choice. Tyler brought her here under false pretenses. He tried to use her to get back at her brother, then to persuade her to take his side against reuniting the town. Yet, through it all, she realized the thing she had the least choice about, no choice, actually, was the perfidious way she felt, light-headed and sort of free, when they were together.

He asked her not to leave town before he returned. In that, she had no choice, either, for if the town were reunited today and a train came tomorrow, she couldn't take it. She had no choice. She couldn't leave without seeing him again.

"No choice?" Madolyn echoed, with such vigor the women started. "That is exactly the point. If the division of Buckhorn had been fair, as the men claim, I would have found lodging at a hotel, and we wouldn't have to meet in secret." *And I might not have met Tyler Grant.*

Another hum of disquietude coursed through the room.

"It's for a good cause," she retorted, scarcely able to conceal her mounting impatience.

"I doubt my Owen would see it that way," Hattie whined.

"Indeed he wouldn't," Madolyn agreed. "That is precisely the reason the world needs changing, ladies. Men control our lives. That simply is not acceptable."

"Easy for you to say," Inez Bradford chimed in. "You don't have a husband to worry about."

"For good reason," Madolyn replied, lifting her eyes from the wedding-ring quilt. "I chose not to subjugate myself to another human being."

Loretta James's black eyes flew to Madolyn's, while the married women favored one another with a kinship Madolyn realized quite suddenly she would never feel. Well, good riddance. She did not need marriage and its attendant horrors.

"It isn't all bad," Inez ventured.

"No, it isn't. If I hadn't married Owen, I wouldn't have little Huey and Margaret Elizabeth."

"Without Victor I wouldn't have my children, either. But on a more selfish note, I kinda enjoy havin' a man to fuss over."

Nods of understanding were followed by Camilla's adding, "And someone to sit with after the evening meal is done and the dishes washed. Someone to share the day's activities with."

"Someone to paddle the boys when they need it," laughed Inez.

Madolyn didn't remind her that without her husband, she wouldn't have four rapidly growing boys to need paddling. Morley, blast him, had proved for all to see, that right or wrong a woman did not have to be married to bear children.

The indecency of it never failed to bring a spot of heat to Madolyn's cheeks. And a pain to her heart. Her brother, father to six illegitimate children! Even her own father couldn't claim such a travesty. At least, not that the family ever knew.

As the days passed, the quilt progressed nicely, but Madolyn was even more pleased with the way the women's attitudes progressed. While they stitched, she read them articles written by Miss Abigail and other suffragette leaders across the country. Not that the women of Buck agreed with all the ideas, but a lively discussion developed, and day by day they learned to speak their minds—on the third floor of the local house of ill repute, leastways.

Their confidence gained, the time had come to move on. A week after the clandestine meetings began, the ladies climbed the back stairs of the House of Negotiable Love to discover that their unfinished quilt had been carefully folded and put away, the quilting frame dismantled. In its place, Clements had erected a worktable; Madolyn provided the paints, brushes and canvas, ordered from Saint Louis.

Goldie stood beside Madolyn, greeting each woman as she entered. It was Goldie's first meeting since the schoolhouse. She wore a high-collared white batiste waist with vertical tucks and a black faille skirt, the creations of Frances Arndt.

"I'm not much of a quilter," Goldie had offered as an excuse every time Madolyn invited her to join the group. Lucky finally explained the reason Goldie refused to attend.

"Ain't got but one street dress. Says that bright pink outfit she wore to the schoolhouse wouldn't be fittin' for receivin' ladyfolk in her own home."

"Excuses," Madolyn exclaimed. But Lucky had a point. And certainly none of the women would be comfortable if Goldie wore her brassy gold kimono.

Upon learning that Frances Arndt took in sewing, Madolyn realized she had found a solution. When she approached her privately about fashioning something for Goldie to wear, the parson's wife agreed to sew a few garments for the madam, if Madolyn could obtain her requirements.

"I'm sure she wouldn't want to come to the parsonage to be measured."

Taken aback, Madolyn squelched the temptation to inquire how, if a madam wasn't welcome at the parsonage, her soul could ever be saved, but she held her tongue. Their work was cut out for them, and without cooperation among the women, it would be difficult, if not impossible, to reunite the town.

"I don't understand it," she pined one evening after the women departed. "The men should be eager for us to succeed. We're trying to save their businesses."

"Men are kinda like sheep," Goldie mused. "They stick together."

"Are you saying they will stand by Tyler even if it means losing their livelihoods?"

"Sheep generally follow blindly where the leader leads—even if that's off a bluff."

"That abominable man!"

"Now, now, Maddie. Don't go blamin' Tyler. He didn't have a chance to nip this in the bud. He was off in Mexico when Morley took his notion. By the time Tyler returned, the town was divided, loyalties, too. To change things, he would've had to start a shootin' war."

"That's what he said. I thought he was exaggerating."

"Tyler Grant usually speaks the truth, Maddie. He's an honorable man."

"No man is an honorable man, Goldie." Madolyn hoped Goldie couldn't see the glow that burned inside her at the mere mention of the man's name. "You, most of all, should know that."

"Quite the contrary. My customers are some of the most loyal people in the world."

"Loyal to whom? I doubt their wives consider them either honorable or loyal."

"You have a point there, honey. You surely do."

Daily, the women painted canvas signs with slogans Madolyn helped them compose:

BUCKHORN REUNITED! REUNITE IT NOW!

And: OUR CHILDREN DESERVE MORE!

And: LET FREEDOM RING!

While they painted, Madolyn taught them songs. Some,

like "Onward, Christian Soldiers" and "Rise up O Men of God," were favorite marching hymns from other campaigns. Others Madolyn helped the ever-more-eager women adapt: "Shall We Gather at the Depot" and "Were You There When They Tore Apart Our Town?"

By the time the ladies in Buck had been thoroughly introduced to the methods of marching and demonstrating, Madolyn realized it was time to take her campaign across the tracks to the ladies of Horn. Without cohesiveness from the women on both sides of the tracks, nothing could be gained.

This second phase, as it were, proved tricky. Madolyn's original idea—rather, Goldie's idea—had been to use the men who slipped across the tracks to engage her girls' services to spread the word on the Horn side of town. But those men weren't thrilled about having their nighttime trysts made public, which would be a possibility if they served as couriers; by the same token, Goldie wasn't eager to scare off her Horn customers by insisting they aid the campaign.

Madolyn searched for an alternative method. The only one that presented itself as feasible required Madolyn, herself, to slip across the tracks. It was the only workable solution, since only Madolyn could teach the ladies of Horn the slogans, chants, and practices they would need when the hour came for reunification.

So, on the next dark night, Madolyn slipped across the tracks, armed with names of friends the ladies of Buck had not seen since the towns were separated. Clements led the way, a lantern held high to light a path through the briars and brambles at the southern edge of town. She arrived with dust clinging to her black skirts, and ringlets torn from her tight bun.

The ladies of Horn were as reticent, yet as eager, as the ladies in Buck had been. They met in the back room of the Bank of Buckhorn, where Constance Allen, wife of banker Sam Allen regularly conducted deportment classes of an evening. Every night for a week they met, and their numbers grew. They painted signs and patiently learned every word of the slogans and songs Madolyn had taught their Buck counterparts.

According to plan, the campaign would begin slowly, leading up to the combined rally day, the date of which would be held in strictest secrecy. Already several of the more courageous Buck women had gathered to march through their dusty streets, past businesses where they drew attention to their cause with their shouted slogans and adapted marching hymns. Their short marches always ended with one pass along the Buck side of the railroad tracks. But they never attempted to cross over.

After Madolyn's fourth clandestine visit to Horn, those ladies took up the march. On her instructions, they were to pay no heed to the women across the tracks; indeed, they tried to time their marches for different parts of the day.

As she had done in Buck, Madolyn put the march date to a vote in Horn. Democracy, after all must be preserved. The ladies in both towns saw the appropriateness of the date.

"Independence Day! We'll give it new meaning!" Nancy Peebles, wife of the Buckhorn Hotel owner enthused.

"Or lose what little independence we have," Angie Thompson fretted.

"Ladies, ladies," Madolyn cautioned. "We only lose that which we are willing to forfeit."

The slogan sounded like it had come from Miss Abigail's own mouth, Madolyn thought proudly, when, in fact, she had composed it herself. But the long hours quickly took their toll. Days in Buck, nights in Horn left little time for necessities, such as sleeping and eating regular meals.

Not only did this double duty exhaust Madolyn, but she felt continually grimy after her clandestine treks through underbrush and down dusty streets in the dead of night. To make things worse, with the onset of summer, water usage had to be more closely restricted.

Conscious of the worsening water shortage as summer grew ever hotter and drier, she dared not ask for a bath in the middle of the week. Primarily, because she knew Goldie and Lucky would oblige her. Everyone was dirty and needing baths. She could not, would not ask to be the exception. If only it would rain. But that, too, seemed improbable. During her almost six weeks in this wilderness, it had not rained once.

Night after night, she bathed in her little wash basin, and, tired as she was, she fell asleep without really minding that she was dirty. On Goldie's suggestion she took up the hours of many of the girls in the House of Negotiable Love—she slept until noon, at which time Lucky brought a light luncheon. While she ate, she prepared for her afternoon session with the ladies of Buck.

By Friday of the second week after undertaking such a marathon schedule, the heat had become heavy, sultry, almost unbearable. Even though she stripped down to chemise and bloomers, she found it difficult to sleep that morning. Clyde Thompson, mayor of Horn, had discovered his wife's involvement in the cause and forbade her to continue meeting with the group, to the end that the other Horn women were so fearful of Mayor Thompson telling their husbands, that only two women showed up for the meeting. Fear of failure took on a realistic face.

A face that plagued Madolyn into the early morning hours. Even the dusty air that blew in her open windows felt heated. She tossed and turned on damp sheets, then finally gave up trying to sleep. Perspiration and dirt had worked their way into her hair like a curse.

Selfish or not, she decided, she could not wait one more day to wash her hair. Not one more day, even though, this being Friday, tomorrow was bath day. She wasn't first in line for the bath water this week, anyway.

Dawn was fast approaching, and with it the breeze had died down. Her lace undercurtains hung limp. Cautioning herself to use as little water as possible, she carried a pitcherful from the container outside her door and poured it into her hand basin. She dipped her head into the basin. What luxury! The coldness inched up her scalp, jarring her senses, then relaxing her. She scrubbed her head vigorously, working the rose-scented soap into a fine lather.

It called to mind her scented baths, and she decided then and there that the first thing on her list when she returned to Boston would be to soak for two full days in a warm, scented bath. When her eyes started stinging from the soap, she squinched them closed. The second thing she would do when she got back to civilization would be to wash her hair in a tub where she wouldn't get soap in her eyes, and rinse it with a whole barrel of rainwater.

For now, however, there was nothing for it but to finish. The water was soapy, her hands were soapy, and she didn't have any clean water. Then, as though in answer to her prayer, Lucky came to her rescue.

At the welcome knock, she sighed contentedly. "Would you fetch me a pitcher of clear water, Lucky, please? I'm in a tight place."

Feeling a bit on the giddy side, now that help was on its way, Madolyn continued to scrub and as she scrubbed, she hummed the latest marching tune she had taught the ladies.

> On our way rejoicing,
> Gladly let us go;
> Conquered have we ladies,
> Vanquished is our foe.

Tyler stood outside Maddie's door, trying to decipher her request. She needed clean water. He understood that. But why?

When she started to hum, his senses did, too. What would he find on the other side of that closed door? Dare he open it to see? The answer to that question was never in doubt.

He dashed back to his own room for a pitcher, dipped it in the communal container, and, taking a deep breath to still his pounding heart, opened the door.

His heart almost ceased altogether at the sight—Maddie, bending over the wash basin, her hair soapy, her eyes squinched shut. Her body was barely covered in a chemise made of tissue-thin batiste and bloomers nearly as revealing.

"You came in the nick of time, Luc—" Her head flew up. Long strands of wet black hair slung soapy water around the room. Most of it landed on Tyler, on his shirt, in his face.

"What are you doing here?" Her voice was scarcely louder than a squeak. As quickly as she had opened them, she squinched her lids shut again.

"Let me help." When he took her by one shoulder, she attempted to pull away, but he held fast. "Whoa, now, Maddie. Simmer down. Let me get the soap out of your eyes." Dipping a corner of his clean shirttail in the fresh pitcher of water, he proceeded to bathe her eyes until she opened first one, then the other.

"That better?"

She didn't respond. Not in words. Her eyes fastened on him like she had seen a demon or some fool thing.

"I thought you were Lucky."

"I know." His eyes left her face and traversed her scarcely clad form.

Instantly she flung her head down, as though to verify what he saw. Wet through and through, her chemise and bloomers clung to her skin. Two rosy nipples puckered beneath the wet fabric, beckoning him, before she crossed her arms over her chest.

"What are you doing here?" Her eyes returned, imploring him—to leave, more than likely. "You're supposed to be in Mexico."

"We drove another herd in last night. Raúl and Sánchez have 'em bedded down outside town." Even dashed with cold water, his body heated in a slow burn. "I rode on into town, late, to, uh . . . to see if you were still here."

She stared at him a moment, as though she didn't comprehend. "I'm still here."

"And if you were real . . ." Speaking, he took up the flannel towel from the dresser and began squeezing water from her hair.

"Real?" Now, she really didn't understand. Hell, neither did he. He chuckled at her confusion.

"I decided you were an apparition."

"An apparition?"

She wasn't used to being teased, he could tell. Sometimes he was able to make her laugh; he loved seeing her laugh, hearing her laugh. But this time he wasn't joking.

"You haunted my dreams, Maddie. Damned if you didn't haunt 'em . . . night and day."

She ducked her head, a sure sign she was hiding something.

"You thought about me, too, didn't you?"

After a long moment, she faced him again. "Does it matter?"

"Does it matter?" He dropped the towel, clasped her face in his hands, and kissed her, long and deep and wet, like he had dreamed of doing for two long weeks. *Did it matter? Hell, yes, it mattered.*

But it shouldn't. Couldn't.

By the time he released her, he had a grip on his runaway brain. "This is what matters." He kissed her again. "Don't tell me you didn't think about it, too."

She nodded, a jerky sort of nod, which he took to be affirmative.

"Did what?" he prompted.

"I thought about it . . ." She grinned up at him, then added, ". . . Tyler." His body tightened at the soft, sensual sound of her saying his name, and at her rare attempt to tease. But even as she made the admission, she struggled to free herself.

He pulled her wet chest to his. Her arms were crossed between them, denying him the contact he craved.

"This isn't right," she whispered against his wet shirt. He felt her heart beat rapidly against him. Or was it his? Or both their hearts, throbbing in unison?

"What isn't right?" Gently, he tugged her arms up and around his neck. When her fingers curled into his hair, his head began to hum. Then he pressed her chest to his and was unable to suppress a shudder, for at last he felt what he had dreamed of feeling, her nipples. They were hard as juniper berries, but he knew from experience they tasted a whole lot sweeter.

"This," she mumbled.

"Cuddlin'?"

"This is more than cuddling."

"Didn't I tell you there was more?"

"Yes, but I—"

"Didn't I tell you it was even sweeter."

"Yes, but—"

"And didn't I promise to show you?"

"Um-hum."

"How 'bout I show you right now?"

He felt her tense. "Now?"

"Unless you think Lucky might walk in on us."

Her breath caught against his chest. "No."

"No what, Maddie?"

She took her time responding, and when she did, he could tell she had made up her mind. Her decision surprised him. And pleased him.

Hesitant green eyes rose to his, and in them he saw determination. He watched embarrassment stain her creamy cheeks with splotches of red. When she spoke, her full lips moved in a slow, sensuous dance.

"Lucky won't come until noon."

That was a curious change in schedule, but one that scarcely tickled his brain. For his brain was full of Maddie. His brain and his arms, and his body yearned for the same sweet fulfillment.

With infinite care he lowered his lips to hers, and for the longest time—too long, his body insisted—he kissed her. Nothing more. Except that it felt like more. Never could he recall a kiss holding so much promise. As if it were an act of lovemaking unto itself, he allowed the delicious agony to build, savoring the fast-approaching crescendo.

Only after her heartbeat matched his own, only after her lips reached and stroked in response to his, only after she melted against him in unmistakable invitation, did he lift her ever so gently in trembling arms and carry her to bed. She felt like a bird in his arms, little and delicate, as though she needed protecting, and loving. With a jolt, he realized that was exactly the way he had remembered her. He had dreamed, not of the militant, meddling Maddie, but of the vulnerable Maddie who had been rejected by her brother and who couldn't bring herself to hug her own nieces and nephews, when it was clear as creek water how badly she wanted to.

And more. He dreamed of the passionate Maddie, the Maddie who took courting lessons from Goldie and used them to set his soul on fire.

Except for a shaft of light from the parlor, the room was dark. He could barely make out the bed, a sight all the more enticing because it was still rumpled. Their lips dislodged when he placed her in the center of it. Her eyes flew open. Lowering himself over her, he claimed her lips again, only to have her fling her head aside.

"No." Hands pressed against his chest, she pushed him away. "No, please."

He lifted himself mere inches, propping his hands against the mattress on either side of her head. "No, what, Maddie?"

"No, I can't . . . I can't . . ."

"All right." Disappointment speared through him. He had been afraid of this; he tried to tell himself it was best. He kissed her tenderly. "All right. If that's what you want."

"It isn't . . . but . . . I can't."

"Why not?"

"I don't know. I just can't . . ."

"You can. If you want to. Do you want to, Maddie?"

"No."

"Truthful, Maddie; be truthful."

"It's wrong to want to."

"But you do."

"Yes."

"What's wrong about it?"

"I don't know."

"If it's so wrong, why do we feel this way? Why do we want to be together . . . *really* together?"

"I don't know."

"You think it should be saved for marriage?"

"Marriage!" She flung her head aside again.

He heard the terror in her voice, felt its echo in his heart. If making love to Maddie meant marrying her, he would have to resist, too. But oh, how sweet she was. How sweet and inviting. Bending, he nudged her face up, kissed her lips. Little nips that finally succeeded in eliciting a response, of which he took full advantage, kissing her deeply, ending by moistening her lips with the tip of his tongue.

"I shall never marry," she vowed.

"I know. You told me. And I told you I won't either. But why should we deny ourselves . . . this . . . when we both want it . . ."—he kissed her again—". . . so badly." Lowering himself he allowed his fully clothed body to skim her almost-nude one. "I want you so bad it hurts."

"I want you, too."

And she did. With every fiber of her being, Madolyn wanted him to continue this sweet and sensual madness.

And madness it seemed. For even before she raised her head out of the wash basin to see him standing in her parlor, she had known it was Tyler. Something alerted her. Not a sound, or even a smell, she had *felt* his presence. Deep inside, then prickling her skin, like that day at the schoolhouse. It confirmed her dreams—and her nightmares. Yes, she wanted him, but in a way she could neither define nor explain. And at what cost?

In his absence she had been able to convince herself that her feelings were blown out of proportion; that he wasn't the all-encompassing, integral part of her life he seemed to have become; that his body hadn't excited her; that his kisses hadn't been the mysterious harbingers of some intoxicating ritual; that she might die were she forced to go through life without experiencing it.

Now he was here, hovering over her, filling her bedchamber as he had filled her mind, threatening to solve the mystery, to make her whole—and all she could do was tremble.

She felt his fingers fumble with the ribbon on her wet chemise. She heard the wet satin squeak when he untied it. She inhaled a deep draft of his scent, his wonderful clean, masculine scent. In that instant, the image of Annie sprang to mind, Annie twirling her finger into Tyler's navel, Annie . . .

Without one smidgen of light, he deftly slipped the tiny buttons out of their loops, opening her camisole down the middle. Just as dexterously, he laid the two halves aside, pushing them off her breasts. His rough hands slid over her skin, cupped her bare breasts; his lips followed. With a low moan of satisfaction she couldn't have stilled had she known it was coming, she clasped his head and pressed it to her. This was what she had craved, yearned for—but now, strangely, receiving it only called forth deeper, more intense yearnings.

But as her emotions soared, the image of Tyler and Annie returned. She recalled the first time she ever saw the girl, dropping her kimono, exposing breasts twice the size of Madolyn's. She spoke out of desperation, without design or forethought. "Is this what you do with Annie?"

Tyler reacted as though she had slapped his face. Jerking his lips from her breast, he sat back, straddling her. His face was lost in shadow, but his wonderful presence loomed over her. Light from the parlor silhouetted his head and wide shoulders.

"Say that again."

"Is this what you do with Annie?"

"Damnation, Maddie! What a thing to ask."

"I'm sorry. The idea was . . . I mean, suddenly I remembered seeing her in your room."

"In my room?"

"In the doorway. That first morning. When you were so brusque."

"Brusque? With Annie?"

"With me."

"I was never brusque with you."

"Yes, you were. After Annie left."

"Maddie . . ." His voice caressed her like a warm spring breeze. "I've never . . . been with Annie."

"You were that morning."

"The first mornin' you were here? She brought my breakfast. And my ironin'. She does my ironin'. For pay. Money."

Money. Oh, my. Relief soared inside her. But she couldn't help pursuing the topic. "It looked like she spent the night."

"With me?"

"Sounded like it, too, by the way you shouted at me."

"I didn't shout at you." Suddenly, he dropped his arms, clasped her to his chest, and rolled them to the side. She felt his heart thrum against her. He spoke into her damp hair. "If I did, it was because I didn't want you to think I had slept with Annie."

"When you had?"

His arms tightened. "No, I hadn't. I've never slept with

Annie. I've never been on a bed with her. I've never . . ."
He rolled her back, slipped the wet camisole from her body
and cast it aside. Tenderly, he cupped her breasts.

"I saw them once," she said.

"What?"

"Her breasts."

"Annie's?"

"Yes."

Tyler groaned. "This isn't the sort of conversation we
should be havin' right now."

"The first day you brought me here. Lucky explained the
shortage of water. After my bath, I offered my water for
someone else . . . another woman."

"Lucky brought Annie up here? To your room?"

"It was before I knew . . . what went on here."

He groaned again.

"Annie marched right in and dropped her kimono to her
feet. There they were."

"They?"

"Her breasts."

"Maddie . . ."

"I'd never seen another woman . . . unclothed. They were
large."

"Maddie, don't."

"Much larger than mine. Does it . . . matter?"

"Matter?" His hands stilled on her breasts. For a long
time he didn't answer the question he had repeated. When
at length he spoke, his voice was low and husky. "I've never
seen Annie's breasts. Never touched them . . . never . . .
But they couldn't be as beautiful as yours."

Her heart stopped. As if to resurrect her, he began to
caress her breasts, showering her with sweet agonizing sensations. When he bent his head and took one in his mouth,
she held his head as though she feared he might let her go.

There was no chance of that, not through the ensuing
hour. While he stripped away her bloomers, then his own

clothing, he kept up a gentle prattle, reassuring her, soothing her. At least, she decided that was his purpose. She could have told him he was wasting his breath. Her head spun in dizzying circles, dizzying, sweet, sensual circles all filled with Tyler—his hands, his lips, his low husky voice.

Tyler can teach you, Goldie had said, but until this morning, Madolyn hadn't imagined what lessons were to be learned.

She was lost from the first, for time after time her body overrode her brain's objections. The first contact of his nude body with hers was so startling she almost jumped out of her own skin.

"No. No."

"There, there, Maddie. I won't hurt you. Get used to me." Clasping her hands in his, fingers entwined, he eased his body over hers. His furry, muscled legs entrapped hers. She seemed aware of each silky hair.

The effect was astounding. Much like when she dipped her head in the basin of cold water, the shock to her system was followed by pure, sweet acceptance.

For the longest time he didn't move, then when he did, it was to kiss her lips, a soft, tender kiss. She felt her breasts peak into his chest hair; she felt her heart throb against his ribs; she felt his heart pound in echo.

Then suddenly she knew no more. Her senses reeled with lovely, fiery, nonsensical things—the ragged sound of his breathing, the faint scent of his shaving soap, the salty taste of his skin, and the feel of him, the wonderful, vitalizing feel of his skin touching hers—his hands, his lips, his legs.

None of it threatened, which was a surprise, albeit one she couldn't investigate, since her ability to reason was curtailed by the intense passion he drew from her.

His large, skilled hands roamed everywhere, tracing gentle, fiery caresses over her body, across her body, inside her body. Before he was through, she knew his body better than she knew her own. She could recognize the feel of each finger, his index finger from his pinkie, and wherever each touched, it burned.

Every touch of his lips became the loving answer to a new, yet familiar quest. He kissed her lips, her face, her neck, her breasts; then lower, his tongue traced a wide and rugged trail across her abdomen.

Her breath caught, her hips lifted, and her brain soared out of control. By the time she felt him burrow his way, hot and rigid, into her begging core, she was in agony.

"It'll hurt a little, Maddie," he crooned into her ear. "Don't be frightened."

Frightened? How could she be frightened, when she had never wanted anything so badly in her life. Having never considered such a thing, she was nevertheless positive this and this alone could satisfy the fierce craving that consumed her. In search of an ancient elixir, she tightened her hold around his neck. "Don't stop, Tyler. Please."

It hurt a little. But the hurt was nothing compared to the stunning sense of joy that seared through her. He lifted her slowly heavenward, then thrust her into oblivion—again and again, until her passions exploded, completing her quest, leaving her breathless and trembling and more joyous than anyone could ever possibly have been, ever on the face of the earth.

He lay beside her, close beside her, cradling her in his all-encompassing embrace. His breath gusted heavy and humid into her hair. For endless moments they lay bound together in silence; indeed, she had trouble thinking, much less speaking. She had never felt such oneness.

When she found her voice, it rose in thanksgiving—for the joy, for the pure joy of what he had given her. "I didn't know anything could be so powerful, so personal. I'm glad you never did anything like this with Annie."

His damp arms tightened around her. "Even if I had, it wouldn't have been makin' love."

It took a moment for his words to penetrate the emotional barrier left over from their . . . Their . . . ? "Making love!"

"Whoa, Maddie. I didn't mean . . . uh, I mean, damnation! It's just an expression." Lifting himself on an elbow, he tried to brush a curl off her forehead, but his familiar presence had suddenly become ominous, threatening. She pushed his hand aside.

The spell had been broken. Shattered. By reality.

She bolted up, dropped her feet to the floor and reached for her dressing gown. *"Love* is the most horrible word in the English language."

Thirteen

Long after Tyler left the suite, Madolyn lay on her bed, draped in her dressing gown, pondering the disastrous turn her life had taken.

Every sinner paid the piper, Miss Abigail was fond of claiming. Of course the founder of the Boston Woman Suffrage Society hadn't been talking about one of their very own, a woman tapped to follow in her own giant footsteps.

That was one thing Madolyn would never do now—follow in Miss Abigail's footsteps. She wasn't worthy to clean the woman's privy. Not after the disgraceful way she had followed Goldie's advice and the disastrous consequences.

Making love! The term showered her with sweet waves of longing, chased by utter despair.

The morning had accomplished one thing: A question that had troubled her for far too long had been answered by that marvelous experiment in her bedchamber. A question that had haunted her every time she recalled her mother's nocturnal screams, or consoled a bruised and battered wife.

Why did women fall into the trap of marriage? Why, when the consequences were so dire? So deadly?

Why, indeed? Now she knew the answer to that question, and it was as she suspected that first night, when Tyler kissed her into oblivion.

The male species used the most devastating weapons of

all—tenderness and a sensuality that snared a woman the way a spider web trapped a fly.

"Come into my parlor," the nursery rhyme invited. And women came, by the droves, convincing themselves against overwhelming odds that this was one man who would remain true to his courtship lies. That hers was the man among men who would remain tender and loving after the vows were exchanged.

Hogwash! Madolyn had seen the results of too many such experiments. Oh, there were women who claimed to be happily married. But were they? Really? Behind the closed doors of their homes, of their bedchambers, were they truly free, as human beings were born to be free?

Perhaps a woman with no experience to the contrary could be excused for falling into the tender trap. But not one as world-wise as Madolyn.

Not one who had grown up to the sounds of reality being played out in her own home night after terrifying night.

When a knock came at her door this time, Madolyn called for identification, even though she was sure it would be Lucky.

Tyler wouldn't return. Not after the way she sent him off. Oh, how it had pained her to do so. She had been unable to control her tears. They had run in embarrassing streams down her cheeks when she told him to leave and to never, never touch her again.

"Damn, Maddie, I didn't go to upset you. You said you wanted it, too."

"I did."

"Well . . . wasn't it good? Didn't you enjoy it? Did I hurt you?"

"Not yet."

"Not yet? What the hell does that mean?"

"You know perfectly well, although I've never known a man who would admit it."

"You're not makin' sense, Maddie. You wanted it. I

tried . . . I thought you enjoyed it. A woman doesn't usually enjoy the first time she makes love, but I promise . . ."

"There you go again. Calling it . . ." Her voice broke, but she forged ahead, for she wasn't one to leave a person with no explanation. ". . . what it was."

"Maddie, I'm sorry. I didn't mean . . ."

"I know what you meant and what you didn't mean. I've known for a long time how men get their way with women. Of course, I never experienced it firsthand until today."

"I am not deceitful!"

"You're a man."

"And damned proud of it. I wouldn't be a . . . a . . . fragile, weepin' female if God made me that way."

He slammed the door so hard when he left, Madolyn feared he had called the girls, but no one came. Until now. The brilliant light of midday streamed through her parlor windows. The clock on her bedside table showed it to be noon. Lucky would be bringing luncheon.

And she must get herself up out of her bed of pity and eat. She had work to do. Plenty of work. For now one thing was abundantly clear. She must take the next train back to Boston, regardless of what Morley did or did not do. But she couldn't leave the women of this divided town in the lurch.

"It's me, Maddie. Goldie. Lucky was busy in the kitchen and asked me to bring your tray."

"Oh." Jumping from the bed, Madolyn secured her robe, although she feared it would still reveal her nudity. "Coming." She ran fingers through her damp, disheveled hair, then tucked strands behind her ears. But when she opened the door, it was to Goldie's knowing gaze.

Ducking her head, Madolyn stepped aside. She pretended to be interested in the food Lucky sent. "You can set it over there. I'm half starved to death."

Wordlessly Goldie deposited the luncheon tray on the tea table, but neither of them reached to remove the cup towel.

"May I sit down?" Without waiting for a reply, Goldie took one of the two chairs and studiously smoothed her brassy gold kimono over her knees. Her painted face was all innocence when she spoke. "We haven't had a chance to visit in such a long time, what with the hours you've been keepin'."

Madolyn sat across from Goldie without meeting the madam's eye.

"Go ahead and eat, honey, don't let me stop you. I've already had my dinner."

Madolyn removed the cup towel, revealing two pieces of crisply fried chicken, a mound of mashed potatoes covered with gravy, and turnip greens. Her stomach tied in knots at the thought of taking a single bite.

"Ummm. You said you were starvin'. Good thing Lucky added an extra chicken leg."

Madolyn spread her napkin on her lap, but the very touch of it brought a rush of tears. Images, in vivid color and poignant detail, assailed her. Annie ironed his shirts. For money. He hadn't slept with her . . . hadn't made love with her. *Love!*

Goldie, as was her nature, got straight to the point. "Where'd Tyler head off to in such a stew a while ago?"

Madolyn, taken off guard, glanced up. *Goldie knew. Tyler told her! How could he have?* "I wouldn't know."

"Oh, well . . ." Speaking, Goldie peered into the bed-chamber beyond Madolyn. She felt herself flush.

What had he told her? Dear God, what had he told her?

"I think maybe I owe you an apology, Maddie. A bit late, I dare say, but . . ."

"Apology?"

"I should have kept my big mouth shut." The madam shrugged, setting her mass of henna-tinted hair to flying. "I wouldn't have hurt you for the world, honey, but you asked my advice and I'm one for handin' it out. Can't keep my blabbermouth shut when it comes to men and women."

"I don't know what you're talking about, Goldie. You have nothing to apologize for. Absolutely nothing."

Goldie reached across the table, captured and squeezed Madolyn's hand. "Oh, but I do, honey. I didn't run into Tyler, and Lucky wasn't too busy to bring your lunch. Truth is, he looked me up and asked me to see about you."

"To see about me?" Indignation rose in billows. Indignation and embarrassment. As was often the case where Tyler was concerned, she didn't know which to give into first. Anger, she knew, would serve her better.

Withdrawing her hand, she stiffened her spine. "As you can see, I'm perfectly fine. I can't imagine what Mr. Grant might have told you, but don't believe a word of it."

"Honey, you don't have to put up such a strong front. Even if he hadn't told me, I could've seen for myself. Why, didn't I tell you weeks ago it was plain as the nose on your face?"

Madolyn covered her mouth with her napkin and wished she could bury her face in it. Or her head in the sand. Or disappear all together.

"Don't go thinkin' Tyler told things best kept between the two of you. He didn't. I told you he was a gentleman, and I still believe it."

"It's like I suspected all along, this country is hard up for gentlemen."

"I recognize the hurt, honey. That's what I'm here to apologize for. My advice, well it would've been all right for some women, but others . . . well, there are women who can't deny love."

"Deny love? Who said anything about love? If Tyler said—"

"Hold on, Maddie. He didn't. I'll swear on it. In fact, I'm sure he would react about like you're doin' if I said this to him. Unless I miss my guess, this little relationship is a double-rutted trail."

"This little relationship doesn't exist, Goldie."

The madam smiled, wanly. "You're both fightin' it, that's for sure."

Unable to resist, Madolyn let her curiosity get the best of her. "What did he say?"

"That I'd better come up and see about you. That you were as mad as an ol' wet hen."

"For once he was right about something."

"Want to talk about it?"

"No."

"That's fine; just fine. But if you decide you want to, I'm here to listen. I can keep my mouth shut, an' I'm through givin' advice. I should never have taken it on myself, not in my profession, to talk to a girl about love."

"Don't feel bad, Goldie. You didn't talk to me about love. You told me how to enjoy myself." She wiped her mouth and grinned across the table. "And I did." That said, tears brimmed again.

"Oh, dear, honey. Whatever have I done?"

"Nothing. It . . . it would have happened anyway. It was . . . It was like being addicted, wanting more, always more. Then I got more and what did he do?"

Goldie sat wide-eyed across the table. "What did he do? Oh, honey, I was so sure he was a gentleman."

"He called it *love* . . . making love."

Goldie's mouth dropped open. "Makin' love?"

Madolyn nodded.

"That's wrong?"

"No. It's true. That's what's wrong."

Goldie slumped back in her chair. "Let me see if I understand. You think you're in love with Tyler?"

Madolyn nodded, her lips pursed, her eyes brimming.

"And that he's in love with you?"

Again, she nodded, vigorously this time.

"And that's bad?"

"It's terrible."

"Terrible? I have a houseful of girls who would give their

eyeteeth for somethin' so terrible as bein' in love and havin' that love returned."

"But it can't go any further. For either of us."

"He agrees?"

"I don't know. He did, but I'm not sure now. He was so . . . so tender . . . and kind . . . and loving." The last word was lost, as Madolyn lost her battle with tears. She sobbed into her napkin.

Goldie rose to comfort her. "Now, now, honey. You just weren't expectin' it, that's all. It's a surprise, findin' someone like that to spend your life with."

"No." Her head jerked up. "Oh, Goldie, I can never marry."

Goldie pulled her chair closer, sat down, and took both of Madolyn's hands in hers. "I think it's time for you to talk about this, Maddie. Why can't you marry?"

"Because I know how men are, what they do to women after they marry them."

Goldie didn't respond for a time. When Madolyn didn't continue, she prompted. "How do you know all this?"

"I lived with it all my life. I heard my mother's screams; I saw her bruises. He broke her arm one time. Many times, so many times I couldn't count them, he bruised her face. Night after night I heard her screams. Sometimes I heard loud thumps, like she was being thrown against the wall. Chairs were always being broken mysteriously. For days at a time she wouldn't come out of her room. After Morley left home, it got worse. I blamed myself. Until I met Miss Abigail and she convinced me otherwise. She said men are basically evil. She said their primary mission in life is to get back at Eve for tricking them into leaving the Garden of Eden. So, that's why I will never marry, Goldie. That's why."

"A good reason," Goldie soothed. "But I can't see Tyler beatin' you or anyone. I've known him a long time and he's never shown a violent side."

"They hide it. That's what Miss Abigail said. I often wondered how they could trap women into marriage. Miss Abigail said they're wily, like foxes. They woo women with weapons of the heart—that's what she called them. I didn't know what she meant until . . . until I took your advice and . . . and engaged in courtship with Tyler."

"Now you know?"

"Yes." Madolyn inhaled deeply trying to rid herself of the sweet longing that suffused her, just thinking about being in Tyler's arms. "I suspected it that very first night when I . . . we . . . uh, kissed. I mean I began to suspect then, that the weapons of the heart Miss Abigail preached about were tenderness and gentleness and sweet fiery passion. Weapons of the devil, that's what they are!"

"Maddie, honey, it doesn't have to be that way."

Madolyn stared across her untouched plate, out the window. Her gaze was snared by the intricate pattern of the lace curtains. "You're suggesting I take a chance?"

"I couldn't give you that kind of advice, could I? But I can tell you what your life will be like if you deny love. You'll end up sleepin' in a lonely bed with a cold heart for company."

Madolyn couldn't meet her gaze. "I'm so frightened."

"I know."

"I have to leave here. On the next train, Goldie. But I can't leave the women. They're counting on me. Will you help?"

"Anything, just ask. But what about your inheritance? Don't you still need Morley's help?"

"I'll go out there again. One last time."

"What if he won't agree?"

"Maybe I can persuade him to give me passage back to Boston, and enough to live on until I can find work."

"I hate that it turned out this way. You're a strong woman, though. Even if I'm wrong about Tyler, which I can't see, but sayin' I am, I'm sure you could hold your own."

"I don't want a lifetime of fighting. I've already had that. But don't worry about me. One day I shall be grateful for the experience. It'll help me in my work. Now, I know first-hand about weapons of the heart."

"I don't think it's that cut and dried, Maddie."

"Maybe not. But I can't take that chance."

Tyler rode away from Buck, leaving his tophand in a state of confusion. What the hell? He was in a state of confusion, himself.

"You're gonna run off an' leave us in charge of the herd?" Raúl had questioned when Tyler rode into camp with word that he was headed north.

"You an' Sánchez are able of mind and body, Raúl. No reason the two of you can't drive this herd to the railroad trap, and when the train rolls in, load 'em up an' ship 'em out."

"Sure we can do it, Grant. That's not the point. You're the one needs to dicker with the buyer about prices."

"Reckon *el jefe's* been dickerin' with that little filly," Sánchez quipped.

"This may be about a filly, Sánchez, but not the one you think." He tugged the brim of his Stetson low, pulled the reins around, and headed north, shouting a last command in his wake. "I'm off to see a man about a horse. Take care of the herd, and stay out of the cantinas until the train pulls out. I'll meet you back at the dugout."

The idea had come to him after he stormed out of Maddie's room, his life in turmoil. That, alone, wasn't such a surprise. Truth known, he'd seen it coming. Even though he had vowed not to act out his fantasies, he knew this relationship was developing into something akin to just that—a relationship.

But damned if it wasn't her fault. All he'd intended was to knock on her door and see if she was still around. Hell, he'd come in too late the night before to disturb the house, or so he reasoned. To be honest with himself, he hadn't wanted Goldie and the girls to know the extent of his turmoil. It wouldn't have taken two words for Goldie to figure that he'd spent the last few weeks pining over Maddie Sinclair.

Pining over her. Agonizing over her. But he hadn't intended to end up in her bed. Not by a long shot. Not until he opened that door and saw her standing there in all her glory and nothing much else.

One sight of her bending over that wash basin in her chemise and bloomers, and what little sanity he had left, fled. All he could think about was touching her, kissing her, filling her body with his, like his mind had been filled with her ever since he rode off and left her standing on that back staircase.

And before. Ever since that first day, when he stood across the tracks watching her tap that impatient toe of hers, he had been haunted by one thing—taking Maddie Sinclair to bed.

Well, damn him, now he had done it. And what had it accomplished? Besides a momentary relief—what sweet relief!—he had managed to snarl up the whole affair.

Not that she hadn't asked for it. She had. She had been a willing participant in the lovemaking. And afterwards she acted like every other female out to snare a man.

I'm glad you haven't done anything like this with Annie.

Glad, was she? Didn't that tell the tale in a nutshell? If she didn't have designs—long-term designs—on him, why would it matter whether he had bedded Penny-Ante Annie or any other woman in or out of the House of Negotiable Love?

And damned if he hadn't played right into her hand, which as things turned out, had been a mistake of gigantic proportion.

Even if I had . . . it wouldn't have been like this . . . it wouldn't have been makin' love.

Making love? He had never seen two little words send a person into such a fit. Making love. Didn't she know it was just an expression? A figure of speech? What had she wanted him to call it? Hell, he couldn't talk to her like a feller'd talk to the girls downstairs. Maddie was a lady.

And therein lay the root of his dilemma. Buck or Horn, or both of them put together, was no place for a lady.

He had just proved that to the woman suffragette.

But it hadn't ended there. The dilemma escalated with her shrill observation that love was the most horrible word in the English language. The fact that he shared that view didn't make it any less troubling to hear the sentiment expressed by a lady of such tender and passionate sensibilities. What had caused her to take such a contemptuous view of a condition folks generally held to be wonderful, even necessary? That's where he was headed—to get some answers. Morley Sinclair had some explaining to do.

That Morley's sister owed explanations of her own became clear as a summer sunrise, when one after the other of Morley's sons challenged him. Each grinning boy wore stiff new boots and bright red calico shirts. Each one greeted him, not with a leveled shotgun, but with an eager question.

¿Donde está Tía Maddie?

All except little Jeff, who sounded like he might cry when he asked, *"¿Donde está mi tía?"*

Where indeed was his aunt? Did Maddie know how she had worked her way into the hearts of these children? Did she know what would happen when she left? Did she know—

What the hell business was it of his?

Tyler had barely stepped down from his horse, when Morley spied him. His irate former partner stomped up from the barn, barking orders. "Don't you understand plain English, Grant? You ain't welcome here. Git off my land."

Tyler watched in disbelief. How could a man of such surly temperament be Maddie's kin? Suddenly, beyond Morley, he spied Jed riding 'Pache Prancer out of the corral, and his morning's worth of discontent jelled into a single mass of anger.

And energy. Stepping forward, he swung hard enough to fell a giant oak. His fist landed on Morley's jaw, stunning the man; Morley stumbled backwards, lost his footing, and fell to the hard-packed earth. His head bounced once. He looked up at Tyler, blinking.

"What the hell was that for?"

"A lot of things." Tyler grabbed a handful of Morley's shirt and pulled him to his feet. Morley staggered a minute. Tyler could see his anger building.

"Maybe I'm just tired of bein' bullied by you."

Morley rubbed his jaw. "It's that damned filly. I knew it'd get your goat, me buyin' her like that. Why'd you think—"

"What happened in Boston, Morley? What happened to Maddie?"

"Maddie, is it?"

"What happened to her?"

"How the hell would I know? I've been gone from there for twenty years."

"Why did you leave? Why won't you have anythin' to do with her? She came all this way and you won't give her the time of day. Why?"

Morley eyed Tyler with fire in his eyes. "Never took you for the meddlin' kind. She put you up to this?"

"Nobody fights my battles, Morley. And I usually don't draw a hand in those of other folks. But this is different."

"Yeah, I can tell. You got skirt fever."

"We're not talkin' about me. We're talkin' about Maddie. What made her like she is?"

"How's that?"

"She's flat scared to death of anyone who wears pants."

Morley's mouth dropped open. His weathered face went slack. His gaze turned cold. "Leave it alone, Grant." His voice was low this time, no longer blustering, deadly serious. "Send her back to Boston. Or keep her here. But stay away from me. I told her an' I'm tellin' you, I want nothin' to do with that old man." Dusting his hat, he crammed it back on his head, and turned to walk away.

Tyler caught him by the shoulder, and for the second time in their long friendship, he knocked his partner—former partner—to the ground. Looking down on the stunned man, Tyler barely resisted kicking him. "I don't know what happened, likely I'll never know, but you're no better than the man you refuse to call father. You're her brother. Her only livin' relative. And damnit she needs your help."

He turned to walk away. Jed sat 'Pache Prancer, watching his boss struggle to rise.

"Help him up, Jed. He's not man enough to rise on his own."

Jed dismounted obediently, and a sudden and wild sensation gripped Tyler. Taking the reins from Jed's unsuspecting hands, he stepped up on the honey-colored filly and sank spurs. The thoroughbred sprung into fluid action.

"What the hell're you doin', Grant?" Morley bellowed.

"Takin' what's mine, Morley," he called over his shoulder. "Takin' what's mine."

Tired as she was, Madolyn could scarcely find the heart to sleep in her bed after Tyler left it. But she tackled that problem the way she tackled everything else—with gritty determination. No one would drive her from her bed. Least of all, a man.

Men! They were all alike—no damned good. She had

known that before arriving in this barbaric land. She hadn't needed Tyler to teach her that.

But he had taught her many things, and in her heart she knew they were far from disgraceful. The time she spent with him had been the most glorious time of her life, and would remain so to the end of her days. She would carry the memory of that morning on the long and lonely road ahead. However painful that memory was at the moment, it wouldn't remain so.

But for now she had enough to do to take her mind off her troubles, things that must be done before she returned to Boston. For that was her decision. Right or wrong, she had made it and would stick with it. She would return to Boston on the first train to leave this deplorable place—after she helped the women solidify their plans.

To that end Madolyn spent long hours instructing the women of both Buck and Horn in everything they needed to know to mount a successful demonstration.

She didn't see Tyler again. He didn't return to the house, unless it was to sneak in while she was away or asleep. No one mentioned him, especially not Goldie, who probably still felt bad about her part in the debacle.

When the train arrived, she wasn't ready. So many things remained to be done before she could leave. Afraid she might run into Tyler at the station, she didn't dare venture to the depot to see whether her order had arrived from Abilene.

He might be at the railroad trap loading his cattle. She might run into him like last time. Her heart pounded painfully, remembering the pleasure they had shared, imagining all the pleasures they would never share.

Night after night, returning from Horn, she lay awake reliving the hours she spent in his arms. If she had one regret it was that their lovemaking had occurred in the dark. She hadn't seen his body. Not that she would have been able to make herself look. She would have been far too self-conscious. But, oh, she wished for that additional memory. The touch of his skin, of his muscles, of his hair was real to her and would always be. She would even remember the slightly salty taste of his skin. She wished she had a vision to carry away, too. Other than the one of Tyler and Annie. Her relief that he hadn't slept with Annie was short-lived, for he probably would, now that she was leaving.

As soon as she was certain the train had departed, she forged ahead with her plans. Although she dreaded it almost as much as she feared seeing Tyler again, she had to try one last time to convince Morley to secure her inheritance. After all, that was the reason she had come to Buckhorn in the first place.

"Sure you can drive a rig like this, little lady?"

"Of course I can handle a team and wagon, Mr. Melrose." She pierced the hostler of Buck's only livery with an expression designed to intimidate, a lesson learned from Miss Abigail.

Determined to get a head start on her trip to the ranch, she had arisen early. Already beleaguered by tired muscles and a worried mind, she didn't intend to allow this chauvinistic little man to stand in her way.

"Where'll you be headin'?"

She started to retort that it was none of his business, but reconsidered, since he was already concerned about her ability to drive his wagon and team.

"Out to my brother's."

"Sure you know the way?"

"Certainly, Mr. Melrose. Now, if you please, the morning is wasting. I would like to complete my journey before the sweltering part of the day."

"How long you aim on bein' gone?"

"I shall return before sundown."

"That'll put you on the road in the heat of the day, sure enough, miss."

"Be that as it may, sir, those are my plans. And they are carefully laid. If you will excuse me, I shall be on my way."

The drive started out well enough, better than that, actually. It was a still morning, about eight o'clock by Papa's watch when she set out. The sun had barely climbed over the far ridge of mountains. The coolness of evening lingered on the earth; sunlight glistened from scant dew-laden grass, and highlighted the few night blossoms that had tarried too long, as if in enjoying their freedom, they had failed to see the approaching dawn. A sobering thought.

One she feared might have some relevance to her own plight. Had she tarried too long in this wild country, and would her leaving be too late?

The question lost its rhetorical nature when Jorge jumped into the roadway, his eyes dancing.

"*Hola, Tía.*" The boy plucked at his red calico shirt. "*Gracias.*" He kicked one booted foot in the air, then the other, repeating as the chorus in a dance. "*Gracias. Gracias.*"

"*De nada, Jorge.*" The delight in her nephew's eyes was worth every hour spent learning his language.

"*Muy bien,*" he complimented. "*Hablas español muy bien.*"

She probably didn't speak Spanish very well, she thought, but she had learned enough to communicate with her family. Again, as on her first visit, she was struck by how much Jorge favored his father. And by the desire to jump off the wagon seat and hug him. She didn't. On her return trip, she promised herself. Yes, she must gather courage enough to hug her nephews and nieces once before leaving them. Oh, my, yes. She must.

Before she could set off again, Jorge stopped her with, "*Tía?*" She watched him dig into a pocket.

"*Para ti.*" He held an open hand toward her.

For the longest time she could only stare at the small carved figure of a horse that rested in her nephew's dirty palm. When he moved closer she took it, squeezing his hand, while tears brimmed in her eyes. Once again her vocabulary failed her. "You made this?" she asked, exaggerating every syllable and accompanying the words with facial expressions.

He must have understood, for pride shone in his green eyes. *"Sí, tía. Para ti."*

"For me? Oh, my. My, oh, my. *Gracias, Jorge."* To show she felt more than simple gratitude, she pressed the perfectly carved little horse to her breast.

Her heart still palpitated out of control when she arrived at the next boy, who, like Jorge, wore a red calico shirt, fashioned from the piece goods Madolyn had intended for their mother to make into a dress. Oh, well, didn't it prove that Carlita was a good mother in spite of her submissive nature—and not being married to their father?

Perhaps most of all, Madolyn hated to leave without effecting a change in Morley's despicable situation. Thinking on it as she continued, she realized she could not run out on this one last responsibility: She must see Morley and Carlita married, for their children's sake.

Each boy in turn beamed with delight when Madolyn spoke to him in Spanish; and each wore a red calico shirt.

Even Little Jeff, who did not wait for Madolyn to find the courage to hug him, but jumped up on the wagon seat and hugged her. Filled with melancholy, she cradled him to her bosom.

"¿Donde está tío?" he wanted to know.

"Tía," Madolyn corrected. *"Estoy tía."*

"Sí." Little Jeff tapped her chest. *"Tía Maddie."*

"Sí."

"¿Pero, donde está tío? Tío Tyler."

Uncle Tyler? Madolyn's heart lurched. She hugged the child closer. Uncle Tyler, Aunt Maddie. Spoken together the words sounded like lyrics to a song, a sad and beautiful song—a requiem.

By the time she struggled with the brake, climbed down, and tethered the team at the hitching rail, her commotion— or Little Jeff's chattering—had called Morley from the barn.

She stood her ground, watching him stride toward her. She felt none of the eagerness to rush to him that had fairly smothered her on her first trip out; none of the eagerness to hug him, that she felt for the children.

His gaze riveted on the back of the wagon. "What're you bringin' now, Maddie?"

"Not as much as before."

"Good thing, that damned table takes up all the room."

"Just books and things this time. The rest is still in town." Stepping to the side, she withdrew a book from the top box. "Little Jeff, run inside and tell your mother I'll be in directly."

Morley eyed the book, which she kept in her hands. "Rest of what's in town?"

"Beds and things."

"Beds! Not for me."

"For your family."

He frowned. "We don't have room for beds, Maddie."

"You will have." He must be getting used to her, she decided. Although he still bellowed, he was less belligerent by half than when she had brought the table. Drawing a steadying breath, she handed him the book.

"Look over these mail-order houses, Morley. You and Carlita sit down together and pick out the one you want. Goldie will store the beds and things until the house comes in."

"HOUSE? House! Damn you for a meddlin'—"

"I am not meddling, Morley. I'm concerned about my family. In fact, I'm on my way back to Boston."

"Boston?" He squinted at her, taken aback. Or did she imagine it?

"Yes. As soon as I finish my business in town."

"I've heard about that business. There's only one way for

you to reunite Buckhorn, and that'll never happen, not in a million years."

"You mean you and Tyler would have to make up?"

"Don't hold your breath."

She ignored his warning. "It's a wonderful idea, Morley. I know exactly how it can be accomplished."

"I'm sure you do."

"When Parson Arndt comes out to marry you and Carlita, Tyler can stand up for you. That'll cement your relationship—"

Morley's belligerence returned in full force: His face turned purple; his eyes narrowed to two dark green pools; and when he spoke he bellowed loud enough to call the cows from the back forty, an expression Lucky was fond of using when Goldie's girls hollered to one another down the staircase.

But Goldie's girls were rarely angry. Morley was furious. "Madolyn Sinclair, you listen to me. There will be no weddin'. If Parson Arndt shows his face around here, he'll get his butt filled with buckshot."

"Morley! It's for these precious—"

"Who asked you to judge me an' mine?"

She straightened her bonnet and stiffened her spine. The sun had climbed to high noon, and she wished for her parasol, but not enough to quit the fight when she smelled progress.

"Claiming the children is definitely an improvement, Morley. After you marry their mother—"

"I am not marryin' their mother. Do you hear me? I'm not the marryin' kind."

"You should have thought about that before . . . before . . ."

Carlita came out the back door. Unlike on Madolyn's previous visits, Carlita approached her with a warm, if quiet, welcome. *"Beinvenida,* Maddie. Dinner is on the table. You will eat, *sí?"*

"Carlita," Morley hissed, "get on back to the house. Maddie's leavin'."

"I'm in no rush, Morley. Really. Carlita and I must discuss wedding plans before I leave for Boston."

"Damnation, woman! You don't have the sense God gave a goat! There will be no weddin'."

Madolyn linked arms with Carlita. "As soon as the date is set, Morley, you can find Tyler and invite him to stand up for you."

Morley grabbed her arm, jerking her around. His eyes were afire. "Maybe you don't hear very good. Else you just don't listen. There will be no weddin'. And definitely, no makin' up with that sonofabitch Grant." He glared at her. "I know what you're up to, but it won't work. You're hell bent on joinin' those towns up again. An' you can't win unless Grant and I . . ."

Morley's eyes bore into hers, but Madolyn could tell his thoughts had changed horses in midstream. Of a sudden, he pulled her toward the wagon, where he grabbed her around the waist and tossed her to the hard wagon seat. Her bustle collapsed.

"Keep my dinner hot," he barked at Carlita. Then without so much as a by-your-leave, he climbed up beside Madolyn and whipped up the team.

Madolyn held on for dear life. Fury swept through her. "I can drive myself back to town, Morley Sinclair. I managed to find my way out here."

"Once and for all, Maddie, I'm gonna git you outta my hair. If you're so het up to see Tyler Grant, I'll take you."

Fourteen

Strive as she did, Madolyn couldn't summon an ounce of indignation at Morley. Indeed, during the whole bouncing, bumping ride, her emotions vacillated between anxiety over how she would face Tyler—would she be able to look him in the eye?—and euphoria at having one last chance to see him.

An hour or so later Morley drew rein in the middle of nowhere. At first Madolyn was scarcely able to see the landscape around her, so frightened was she of her own wicked self. Then, when she could see, she decided he must be resting the team. From the way he had driven them, they surely needed it.

"Where are we?" she asked, only to have Morley interrupt her with a bellow aimed at the sheer side of a rocky cliff.

"Tyler Grant, get your damned ol' carcass out here!"

Before Madolyn recognized the slab of weathered wood for a door, it opened, and Tyler stepped out of the side of the hill. Her breath caught at sight of him. He filled the space, wide-open though it was. He was bare to the waist; her first coherent thought was of her wish to see him nude. Next she recalled the morning she had, the morning Penny-Ante twirled her finger in his navel. Sitting primly, parasol hoisted against the blazing sun, Madolyn wondered what it would feel like. Her finger twitched and she gripped the parasol tighter. And her wits.

It was the way he looked at her, she reasoned, that caused such a scandalous, unwelcome notion to take control of her sanity. He just stood there, slouch-like, even though there wasn't anything in sight for him to lean against. In truth, he could have been part of the hill itself. But his attention was on her, and his expression was one she knew well. He wasn't quite grinning, but his eyes danced over her, mesmerizing her, tantalizing her, setting her senses to humming like locusts on a still summer night. Morley bellowed again, bringing her back to reality.

"I've come to take you up on that trade you offered."

"What trade?" Tyler asked, but his eyes never left Madolyn.

"Day you drove Maddie out to the house."

Tyler blanched. His eyes darted to Morley. Madolyn looked around in time to see the set to Morley's jaw. He looked like the cat who had just eaten the proverbial canary. Although from the gloating way he grinned, she figured it must have been more like a buzzard.

"What trade?" Even as she echoed Tyler's question, an uneasiness crept into her euphoria. Before Morley could answer, Tyler spoke again.

"You know the conditions, Morley." His words sounded strained. Turning, Madolyn saw that his face had lost its color.

"A filly for a filly," Morley hissed. "Where's my damned horse?"

Her uneasiness turned to disbelief. She glared at her brother, furious, embarrassed. Sick, her only wish was to disappear, to crawl under one of the numerous stones and hide.

Since that was out of the question, she jumped into the fray. "How dare you, Morley Sinclair? You're a beast!" Her brain, however, replayed Morley's opening statement—that he was taking up *Tyler's* offer.

Tyler had offered to trade her for the horse? *Her for a*

horse? She turned furious eyes on him. As if she were hi
to trade! "How dare you?"

He had moved closer now, and stood within a couple c
feet of her. "Whoa, now, Maddie, it wasn't like that."

"What do you mean, it wasn't like that? What differenc
does it make what it was like? A trade's a trade. A woma
for a horse? Men! Miss Abigail is right, you're no damne
good. None of you! None of you—"

Tyler interrupted her, speaking in a low, controlled voic
"Have you fulfilled the rest of the bargain?"

"A filly for a filly," Morley repeated to Madolyn's ever
lasting chagrin.

"Not quite. The offer hinged on you securin' Maddie'
inheritance."

Madolyn's eyebrows lifted.

"Not on your life, Grant," Morley bellowed. "I said—

"I know what you said, Morley. And I know what I saic
My offer was to see Maddie off to Boston, after you gav
me 'Pache Prancer and secured her inheritance."

Madolyn watched Morley grip the reins in tight-glove
fists. His jaws were clinched. He frightened her. She wante
to climb off the wagon seat, to run from him. But she dare
not.

"Where's 'Pache Prancer?" Morley was demanding.

Tyler laughed. That easy, deep-throated laugh Madolyr
had so envied him. "You think I'd keep her around for yo
to find? I'm not stupid. I knew you'd come after her soone
or later. You're as easy to read as *McGuffy's Primer.*"

"That so? That damned so?" Twisting the reins aroun
the brake handle, Morley lumbered down from the wago
seat. "Get on down from there, Maddie. Stretch your legs.'

She did need to do that. Her knees were stiff from th
hour's ride over rutted terrain, and her bottom ached from
bouncing on the hard wagon seat in her collapsible bustle
An equally harrowing ride awaited her when they starte
back to town—or wherever her brother took her next.

"Go ahead, Morley," Tyler was saying. "Look around. See what you find." He winked at Madolyn and she went weak.

"You, too, Maddie. Climb on down." He reached for her parasol. Her hand was so limp, he took it easily, closed it, and tossed it to the wagon bed. When he reached to help her down, her arms trembled.

"Welcome to my humble abode." His voice flowed over her. Her resolve to remain aloof weakened. When had she ever been able to keep her wits around this man? He filled her senses. And this would surely be the last time she ever saw him on this earth. Curiosity nudged the edges of her anxiety. She watched Morley disappear around the edge of the cliff.

Tyler pulled on her arm. Although it was no more than a tug, it triggered the glow inside her. She stepped from the wagon seat, lost her footing, and tumbled into him.

Into his bare chest. Her body quivered as if she had landed in a prickly pear patch. She glanced up inadvertently, and in that instant, she knew he had done it on purpose. Stiffly she tried to pull back, but he had her by both arms now.

"Maddie."

That was all he said, one word, *Maddie,* but it left her breathless. His eyes held hers until she could resist no longer and cast her gaze over his face, taking in every feature. The eyebrows she had stroked, the eyes she had kissed, the dark hair that was always so neatly trimmed yet never seemed to stay in place, the lips . . . Her knees went weak. Why didn't he kiss her? Didn't he realize this might be the last chance they ever had? *Ever?*

"Sorry about my attire—or lack of it. I was just fixin' to . . ." His words drifted off; his gaze danced over her. Her throat constricted. She pursed her lips. Did he know how she felt? Could he tell what the sight of him had done to her?

"Want to look around?" His voice was husky, dangerously low, underscored by an ever-so-slight tremor.

She glanced toward the edge of the cliff. "Where's Morley?"

"Lookin' for that damned horse."

"Will he find her?" She tried to move aside, but couldn't. She felt as though her feet were rooted in the rocky soil.

"Not likely. Come on. Let me show you my house."

Curiosity claimed a bit more of her discomposure. She squinted toward the cliff, where the only thing that looked like it belonged on a house was the door. "Is that it?"

"It's a dugout. Sort of."

She stared at the heavy wooden door—more like the corral gates she had seen in Buck, large, solid, with steel hinges and a leather thong for pulling it open. It fitted into an opening that had obviously been chiseled just to accommodate it.

"God, Maddie!" He released her suddenly. "I wasn't expectin' company. I'll be right back."

She watched him cross the short distance. Reaching the cliff, he pulled the latch and disappeared behind the heavy wooden door, leaving it ajar. Curiosity nudged again.

What harm could it do to look? One look. One more image to carry back to Boston inside her locked heart. Without further consideration, she followed him to the door, where she stood outside the opening, staring inside.

She wasn't sure what she had expected. Everything had come upon her so suddenly she hadn't had time to speculate. But looking into the interior of the dugout, she knew she would never have imagined, not in a million years, the scene that stood before her.

It was filled with Tyler, the essence of him. She inhaled deep drafts of his own personal scent—a mixture of soap and baywood and man. She would have known he lived here if she didn't have sight.

The furnishings were a further surprise: A pot-bellied

stove with flue extending through the limestone roof; pine table, simple but serviceable, and matching chair; kerosene lantern, and books—books stacked everyplace, enough books to fill all the shelves in the library in her home in Boston, or so it seemed.

But it wasn't the books that captured her attention, it was the bed—an iron bedstead, fitted with a mattress that looked substantial, topped by a Mexican serape.

Everything was neat as a pin; she would have expected no less, neat and clean and proper. But her thoughts were not proper, not by a long shot, as he would say.

Midway down the length of the room, Tyler stood with his bare back to her. Without warning, he turned and caught her watching him struggle into a shirt.

"Come in, if you want . . ." He looked disconcerted. For what reason she couldn't guess. It was she who should be disconcerted. She, who was.

Returning his attention to his shirt, he finished buttoning it, and tucked it into his waistband as best he could without unbuttoning his fly. The thought helped Madolyn move her gaze from him to his house.

"It's nice." Her voice wavered somewhere near the top of the scale.

"Nice isn't the word I'd use," he said, "but then I didn't grow up in confined quarters."

Suddenly she was filled with questions: Where had he grown up? In town? In the country? What kind of house had he lived in? Who were his friends? What games had he played as a child? What food had he liked? What girls—

"Caught me ironin'."

She glanced back at him, astonished. "Ironing?"

Moving aside, he picked up a smooth flat rock to which he had attached a wire handle. Curiosity nudged her into the room. He handed the iron to her.

"You made this?"

He nodded. "It's flint. Feel it . . . smooth as any ol' iron you ever saw."

She weighed it in her hand. "It's a lot heavier than one made of iron. How does it work?"

Taking the iron back, he placed it on the flat surface of the pot-bellied stove. "Set it right here and before you know it, you've got an iron hot enough to smooth out the most stubborn wrinkle."

She laughed. "I've never known a man who cared so much for . . ." She looked up. His intense scrutiny stopped her words. "I mean . . ."

His gaze held hers, refused to release hers. "What, Maddie?"

Her heart pounded. Suddenly she knew if she didn't get out of this dugout, she would end up in his arms. *In his arms.*

Where she desperately wished to be.

Pivoting, she exited through the improbable door and breathed in a lungful of dusty summer heat. Casting about, she searched for Morley. Where had he gone?

Tyler caught her by the arm. "Can't we talk?"

Talk? "No."

"I've been thinkin' a lot, Maddie. About us. We can work things out."

Work things out? That confirmed her worst suspicions—he felt the same miserable way she did. "No." She shook her head vigorously, as if to convince herself. "Never."

"Never's a long time; I don't think you know how long."

She recalled Goldie's claim, that to deny love left one with a cold and lonely life.

"Never means forever," he said in a low, quiet, desperate voice.

"I know what it means." Frustration turned to anger. "You do, too. We pledged the same thing. That's the reason, the only reason, it was safe for us . . . safe for us to—"

"Safe?" He hissed the word. Tightening his grip, he drew her around to face him. "Pledges can be broken."

She refused to meet his eyes. "Spoken like a true man."

"I am a true man, Maddie. A true man who's in love with you."

"Love?"

"It isn't the most horrible word in the language; it doesn't even have to be frightenin'. Let me show you, prove to you—"

"No." Panic made her breath come short. "I'm going back to Boston. On the next train." She felt him flinch. When he responded, his voice was barely audible.

"Morley came through?"

"No, but I'm going anyway."

"Why?"

One word. One simple word, yet she felt as if the mountain had caved in on top of her. In one short, simple word he asked the impossible of her—the truth. Rather than lie, she refused to answer.

"Why, Maddie?" he persisted. "Say it. You're runnin' away from somethin'. And you can't do that. I'm here to tell you, you can't run away."

At that moment Morley stormed back around the corner of the cliff. He stopped beside the wagon. "What'd you do, Grant? Take that little filly across into Old Mexico?"

"I'm not thickheaded," Tyler retorted. " 'Pache Prancer's safe an' sound."

"And she's mine. Where the hell is she?"

"In due time, Morley. See what you can do about gettin' Maddie that inheritance, then we'll talk."

"Threaten all you want, Grant. You can't win. Haven't you learned that much about me?" Morley climbed up on the wagon seat, ranting all the way. "Should've learned that by now."

Suddenly Madolyn grasped the situation. Morley was

leaving. "Wait." She tore free of Tyler's hold and ran for the wagon.

But Morley had already released the brake and whipped up the team. Turning the wagon in a wide arc, he shouted over his shoulder. "I told you to ship her back to Boston, Grant. You're the one chose not to, so you deal with her meddlin' for awhile. Maybe then you'll see the light about that thoroughbred."

Madolyn couldn't believe what was happening. Desperation choked in her throat. Desperation, which she didn't have time to analyze. Lifting her skirts, she ran faster, but succeeded only in catching her hem on a rock. She heard a rip, but kept going.

Finally, Tyler's firm grip brought her to a halt. Together, they watched Morley and the rented wagon disappear in a plume of dust. "He'll come back," she said, half to herself.

"Don't count on it."

"But why?"

"Why? Hell, Maddie, he's a mean, ornery sonofabitch, that's why."

"You mean he brought me out here to . . . to leave me?" She felt her voice tremble.

Tyler caught her shoulder. Before she could object, he pulled her to his chest, where he cradled her head, crushing the brim of her proper black hat.

"Why else would he have brought you all this way?"

She sighed against his freshly ironed shirt. Without starch, it was soft. She liked it that way. He ironed it himself. She had never known a man to iron before. She was glad Annie hadn't ironed it. She felt possessive of him, and that doubled her distress. But at the moment, here in his arms, she felt possessed by him, too, and heaven help her if she didn't feel safe and secure.

"I don't know." She tried to summon the gumption to tear herself away from him. "He tossed me on the wagon seat and said if I was so het up, those were his words, to see you, he would take me. He didn't say he intended to leave me."

"So het up to see me?"

She heard surprise in his voice. He drew her back and looked into her face, and she saw it—surprise, pleasure, triumph. He laughed.

"This is a mighty interestin' development, Maddie," he drawled. "Mind fillin' in the blank spots?"

She took a deep breath, hoping to still the trembling in her chest. "I rented the rig and drove out to Morley's to deliver some of the things I ordered for Carlita and the children, mostly books. I stored the beds at Goldie's, since they don't have room for them, yet."

"Beds?"

"I took the plans for mail-order houses, though, so he and Carlita can choose which one they want."

"Mail-order houses?"

"You're the one who told me about the scarcity of lumber out here. And they have to have a place to live."

"I don't suppose it occurred to you that they think they have a place to live?"

"That hut? It isn't big enough for a family of eight and you know it."

"No, I don't know it. Neither do you. What's big enough for them, doesn't have to be big enough for us."

His choice of words stunned her, but he didn't appear to notice. "So ol' Morley got tired of your meddlin' and brought you over here?"

"Not at that point. Not until after I mentioned the parson coming out and you standing up and . . ."

"Whoa, Maddie." He placed an index finger on her lips, silencing her. For a long time he just stared at her, as if his mind were miles away. Finally he said, "You know, I've never cared much for meddlin' women. Truth is, I never would have given you two cents for one . . ." His face dipped toward hers; he removed his finger; his lips brushed hers.

She shuddered. His eyes held her so mesmerized that she could tell he felt it, too.

". . . until now," he finished, closing his lips over hers.

It was the most glorious kiss she had ever received. Possibly because she had thought she would never kiss him again, or maybe because this would in truth be their last time together, or possibly because the promise inherent in his wet, hot, stroking lips erased everything from her mind except the sensual pleasure of being with him. She felt like she was soaring among the clouds, pink, fluffy clouds that were tinged around the edges with gold from the setting sun and the gold was racing through her system.

Relief became passion. She returned his kisses with an abandon she had rarely felt. The sweetness of it brought tears to her eyes; the passion it drew from her, drugged her with heady expectations.

When he lifted her in his arms and carried her to the dugout, she clasped him tightly around the neck and tried to hold her fears at bay, bidding herself enjoy it, all of it, one more time. And when he kicked the door shut behind them, releasing all but her lips, she began to glow from the inside out with that special fire only he could light inside her. Her mind was filled with kissing him.

Kissing and cuddling. And oh, so much more. When he began to disrobe her, she held her breath in eager anticipation. If her body could speak, it would be crying, pleading, beseeching him to hurry.

He tossed aside the serape covering the bed, mumbling something about it being too scratchy. She sank into the mattress, which surely was filled with the finest goose feathers. He stretched himself beside her. Close. Touching. Skin to skin. His lips took her breasts and a hand slid between her thighs, into the begging, weeping core of her, and she knew that she would not have to go through life without being loved.

She might not have a life like Frances Arndt or Camilla Crane with husbands to share the day-to-day triumphs and tragedies. But she had been loved.

She might not have a child, like Hattie Jasper, but she—

A child! Oh, dear God, no! She sprang up, fighting his arms, pushing him aside.

"Maddie?"

"I can't." She scooted off the bed. "We can't."

He grabbed her arm, bringing her up short. She sat on the side of the bed. Terror raced through her. He laid his face between her shoulder blades. It felt so good against her bare skin. So good. So right. *So wrong.*

"Yes, we can, love."

The word seared through her. She felt as though he had touched her heart with that flintstone iron of his. "No."

"Why?" His demand was gruff. "Tell me why."

"Because I might . . . I might . . . What if I . . . I can't have . . . your baby."

"Baby?"

She could tell by his voice he had never considered such a thing. Gradually his grip tightened. When he failed at turning her around, he climbed off the bed and knelt before her, cradling his head against her stomach.

"A baby. I never thought . . ." Shifting his face without losing contact with her belly, he looked between her heaving breasts to her face. "Are you carryin' our baby, Maddie?"

She shook her head. He stared at her for ever so long, solemn, serious, as though he had lost something of great value.

After a while, he said, "Oh," and twisted his face to kiss her belly. He pressed his face into it, and kissed her again and again.

The sensualness of it, the intimacy . . . the sincerity . . . took her breath away. Despite her vow to remain detached, she clasped his head with both hands and held it against her. Oh, the beauty of it, of this moment suspended in time, committed to memory, locked inside her heart . . .

But when his movements became not merely sensual, but passionate, she pushed him away. Lacking the strength to stand, she buried her face in her hands.

Still kneeling, he pried them away. "I want you to have my baby, Maddie."

His voice was earnest, so earnest her tears spilled over at the sound of it. Have his baby? Oh, to have his baby!

"No." She shook her head vigorously, as if by her action, she could convince herself as well as him.

"Why not?"

"We . . . we would have to get married."

Against her struggles to prevent it, he pulled her face to his bare chest. She felt the soft hairs, tasted the salt of her own tears, heard his thrashing heart.

"Would that be so bad?"

"Yes!" She struggled to escape. Gaining her freedom, she scooted off the bed on the opposite side and looked around for her clothing. She felt his eyes on her while she dressed, but she wasn't embarrassed, only sad. Infinitely sad.

And frightened. Of herself now. Of her waning ability to resist him. "Take me back to town. Please."

She heard him stomp into his boots, and when she turned he was fully dressed. "Have you ever ridden a horse?" His voice was normal, no longer thick with passion. Thank goodness.

"A horse?" she asked. "No, but—"

"That's all I've got. I'll take you back to town, but it'll have to be astride a horse."

"I can do it." And she could. She could ride a horse to Buck; she could ride a horse to Boston. She could do anything it took to get out of this dugout and out of this country.

The door banged suddenly as someone tried to open it from the outside. The inside bar held fast.

"Morley?" she sighed.

"*Jefe!*" came a call from outside. "Open up. We've got trouble."

Removing the bar, Tyler greeted the vaquero with, "*¿Qué pasa, Sánchez?*"

Madolyn slunk into the shadows, embarrassed at being caught inside Tyler's dugout.

"The Rurales," came Sánchez's reply, "they're plannin' a raid on Las Colinas."

"Damnation!" Tyler's eyes sought and found her back in the shadows. "I've gotta ride, Maddie."

"Ride? Where?"

"Mexico. Las Colinas."

Her heart thudded. Was he leaving her here alone? No. Tyler wouldn't do that. He would send her back to Buck on a horse by herself. "You'll have to show me the way," she said.

"Hell, Maddie, you've never even ridden a horse. You can't ride twenty miles alone, over terrain that all looks the same. You'd get lost before suppertime."

She stiffened her spine. "Don't worry, I'll make it."

"You could lose control of your horse. You could fall off. Hell, the horse could step in a varmint hole. No. There's no way I'll let you ride twenty miles by yourself."

"But . . ." Madolyn stared around at the dugout. "How long will you be gone?"

"Won't know till I get down there an' see what the difficulty is."

"I'll stay here. You have books, food. I can bar the door and . . ." She strove to contain the panic that rose rapidly inside her, cresting in her chest in a stifling tidal wave of fear. She couldn't let him see it, her fear. She couldn't send him off on a dangerous journey with her to worry about. "I'll be fine, just fine, right—"

"I can't let you do it, Maddie. This could be a trap. The Rurales could be trying to draw me away from here, so they can raid the place, reclaim my cattle."

"I thought you shipped all—I mean . . ." The only thing she knew with any certainty about his activities in Buck was what happened inside her suite, in her bed . . .

In her heart.

"They don't know that," he was saying.

"Don't worry." She was encouraged, knowing she had been saved from herself by this unexpected turn of events. Knowing, too, that she sorely regretted it. "I'll bar the door."

"That wouldn't stop 'em. I can't leave you here alone; and you can't ride back to town alone. Damn Morley Sinclair's hide!"

"Go ahead, do what you have to. I'll be fine."

"Damn, Maddie, Indians even come this way time to time."

"I'll be fine," she repeated.

"No. There's only one solution. You'll have to ride with me."

Fifteen

"Damnation, Maddie, with all those trunks, valises, band-boxes and hatboxes, you oughta have some kind of clothes that wouldn't spook a horse."

"I didn't expect to find myself riding a horse today," she retorted, struggling to conceal her mounting terror.

"You haven't, yet." Tyler's drawl wavered somewhere between amusement and aggravation.

She had tried three times to mount the skittish mahogany-colored horse, but it sidestepped and snorted more with each attempt. "Especially not one as temperamental as this."

"Temperamental? Now that's the pot callin' the kettle black."

"I am not temperamental . . . Ahhh! What are you doing—ahhh?"

While she was distracted, Tyler caught her around the waist and heaved her into the saddle, or tried to. But her bustle had no more than collapsed, when the horse reared on its hind legs and nickered loudly. She grabbed for the saddlehorn.

"Don't drop the reins!" Tyler shouted. But too late. In her panic, the reins slipped from her hands.

"Whoa, there, boy, calm down." His tone was anything but calm. "Grab him with your knees, Maddie."

She tried to obey, but just when she thought she would slip backwards out of the saddle, the ornery critter changed directions, bringing its front legs down with a wallop that slung her face-first across its neck; her bustle sprang up in back. Terrified, she grabbed two fistfuls of mane and held on, until Tyler finally managed to drag her off the animal's back and out of range of its kicking hooves.

"Stand over there out of the way," he ordered, "while I figure out what to do."

She dusted off her skirts and readjusted her bonnet with trembling arms, wishing all the while for her parasol. If she'd had her trusty parasol, she could have shown that animal a thing or two. A few good whacks of that parasol had subdued ornery critters of the two-legged variety; no reason it wouldn't work on four-legged ones. But her parasol had gone the way of the rented wagon, and she was caught in the worst predicament of all her thirty years.

She was going to Mexico. A foreign country. She was going to Mexico—with Tyler Grant! Lord in heaven she needed strength. Tons of strength.

Tyler headed for the dugout. "Come on, Maddie."

She shook herself to regain some of her wits and held her ground. Tapping one foot absently against a rock, she watched him turn and beckon to her from the doorway.

"I'm fine out here."

He beckoned from the door. "Come on. We have to find you some clothes that won't spook the horses. Time's wastin'." He disappeared into the side of the hill, leaving her to wonder what in the world he meant by such clothing. Before she could decide exactly what to do, he stuck his head out the door.

"Get a move on, Maddie. Those Rurales won't wait for you to make up your mind about comin' back into this dugout with me."

Casting about, she saw Raúl, who appeared to mind his own business over by the water trough. He could hear, of course, and she had heard him speak enough English—he probably understood. Her face flamed—she felt it, every heated inch of embarrassment that raced up her neck and flushed her cheeks. Sánchez had already set out for Mexico, or he would be enjoying her discomfiture, too. Just what Tyler Grant liked, an audience to witness their battles.

"What kind of clothes?"

He dangled a baggy pair of brown duck britches. "Duckins. Mine," he added with a grin.

She glanced down at her skirts, dirty by now, and tattered. A hunk had been ripped off the hem when she caught it on that rock. No, she would never make it on such a trip in skirts.

By the time she reached the dugout, Tyler was busy filling flour sacks with foodstuffs. Without meeting his gaze, she ventured inside.

He closed the door, then handed her the britches and a clean, ironed blue shirt. She turned it over examining it from all sides, lost for a moment in thought.

"Annie's never touched that shirt, if that's what's botherin' you," he observed dryly.

Madolyn glanced up, chagrined that he could read her thoughts with such ease. "If you're in such a hurry to be on our way, kindly leave me alone to dress."

His eyes narrowed. Dropping the flour sack, he advanced toward her, grasped her by the shoulders, drew her to his chest, and lowered his lips. He kissed her hard on the mouth. Hard and fierce. A kiss that not only spoke to her of passion but screamed it, demanding the same in return.

Then as quickly as he had taken her, he turned her loose. "There, feelin' better?"

"What?"

"That's what you were hankerin' for wasn't it?"

"Certainly not."

He reached for her again. This time his kiss was softer, gentler, but every bit as passionate. When he released her again, it was with his lips, only. His thumbs drew spirals on her upper arms. "Send that high horse of yours back to town, Maddie. We don't need it on this trip."

With that, he began to undress her. She tried to step away but he pulled her back. "Shh. Quiet down. Let's get this over with."

She knew he could feel her arms quiver. "I can dress myself."

"Sure you can." His eyes twinkled mischievously. "But I like to do it." When her fitted basque was unbuttoned, he shoved it off her shoulders and tossed it to the bed. Then he unbuttoned her skirt.

"Step out," he ordered. She complied, wary, berating herself for not summoning the will to oppose him. Next, he untied her petticoats. The bustle confounded him, to her delight. He flipped it back and forth a few times. "Hell, the damn thing folds up like an accordion."

"It's collapsible."

He grinned, springing it to and fro a couple more times. "Wonder why I didn't notice that before—" His eyes found and held hers in a moment of intense mutual desire.

He winked. "Reckon I was too het up for what lay ahead." He tossed the bustle to the bed and turned to her, his eyes smoldering.

She stood before him now in only corset and pantaloons, but when he reached for her corset laces, she stopped him.

"I'll finish, while you get our food together."

Dipping his face, he kissed her chest, just where her breasts started to mound. "I'd much rather do this."

In spite of herself, she laughed. Lightly, to be sure. But she laughed. His eyes held hers. His lips brushed hers. Then, of a sudden, he swatted her on her bloomer-clad bottom.

"Save that laugh, Maddie. It sounds so good, I'm goin' to have to hear it again."

Not likely, she thought. But she kept her silence, and while he finished filling several flour sacks with canned foods and jerked meat, she slipped the britches and shirt over her pantaloons and corset.

"Oh, no," she sighed. "These will never do." She held the sides of the pants wide to either side.

Laughing, he unsheathed his Bowie knife, sliced a length of hemp rope from a coil that hung on a peg hammered into the rock wall, and threaded it through the belt loops. But when he attempted to tie it, his hands stopped on her waist.

He eyed her with that exasperated expression he often got when she pushed his patience to the limit. "Take off that damned corset."

"Not on your life!"

"I don't mean for the reason you're thinkin'. Not that I'm not thinkin' it," he drawled, "but you wouldn't last one day ridin' a horse through the rugged country we'll be travelin' trussed up like a turkey gobbler at Thanksgivin' dinner."

"I've worn a corset all my grown life."

His tone softened. "In all your life, grown or otherwise, Maddie, you've not experienced the hardship you're about to face. Don't make things harder on yourself. Take it off."

Even as he spoke, he began to unbutton the blue shirt. He stripped it off and she let him, as though she had good sense. But when he started on her corset, she moved his hands aside.

"You've already done that once today, and you know where that got us. If you're in such a hurry, go see to the horses. I can finish."

He kissed her quickly. Before leaving the dugout, he tossed an old brown Stetson to the bed. "Take it off. And that city-bonnet of yours, too."

"I will." And she did, but she stuffed the corset into a sack she hastily made from one of her petticoats, tying the corners to conceal the contents.

The straw bonnet she could do without, but she couldn't

go off to a foreign country without her corset. Why, Miss Abigail would be mortified!

Day became night and night became day, as for three days and nights they traveled by the light of the moon and slept beneath the sweltering sun. Sánchez had gone on ahead to Las Colinas, "to check on things," was all Tyler would say. Madolyn had so little knowledge of their situation she couldn't even fill in the blanks.

The terrain was rocky, not a kilometer of it level, she would wager. By the time they reached the Rio Grande the first day out, the sun was setting and she was ready for relief, even if that meant sleeping on the hard ground.

Although they had spent no more than four hours in the saddle up to now, she had never imagined one's backside could hurt the way hers did; she was certain it must be black and blue with bruises. And, if that weren't enough, the skin between her legs had been rubbed raw from sitting astride the saddle.

But Tyler seemed to follow Miss Abigail's dictum, that there should be no rest for the weary. "Night's the only time we can travel once we cross the river," he explained, "so we'll have to keep goin'. You up to it?"

"Yes. Of course." She sat her saddle, hoping she was up to it, whatever "it" turned out to be. He instructed her to remove her shoes.

"Tie the laces together and drape 'em around your neck."

Skeptical, she watched him tug off his boots, then stretch a length of rope through the dog-eared tops and hang them around his neck like a stole.

"Leather dries stiffer'n your spine, madam secretary. Only way to save a wet pair of boots is to wear 'em till they dry. And let me tell you somethin', honey, that ain't no fun."

She followed his instructions, allowing his teasing voice

to dispel some of the jitters that fluttered like a swarm of butterflies in her stomach.

Raúl led off, followed by Tyler, with Madolyn close behind. Tyler continued to instruct her until the moment her horse entered the black waters.

"Hold the reins loosely in both hands, grip the saddle with your knees, and stay close to me. If you get in trouble, holler, I'll save you. Don't be scared."

"All right." Which was easy enough to say, but when she nudged her horse in behind Tyler's, she began to quake from the inside out.

Water sprayed from the hooves of Raúl's mount; it glistened like rubies in the last rays of the setting sun. A stunning, glorious sight. Then her horse plunged in behind Tyler's. The water rose quickly and was icy cold as it climbed up her legs. Her mount lost its footing and swam into the current. By the time they climbed the opposite bank, she was wet to the chin from the skin out. Her teeth chattered.

Tyler turned at the sound. "Cold?"

"It feels good," she managed between chatters. "The weather's been hot for so long I'd forgotten how it feels to be cold." They didn't stop or even slow down, but rode off into the gathering darkness.

"Where we're headed, you may see snow," he told her once.

"Snow? In June?"

"From a distance. The mountains that ring Las Colinas are topped with snow year round."

Raúl set a rapid pace and held it until almost sunup. From time to time Tyler handed her food.

"Jerky," he explained what the dried slivers of meat were. "Made from mule deer."

"Mule? Or deer?"

He laughed. "Mule deer. They're deer with long, floppy ears."

They each carried a canteen, and Tyler reminded her to drink. "Take little sips along; that'll keep you from gettin' really thirsty."

"What about Raúl?" she asked once when he handed her another piece of jerky.

"He carries his own food. Don't worry about him. Just watch where you're goin'."

Several times during the long night, Tyler left her with Raúl and rode into the rocky, cactus-clad foothills, sometimes ahead, other times to the north or south. Once when he returned, it was to direct them to a camping place back in the hills.

"There's a stream and shade and some caves where we can stake the horses out of sight. We'll rest there until nightfall."

The sun was well up by now, and the terrain was a surprise. It looked exactly the same as the land around Buckhorn. The campsite Tyler had chosen was on a rocky hillside with no more trees than in Texas. She found it strange that they had crossed a river, entered a foreign land, ridden throughout the long night, and still remained in a desolate, almost barren desert.

No sooner had they dismounted at the campsite, than Raúl stripped the horses of their saddles and led them to water, after which he took them up the hill to the cave Tyler indicated. Madolyn didn't see him again.

"You can fill our canteens in that stream, if you want," Tyler suggested. When she returned, he had taken a sack of food from his saddlebags and spread their repast on top of a tarp. "What're you hungry for?"

She came forward, laughing. At the sound, he glanced up, capturing her gaze with a heated look that caused the sound to catch in her throat.

He took the canteens and set them aside. "You didn't forget."

"You told me not to."

His brows shot up. "When'd you start doin' what I tell you to?"

She laughed again. Dropping to the ground on a nearby log, she decided she must be giddy with weariness. "I don't, unless it suits my fancy."

"Suits your fancy, huh?" He handed her a tin plate. "Hope cold biscuits and jerky suits your fancy. We can't risk a fire."

Reminder of the Rurales sobered her. "What would they do if they caught us?"

Tyler settled down on the log beside her. "Shoot us, I reckon."

"Shoot us?"

"Don't get excited. I won't let 'em shoot you. That's a promise."

"One that might be difficult to keep, since they would probably shoot you first."

He glanced up from his plate with a grimace. "I'm sorry. Bad joke." He grinned. "Try not to worry. I wouldn't have brought you if I didn't think I could protect you."

She listened to the creek lap against the bank and felt the strange sensation of sitting here, who knew where, beside this man who had become such an integral part of her life that she truly didn't worry too much about her own safety. Here they were, in a foreign country, faced with the possibility of being set upon by foreign soldiers, yet none of it seemed real—except the man beside her, except her feelings for him.

"I'm mighty proud of the way you made it through all that rough country," he told her.

She smiled, inordinately pleased that he had noticed. "Thanks. I'm proud of myself, wrong as that is."

"Wrong? You're entitled to be proud. Anyone who saw you would say the same."

"Not Miss Abigail. She says pride—"

"To hell with Miss Abigail." He kissed her softly on the lips. "We'll lay our blankets back in that thicket."

She tensed before his words were out. Hadn't she dreaded this moment all day? "No."

Tyler studied her, serious. "When we get back to Texas, we'll divvy up the authority in this relationship, Maddie. In the meantime, you have to do exactly what I say."

"But . . . ? Where's Raúl?"

"Keepin' watch. In a few hours, I'll join him. Until then . . ."

Panic-stricken, she scrambled to her feet. "Until then, nothing, Tyler Grant. We don't have a relationship. And nothing, absolutely nothing, is going to happen between us."

"Maddie, Maddie, calm down." Rising, he caught her by the shoulders. "Nothin'll happen, I promise." In spite of that promise, however, he kissed her, a long, wet, passionate kiss that left her heart palpitating and her body wanting more. But to her surprise, she didn't get it.

"There, that'll have to do for today, love. I'm near as tuckered out as you."

They spread their blankets several feet apart on a matting of leaves that only partially softened the rock-solid ground.

"Where will Raúl be while you keep watch?"

"Up yonder by the cave. He's good with horses. If someone comes, he'll be able to keep 'em quiet."

If he's awake, she thought. But she kept her worries to herself. Tyler had enough on his mind. "Do you always take this route?" she questioned after laying her head on her saddle like he had showed her. Funny how the curve of the seat fitted her neck; sleeping on it wasn't nearly as uncomfortable as she had feared.

"Depends," he responded from his own blankets. "I like to vary things, keep the Rurales on their toes."

"Do you think they know we're coming?"

"Not likely." But he had waited so long to answer, she decided his response was for her benefit.

"Don't worry, love," he added. "We're gonna be just fine. I'm anxious for you to see Las Colinas."

His soft drawl lulled her. Quickly, before her will weakened, she turned her back to him. "Don't call me that."

"What?"

She stared into the distance, to the hills, breathless, as though she had just run up one of them. "You know what."

"Say it, Maddie."

"No," she whispered. "Never. Please, don't say it again."

He didn't respond, and she knew he would do what he wished about it. He always did. Which was one of the things she loved about him. *Loved,* when she should have feared for her life.

Two mornings later they arrived unmolested at the most beautiful place she had ever seen, or even envisioned. Together they watched the sun top a near tier of hills, splashing its golden light across the valley below them, turning dewdrops to diamonds, and the little creek that meandered its length, into a gem-studded belt.

Fatigued in body and mind, she saw a rider race up the hill toward them and turn. It was Sánchez, bringing word that the way was clear, no Rurales in sight. She walked her horse beside Tyler's down a grassy slope, coming at length into the verdant valley.

"The creek runs out of the hills, yonder." He pointed to the distant mountains, which were so far away they looked black in the clear fresh light of dawn.

"Snow." She pointed to white peaks in the distance.

"Didn't I promise you snow?"

"Yes." Her breath caught, but her pulse raced. "What a beautiful place! It feels like a whole new world."

Tyler took his time answering. When he did, it was in a subdued tone that echoed her own wonderment. "I feel that way, too. Always have. The first time I set eyes on this

valley, I felt like I'd come home. I get that same feelin'
every time I ride down this hill."

Sánchez and Raúl had ridden ahead and were now no
more than stick figures among the cattle that grazed by the
stream. "The Rurales haven't taken your cattle."

"Not yet. Let's go. I need to get 'em movin' before we're
discovered."

Strangely, for she had never considered herself overly
brave, she wasn't afraid of the Rurales. If they came, Tyler
would protect her. She trusted him—with her life. And that
frightened her more than a battalion of Rurales could ever
have done.

But riding beside him down the hill, she was unable to
think of anything except this one magnificent moment. For
the few minutes it took them to reach a large structure that
rose in the distance, she allowed herself to revel in the experience of being alive and riding through the coolness and
the beauty beside this man who made her feel things she
had never expected to feel.

Memories, she insisted. She was making memories for
the cold and lonely nights back in Boston. But she didn't
feel like she was making memories. She felt like she was
living life. How easy to pretend they were coming home
from some exotic journey, returning side by side to their
beautiful cattle and their beautiful valley. When Tyler drew
rein beside a burned-out adobe structure, she did the same.

He dismounted, took her reins, and pulled both horses
into what she supposed had once been a walled courtyard.
Securing the reins to an exposed beam, he lifted his hands
for her to dismount. "You'll have to stay here, while I help
those vaqueros round up."

Setting her on the ground, he turned to his saddlebags
and withdrew a pistol. After checking the load, he handed
it to her. She eyed it skeptically.

"A precaution, Maddie. Sánchez has arranged for friends
to guard the valley."

She glanced around, striving to quiet the panic that had begun to gnaw through her fantasy.

"Take it," he urged. "You don't have to shoot anyone. Fire a warnin' shot. I'll be right out there with the cattle. One shot and I'll be here."

She took the pistol, but refused to let herself look at it.

"I'll be back before nightfall," he told her.

In an effort she recognized as defensive, she scanned the crumbled walls and toppled black beams. "What is this place?"

"My home." He draped an arm around her shoulders and drew her through an archway. Both adjoining walls had crumbled to the tiled floor. "What's left of it."

"Your home?" Madolyn caught her breath. "I thought . . ."

"That I'd always lived in a hole in the side of a hill?"

"No. I mean . . . What happened?"

"Rurales burned me out."

"When?"

"Six months back."

"Six months?"

"Yep." He nodded toward the valley. "Those cattle out there are the ones Morley Damn-his-hide refused to let me move to Texas."

"I don't understand what happened to Morley," she sighed. "He was a wonderful brother, kind, considerate. Now look at him. He's become a mean old man. What happened?"

Halting beside a fire-blackened fountain in what must have been an enormous patio, Tyler turned her to face him. He clasped his hands lightly behind her head, gazed into her eyes. "I don't know, love. But I have a hunch it's tied up with what's eatin' at you."

"Me?" She pursed her lips, allowing his endearment to caress her senses a moment before she rejected it. "Nothing's eating at me, as you say."

"No? Then why is my love so hard for you to accept? Why can't you give me yours?"

Her heart thudded against her ribs. Again he had asked for the impossible, the truth. Turning away, she stepped through an archway, entered another littered room, this one with a partial roof and two good walls.

Tyler caught her by the shoulder and pulled her around. His warm brown eyes implored her to respond. "Why, Maddie? What happened to you? What happened to Morley? I'd bet this ranch they're connected."

The truth hammered in her head. "You don't have this ranch to bet," she retorted. "Even if you did, you would lose." She steeled herself against the warring emotions that mushroomed inside her—fear, hatred, loneliness, and most threatening of all, the overwhelming love she felt for this man. "Stay out of it, Tyler. It's none of your business."

She could tell in an instant that she had wounded him. He recovered by a method she knew well, one she often used herself. He launched a counterattack.

"Now there's another case of the pot callin' the kettle black—you tellin' someone else to mind his own business. You, the most meddlin' woman I've ever known."

"If I'm so disagreeable, then leave me alone. Stop . . . stop . . ."

"Stop what, Maddie?"

"Everything," she cried. "Everything! Beginning with . . . with your miserable kisses and ending with calling me that . . . that horrible word."

He left her standing there. Right there, in the middle of his burned-out house, in the center of this beautiful valley, inside a foreign country. He stormed through the rubble, stepped into his saddle, and rode off, leaving her standing there. Alone. And empty.

And miserable.

Damn him! He was good at that. He was good at so many things. Too many things.

But he returned at dusk, like he promised. She hadn't been afraid in his absence, not really, only a little nervous. Throughout the day, between excursions to explore the sprawling structure Tyler called home, she watched him work cattle alongside Sánchez and Raúl and three other vaqueros. They drove them in bunches off toward the north.

The house had been a mansion; the ruins were that large. Although the roof was caved in and several of the major walls lay crumbled on expansive tile floors, the grandeur of the place was evident. Courtyards and fountains and overgrown shrubbery bespoke opulence. In contrast to the blackened beams, brilliant blossoms of scarlet and magenta clung to smut-streaked adobe walls, as plants she had no name for struggled to survive without the care they so badly needed.

She identified with them, with the straggling plants, for she felt that with a little tenderness and attention, she, too, could thrive in this magical world.

It was a thought at once disquieting and inviting. How tempting to think that here in a far distant land she might slip into different skin and become a new person.

A person who could give joy and receive it; give love and receive it. That here in this magical world, cruelty and fear could not find her.

With the sun gone, a chill set in, and Madolyn took a serape from her saddlebags and slipped it over her head. In the gathering darkness, she wandered alone through the numerous rooms, trying to decide what each might have been. It was difficult, for no furniture remained.

Who had built it, this mansion? For no apparent reason she sensed it must have been built long before Tyler left Georgia. Goldie said his wife had died. He called her Susan.

Had Susan died here? Had they lived together in this fantasy land? The idea of it left her sad, and even more lonely.

By the time Tyler returned, she was filled with questions, so many questions they cloaked her other concerns. Indeed, her other concerns seemed to have been left at the border, or at the very farthest, at the edge of this magnificent valley.

A world unto itself, this valley. A world where anything was possible, for a little while. And therein lay the danger. She must remain vigilant. She must not allow herself to lose sight of the predicament she could find herself in by becoming too enamored with this fantasy land and with the man who brought her here.

She felt his presence before he spoke. As at the other times, it started deep inside, an awareness that traveled outward, prickling her skin. She tried to shake off the concern this caused, but the best she could do was to convince herself to store it away, to worry about it later. When his hands touched her shoulders, the prickles turned to desire.

"We'll have to see about gettin' you some more clothes. I mistook you for a peon."

Beneath his palms, her shoulders felt like live coals. She savored the intensity of it. "A what?"

"A worker."

"I am a worker. If you had left food, I could have had a hot supper waiting."

Laughing, he dropped his hands and looked around. "Here?"

"Of course. I counted at least ten fireplaces. I could have cooked in any one of them."

"You've cooked over an open fire?"

"No. But I could. I can do anything I set my mind to."

Without warning he turned serious. Drawing her around,

he pulled her close, mumbling, "I know, love. That's what I'm bankin' on."

Before she could question his meaning, he kissed her. Once. Then he took her hand and led her out of the rabble-strewn courtyard.

"Where are we going?"

"Back into the hills where the Rurales won't be as likely to find us."

Disappointment speared through her, sudden and unexpected. "I thought we could stay here."

He glanced around. "You like the place, huh?"

"I love it."

His gaze captured hers. For the longest time he held her mesmerized by the sheerest thread of intense desire—his or her own? "That's a start," he whispered. Then with a sigh, he added, "María told Sánchez the Rurales have been watchin' this place."

"María?"

"Sánchez's . . . uh, his . . ."

Madolyn laughed. "I don't know why you're hemming and hawing. I live in the House of Negotiable Love. Nothing can shock me."

He raised an eyebrow. "We'll see."

She followed him to the horses, mounted, and rode with him through the haze of dusk. They headed across the valley, traveling north in the direction where she had watched the cattle disappear earlier. The softness of evening combined with the ethereal beauty of this place and the mesmerizing warmth of his presence to form a cocoon, in which she felt whole, complete in a way she had never known.

"You moved all the cattle?"

"Yep."

They rode in companionable silence.

"So you like the place?" he asked at length.

"It's magnificent. Yet so awfully sad."

"Sad?"

"That you've lost it. That the house was destroyed. That . . ." Hesitating to ask personal questions, she forged ahead, aided by the cover of darkness and the closeness she felt with him. "Is your wife buried here?"

"Susan? No, she died long before Morley and I arrived here. She's buried back in Georgia."

"Oh."

"Why'd you think that?"

"The house is so grand."

He laughed. "Too grand for a couple of ornery ol' cow-pokes like Morley an' me?"

She laughed in return. "Since you put it that way."

"Well, I agree. It was historic, one of the first of the grand haciendas built durin' Mexico's colonial heyday."

"I wish I could have seen it before."

"So do I, Maddie." He spoke into the wind and when the words blew back to her, they sounded more like a wish and a statement and she knew she wished the same.

And she knew she shouldn't.

They entered a narrow, winding canyon. The moon had come out now and lighted their way, if dimly. Tyler led the way up the steep trail. She followed him, gripping the reins and grateful for her serape with the evening chill setting in. She thought of the snow-capped peaks and shivered. But it was a good feeling, the best she could recall, if the strangest. Indeed, she felt as though they had left the real world behind. Already a weight seemed lifted from her shoulders. She felt light-headed and lighthearted and wished it were just because of the altitude.

Tyler didn't stop again until they had climbed well above the valley floor. Then, of a sudden, he drew rein on a rocky ledge.

"What is it?" she asked, thinking of Rurales.

"I want to show you somethin'." He helped her dismount. With an arm draped over her shoulders, he drew her back the way they had just come. Together they stood on the edge of the hill and looked down into the valley.

All was black now, like velvet. The little stream glimmered in the moonlight even brighter than at dawn.

"I've never seen anything so beautiful," she whispered. "Not in all my life."

He remained silent, but the way his hand squeezed her shoulder, she knew he felt the same. The poignancy of sharing this special moment, this special place, with this special man was almost too much to bear. She blinked back tears, admonishing herself to get control. To keep control.

"How long will it take the Rurales to miss the cattle?"

"Not long enough." He pressed her to his side. "I didn't mean to frighten you. Even if they find the cattle, they won't find us."

"Why not?"

"They don't care about us. They're after the cattle."

"I see." But she didn't, not really. Even if they weren't staying with the cattle tonight, they would eventually have to connect with them to drive them back to Texas. But Tyler's mind wasn't on cattle, nor even on Rurales, she discovered.

"Maddie." His solemn tone alarmed her. Had he saved the bad news until they were safely out of the valley?

"What is it?"

"You tell me," he answered. His voice was low, desperate. "I have to know. It's been eatin' at me all day, and longer, for a long time now." Both arms went around her. He cradled her close, as though to protect her from some demon that might pounce on them out of the darkness. And she knew he would. Right or wrong, she trusted him.

"What happened to make you so afraid?"

Tensed, she stared into the black night, seeking some safe haven, but all she saw was blackness. Blackness. Like her life had always been.

Like her life would always be without Tyler.

"I need to know," he said. "I deserve to know."

"I know." He was right. But how could she say the words? "Not now. Not here. I can't talk about it standing here on this rocky ledge."

He turned her by the shoulders. Moonlight glinted from the moisture in his eyes. "I need to know now. At the end of this canyon we'll come to an old adobe stable, where we'll stay the next few days, while I dip cattle."

"I'll tell you when we get there."

"No. There'll be people there. I can't wait any longer."

And he couldn't. It had come upon him suddenly, and without half thinking he reined in his horse and confronted her. He had to know. Now.

Earlier in the day when he rode away from her, it had been from necessity; he'd had to get out of there. Fast. Coming home had been hard enough. Oh, he had seen the house since the Rurales set fire to it, but each time was like pouring salt into a fresh wound.

His home. No woman had shared this home with him. Except for an occasional serving girl, no woman had shared his bed. That wasn't the meaning of this valley. It had nothing to do with the physical world, hardly even with the cattle he and Morley raised here. This valley had been his place of refuge from memories that had haunted and plagued him.

Maddie said it reminded her of another world, and it had been that for him. A new world. A world in which to escape. A world in which to heal. This valley had transcended his physical needs.

Until today. Today when he stood beside Maddie, looking at the remains of the burned-out hull of his home, he knew his old wounds were healed. It was as if he had been washed clean in the icy spring that flowed through the land.

Standing there beside her, it had come to him. The truth. That this woman, this meddling, toe-tapping sister of his arch-enemy was the woman he had to spend the rest of his life with. He couldn't let her slip away. Or run away.

Standing there in the valley with Maddie, he felt like a new man with a new life to spend with the first and only woman he would ever truly love.

He wanted to tell her. He ached to tell her. To convince her of the truth, that she felt the same way. That they had been touched by some magical and unseen hand, selected out of all the men and all the women in the world, just for each other.

But he couldn't tell her any of that. Not until he knew what kind of problem she faced; what kind of problem they faced.

He cradled her head against his chest. "Please don't close me out. Not any longer. I want to help you, Maddie. I want to rescue you from whatever is causin' you such pain."

She felt his heart throb steady and true, against her. *Rescue her?* He spoke as though he were a knight of old and she a damsel facing a dragon. But he was asking for the truth, and the truth was not a fairy story. The truth was reality. Reality, harsh and cruel.

Rescue her. Could he? Had she been right earlier? Was anything possible in this land of magic? Was he her knight in shining armor ready and willing to dispatch her demons? The world's demons, Miss Abigail would say.

She felt safe in his arms. No question about that. Safe and secure . . . and loved. But that wasn't all. If it were, she could control the situation.

He felt the same way she did. She had known as much, even before he said it. His feelings for her showed in a myriad of tiny details—the gentle touch of his hands, the softness when he spoke her name, the lighthearted way he laughed and encouraged her to laugh. She saw it in his warm brown eyes, felt it in the erratic beat of his heart against hers, experienced it in the passion he was so quick to express and so helpless to conceal. She knew it by the way he called her "love," so tenderly, so naturally, making her feel special, and, yes, loved.

She knew, but she couldn't let him say it again, not ever again. So she fought him with words, carefully chosen words, knowing in advance she could cool his passion with platitudes that no longer rang true, even to her own ears.

"Miss Abigail says when a man sets out to rescue a woman, she had better watch where she steps, else she's likely to find herself caught in a trap."

Sixteen

"Damnation, Maddie! Would you stop hidin' behind the chastity belt of that old biddy!"

"I'll thank you not to swear when you speak of Miss Abigail."

"And I'll thank you to get off your damned high horse." Turning abruptly, he stalked away without a backward glance.

Stunned by his harshness, she refrained from trying to get the last word. She had made him angry this time, really angry. And she regretted it. Not standing up for Miss Abigail's good name. She would never regret that. But the magic of this day had suddenly vanished, as if it had been no more than a soap bubble. She had burst the ephemeral fantasy.

Leaving her alone. And lonely. For the first time today this land seemed foreign instead of magical. Which is what it had been all along. All the joy and beauty drained out of her, leaving her cold and empty. Like she would always be.

Her trepidation grew when Tyler remounted without waiting to assist her. But she struggled into her saddle, knowing he wouldn't leave her; that knowledge was little comfort.

He waited, but barely, heading up the canyon before she had good control of her horse. He rode ahead, like before, straight and tall in the saddle, and she followed, imagining him stiff with anger. The silence became heavy, foreboding. She should not have angered him. She, who knew all too well what to expect from an angry man.

Darkness enclosed them, surrounding them with its blackness the way the waters of the Rio Grande had closed around her horse when it gave up its legs and started to swim. The only light came from above—from stars that glittered along a narrow strip of black sky—all that was visible from the bottom of the canyon. Like a river of stars, she thought. They followed that river in silence.

The next time he stopped, it was before an enormous adobe building, similar to the burned-out hull of his home, except this one wasn't burned-out. It looked deserted.

Madolyn drew her horse to a halt beside Tyler's, then sat in stunned silence until she realized he was waiting for her to dismount on her own. He had lost patience with her before, but never to this extent. Fear began to inch its icy fingers up her spine. She tried to make the best of things. He would come around. He couldn't stay angry forever.

He won't stay angry forever. The words chilled her, even thinking them. For they were not her words. They had come from her subconscious. They came to her now in her mother's voice.

"Don't mind Papa," her mother would say through swollen lips. "He'll come around. He won't stay angry forever."

Desperately, she shook off the past, girded herself to face the present. To survive the present—until she was back on familiar soil.

"What is this?" she asked in as cheerful a tone as she could muster. "It doesn't look like a stable."

He met her questions with a sullen shrug. They entered the building through a massive archway and walked together, but separately, down a wide dimly lit aisle. To either side she saw dim outlines of stalls. When he stopped, she stopped. He opened a half-door and motioned for her to lead her horse inside.

After depositing both horses they continued down the hay-strewn aisle, toward a light that gleamed at the far end. At least, she suspected that was their destination. She had no one to ask.

No more than a pinpoint at first, the light grew as they neared, coming finally into a large space that was sparsely furnished with a table, some chairs, and a huge fireplace fitted with cooking rack and pots. Spicy aromas combined with wood and cigarette smoke.

Several people gathered around the fireplace. A couple of women tended a spit on which an animal too small to be a calf roasted. They wore loose black dresses, with coarse black rebozos wrapped around their shoulders, the ends dangling almost to the rock floor.

"What are they cooking?" she tried.

"*Cabrito,*" Tyler responded.

"What's that?"

"Goat." He eyed her sternly. "I expect you to treat these women with respect."

Her trepidation grew, and along with it, her ire. In spite of her fear, she could not hold her tongue. "How dare you, sir!"

"Don't sir me, Maddie. I'm gettin' damned tired of it. If you want some food go ahead. They'll serve you a plate."

He didn't introduce her, and she was so angry she wasn't sure she could remember enough Spanish to accomplish the task. But she needn't have worried. The women introduced themselves.

"*Soy María,*" the younger woman said. "*Bienvenida, Maddie.*" She sang Madolyn's name so it came out sounding like Mad-dé. Turning to the older woman who stooped over a huge copper kettle that bubbled on the coals, she explained, "*Mi mamá, Hortensia.*"

"*Hola, María. Hortensia.*" She took the offered plate and

thanked them, while Tyler disappeared into the darkness without a word. Where he went was a mystery. A group of men sat just beyond the circle of light, she could see the glow of their cigarettes and hear their low murmurs. If he joined them, she couldn't make out his voice.

When she removed her brown Stetson her hair fell around her shoulders. Most of her hairpins had been lost somewhere between Tyler's dugout and this faraway place. She placed the hat on the table and sat in the chair Maria motioned her to and began to eat. The meat was stringy and delicious, although bear meat would probably have tasted good on this night. She was that hungry.

But even as she ate the *cabrito,* beans, tortillas, and drank thick black coffee, she felt empty inside. Now that they were around others, strangers though they were, her fear began to dissipate. Taking its place was a mounting sense of loneliness. She knew she should be grateful that he hadn't left her in the countryside. That hadn't worried her.

It wasn't as if he hadn't ridden or walked off and left her before. But recalling those other times now, she knew there was a difference. A vast difference. She had done more than stretch his patience this time. She had offended him, intentionally. She had taken his precious gift of love, his offer to make her whole, and had flung it back in his face.

And she was sorry; she wanted to apologize. She wanted to tell him he was right. She loved him. Oh, my, how she loved him. But in the long run, that would only hurt him more. For she could never give herself to him—and she could never explain why. He was, after all, a man. A man who caused her heart to race and set her pores on fire, true. But a man, nonetheless. No, this way was best. The more distance she kept between them, the better for both of them in the long run.

Although her newly acquired knowledge of the language

did not extend to domestic chores, Madolyn made herself useful by washing her plate in a bucket where Hortensia had washed others. When she continued to wash the accumulation of dishes, the women tried to stop her, but she steadfastly resisted.

"No." She shook her head, trying to smile. The women left her to her task, and in the ensuing stillness, the men's talk floated toward her like campfire smoke drifting on a breeze. She recognized Tyler's voice now. He spoke with that lovely fluency she had observed the day he drove her out to Morley's.

That first day. How long ago it seemed. How far away. For the first time since they left his dugout, she recalled the struggle to reunite Buckhorn. Were the women still working on their Independence Day demonstration? She hoped so. They needed her help. She wondered whether she would return in time to help them. She wondered whether it really mattered or why she cared or how she would survive in this foreign land with only an angry, sullen man as a guide.

And he *was* angry. There was no doubt about that. When at length he came to her and indicated with a jerk of his head that she was to follow him, her first impulse was to refuse. But she rose in spite of herself, and in spite of herself, hope sprang to life in her breast.

"Where are we going?"

He nodded toward an open archway that led out into the black night. Her heart thudded against her ribs. She was afraid.

For the first time since she had known this man, she was afraid of him. But she followed him out the door, like she had good sense. He wouldn't hurt her, she insisted. Not Tyler.

He carried a lantern, and she followed him around the side of the building and up a flight of stone steps, her serape gripped in tight fists against the chill of night, against the chill of fear. *This is Tyler,* she reasoned. *He loves you.*

He won't stay angry forever, her mother's voice whispered through time and memory.

At the top of the steps, they entered a large, vacant room with a floor of rough-hewn logs that had been worn smooth by time. It smelled of hay and only faintly of horses, a bit dusty, but clean and smoke-free. By the light of Tyler's lantern, she saw her bedroll in a far corner, and next to hers, his own.

Her suspicions turned to certainty, when, with another jerk of his head, he motioned her toward the bedrolls. Whether he intended for her to sit or lie, she had no idea. But she knew what he would do.

At least, she thought she did. Everything in her past prepared her for what was to come—an experience she had vowed would never be repeated in her own life.

Yet, here she was. *Run!* she cried inside. *Run! Down the stairs, into that room full of people. Run!*

But she didn't. This was Tyler. Inside her, anger built rapidly. Anger at herself. Anger, that she could not keep herself from submitting to this moment—to this man. Yet, she loved him and in the name of that love, she had followed him to this room, leaving herself open to whatever form of retaliation he intended to extract.

Night after night she had seen this script played out. She knew it by heart. Like a theater patron who had witnessed the same play a thousand times, she knew what to expect. Night after night, year after year, she had watched her mother climb the stairs behind her father. She thought she had learned from the despicable experience. Yet, she hadn't. For she followed this man to this dark, secluded room, and she remained here, incapable of running from him. In the name of love.

"Sit, Maddie." Without waiting for her to obey his command, Tyler sat on his own bedroll, cross-legged. He placed the lantern on the floor at the head of their beds.

She sat, too, although everything inside her screamed for her not to, for her to run, run for her life. He had never seemed so large. His presence loomed before her, heavy, oppressive. Her arms trembled and she held onto them to keep him from seeing her fright.

"Now, talk," he ordered. "And none of that highfalutin nonsense about Miss Abigail. I want to hear about you. What happened to you? I want to know."

"What?" The word quivered out, and she thought suddenly that now she would learn the answer to a debate that raged at the society: Which enraged a man more, defiance or weakness?

"Start talkin', Maddie. I'm prepared to sit here till hell freezes over."

"Sit here?"

"Right here. Now talk."

"Talk?" As a preliminary to what? Did he interrogate his victims before extracting vengeance?

"Talk!" he shouted.

"Then what?"

He didn't respond for a time. When finally he did, his lowered tone emphasized his exasperation. "All I'm interested in is the truth. You owe me that. So get started."

Comprehension came slowly. "Just talk? That's all?"

"Hell, isn't that enough? You've resisted talkin' about this for the last time, Maddie. Like I said, I'll sit here as long as it takes. And you will, too."

Relief shot moisture to her eyes. She quelled it with the admonition that this confrontation was far from over. But relief would not be denied, and it took the form of anger.

"How dare you?" she cried in a choking whisper.

"How dare me what?"

"Frighten me like that."

"Frighten you? What did I do?"

"You're angry. You've been angry ever since we left that ledge."

"Damn right, I'm angry. *Mad* is a better word. Way I see it, I have every right to be mad as hell."

"Don't talk to me about rights. I should never have come up here with you. I should never—"

His voice softened. "What's goin' on, Maddie?"

"You're angry."

"So what?"

Reality closed in, smothering her. She gripped her arms tighter. "I know," she whispered.

"What do you know?" he asked gently.

"What men do when they're angry. Don't deny it."

For a long time he just stared at her. "Hell! If you're talkin' about . . . If you thought . . . Hell." He shook his head as if unable to believe what he had heard. "For your information, I have never struck a woman in my life." He sounded offended.

She watched him, wary.

"That's the honest-to-God truth," he swore. "I have never struck a woman." When he reached toward her, she dodged his hand. "I sure as hell wouldn't start now . . . with you."

She wanted to believe him, and part of her did, for she sat there, unable to run, angry at herself for it. She kept her eyes on the strip of floorboard that stretched between their bedrolls, her senses acutely tuned. She tried to think she was poised to flee, ready to jump up from the bedroll at a moment's notice. But she wasn't sure she would be able to. You had to want to run away from someone, she realized now. She didn't want to run from Tyler. She wanted, desperately wanted, to believe him.

Worse, she wanted to throw herself in his arms. Was that the reason her mother followed her father into their bedchamber night after night? Were women indeed that stupid, that dense, that hungry for love?

"That's it, isn't it?" Tyler was saying. "That's what happened to you."

She glanced up, confused. Tears spilled from her eyes. She tried to blink them back.

"Who was it, Maddie? Who hurt you? Your father?"

His voice was tender, gentle; it held her mesmerized. For a moment she forgot he was a man, a hated, feared man. He was Tyler, tender, gentle, loving Tyler.

No! her brain resisted. *He's a man!* She ducked her head. When his fingers touched her chin, she tried to keep him from lifting her face, but he was the stronger.

Men always were.

"Did he beat you?"

She heard his voice break somewhere in the middle of the question. She dared not meet his gaze.

"That damned Morley. Did he run off and leave you in the hands of an abusive father?"

She found her voice, although she was still unable to stem the flow of tears. "He didn't beat me."

Before she knew he had moved, Tyler held her face in his hands. His gentle hands. They stilled on her cheeks at her reply. "God! What did he do?"

"He . . . he beat her."

"Her?" Tyler's hands relaxed; his voice broke, in what sounded like relief. "Your father beat your mother?"

She tried to reply, but the dreadful admission choked in her throat. She nodded, her eyes downcast, from both fear and shame.

"Tell me about it."

"No. I can't." Suddenly she was no longer able to control her trembling. Truth and fear tumbled together, shaking every part of her. Her entire body trembled and she could do nothing to stop it. Tears poured from her eyes, and she could not stop them, either.

Then she was in his arms. He held her tightly against his

chest. Tighter than ever before. Yet, gentler, too. Tighter, gentler, it didn't make sense.

None of it made sense. Here she was in a foreign country, a world away from Boston, years away from the trauma she had endured, yet she felt it as plainly as when it first occurred.

"There, there, Maddie. It's okay. I won't ask you again. Not anymore. It doesn't matter."

Gradually her brain began to clear. Her lifelong determination to deny the past a purchase on her life and Miss Abigail's doctrine on self-reliance came face to face with Tyler's extraordinary compassion, teaching her another truth on this night of truths. Love was stronger than fear. "I have to tell you. You deserve to know."

Moving out of his protective embrace, she sat on her bedroll, he on his. Their knees touched through her baggy duckins and his, as she sat cross-legged, like he did. Unladylike, improper, the first time she had ever sat that way in her life. That she allowed herself to do so now, added to the gradual sense of power that had begun to seep into her.

"In the beginning I didn't realize what was happening. Mother always made up some story to account for her tears and injuries. Even when I was young, I didn't believe her. I thought I had done something to hurt her."

Tyler reached for her, but she offered only her hands, which he clasped and held tightly between them.

"In time I understood that I didn't have anything to do with her pain."

"But it had already affected you."

"Yes. I hated her for submitting to him. Oh, I pitied her, too, and I loved her. But I hated what she was, her submissiveness. Tonight, for the first time, I understand."

"Tonight?"

"I followed you up those stairs. I sat where you ordered me to sit."

"I wasn't goin' to hurt you."

"I didn't know that."

"Of course, you knew that."

"No, I didn't. You were angry, and I climbed the stairs behind you, just like my mother climbed the stairs behind my father night after night. All he had to do was nod toward the bedchamber and off they went. I used to make up excuses for her to stay behind—

" 'You haven't heard my sonata, Mother.'

" 'You haven't seen my embroidery.'

"Inside I was screaming, 'Don't go! Don't go!'

"She understood. She heard my silent pleas. 'I'll hear it tomorrow, Madolyn,' she would say. 'It'll be all right.'

"Then Papa would order me to my room."

Tyler's eyes widened as the tale grew. Horror played across the planes of his face. When she finished, he sat, silently squeezing her hands. What was he thinking? Had the tale made him sick? Sick with shame, like she had been for so long?

"You came up here, thinkin' I was goin' to . . . ?" His voice was low, husky, and it broke several times. "God, Maddie, that's so horrible, I can't even say it."

"I know. All my life I swore I would never, ever submit to a man; I vowed to spend my life saving other women from such relationships. And I meant it, Tyler. I still do, I guess, but when you jerked your head toward the back of the stable, I rose and followed you, and when you told me to sit on this bedroll, I sat on it."

"You knew I wouldn't hurt you," he insisted again.

"No, I didn't."

Before she could stop him again, he pulled her across the space and into his arms. He pressed her head to his heart, and she felt it pound. He buried his face in her hair; she felt his lips on her scalp, then his tears, hot and wet. He held her so tightly she began to feel safe.

"I'm not like your father, Maddie." He spoke against her

head; his voice rasped into the stillness. "Please listen. Please hear. Please believe me."

She sat back, but remained in the loose shelter of his arms. "It wasn't just Papa. I've worked with women who were abused. You can't imagine how many there are."

"You can't imagine how many decent husbands and fathers there are, either."

She touched his face with the tips of her fingers. "I want to believe that. I wish I could."

"You can, love. I'll teach you. I won't ever give up. I love you, Maddie. Don't ask me not to say it; I can't keep the words inside. I love you. And I want you so bad."

"I want you, too, but . . ."

"No buts. I want to marry you."

Terror swept through her like an icy wind. "No, please . . . Don't say that again, not ever."

"Okay, okay. I won't say it again. Tonight."

"Not ever," she insisted.

"Don't ask me that, Maddie. How 'bout we take things one day at a time?"

"Okay."

"And one night at a time."

She tensed. "No."

"Beginnin' tonight, love."

"No." Her heart beat to a wild and terrified cadence.

"There's nothin' to be afraid of, Maddie. Nothin'."

"Having a baby."

"You won't have a baby. I promise."

"You're full of promises."

"And you're full of doubts." His lips touched hers, setting off a fiery streak of yearning. A shudder raced through her, releasing some of the tension that had built while she told her awful secret. His lips covered hers. Inside she began to glow.

"Let me help you, Maddie," he mumbled against her skin. "Let me free you."

By the time he had her clothes unfastened, her head was buzzing, but when he tried to lay her back against the bed-roll, she found strength to resist.

"No, Tyler . . ." He stroked her breast; she ached for more. "No . . ."

"How 'bout we leave your clothes on?" He kissed her lips, little passionate nips. "And mine." His lips moved down her neck. "I won't even unbutton my duckins."

His lips found her breast. She whimpered and felt sub-missive but was powerless to object. As though she were clay, he sculpted her emotions, building her passion by in-crements, chasing her fears into a distant corner of her brain. His open palm laved her skin with heat; his fingers seared fire to her very core; his lips devoured, invited, pro-voked, incinerating her fears, leaving only love to rise through the ashes of her past.

Love for this man, who, with his lips and hands and softly murmured reassurances brought her passion to a shattering crescendo. When her tremors subsided, he held her close, so close she felt the rigid evidence of his own need, which he held in check behind a barrier of clothing.

Not once did he complain. Instead, he whispered soft, crooning words against her skin and nipped kisses across her face. She held him fast. She had never felt so loved, so secure, so safe.

"I hate the way you make me feel."

He chuckled. "I can tell."

"I do."

"What do you hate about it, love?"

"I hate feeling safe with you; I hate feeling like I can't live without you."

"Oh, Maddie, love, please—"

"Don't call me that."

"Then I'll have to prove it, won't I, how safe you are? As far as not bein' able to live without me, or any other man, you've already proved you can. But just because you can, doesn't mean you should. Why do you think the Man Upstairs put man and woman on this earth, if not to be together?"

"I want no part of the togetherness I've seen."

"It doesn't have to be like that."

She drew back, confused, yet desperate to make him understand. "Look back through the ages, Tyler. Pick any part of history you want, and what do you find? Women subservient to men. I can't live like that. Not only because I'm afraid; I don't want to live like that. I told you how I hated my mother for being submissive. Well, I hated myself, too. Earlier tonight, I hated myself for blindly following you up those stairs, for sitting where you told me to, when you told me to, even though I expected the worst."

He stroked her head, sifting fingers through her thick hair. "I don't have an answer for that," he admitted. "Not a new one. But I'll tell you the way I see it. Yes, there are husbands who abuse their wives. But they're not the majority. There are husbands who think their way is the only way, they make the decisions, that's pretty standard. But it doesn't have to be like that. I told you back on the trail that as soon as we get back across the border, we'll sit down and divvy up the authority. We will. I want to marry you—"

"You promised not to say that."

"I can't help it, Maddie. I want what I want."

"Like a true man."

"Hell, yes, like a true man. I ache like a true man, too." He held her close, running a possessive hand down her spine, pressing her body against his, as if to illustrate exactly where and how much he ached for her. "Tell you what, we won't talk about this again till we're back on Texas soil. How's that?"

"Fine."

"We don't need to talk all that much, anyhow." As if to

prove the point, he kissed her again, the tenderest, deepest, wettest, most passionate kiss she had ever imagined.

And in the following days, he continued to prove that point. Madolyn had never imagined two people could engage in so much kissing! Why, who ever heard of such a thing?

Certainly, Miss Abigail would have been mortified, had she known. Fortunately, Miss Abigail wasn't along. Once they returned to Texas, Madolyn reasoned, she could worry about regaining her sense of right and wrong. Later, she would find the strength to do what she knew all along she must do.

But for the time being, she did exactly what Tyler said; it wasn't submitting, she reasoned, when she wanted it, too. Like an old reptile skin, the strictures of her civilized world sloughed off, leaving her free to enjoy the fantasy of loving and being loved. And enjoy, she did. She would repent later, but for now, she was having too much fun.

Their first morning in the stable, Tyler brought her two dresses. She had slept soundly and awakened to find him gone. He returned soon after, bearing a package wrapped in brown paper.

"María went into the village overnight. See if these fit. I told her you were about her size."

"And how did you decide that?" She had awakened light-headed and still giddy from her night with Tyler. That she could tease him about a topic as serious as another woman, delighted her.

He pulled her to him. The package squashed between them. "Not the way you think, Maddie, love. She's Sánchez's woman, and even if she weren't . . ." He kissed her then, an all-consuming, proprietary kiss that rendered his final words useless. ". . . you're all the woman I need, now or ever."

To cover her distress, Madolyn tore into the package, pulling out two cotton shifts. One black, one white, they were fashioned the same—loose-fitting, with colorful embroidery decorating the yokes, and belts to tie or not.

"Now, all I need is a bath," she said, only half in jest. She couldn't recall ever being so dirty, not even as a child.

"Run down to the river," he suggested. "I'm fixin' to take the men off to dip cattle. You won't be disturbed." He kissed her again. "Not that I wouldn't give my eyeteeth to join you."

"Tyler!" But, far from being offended, she was pleased. Never had she imagined herself engaging in intimate jesting with a man, a man who loved her. And, dear Lord help her, yes, a man she loved in return.

Cypress trees formed a natural cove around a bend in the little river that meandered down from the hills. Although the water was cold, it was also invigorating, and she scrubbed with the harsh ash soap Hortensia had provided, after a discussion that consisted mostly of hand signals.

She scrubbed her hair and her body and never once wished for hot water or rose-scented soap. With lacy leaves forming a canopy overhead and embankments to either side of the swiftly flowing stream, she had her own private bathing glen.

Beauty suffused her, and here, alone in this place, peace begin to seep into the void left by unburdening her soul to Tyler. She sat on a rock slab to dry, letting the soft, cool breeze blow across her naked body in a free and open manner she could never have imagined herself doing in the past.

At Tyler's insistence, she had purged herself of those dreadful memories, leaving not an empty, useless shell, but a receptacle for his love. And he filled her with it, a love so complete, so gentle, so selfless that it took her breath, just recalling it.

The intimacy, the splendor, the gifts he had given.

The gift of acceptance, listening to her story without rejecting her for her parents' shameful behavior.

The gift of fulfillment, when he was so obviously in need. But he didn't complain. Not even when it was over and he pulled her close and she felt the rigid evidence of his own need. She had lain in his arms, filled with joy and relief and a great sense of sadness, that she could not give him gifts in return, one above all others, the gift of her love.

She spent the day alone, wandering the riverbank, sitting beneath a shade tree, watching fish jump in the water, birds light on branches overhead, hearing their song, the lapping of the water, the wind through the trees. And she began to heal.

By the end of the day the jagged edges of her memories were not as sharp. Then he returned and the sight of him sent fear chasing the longing she had felt all day. Her longing to give in to him, to love him, once more became entangled with her lifelong fears. He stood in the door to their room, and she stood still as a held breath in the center of it.

He was clean; his hair still dripped. She wondered whether he had bathed in the same secluded spot as she. She recalled his teasing that he wished they could bathe together.

That wish had stayed with her the day long, while she bathed, wishing he were there; while she sunned on the rock, the soft air drying her body, she wished for him.

Now he stood before her, and she knew what he wanted, and she trembled.

In two steps he was beside her. "Told you they'd fit," he mumbled, just before he kissed her. It was a strong, solid kiss that spoke of the day's separation and the coming together they both wanted. His hands skimmed down her arms, found her breast.

He drew back, eyebrows arched. His hands slipped to her

ribs. His warm eyes danced over her face with a combination of laughter and chagrin.

"Where the hell did this come from?"

"What?"

"What?" he mimicked with a grin. "You know damn well what. I told you to leave that corset behind."

"No, you didn't. You said I shouldn't wear it riding horses, and you were right. But now, with a dress, and . . ."

While she spoke, he edged the dress up her body, scrunched it around her neck, and went to work untying her corset.

"Tyler?"

"Maddie," he mimicked again. Then his hands were on her skin. His gentle, rough hands that worked magic on her body. He cupped her breasts in his palms and looked into her eyes.

"Thought you liked the feel of my hands."

She returned his stare, direct, proud. The glow spread through her. "I do."

He fumbled with the tie on her bloomers. "Then don't girt up so I can't reach you."

"Tyler?"

Her bloomers fell to the floor. His hands possessed her; his lips took a breast. All sense was lost to her. Only once, when he lifted her in his arms and carried her to their bedroll, did she manage to object.

"Don't worry, Maddie. Nothin'll happen."

"But you? I want it to be good for you, too."

He smiled into her bewildered eyes. "I have you, love. And I have patience. For now I'll settle for those two things."

As the days passed in this idyllic land, as the nights passed in the arms of this perfect man, Madolyn grew ever more secure. She lived each day for his return and spent each night locked in his arms. Eventually that was not enough. She loved him, there was no denying that. And he loved her and deserved more of her, all of her. And she wanted, oh how she wanted, to give herself to him. To ease his aching body and troubled mind. To cast caution to the wind, to swear her love and allegiance for now and forever. Still, she was unable to do so.

She did finally, however, persuade him to let her watch the dipping process. He hadn't wanted to, she could tell that.

"It's dangerous, Maddie. The Rurales could come upon us at anytime. I don't want you in the middle of a shootout."

That convinced her, as nothing else could have. She had to go. She could not sit idly back at the stable, while Tyler faced the Rurales. Although just what she could do to prevent a shootout evaded her comprehension. She didn't let him see her concern, however, but laughed it off with a wave of the hand.

"Pshaw! We haven't caught sight of the Rurales since we've been here. If you think you can leave me with the women by using that timeworn excuse, think again."

By the time she ended her little speech, he was laughing. "Pshaw? I've never heard you use that word."

"I haven't either," she admitted. "My grandmother used to brush things off with it."

"So did mine." His gaze ignited fires inside her. "There's somethin' else we have in common, case we're still lookin'."

She kissed him, proud of herself for acting so boldly, especially when she saw how it pleased him. "You're awfully good at that," she murmured.

"What's that, love?"

"Changing the subject. When can I watch you work cattle?"

"Soon." And he kept his promise.

Several days later, he allowed her to come with them to the box canyon. It was a comfortable, lazy sort of day. At least for Madolyn.

She sat back on the hillside beneath a stand of cotton-woods, watching the work and eating tortillas and chorizo left over from breakfast. The difficulty of the work astounded her, especially since she knew how hard it was to stay on the back of a horse. When Tyler joined her at midday, it was for only a brief respite. He plopped down beside her, pecked her on the cheek, and took the tortilla she rolled around a hunk of the spicy sausage.

"How much longer?"

"Till we finish," he responded, explaining. "This is the last bunch. By dark we should have them headed for Texas."

"We're leaving?" For days now she had expected this. No fantasy lasted forever. With each day that passed, she dreaded leaving this wonderland more.

"Raúl and Sánchez will start the cattle on the road tonight. You and I will go back for our gear. We'll leave in the mornin', meet up with them tomorrow night."

Tomorrow. One more night. Dismally she pulled her mind off the future. She couldn't ruin what time they had left. She handed him another roll of chorizo. "I've never seen men work so hard. You must be exhausted."

"You said it." In a heartbeat his eyes had found hers, held hers. He winked. "For just about everythin', love."

That's all it took for the glow that burned constantly inside her now to burst into flame. She didn't mind him calling her love, anymore. She savored the sound. It made her feel wanted, like she belonged to someone, someone who would protect and cherish her. And love her.

"You have work to do," she hedged.

"Afterwards?"

Afterwards? Her heart leaped at the thought. She should refuse. She must refuse. Then again, what harm could it do? One time. One more time.

She had been over and over this, in argument with herself. Tyler hadn't begged or even asked her. Oh, he teased about it, like now. She knew he was serious, but he never pressured her.

She pressured herself, and her latest argument against abstaining could well be her downfall. One time. What harm could one time do?

Plenty. One time was all it took. One time and she could conceive Tyler's baby. But for the life of her, she was unable to dredge up one ounce of concern over that. What harm would having his baby do? Indeed, if she couldn't have him, wouldn't his baby be the next best thing?

"Humm," he was saying, nudging her cheek with his nose. "What's on your mind, love?"

Her heart throbbed in her chest. It always did when they were close, and more so when she thought about making love with him. She knew he knew.

But like the gentleman he was, he ignored it. She turned her face until her lips touched his. "We'll see."

He went back to work after that, and she sat the whole afternoon on the hill beneath the cottonwood trees. She watched the vaqueros, but did not see them. She argued with herself, tried to talk herself out of this thing she wanted so badly. When Tyler came once in the middle of the afternoon for a cool drink, she knew he recognized her dilemma; she knew he shared it.

She couldn't meet his eyes. She felt stiff, awkward. He didn't stay long, just long enough to kiss her cheek and whisper, "What's on your mind, Maddie, love?"

The sun had sunk halfway below the hills before they finished dipping. Raúl and Sánchez headed the herd out of the canyon. Maddie prepared to leave, but Tyler remained at the creek. She watched, mesmerized, while he stripped and bathed. She was too far away to see details of his body, but she imagined them. And she longed to see him, to feel him.

Then he was sauntering up the hill, his hair still dripping, his shirt slung over one shoulder, a grin the size of Texas

on his face. She couldn't take her eyes from him. The top
two buttons on his duckins were undone. She thought about
that first morning when she caught him standing in his
doorway, half dressed, flirting with Annie. When she left
he would have Annie again. But today . . .

Reaching her, he knelt on one knee, his beloved, all-
consuming presence spilling over her. When he spoke it
was in a playful, teasing tone, but his eyes were earnest.
"Think I'm clean enough to make love to my lady?"

Make love. Her breath caught at the words, at their im-
plication, at the way the glow inside her flamed at the
thought. Before she could consider refusing, she caught his
face in her hands and pulled his lips to hers.

He kissed her until she was dizzy. Then he drew back
mere inches. "Want to wait till we get back to the stable?"

"No."

She saw at once how pleased he was. His eyes danced
in a glaze of moisture, and she felt tears gather behind her
own lids.

His hands trembled when he skimmed the white shift up
her body, stripped it over her head, and discarded it. His
eyes worshipped her while his fingers fumbled with the ties
on her chemise and bloomers. His hands spanned her rib
cage, and she knew she never wanted anything else to touch
her there ever again . . . only Tyler's hands.

"I gave María the corset," she whispered.

He chuckled. "Poor ol' Sánchez."

Timidly, she reached to touch his bare chest. The muscles
quivered when she sifted her fingers through the silky hair.
Following her hands with her eyes, she traced his ribs, while
he bracketed himself over her, stiff-armed, forehead drooped
to hers. Her hands skimmed his waist. Then she did it. She
twirled her index finger into his navel, twisted and rolled it.
Delighted, she found his eyes, grinned, and admitted, a bit
sheepishly, "I've wanted to do that for such a long time."

He laughed, deep, full-bodied and husky, while his eyes

smoldered. "Why, Miss Madolyn Sinclair! Shame on you. What would Miss Abigail say?"

Thinking about Miss Abigail at this particular moment was ludicrous. Madolyn laughed. "Miss Abigail is in Boston, Tyler. And I'm here . . . with you . . ."

While she teased, he kicked off his britches, and by the time the words died on her lips, he had buried himself deeply into her core. "And I'm inside you, love, and dang if I don't want to stay forever."

She couldn't respond; she couldn't even take her eyes from his. She glowed like the sun at high noon. Her body hummed, her head spun in dizzying circles, and as his body filled hers, stretching and probing and thrusting, her heart filled to bursting with his love.

The force of his passion mesmerized her. She saw the power of it reflected in his desperate gaze, in the grim set to his mouth. He had filled her mind, her life, these last few months, and now his body filled hers with a driving passion, fiery, throbbing, and all-consuming. It mounted, intensified, and carried her higher and higher and higher.

Until mere moments later, he exploded inside her, filling her with a love so powerful she knew she could never live without him. She held him close, fiercely, as he had loved her.

After another few moments, he collapsed, rolled them to the side, and kissed her tenderly. His breathing came in heavy bursts. "Are you ready to say yes?"

She clung to him while the soft breeze cooled their damp skin. "I want to in the worst way."

"Not any worse than I want you to, Maddie. I'll be a good husband. I swear it. I can't promise you luxuries—"

"That doesn't matter. What if I couldn't be a good wife?"

His eyes caressed her face, while his hands stilled on her cooling skin. "No chance, love."

"But I don't know how. I mean . . . I've never known anything except . . . I won't be submissive, Tyler."

"I don't want you to be. We'll argue some, but we'll laugh more. And we'll have love, lots of love, every day, every night, forever."

She kissed him, then grinned. "And lots of babies."

"If that's what you want, we'll have a houseful of the little critters."

The ride back to the stable was idyllic. Even facing the dangerous trip to Texas, she couldn't dredge up the slightest regret over her journey to this magical land. Indeed, since her afternoon in Tyler's arms, she felt renewed, like she might be able to overcome her fears. Like she might be able to live a normal life. A life filled with love and one perfect man.

The test would come later, after they returned to Buck. After they left this paradise. But how could he be any different there than here? He was honest, open, he didn't hide anything. How could he have a dark side? She had been with him night and day. Never once had he resorted to violence.

Oh, she didn't doubt he would defend himself, or her, should the Rurales attack. But he didn't go looking for a fight, like her father had done. He didn't blow up every time she challenged his thinking or took an opposite point of view. He actually seemed to appreciate her independent nature; he said he did. And he acted like he spoke the truth.

By the time they arrived back at the stable, the moon had come up, round and white. A beautiful full moon, a seal of approval for her decision to take a chance on love, on Tyler.

"Sonofabitch!" His oath startled her. "Who the hell . . . ?"

Madolyn followed his gaze to a plume of dust that moved swiftly away from the stable in the opposite direction. No more than the silhouette of the rider was visible in the moonlight, but that was enough.

"Rurales?" she questioned.

Tyler gave no answer. Instantly wary, he reined in and indicated that she should halt, too.

"I've got to check this out, Maddie. And I want you out of the way while I do it." She watched him glance up the stone staircase to the room they had shared the past week. All was dark, still. "Slip out of your saddle and get up those steps. Be quick and quiet."

"Are you in danger?"

"No. Now go. I'll take care of the horses."

She obeyed, never questioning, and when she gained the safety of their room, she was proud of herself. She had not questioned or argued, and she didn't feel submissive for the lack of either. She didn't light the lantern, knowing she shouldn't do so until Tyler returned. She hovered near the window, listening, watching.

In the pale moonlight, she saw him leave the horses back in the oaks. When he exited the trees, his right arm was cocked, like he carried something. *A gun.* Her heart stopped. She wanted to run down the steps, but restrained herself— her actions, not her imagination. He couldn't face danger alone. She couldn't let him.

But she must. Anything she did could— A series of shouts erupted below. Tyler. He spoke in Spanish, rapidly, angrily, words she didn't understand, except for a few, like Rurales, Sánchez, María. She had never heard him so angry. But he wasn't the only one. As though engaged in a duet, a woman's voice shouted back, giving him tit for tat, or so it sounded.

Then the woman screamed. *"¡NO! ¡Por favor, no!"* The screams continued; the woman sounded for all the world like María. Madolyn could stand by no longer. She was needed. Tyler couldn't deal with a terrified woman, angry or otherwise, and Rurales, too. She slipped out the door

and down the steps, keeping her back to the wall to elimi-
nate showing her profile. At the bottom she edged along
the adobe building in the same manner, coming at length
to the door through which Tyler had led her that night so
long ago. At least it seemed long ago.

She had been the one frightened that night. Of him. Outrageous even to think such a thing now. Not only had she
lost her fear of him, she had learned to trust and admire
him. She had always loved him, or so she felt.

Then she peered around the corner into the kitchen, and
her world was shattered by the hand of the man she loved.
In horror, she watched María recoil from an open-handed
blow to the side of her face; she fell to the stone floor,
sobbing.

But Madolyn's attention was on María's attacker. She
clutched at her chest, suddenly unable to breathe. Her gasp
drew his attention.

"Maddie!" Tyler looked as though he had seen a demon.
He rushed toward her.

She backed away but was unable to run. It had nothing
to do with submissiveness now. She was gripped by the
horror of what she had witnessed.

"Maddie, listen. It isn't like you think."

Suddenly he was the demon. She stood riveted to the
spot, while inside, her heart splintered.

"She's sleepin' with one of the Rurales—or several of
'em. That's who we saw leavin'. She brought us here on
purpose. She told them where to find us."

Madolyn struggled to keep her balance, to breathe, to
work through the haze. Her heart might be broken, but she
must force her brain to function. *Now!* "What excuse will
you use next time?" Before her tears could break loose, she
turned and fled up the stairs, conscious only of escape.

Seventeen

"No, miss, I can't rent you no room in this place." Henry Peebles, portly proprietor of the Buckhorn Hotel, stood behind his pine counter, squinting down his nose in the general direction of Madolyn, unable to meet her eyes.

She had known when she walked into the hotel, slapped her reticule on the desk, and demanded a room, that she would have a difficult time convincing Mr. Peebles to rent to her, since Morley had forbidden anyone in Horn from even speaking to her. But she had no choice. She could not remain at Goldie's one single night and retain a semblance of sanity. Not with the memories that place held. Not even if, as she feared, the women of Horn denounced her for a harlot for spending two unchaperoned weeks in the company of a man.

But the women of Horn had not condemned her. Rather, they stood behind her, a single pillar of support. Madolyn tipped her chin. "Then I shall sleep on the boardwalk, sir."

She paused to allow the proprietor to hear the gasps of these brave women. They had gathered piecemeal, after learning through the swiftly moving grapevine that she had crossed the tracks, bag and baggage, in broad-open daylight, headed for the Buckhorn Hotel. "The last few months have inured me to hardship," she added. *And to heartbreak.* Her will to fight wavered.

But behind her the women crowded near, like schoolchildren seeking the presence of a revered teacher. They wouldn't have gathered in defiance of everything their husbands believed had she not taught them to stand on their own feet. A swelling of pride struggled to replace her anguish.

One day it would, she insisted. One day she would forget all about Buck and Horn and Texas and Mexico and Morley and . . . *Yes!* She would even forget Tyler Grant. One day she would forget everything about him, except the lesson she learned in Mexico, a lesson she would pass on to other women who found themselves attacked by weapons of the heart.

"That boardwalk out yonder ain't no place for a lady to be sleepin', Miss Sinclair. An' well you know it."

"Then how about one of the benches down at the depot, where passengers on incoming trains can see how Horn, Texas, treats a lady?"

"Ladies," corrected a timid voice behind her.

Mr. Peebles's eyes bugged. "Miz Handleman? Mind what you say. Your husband's jest next door cuttin' hair—"

"I know where my husband is." The woman's voice gained strength; she took a step forward. "And I know where I am. Standing right here beside the most courageous woman in all the world." She gazed up at Madolyn with undisguised adoration. "I shall be honored to share a bench with you, Miss Sinclair."

Madolyn's heart swelled.

"And I."

"Count me in."

"Me, too."

"Ladies! Ladies!" Mr. Peebles stretched pudgy hands toward the women, as though bestowing a benediction. "No use gettin' riled—"

"We've been riled for some time now, Peebles." The voice belonged to Thelma Rider, who stood eye to eye with Madolyn, but outweighed her by a good fifty pounds.

Madolyn watched the portly proprietor of the Buckhorn Hotel fidget with the register. Before he could overturn the bottle of black ink, she interrupted him.

"All you have to do is rent me a room."

"I've got my orders, miss."

"From my brother. Nevertheless, I must have a place to stay until after Independence Day. I promise to take the first train that leaves this station after July Fourth, eastbound, that is. I have seen enough of the West, thank you. In the meantime, Mr. Peebles, all I'm asking is for a room."

"I take it you ain't full-up," Emma Butler observed.

Mr. Peebles rolled his eyes upward, toward what Madolyn knew must be a nearly empty establishment. This far from civilization and irregular as the train service was, the hotel had probably never been full one day since it opened.

"You aren't averse to making a living, are you?" Angie Thompson questioned.

"No, we are not," came a feminine reply from the back of the crowd. A slight woman with mousy brown hair topped by a yellow straw bonnet pushed to the front and stood defiantly before Henry Peebles. It was the death-blow.

"Nancy?" he mouthed, for his voice deserted him at sight of his little wife in company with the rebellious women.

"Give her room ten, Henry. It's nicer and further away from the smoky parlor." Nancy Peebles's tone could only be described as sweet.

Weapons of the heart? Miss Abigail's phrase came back to Madolyn like a slap in the face. Did women use them, too? If so, she decided, pulling her wits together, they were well justified, what with the havoc wreaked on them by the male race.

Henry shook his head. "Morley ain't gonna like it."

"I suggest you let my brother do his dirty work, Mr. Peebles," Madolyn said quietly. "Now, while I move into room ten, will you please send someone out to Morley's with word that I must speak with him immediately?"

Capitulation was difficult for Henry Peebles; Madolyn could tell that. But he turned the register to face her. "Sign here, miss. Until Independence Day, you say?"

"One week from today, sir. After which, I shall board the first eastbound train."

Taking up the key to room ten, Henry Peebles led Rolly up the stairs with the first of Madolyn's baggage. She took the private moment to thank the women.

"I appreciate your courage in standing up for me."

"We're honored to have you on our side of the tracks," Angie replied, as though prompted by her position as wife of the mayor of Horn to issue a formal welcome.

"And we're mighty glad to hear you're not runnin' out before the march."

"I wouldn't run out on my sisters." I couldn't. Even though every moment spent in this barbaric land was a moment of self-inflicted torture.

"We have a lot left to do," Constance Allen confided.

"Like coming up with that contingency plan you mentioned, Maddie. Case all else fails."

Madolyn couldn't recall ever saying anything of the sort, but then her brain had been damaged. It would recover, she vowed. "I'll put my mind to it, Emma."

"When shall we meet?" Nancy wanted to know.

"As soon as I'm unpacked."

"Where?"

Madolyn scanned the parlor of the Buckhorn Hotel. Smoking room would be a more apt term for the dimly lit area adjacent to the entrance. "If you don't mind the smoke—"

"How about our barn?" the mayor's wife whispered after a glance up the stairs. "That's where we've been painting."

"We'll have privacy to practice our songs."

"Wonderful," Madolyn agreed. "I'll meet you there."

"You're invited to my house for supper," Constance Allen told her. "We're having chicken and dumplings, if they haven't burned while I've been upholding my rights."

The other women laughed. They exited together, leaving Madolyn alone in the foyer of her brother's hotel, feeling lighter than she had in days. A dinner invitation, for heaven's sake. When she had expected condemnation, or at best disapproval. The camaraderie she had developed with these women warmed her heart.

But her warm heart quickly turned cold again once she was alone in the modest room on the second floor of the Buckhorn Hotel. The unadorned oak dresser and iron bed with its lumpy cotton-batting filled mattress couldn't compare with Goldie's carved walnut furniture and plump featherbed. With unbleached muslin curtains and bare pine flooring, austere was too fancy a term for the accommodations at the Buckhorn Hotel.

But didn't that match her life? Austere. She should never have traveled to this barbaric land. She should never have allowed Tyler Grant into her heart. She should never have crossed those railroad tracks. That had been her first mistake.

But the mistakes that followed made her first stumbling trek across the tracks look like baby steps. The mistakes that followed were the most devastating of her life. They ruined her future. Now she would be forced to live with them forever.

Forever is a long time, Tyler once said. Forever meant never.

Forever meant always.

But she would make it! She would throw herself into her work. The momentary lift she received from the support of the brave women of Horn gave her heart. She would throw herself into her work and receive strength and renewal from her sisters. One day she would forget her terrible mistake in Mexico. Her terrible mistake—trusting Tyler Grant.

Trusting any man!

She had fallen for his lies. The oldest lies in the world. And now she must pay the price. Loneliness, Goldie claimed. Already, she felt it. But for the time being, she was cursed by not being able to erase the scene at the stable from her mind. María's screams; Tyler's pleas.

"Damnation, Maddie," he had argued, "she put our lives in danger." He had never seemed larger, looming over her, his once warm brown eyes dark with emotion.

Short of breath, Madolyn could but gasp, "You struck her."

"Damn right. If she'd been a man I would've cold-cocked her."

"At least now I know you for the violent man you are."

"Violent? You want to see violence? Well, you just might. The Rurales know where the cattle are. That little wench told them. Raúl and Sánchez are with the cattle. The Rurales could kill them. They could kill us. They could kill *you.*" Sadness softened his expression. She backed away.

"You solved all that by striking this woman?"

"Hopefully. Now I know what she told them. She had refused to tell me. Damnation, Maddie, I had to know what she told them. I'm responsible for my men, for you." He stepped toward her, tentatively, as though he didn't know how to act.

"I'll thank you not to include me in your list of responsibilities, Tyler Grant, not ever again."

When he reached for her, she fled, although later she wasn't sure whether she had fled him or herself. For even then she had wanted nothing except to throw herself in his arms. Ah, the weapons of the heart. What destruction they wrought.

The Rurales hadn't killed anybody, much to Madolyn's relief. But only because she and Tyler left the stable immediately and reached the herd ahead of them.

The skirmish that followed took place by the light of the

moon. Tyler left her back in the hills well out of harm's way, with instructions not to move a hair on her head until he returned.

She had never seen him so furious. But when she said as much, he retorted.

"Damn right, I'm mad. I shouldn't have trusted that woman. I should have been suspicious when she wanted us to move to the stable. I shouldn't have trusted Sánchez. He never did have a brain where women are concerned."

During the ensuing gunplay, she had huddled in the darkness, worried, angry, heavy-hearted. When they returned, it was with few casualties. The Rurales recaptured the cattle, and they shot Raúl's horse out from under him.

"Raúl will take your horse, Maddie. You'll double with me."

It was torture of the worst kind, riding behind Tyler's saddle, forced to hold onto him to keep from falling off. But it was the only way back to Texas. She occupied her mind, or tried to, by planning her trip from Buckhorn to Boston on the very next eastbound train.

"How can I convince you?" Tyler asked once before they arrived back in Buck. "It was the only way. If I hadn't learned the truth from María, we would have lost a lot more than cattle. I'm not a violent man, Maddie."

"Convince yourself if you can," she retorted. "I'll thank you not to speak to me again."

"Then so be it. I'll count myself the lucky one. If I had to weigh and measure every single action by your unrelentin' standards, livin' with you would be a curse!"

Living without him was to be hers.

Morley didn't come at her first summons, but Madolyn was so busy she didn't have time to worry about it. She had but a week to get the women ready for their big demonstration. They worked long into the night, practicing songs, painting signs. She instructed them on how to walk, how to look, what to expect from the onlookers—their husbands. It took her mind off Tyler.

In part, it did. She was good at controlling her mind; she had learned early and well. And it took all her knowledge, experience, and training to keep his overwhelming presence out of her thoughts moment by moment, day by miserable day.

The nights were her downfall. She came to dread the few hours left to her for sleep. For in sleep, she dreamed. And her dreams were filled with Tyler. In her dreams she relived everything they had done together and many things they had not.

They made love on the cushiony bed in his dugout. And she awoke on the Buckhorn Hotel's lumpy batting-filled mattress, alone and lonely, the way Goldie had predicted.

She dreamed about Mexico—the adobe hacienda was new and she was its mistress and he was her hero. She awoke to the grim reality that he was, in truth, the villain in her life's story.

She dreamed that they bathed together in the icy little stream. Afterwards they made love on the rock with the breeze drying their bodies while the heat of their love consumed them. And she awoke alone and lonely.

In her dreams he was her lover, her protector, her life.

In the harsh cold light of day, he was to become her nemesis. She could not leave this barbaric land soon enough. She prayed that when she did, she could leave his presence behind. She worried that that might be the hardest of all.

The Independence Day march was fast approaching, and no word from Morley. She was certain that Morley had run away from their abusive home. But, as was too often the case, he had become like the father he hated, and she must stop that. For the sake of Carlita and the children, and for Morley's sake.

Two days before the march, when he still hadn't arrived, she resorted to a fabrication. She sent him word that she was ill. She hated to lie, especially after rebuking Tyler for doing so. But this was different, she reasoned. She must talk to her brother before she left this country, and she could think of no other way to persuade him to come to town.

It occurred to her that she could march over to the livery, hire a rig, and ride out there. By moving from Goldie's to the Buckhorn Hotel, she had effectively put an end to the hogwash of not being able to cross the railroad tracks. If she dared, she could come and go between the two towns as she pleased. Yes, she could walk to the livery and hire a rig and ride out to Morley's. In fact, since her experience in Mexico, she could ride a horse. But she had never been successful at talking to Morley at the ranch. Perhaps in town, she would have better luck.

Besides, she was reluctant to venture into the country again. It reminded her of Tyler even more than the Buck side of town did. He was a part of it, this country, and for a brief time she had been, too.

So, two days before the march, she sent word to Morley that she had contracted some dreadful disease in Mexico and would he come to see her one last time. As an added touch, she asked to be buried in the Buckhorn Cemetery, saying she wanted to go to her final rest in a place where her beloved nieces and nephews could care for her into perpetuity.

In truth, she never wanted to see Buckhorn, Texas, again, alive or dead. Her last sight of it would be from the window of a passenger car headed east. She certainly did not want to have to look down on it from heaven above.

But by the time she awoke on Independence Day morning, Morley still hadn't arrived. Dismally, she knew she shouldn't expect him. Although the demonstration wasn't scheduled to begin until just before noon, she dressed quickly, twisting her hair into a tight knot.

Already celebratory shouts and laughter filtered through her windows, making her doubly eager to spend this day outside. It would be her last. After today, she would not venture outside the hotel again until she boarded a train bound for Boston.

She wasn't concerned about running into Tyler today. He knew about the demonstration, and he could be no more eager to see her, than she, him. But after today, if they succeeded in rejoining the town, he would be allowed to cross the tracks at will. So after today, she would stay indoors. She could not, would not, chance meeting him on the street. His presence in her dreams was hard enough to bear.

Then as she watched the growing number of revelers from her window, her hands stilled on the black straw bonnet she had but lifted to her head. There he was.

Morley. Seeing him, her heart lurched, for he reminded her of Tyler. Which was absurd, since they looked nothing alike. But they were alike. In one momentous way they were exactly alike—they were the only two people on earth she had ever loved. Truly, truly loved.

Her last image of Tyler was burned into her brain. He left her on the back steps of Goldie's, after she refused to allow him to accompany her upstairs.

"Well, Maddie, I guess this is it."

She struggled to hold back her tears, now, recalling how hard it had been to keep from crying then. She was so full of them, of the sadness and the already-creeping loneliness, that she hadn't dared reply. Instead, she turned and fled up the steps. Where he had gone, what he had done, she didn't know. To prevent hearing his name, she moved to the Buckhorn Hotel that very afternoon.

The move hadn't prevented her wondering where he was, though, whether he was in his dugout, whether he had returned to Mexico to recapture his cattle. She tried not to worry about him. But María had betrayed them once. Would someone else betray him? Would he die down there and she never know?

It had occurred to her one morning upon dragging herself out of a stupor induced by an unusually poignant dream that she didn't know anything about him. Not really. They had never discussed Susan, and why her death had devastated him. She didn't know where he grew up, where he went to school, whether he had brothers or sisters or aunts—

She didn't know anything about him except that he could be tender and selfless and passionate—and that she loved him.

Dismally, she realized that she would always love him. Whether she was buried in Buckhorn or Boston, she would go to her grave loving Tyler Grant.

"You don't look all that sickly," Morley accused when she opened the door to him. "Figured you was pullin' some sort of stunt, after what happened in Mexico."

Her heart lurched. "What happened in Mexico?" she echoed. Had Tyler revealed intimacies that should never have happened in the first place? Before Morley could say more, she charged ahead. "Whatever happened—everything that happened—it's your fault. If you hadn't left me out there . . ."

"Whoa, now, Maddie."

He sounded so much like Tyler, it startled her. She regained quickly. "I apologize for the fabrication, Morley. But the truth is, I had to talk to you, and I knew you wouldn't come just to talk. I'm flattered that you would come to see me on my deathbed. Even if you did wait until time was short." Picking up the timepiece from her dresser, she flipped it open.

"Papa's?" Morley's tone was harsh.

She glanced up to see him lost in thought. "I keep it to

remind me that men are no damned good." She should have
consulted it more in recent weeks, she thought, angry with
herself. "That's what I want to talk to you about."

"No need bringin' up that inheritance again, Maddie. I
haven't changed my mind, an' I'm not fixin' to. I'm prepared to pay your way to Boston, though, if you still want
to go—"

"If I still want to go? Why shouldn't I want to return
to . . . to civilization?"

"Love sometimes civilizes the most heathen place."

"Love?" *A lecture on love from Morley?* Regrouping, she
turned away, lest he see the truth. "Yes, I want to return to
Boston, but that isn't what I called you into town to discuss.
In Mexico, Tyler brought up something that—"

"I'm not here to listen to Tyler Grant's—"

She swirled on him. "Damn you, Morley, shut up and
listen. I'm talking about you. And me. And Mama and
Papa."

His face turned florid. "I refuse to talk about that, any
of it, especially that damned old man. If there's nothin' else
on your mind, I'll wish you a safe trip."

She ran to the door, flattened her back against it, as
though she could hold him in the room by sheer force.
"There is more, Morley. I know now why you left home."

"Bully for you."

"Tyler said it first. He said my fear of marriage stems
from the same thing that drove you away from Boston."

"What's he settin' himself up like, some goddamn fortune
teller?" But the color had drained from his face.

"He's right, Morley. Papa was a mean, hateful, violent
old man. He always was. That's why you left."

He glared at her. She rushed ahead, desperate to say what
was on her mind before he set her aside and charged out
of her life. Again.

"Papa told me you died at sea. I was heartbroken. You
left me alone, all alone in that house with him . . . and

with her. I couldn't stop crying. So, he told me you died at sea. That a sailor brought word. Do you know what I did? I went to the docks everyday, rain, snow, sleet. I went and stood there and looked out at sea and cried. I loved you with all my heart. You were all I ever had—the only person I ever loved or who ever loved me. And you left me all alone."

"Damnation, Maddie!" He turned away. "You couldn't expect me to've stayed around."

"You could have said good-bye. You could have told me where you were going. You could have written."

"I did."

"Once. Papa hid the letter. I found it in the lockbox after he died. Three months ago, Morley. That was the first time I knew you were alive. Three months ago."

Morley's arms went slack. He turned back to the room, crossed to the window, stared out at his town. "I'm sorry, Maddie. I'm really sorry. I didn't know they told you that. I knew you'd worry. I hated to leave you there. But hell . . ." He paused, drew a deep breath. "I was only sixteen. I couldn't have taken care of you. I could barely take care of myself. And I couldn't take it any longer. That may sound weak, but it's God's own truth. I couldn't take it. I'd have ended up killin' him."

"What about Mama? She had to take it year after year."

When he turned, she could tell the fight had gone out of him. He looked more like her brother than he had since she arrived. "It was her choice," he said.

"You can't believe that. He broke her body and her spirit. She didn't want that."

"Then why wouldn't she leave? Tell me that, Maddie. Why wouldn't she leave?"

"She couldn't."

"She could have. I offered to help; I begged her to leave."

Madolyn felt as though someone had struck her between the shoulders, knocking the air out of her lungs. "When?"

"First time was before I left. I begged her to come with me, to bring you and come with me. Together, we could have made it. But she wouldn't. Said it wouldn't be right to leave him; it wouldn't be right to take you away from your home."

"My home?" The words quivered out.

Morley slumped to the edge of the bed, where he sat with elbows propped on his knees. He stared at the bare pine floor. "I tried again after Grant and I settled here. I sent her money in care of Grandmother Sewell, so the old man wouldn't know about it. I sent directions and enough money for the two of you to come out here and live with me. But do you know what she did? She sent the money back, thankin' me, but sayin' she was fine, that things had worked out, and that you were fine, too."

Madolyn sank to the bed beside him. "If only I had known."

"What could you have done? She wouldn't have listened to you, either."

"I could have left before I became a miserable old maid."

Slipping to his knees, Morley knelt before her. He crossed big callused hands over her lap and peered into her face. When she looked in his eyes, she saw her brother—concerned, loving, sharing her shame and agony. Sharing, at last, after all these years of bearing it alone.

"Oh, Morley, isn't it terrible? Look what he's done to us."

"To you, little girl." He used the appellation he had teased her with so many years before. She'd hated it, then, insisting she wasn't little. And she grew up to prove that point. "He didn't do nothin' to me," Morley added.

"Yes, he did. You're like him in so many ways. You can't call him father; well, your children don't call you father. I don't know whether you beat Carlita, but she's as submissive as Mama. You married your mother, and you treat her like Papa—"

"It's different. Their culture's different, damn it."

She squeezed his hands. "You could have changed that. You, of all people, know what she needs—respect and kindness . . . and your name. Obviously you love her. Why else would you have stayed with her fourteen years and fathered six children?"

"There're other reasons for a man and woman—"

"I lived at the House of Negotiable Love, Morley. I'm aware of the reasons men and women . . ." Regrouping, she returned to the topic at hand. "If you didn't love Carlita, you wouldn't keep her around. And since you do, for her sake, for the children's sake, and for your sake, you must marry her."

Morley shook his head. "Grant's right, you're one meddlin' female."

"I'm also right."

"Maybe."

"Maybe? Now, there's progress. But the truth is, I don't have time to bring out the best in you. You'll have to do it yourself. I don't want to leave until you've come to grips with things, but if you don't hurry, I might have to."

"What're you leavin' for?"

"I . . . I have a life back there."

"Some life. No family. No home. No one to love."

"I have the women at the center."

"I don't reckon you've taken to sleepin' with 'em."

"Morley!"

"Likely you won't get half the pleasure out of marchin' around town with a bunch of spinsters shoutin' things like 'Down with men!' as you would snugglin' up to Tyler Grant."

"Morley!"

"Go ahead, Maddie, work yourself into a righteous rage, but you can't deny the truth."

"I shall never give up my work for women's rights. I'll thank you to remember that."

"Okay, okay." He grinned. "Just thought I'd give you a little of the tongue-lashin' you've been givin' me."

"Oh, Morley." She swiped at the tears running down her cheeks. "I didn't come out here to meddle in your business."

"I know, little girl. Come here." He pulled her into his arms and she sobbed against his chest; Morley, her brother who had always consoled her, dried her tears.

She was no longer a little girl. She was a grown woman, a spinster. And he was right, she did love to snuggle up to Tyler . . . and so much more. If only . . .

"You weren't really meddlin'," Morley was saying. "Like you said, we're your family." He pulled her back and wiped her tears with the rough pads of his thumbs. "And you're our family. Carlita and the kids, well, they think you hung the moon."

She grinned.

"And there's another feller aroun' somewhere who feels the same way, 'less I miss my guess. Bad as I hate to admit it, he'd make a hell of a good husband for my baby sister."

"Oh, Morley." The tears flowed again.

"He asked you, didn't he?"

She nodded.

"And you're runnin' away. Why?"

"Why? After what we know about marriage, how can you ask?"

"So, marriage is all right for me an' Carlita, but not for you. That doesn't make one damned bit of sense."

"You and Carlita have a houseful of children. I don't." Not yet, she thought; pray God, she wasn't carrying Tyler's baby.

"Maddie, Maddie, don't run away from life. That man has it bad for you. I saw that when he came out there and cold-cocked me for not gettin' your inheritance."

"There you go. There's your answer. He's violent."

"Hell, Maddie, he's no more violent than the next man."

"I know what the next man does, thank you, and I don't want any part of it. Besides, he came out there to get 'Pache Prancer. Don't try to make things what they aren't."

"You're wrong about that. He came to confront me about bein' so hard on you. And I have been. And I'm sorry."

She smiled, wanly.

"Seein' you tore me in two, Maddie. I wanted to take you in and make you a part of my family and never let you go. But I was scared, little girl. Scared to death of relivin' the past."

"That's how I feel, Morley. Now you understand."

"I understand, but I'll still say you're dead wrong about Grant. He's in love with you, Maddie. You oughta marry him."

"I can't," she repeated, wishing all the time that she could. "In Mexico, I saw . . . I saw him slap a woman. He knocked her to the ground and she screamed." The memory was still the clearest of any in her mind, and the most terrifying. It was raw, like a new wound, and she feared it would never heal.

"Musta had a damned good reason," Morley was saying.

"Spoken like a true man."

"Hell, Maddie, cut us some slack, will you? In straightforward terms, why did Grant slap that woman?"

"She . . . she told the Rurales where we were."

Morley's green eyes hardened. "You're holdin' that against him? The wench deserved more'n a slap."

"Tyler said, uh, he didn't slap her because she did it; it was . . . she wouldn't tell him what she told the Rurales and—"

"You don't understand that? You'd have to be a dunce not—"

"I understand, Morley. But I'm scared. Too scared to take a chance that he might be . . . like Papa."

"He isn't like that old man. I'd bet my life on it. And

you aren't like Mama. You aren't submissive, Maddie. You'd never let him get the upper hand, even if he tried."

"What if he did try? Maybe he is good, tender, kind, like he acts. But I can't—"

Morley tucked a loose curl back behind her ear. "Take a chance, little girl. That's what life's made up of, chances. Don't run away. From what I hear you're good at fightin' other folks' battles. Stand up and fight for yourself."

"I don't know . . . I can't . . ."

"At least, talk to him again," he urged. "Don't run off to Boston without tryin' again. Come on. Let me take you out there. I have a horse to get from him anyhow."

She was tempted. Oh, my, she was tempted. What she wouldn't give to see Tyler again, to look into his eyes again, to feel his arms around her. The old glow returned, just thinking about it. But, oh, the pain it would cause later.

Commotion in the street became louder. Madolyn gathered her wits. "I can't, Morley. I don't have time."

A knock at the door was followed by a feminine voice. "You ready, Maddie? Time to get over to the barn."

"Coming, Angie." She hugged Morley, then stood back and rubbed tears from her face. "Thank you for coming to town. It's so good to talk to you again."

"I've missed you, little girl. Wondered about you. Worried about you." He held her by the shoulders and grinned into her teary-eyed face. "You've made one hell of a woman, Maddie. I'm proud as can be of you."

Angie Thompson called again.

"I'd better get along, too." He snatched his Stetson off the dresser. "I've got work to do."

"On Independence Day? You should stay around and enjoy the festivities. You should have brought your family."

"They're out there," he acknowledged with a wry grin. "Biggest fit Carlita ever pitched. Wouldn't hear of not comin' to town today an' bringin' all the kids."

Madolyn took heart. "Don't you run off, either, Morley. I promise you, this is one Independence Day you will never forget."

"She's long gone." Goldie stood in the foyer tapping an impatient foot. Tyler raced down the central staircase. Maddie's rooms had been cleaned out.

"What the hell do you mean? Where'd she—"

"Moved across the tracks, lock, stock, and barrel. Into the Buckhorn Hotel. Didn't spend one night after you brought her back from wherever you'd taken her. Wanted to get as far away from you as possible, I reckon."

"She said that?"

"Didn't have to. It was written plain as day all over her face. Morley's accommodations likely aren't as fancy as mine, but at least she can go to sleep without worrying whether you're across the hall sleeping or downstairs with one of my girls."

"Damnation, Goldie. You've got to talk to her."

"Wouldn't do any good. Besides, I don't have time." She called up the stairs. "Come on, girls, we can't be late." She winked at Tyler. "We're fixin' to take our town back, hon. If you don't want to miss the fireworks, come along."

"Take my town?" But Tyler's mind wasn't on fireworks or towns. His mind was on Maddie. Had been for the better part of the week. Damnation, he couldn't get the woman off his mind. Determined to make one more attempt to talk sense to her, he had come to town, only to find her gone. Hell, it must have taken the whole town to move her and all that paraphernalia of hers. And into Morley Damn-his-hide's hotel.

Independence Day! Wasn't that what Goldie said? He hadn't even realized what day it was. Maddie was gone; that's all he knew. Except that he had to find her.

And he would. If she thought she could hide from him by crossing a set of railroad tracks, she had another think coming. It was a free country, wasn't it? Wasn't that what she was always harping about? Freedom. Independence. Well, he was free, too, and it was high time he started acting like it.

Eighteen

"Quiet, ladies! Quiet!" Madolyn shouted above the chatter of two dozen women gathered in the mayor's barn. "Form your lines," she encouraged. "Four abreast. Time to get started."

They were all there: Constance Allen, Angie Thompson, Pansy Handleman, Thelma Rider and Nancy Peebles.

"Take your places, ladies," Madolyn called again. "Everyone now. Hold hands. We shall march out singing; don't stop until we meet the ladies of Buck at the railroad tracks. And remember what I told you: We have one chance to influence those men out there; today's the day. Today's *our* day. Ready?"

"READY, MADDIE!"

"On three, then. One. Two. Three." The resounding shout raised the mayor's rafters.

"Buckhorn reunited! Reunite it now! Buckhorn . . ."

Chanting as they marched, the women followed Madolyn out into the street. In addition to shouting their slogan, they carried black parasols on which they had carefully lettered the words in white. Each lady held hers aloft.

Parasols had been Madolyn's idea. More women would march longer, she reasoned, if sheltered from the July sun. Also, the parasols would prevent them from having to look into the intimidating faces of their husbands and neighbors.

As Madolyn expected, by the time they rounded the side of the building and emerged onto the main street, a group of men had gathered. Most just gawked. Several chuckled. A few shouted wisecracks.

"Lookit, Jeb. The parasol brigade."

"Ain't never seen nothin' like it."

"Eyes front," Madolyn called, holding the parasol that Constance Allen had painted for her while she was in Mexico. "All together now. Sing it out!"

"Buckhorn reunited! Reunite it now! Buckhorn . . ."

She led the chant, ever faster and louder, until by the time they stood at the edge of the tracks, they were breathing hard. They paused to catch their breaths.

"¡Tía Maddie!" The small voice took what breath Madolyn had left. She glanced toward the boardwalk. Little Jeff stood hand in hand with his sisters and Carlita. Emotion overwhelmed her. Her composure fled. There stood the children she had thought she would never see again. Without a moment's hesitation, she dropped to her knees and held out her arms. Little Jeff broke free and raced into her embrace. His little arms grabbed her in a tight neck-hold. Tears rushed to her eyes.

"¡Donde está tio?" His innocent question tore through her heart, forcing her back to reality.

She stood, glanced behind her, embarrassed. She had stopped the entire procession, for something so personal, so . . . She squared her shoulders, glanced at Carlita. Betsy and Clara stood beside their mother. Morley and the older boys were nowhere to be seen. She wondered whether he had taken them back to the ranch to work. She hoped not. Everyone should celebrate Independence Day. She tried to stiffen her spine, but thoughts of Morley, her brother, and these children, her family, left her weak and weepy. Pride came to her aid.

Morley said he was proud of her. She hoped he was watching now. She wondered whether he would be proud of her after she reunited the town he had split apart in a fit of anger.

She beckoned Carlita. "Come. Bring the girls."

The idea took the very life out of the woman. Like a turtle hiding its head from danger, Carlita cringed into her rebozo.

"There they come," someone behind Madolyn called, drawing her attention back to the march.

"The ladies of Buck!"

"Hooray! Hooray!"

Joyous greetings rang out from both sides of the tracks. The men might sneer at this demonstration, but the women themselves—for the time being, at least—paid them no mind. All were serious, yet it was plain to see that they were enjoying every minute of it.

The women of Buck stopped on their side of the tracks, and Madolyn stood face to face with Goldie and her girls. A desperate longing lodged in her chest. Gripped by emotion, she couldn't speak. What lessons she had learned at the House of Negotiable Love! Above all, that all women are created equal. She prayed she never forgot that.

"Hidee, Miss Maddie. Hidee."

Two-Bit. Daphne.

Penny-Ante.

Goldie. Attired in the fuchsia suit she had worn to that first meeting so long ago, dyed ostrich plumes dipping helter-skelter around her painted face, Goldie's smile wavered, revealing the lack of confidence that always surfaced when the madam ventured out of her domain. Madolyn dropped Little Jeff's hand and embraced her.

Goldie pulled away, disconcerted. Color tinged her face beneath the heavy application of rouge. She patted the sides of her henna-tinted hair, which was pinned into a severe bun today. It did nothing to diminish her aura of sensuality.

"I've missed you, Goldie." Madolyn was unable to keep the words from tumbling out. She looked for Lucky, found her a couple of feet behind Goldie. "You, too, Lucky. And the girls. All of you."

Goldie recovered, tugging on her overly tight bodice. True to her nature, she spoke what was on her mind. "And Tyler? Have you missed him, too, Maddie?"

Madolyn blanched. "No . . ." The lie stuck in her throat. Goldie would have seen through it, anyway. Goldie was a wizard at seeing into one's heart.

"He misses you—"

"No. Don't say it . . ." she begged. Through gritty determination, she regained her composure. She looked around for Little Jeff and saw him clinging to Carlita's skirts.

"Come along, ladies." The position of march director came in handy. "Line up on the tracks. Mix it up. Two from Horn and two from Buck in each line."

The women complied eagerly. Goldie took the hand of Frances Arndt, the parson's wife, and they joined with Angie Thompson and Constance Allen from the Horn side; Bertie and Annie teamed with Thelma Rider and Emma Butler; Nancy Peebles and Ol' Miz Watson joined Lucky and Inez Bradford. And so it went, until the women stood like a brass band down the middle of the tracks, four abreast, more than ten rows deep.

Watching them, Madolyn strove to recapture the joy she had felt earlier with Morley, but Goldie's claim was all she could think about. Did Tyler really miss her? How did Goldie know? *Questions.*

Questions she would never ask. Could never ask. She should have known Goldie would mention Tyler. She should have prepared herself to hear his name.

But she hadn't. Wasn't still. Never would be, from the way her heart fluttered. Loretta James rushed onto the tracks.

"Sorry I'm late, Maddie. I ran into Tyler. We had to settle some things about the school."

Tyler? Lord in heaven. He was in town?

Tyler and Loretta? Loretta James, who surely had her cap

set for him. She would likely catch him, too, come fall when she returned from St. Louis. If not before she left.

If she left.

Oh, the misery of it! The sheer misery. She couldn't be gone from this place soon enough. Dredging her senses from the depths of despair, Madolyn signaled for the instruments to begin. The first few notes effectively silenced the crowd on both sides of the tracks.

"Forward, ladies!" She stepped down the center of tracks to the strains of "Shall We Gather at the River," raw and unschooled though the rendition was.

"Shall we gather at the depot," the women sang.

"Hey, Jack, that Emma playin' your tuba?"

"By damn!"

"Lookee there! That's ol' Miz Watson playin' a fiddle. Who'd've ever thunk it?"

Hearing the comments, Madolyn knew her biggest difficulty now would be to keep the women from being overcome by self-consciousness. Keep them busy, Miss Abigail advised.

"Ready, ladies! One, Two, Three . . ."

And the march began.

"Buckhorn reunited!"

To her relief, the shouts rang loud and clear.

"Reunite it now!"

She led the little band up the tracks past both depots. When they neared the bend that led to the loading pens and railroad trap, she stopped and steeled herself to finish the demonstration. Then, and only then, could she return to her room at the Buckhorn Hotel. The thought had never seemed so lonely.

"Turn around, ladies. We shall sing our way back. Sing your hearts out!" And to her gratification, the marching songs burst forth with the vigor of a camp-meeting choir.

"Were you there when they tore apart our town?"

"Goldie!" someone shouted. "Whatcha doin' in there?"

"Figurin' to improve business, Pete!" Goldie hollered back.

"Hip, hip, hooray!" came the cry of a man from Horn.

Headed east, she passed the dual depots again, determined to remain on the tracks in accordance with the communities' rules until they presented their proclamations to the two mayors.

"We've been that way, Maddie," Hattie Jasper called from behind. "Let's march plumb through town."

Madolyn hesitated. She wanted to present the proclamations first, but she hadn't seen either mayor. Since Tyler was in town, she dared not look too closely on the Buck side.

"Do you see the mayors?" she questioned Hattie without breaking stride.

Her mind remained on its own single track: Tyler Grant. She doubted he would come down during the demonstration, yet . . . Resolutely, her eyes trained straight ahead, she stepped back down the tracks with the women of both towns following.

Then, suddenly, she felt it. The awareness deep inside her. By the time it prickled on her skin, her feet had faltered. She had to force them to move down the tracks.

He was here. Like all those other times, she felt his presence. And it was the most devastating experience of all. For it told her, as nothing else could have, that she would never be free of him. Never.

Always. Whether she went to Boston or China, his presence would be with her always.

She couldn't keep from looking. Indeed, it seemed senseless not to. She spied him through the melee, as though the crowd had parted for that purpose alone. She glanced quickly away. Then back, unable to keep from it. Unable to keep from staring at him. The way he stared at her.

He lounged against the depot in the same arrogant pose that had frightened her the day she came to town, so long ago, a lifetime ago. Would she had remained frightened! Now that look, that man, fired her to her very toes. She tore her gaze away from his.

"Forward, ladies!"

"Join us, hon," Goldie called when they passed him.

"I'd better watch, Goldie. Keep an' eye on my town."

His voice trilled through her; inside, the glow leaped into flame. By sheer force of will, she managed to stiffen her spine and lead her band of determined, unsuspecting women past the depot. At the edge of town, she executed an about-face. As much as she now dreaded it, she walked to the head of the group and started them back up the tracks.

But it wasn't Tyler who awaited them between the two depots. The mayors of Buck and Horn stood shoulder to shoulder, blocking the tracks. Madolyn noted the indignation in the eyes of both men, Buster Nunn, mayor of Buck, and Clyde Thompson, mayor of Horn. Obviously they intended to defend the honor of the men of their respective towns.

Wordlessly—and self-consciously now that she knew Tyler watched from the crowd—Madolyn withdrew the two proclamations from her reticule and handed one to each mayor. Each man studied the paper he held, then glanced at his neighbor's.

"The proclamations are identical, gentlemen," she confirmed. "On this day of Independence, we, the women of Buckhorn declare our town reunited." She waved her parasol in signal for the women to make their planned march through first Buck, then Horn.

Buster Nunn stopped her. "You know the rules, Miss Sinclair."

"Residents don't cross the tracks either way," Mayor Thompson elucidated.

Madolyn gradually lowered her parasol, as if she planned to stand there and argue the point. She trained her eyes on Buster Nunn. She hoped the women remembered the tactics she had drilled them in. Sliding the mechanism of her parasol along the shaft, she closed it, then sighed in relief, at the echoing swoosh behind her. She pictured each lady sliding her own parasol closed.

"Move aside, Mayor Nunn." She kept her voice low, conversational. Miss Abigail had warned about antagonizing men in such confrontations. An antagonized male was more difficult to deal with, by a country mile.

"We are engaged in a peaceful demonstration, Your Honor, which is our right in the United States of America."

"Be that as it may, miss. I can't let you pass."

"And I, sir, shan't allow you to stand in the way of progress." She raised her parasol. "I will thank you to remove yourself from our path."

Mayor Nunn stood his ground.

"Ladies," Madolyn called, "follow me." With a slow, deliberate gesture, learned through both practice and experience, she whacked her parasol across the mayor's arm and held it there, attempting to force him aside. "Ladies," she called. "You know what to do."

Without further delay, the women spread out to either side of her, coming to a stop in the center of the tracks. Then of a sudden her decorum was shattered.

"Buster." Tyler's drawl hit her like a hammer to an anvil. "I'm agreeable to allowin' the ladies who live in Horn to travel into my town today. In the spirit of keepin' this little demonstration nonviolent."

"Nonviolent!" Involuntarily, Madolyn glared at him.

"Can't have you whackin' the good mayor with that parasol, Maddie. I, for one, know how wicked you can be with it."

Angrily, she pulled her gaze from his, lest he see how affected she was by his arrogant, humiliating presence.

After a glance at Tyler for confirmation, Buster Nunn stepped aside. The women prepared to follow Madolyn, but were stopped by another voice.

Clyde Thompson held his ground, or tried to. "You ladies from Horn best be rememberin' your place."

"Let 'em go, Clyde." Morley's voice, like Tyler's, held more humor than anger. "They'll get it out of their systems soon enough in this heat."

But Morley Sinclair didn't know his sister, nor the determination of the women from both towns who had been deprived of their freedom too long now.

"Let freedom ring!" someone shouted.

Other women took up the chorus. "Ring in the new! Ring out the old!"

"It's Independence Day!"

"Our independence!"

Madolyn stood as though rooted to the tracks. Were these two bull-headed men going to defeat her, not by stopping the demonstration, but by belittling it?

"Lead on, Maddie," one of the women urged.

To where? she wondered. These two men, the only two people she had ever loved, had made a mockery of the demonstration. They didn't deserve to have their towns reunited.

"Don't give up on us, Maddie."

"We can't quit now."

"Lead on, Maddie."

Madolyn stiffened her spine, and with it came resolve. No man in either town deserved a one of these good women. And she, Madolyn Sinclair, formerly secretary of the Boston Woman Suffrage Society, could not, would not, let them down. Her heart might be broken, but her will remained strong.

She stepped off the railroad tracks, praying she didn't look as limp and out of steam as she felt. With her first step toward Buck, memories assailed her. She recalled the first time she ever crossed these tracks and the man who had been waiting for her. She recalled the way he looked that day, his face wearing that slightly quizzical expression she had come to know meant he wanted to kiss her.

But Tyler Grant stepped toward her that day wanting more than a kiss. He greeted her with a lie on his lips. The first of more than two months' worth of lies.

When a hand touched her from behind, Madolyn flinched, but it was only Goldie. "Don't let 'em get your goat, Maddie."

"They've already gotten it, and eaten it."

"Not if you don't let 'em," Goldie insisted. "Come on, honey, let's march down to the house an' back. By then you'll have thought of something."

"I'm fresh out of ideas, except the violent variety."

"You'll think of something." And with that the madam raised her voice in an improbable song.

"Onward Christian Soldiers . . ."

Her fellow marchers didn't seem to notice the incongruity, for they joined the madam enthusiastically. Madolyn saw no recourse but to lead off down the street.

Although a few of the more curious followed along the sides, most of the populace remained at the railroad tracks. Madolyn hadn't opened her parasol, and when she made an about-face at the house, she saw that none of the others had, either.

"Open your parasols, ladies. Hold them aloft. We shan't be overcome."

"That's the spirit, Maddie." Goldie encouraged her from close at hand. Goldie, who had been such a support, such a friend. Madolyn made the mistake of looking into the madam's kohl-lined eyes. Tears rushed to her own.

She squeezed her lids.

Goldie took her arm. "Don't let him get you down, honey."

"I hate him."

"No, you don't. You love him. And he loves you. But don't let him goad you into givin' up. We need you. Every woman here needs your support. Don't let us down."

Madolyn listened and knew Goldie was right. Every

woman here deserved to win. No man in either town should be let off the hook, not after the scorn they had shown these good women. Gradually, standing there among the others, her strength began to return, and with it her fighting spirit.

"All right, ladies," she called at length. "Plan B."

That was all it took. The women dug into reticules and pockets and sleeves, withdrawing little scraps of paper, which they passed forward to Madolyn.

She held them as though they were holy, and indeed they were. Priceless, at least.

"Follow me, ladies. I think we have heard the last sneer from this crowd."

Orderliness in the ranks gave way to chaos, but it was a controlled chaos, in which the women linked arms and sang and chanted and laughed, all at once. Sisters to the end, Madolyn thought, glancing back at the lovely scene, which momentarily distracted her from her own dilemma.

She crossed the tracks and headed into Horn with never a look left or right. No sooner had she reached the Horn side, however, than a figure darted from the crowd.

"Carlita?"

"I have rights to march for, too."

Madolyn hugged her, and they marched on, arm and arm. Once Morley reached out to recapture Carlita, but she resisted and Madolyn's bosom swelled. The time had come.

Swinging a wide arc in the middle of the dusty Horn street, she headed back to the tracks. Upon drawing even with the two mayors, she halted her band with a pump of her parasol. As though she were offering a holy relic at an altar, she presented the stack of papers to Clyde Thompson, telling Buster Nunn, "You will want to peruse these, too, sir. They concern citizens on your side of Buckhorn, as well."

Mayor Thompson flipped through the stack. "What the hell is all this?"

"Read some of them aloud," Madolyn suggested. "No

need to consider them private, they will be published in the *Buckhorn News* come morning."

"You're one crazy lady," Buster chimed in. "These don't make any sense a'tall."

"What exactly do you not understand?" she quizzed in her most imperious tone.

Clyde Thompson read the top slip. "I, Nancy Peebles, pledge not to clean another hotel room until my husband demands that Morley Sinclair and Tyler Grant reunite our towns."

"Nancy?" Henry Peebles squeaked from somewhere in the crowd. *"My* Nancy?"

Buster Nunn read the next slip. "I, Frances Arndt, pledge not to prepare Sunday dinner again until my husband demands that Morley Sinclair and Tyler Grant reunite our towns."

"Frances?" the parson was heard to exclaim.

Madolyn signaled her band. "Since we are familiar with the contents, Your Honors, we shall continue our demonstration."

Before Madolyn could lead the march forward again, however, Carlita stopped her with a hand to her arm. "I wasn't able to write down my request," she said. "I will tell Morley now. In front of these witnesses."

Madolyn was stunned. One look at Morley showed him to be more so. "Now hold on a cockeyed minute, Carlita—"

But he was too late. In a soft voice that traveled only to those immediately present, Carlita made her will known. "I, Carlita Ramírez, pledge to move Morley Sinclair out of my home until we are properly married."

Morley's mouth fell open. "Married?"

"And until he promises to see our children educated."

Morley's eyes narrowed on Madolyn. "This is all your doin'."

"I know." She smiled, stepping off again. But the instant she set foot on Buck soil, Tyler intercepted her. He didn't touch her but he might as well have knocked her down, for the impact she felt.

She tilted her parasol forward, blocking eye contact. "I'll thank you to step aside, sir."

He pushed it away. "Or you'll what, Maddie? Take your parasol to me?"

"I might, indeed. These ladies will back me up."

Tyler grinned. "Just what I need. Witnesses. Listen up, ladies, gents."

Before Madolyn realized what he was doing, Tyler caught her chin and tipped it, so she had to look him in the face. She squeezed her eyes shut.

"Open your eyes, Maddie. I want you to look at me so you'll see how serious I am, when I say what I came to town to say. I love you, Maddie Sinclair."

Her eyes flew open. Gasps and snickers and a sprinkling of applause erupted around them.

"I love you. Now I've said it in front of all these witnesses. I'll never take it back—"

The women need you, she thought, furiously trying to regain her thoughts. *The women need you.* Madolyn repeated the litany, shutting out Tyler's words, his face, calling on her expert training. She could not let the women down; she must stand firm.

Acting suddenly, she sidestepped him. "Move aside, sir. We have work to do. Ladies, one, two . . ." A chorus resounded behind her, but nothing could penetrate the thundering in her head.

"Buckhorn reunited! Reunite it now! Buckhorn . . ."

By the time they left the depot behind, Madolyn was quaking. But she couldn't stop the march. Not now. Not at this crucial moment. The women depended on her. They deserved her very best. She picked up speed, led them the length of the once-united main street, past the saloons, past Goldie's, and turning, past the schoolhouse.

The schoolhouse, to which Loretta would return in the fall.

Madolyn stomped the ground so hard dust flew from beneath her swaying skirts. She shouted the slogan loud enough that she could have been shouting at Tyler.

No! No!

Yes. Lord in heaven, yes.

No. She must leave. She was afraid. She couldn't take a chance.

Yes. That's what life was made of, chances.

No.

Yes.

Rounding the depot on the opposite side, she came to a teetering stop inches from the tracks. As though directed by an unseen conductor, the chanting stopped. The women halted behind her. Around them, the crowd fell silent.

Tyler stood before her. In the middle of the tracks. Still as her heart, which had ceased to beat. Before she knew what he was about, he grabbed her in a crushing embrace.

"Are you crazy?" she mumbled. Was every humiliating battle in her life destined to be waged at this depot before a crowd of stunned citizens? Every wonderful . . .

He lowered his face; she blinked back tears. When he kissed her she felt her knees buckle.

"I love you, Maddie."

She could see it in his eyes.

"You love me, too."

Lord in heaven, she did love him so.

"I can't give you up, Maddie. I won't give you up. I'll be good to you, that's a promise. But if you can't accept that right now, look around. Look at Goldie and Lucky and Loretta and Carlita. Look at all these ladies. They love you, too. They'd skin me alive if I ever hurt you. If you can't believe me, trust them to protect you. Give me a chance, Maddie. Give me a chance to prove that I'll love and respect and protect you from harm."

She fought tears, but they were tears of release. Not the release of her fears. She sensed that, even through the dizzying swells in her brain. But she suddenly knew she had to stop fighting him, and her heart.

"I shall never give up my work . . . Tyler."

"So do it. I won't stand in your way. Hell, you can organize all the women in America, if that's what makes you happy. I'll be your strongest supporter."

She grinned, flustered. She dared not look around, for she knew the townsfolk were gaping. And the women. What were they thinking? She, Madolyn Sinclair, avowed suffragette, standing here in the middle of the street in the arms of their arch-enemy.

In the arms of the man she loved, the only man she would ever love. She felt that wonderful, warm glow spread outward.

She pulled away, her chin tipped. "You're right, Tyler, a lot of women need my help. All around the world—"

He captured her face in his hands. "Not around the world. Not in Boston, either. Right here."

"Oh, no," she said. "This battle will soon be behind us."

He rolled his eyes, then turned serious again. "This is a growin' land, Maddie." His tone was grave, sincere. As he continued, she imagined him rehearsing the speech, practicing to make it better. Was he that determined to convince her? Pride swelled to bursting inside her heart.

"The women out here need someone like you," he said. "They need your leadership, your devotion to freedom and independence, your strength." His loving eyes bore into hers. "And I need all that, too."

He kissed her then, so long and hard she felt like swooning, but this was no time to succumb to feminine impulses. When he lifted his face and gazed into her eyes, she had never felt so loved. She had never been so loved.

"I need you, Maddie. For my wife."

She had thought herself past being stunned, but when

Tyler released all but her hands and knelt before her on the railroad tracks, her head began to spin.

"Madolyn Sinclair, secretary of the Boston Woman Suffrage Society, will you marry me and spend the rest of your life tryin' to redeem my ornery soul?"

Madolyn's mouth fell open. Behind her, Carlita whispered, *"Sí, Maddie, sí."*

"Say yes, Maddie," Tyler echoed. "Please, say yes. Hell, I know it won't be easy. You a suffragette and me an ornery ol' cowpoke. But we'll make it. I love you, Maddie."

And with that, he rose and kissed her again. Right there in the middle of this divided town, surrounded by cheering men and women from both sides of the tracks.

I love you, too, Tyler. The words thundered through her head. She didn't speak them, she couldn't. Not standing in the middle of the railroad tracks, surrounded by people.

But he heard her. She watched him smile, relax, grin—a broad, wide, silly, wonderful grin. She didn't speak the words; she didn't even mouth them, but he heard. Heart to heart; mind to mind; soul to soul.

And in that instant of pure communication, she knew she had made not only the right decision, but the only decision she could ever have made. For to walk away from Tyler would have been to walk away from life itself.

Nineteen

Tipping her chin a tad higher, just to let him know it wouldn't be easy, not by a long shot, she smiled. "We'll have to discuss this later, Tyler. The ladies and I have work to do."

"Damnation, Maddie, can't you tell you've won?"

"Won?" Madolyn glanced around the gathering. Her head still spun. Her body hummed. She wanted nothing more than to be carried away from here in Tyler's arms. But she had work to do.

And she wanted to savor the moment a while longer. She didn't want to race through this magical moment; she wanted to savor it bit by bit—Tyler proclaiming his love in front of the whole town; Tyler's pledge to be good and true; Tyler's proposal.

His proposal. Her heart fairly burst. She tried to keep the smile from her lips, but knew she only partially succeeded. Some demonstration this turned out to be. The men gained the upper hand at the beginning, and now they had sealed it.

Yet, they did look somewhat sheepish, she noticed, huddled around the tracks to either side of their parasol-wielding wives.

"You won, Maddie," Tyler said again. "No use rubbin' salt in the wound."

"Spoken like a true man," she retorted. "Well, you won't get off so easily." She scanned the group, her attention focusing at length on the mayors who stood side by side, each holding a stack of ultimatums from the women of Buckhorn.

"Gentlemen," she called. "Mr. Grant says we've won. Are you prepared to meet our demands."

"This is a damned revolt," someone murmured behind Tyler.

"Just what you heathens deserve, bringin' women to the West," another man was heard to grouse. "They'll henpeck a good man 'fore he has a chanct to defend hisself."

"Well?" Madolyn questioned. "What do you say, Mayors? Those are our terms. Please don't doubt that we are prepared to back them up."

"I'll vouch for that, Buster," Tyler put in. "I'm just glad to have her on my side."

"If we find ourselves on the same side, sir, it's because you came around to my way of thinking."

Tyler laughed. That deep, rollicking laugh that started in his belly and worked its way up.

Madolyn stood a little straighter. It was all she could do to keep from laughing with him. The women had spread out behind her, however, committed to their leader and their cause.

The mayors stepped forward.

"What we want to know, Miss Sinclair, is if we side with our wives instead of with the gentlemen who own these towns, will you agree not to publish these terms in the newspaper?"

"Indeed, we will."

"Do we have your word?"

"Now, hold on a cockeyed minute, Buster—"

Madolyn placed a silencing hand on Tyler's arm. "My word, sir, is not in question. First, we must be certain you have reunited the town. I'm afraid I'll have to warn you . . . I speak for all of us, when I say *your* word is not enough."

"Not enough?"

"No, indeed. Women have been lied to and cheated and

subjugated for centuries. Please don't ask us to take your word. We have history to show us the perils of such capitulation."

"Well, now . . ." The mayors studied each other from their respective sides of the tracks.

"Guess we could shake and make up," Buster suggested with a sideways glance at Tyler.

"We could, but . . ." Clyde cast his gaze about the men on his side. Morley stepped up. His eyes were on Carlita. "Get on over here," he ordered. "No need to air our linen in public."

Madolyn reached for his daughters. "Your linen is already aired. Carlita made her demand. Are you prepared to acquiesce?"

"Acquiesce? You've picked up some mighty highfalutin words, Maddie. But yes, damnit, I'm gonna marry her."

"That wasn't all."

" 'Course I'll see those kids educated."

Madolyn persisted. "Your proposal lacked—"

Carlita interrupted her with a whispered, "Maddie, it's all right. I understand him. He puts up a big front, but he's just a soft ol' pussycat at home."

That said, however, Carlita remained right where she stood. "Thank you, Morley. As soon as the town is reunited I'll be happy to marry you."

"As soon as . . . ! You women don't give us much leeway."

"None whatsoever." Madolyn glanced from her brother to Tyler. "I believe the next move is up to the two of you."

"Us?" Tyler turned his attention to his former partner. "Like hell it is."

"Damned right, Maddie," Morley challenged. "You've gone too far this time. This fight is between Tyler and me."

"The whole town has suffered." Madolyn looked to the mayors for confirmation. "I think the men on both sides are waiting to follow your lead. Go ahead and shake hands."

"Not until I get my horse back!" Morley stormed.

"Not until you agree to pasture my cattle!" Tyler returned.

"We ain't got no middle ground, Maddie. Go ahead, reunite the damned town, but leave me out of it."

"Me, too."

"Morley," Madolyn chastised. "Not over an hour ago you told me what a fine husband Tyler would make. Are you refusing to shake hands with the man you tried so hard to convince your sister to marry?"

"He said . . ." Tyler's words sputtered to a stop. He looked to Morley then back to Madolyn. "He said what?"

"That I shouldn't run away from life, that I needed to take chances, one chance—on you."

Tyler scrutinized his former partner, as though uncertain what he was seeing. "You said all that?"

"Damn right. It's true, ain't it?"

"Of course, it's true, but . . ." Tyler squared his shoulders, winked at Madolyn, and stepped across the tracks, his hand outstretched to his future brother-in-law.

"What about 'Pache Prancer?" Morley demanded.

"You'll get her back. And I'll get my pasturage." He crooked his arm for Madolyn. "You don't think this is the end of her meddlin', do you, Morley?"

Madolyn went to him and Carlita followed. They stood in the middle of the tracks, the four of them, looking at each other and grinning. Tyler drew Madolyn to his side and she slipped an arm around his waist, there in the middle of town with citizens from both sides gathered around them.

When a cheer went up, Madolyn thought at first it was for them, for their reunion, then she heard the words.

"Lookit Bob! Take it down, son. Take it down."

And while the two ornery cowmen and the women who tamed them looked on, boys from both sides of the tracks shinned up the posts and tore down the divided station signs.

"Hip, Hip, Hooray!" came the shout. Madolyn and Tyler joined in; Carlita and Morley joined, too.

Suddenly Goldie's voice rose above the confusion. "Listen up, folks. Listen up." When she had their attention, she continued. "This is a mighty proud day for folks on both sides of these tracks. Independence Day will mean something personal to us from now on. And I know and you know that it wouldn't have happened without the fearless leadership of one person. Maddie, step up here and take your bows."

"Oh, no. We did it together."

But the women insisted loudly and Tyler pushed her forward. Holding his hand, she pulled him along, her mind reeling with the speech she was being called upon to give. What would she say? How could she thank them? She squeezed Tyler's hand.

Goldie and Morley most of all. How could she thank them for prodding her until she lost, not her fear, but her need to run away from it? And Tyler, how could she thank him for sticking by her, for not giving up on her?

Suddenly the crowd roared, as though she had just accomplished all the above and more. Tyler nudged her forward.

"Look up, Maddie."

The sight left her breathless. In place of the two divided signs a new one hung from the depot: MADOLYN, TEXAS.

"No," she breathed. "They can't."

"We can and we did," Goldie responded. "You gave us the courage to stand up for ourselves and our town. And those are lessons we don't ever want to forget."

Frances Arndt stepped up beside the madam. "So Goldie and I gathered the women and put it to them." She smiled at the new sign. "That sign will be there to remind us of the lessons we learned from you, Maddie. Day after day we can look at it and remember that you taught us how to stand on our own two feet."

Tyler pulled her close. Just before his lips captured hers, he murmured, "And I'll have *you*, Maddie Sinclair, to look at every single day for the rest of my life. And to love."

"Tia y tío, tío y tía, tía y tío . . ." Holding hands, the children skipped in a wide circle around the inside walls of the schoolhouse. The adults attending the dual wedding reception stayed out of their way, best they could.

All except one of the brides and one of the grooms. Madolyn and Tyler held hands with Little Jeff and their two little nieces and let the children of Buckhorn drag them laughing and skipping around the room. Madolyn felt a little self-conscious, true, but it was her wedding day. Couldn't she let her hair down a bit?

And after the gifts the children had brought—her eyes teared seeing them stacked on Loretta's desk along with the mound of gifts she had received from the women of Buckhorn, including the wedding-ring quilt.

That had been but one surprise among many.

"When did you finish it?" Her eyes widened when she tore away the wrapping tissue. "How did you know?"

"It was Goldie's idea," Frances Arndt explained. "She said there'd either be one wedding or a couple of funerals."

"So we decided to hope for the best and finish the quilt," Hattie Jasper put in.

Madolyn fingered the delicate stitches, the colorful interlocked rings in the design. "Unity," she whispered. "That's what the rings stand for. Unity means more than man and wife." She scanned the group of women, sisters at heart, all of them. "It will always remind me of us, and how we worked together for the good of all."

"And had a good time doin' it," Constance Allen added.

Loretta James hugged her. "I'll have to wish you luck, even if you did steal the best catch in town."

Madolyn was beside herself. From the moment they left

the depot where Pastor Arndt performed the double ceremony, her head had been spinning. She hadn't known what to concentrate on first—the animated chatter of the reunited townsfolk; the way her nieces and nephews played with their new town friends, as if they had always known how to play; the stack cake that had grown out of all proportion, since every woman in town insisted on making a layer to bring to the reception; or the way her new husband—the word took her breath away, she thought possibly it always would—stood to the side in conversation with her brother, once and always his best friend.

When she saw Morley hand Tyler the book on mail-order houses, she joined them. Tyler drew her hand into the crook of his elbow and squeezed, increasing the giddiness that had been growing inside her for the last few days.

"Figured you need it worse'n I do right now," Morley was saying. "I want the damned thing back, though." He scowled at his sister but wasn't quite able to keep a smile from his lips. "Since I just found out I paid for it. And a whole lot more besides."

When Madolyn blanched, wondering what to expect from Morley now, he laughed and drew her into a rough bear hug. "You beat the clock, little girl."

"The clock?"

"The year's not up, and look what you got."

She laughed. "A husband. Isn't that grand?"

"When things quiet down some, we'll see about gettin' that inheritance. Don't reckon we should let it go to some ol' men's club, not with the kinda ideas in your head."

She kissed him on the cheek. "Thank you, Morley. Isn't our life going to be wonderful?"

He cocked his head. "Don't know about wonderful, but with a suffragette for a sister, it's likely to be interestin'." But his voice was so loving she knew he was still proud of her.

Carlita summoned the children, then. They lined up before Madolyn, beginning with Little Clara, the youngest, who held her sister Betsy's hand.

"Para ti," Betsy said, holding out a small package wrapped in tissue paper.

"For me?"

"Y tío," Clara added.

Beckoning Tyler to join her, Madolyn knelt in a puddle of ivory lawn skirts and accepted the gift. *"Gracias."* She could hardly tear herself away from the girls' eyes to open the gift. Inside the tissue lay a doll made of sotol sticks, with yarn hair and black shoe-button eyes. It was dressed in red calico.

"Betsy made the dress," Carlita explained.

"Oh, my!" Madolyn hugged the doll, then impulsively opened her arms and gathered the girls to her bosom. "Oh, my, how could any one person be so lucky?"

Tyler had hunkered down beside her. When she released the girls, Clara threw her arms around his neck.

"Won't be a coon's age between visits anymore, little one." He winked over her black curls to Madolyn. "Think we could have us one like her?"

"Oh!" Madolyn felt her heart thrash with ecstasy and her face flush with embarrassment.

"You will make a wonderful mother," Carlita assured her.

"Oh, my." For a time she couldn't say more. "I'll need your help, Carlita. I won't know the first thing about taking care of children."

"They'll teach you," Carlita vowed. "But we will help."

The boys were next. Little Jeff and Abe had made her a vase from a dried gourd and received sound hugs in return. She rose to receive Tomás's gift, a little basket he had woven from dried grass. He even stood still for his hug, though she knew it embarrassed the ten-year-old. He'll get used to it, she thought. Now that she could hug her nieces and nephews, she intended to do it on a regular basis.

Then Jorge was standing before her, looking for all the

world like Morley had looked so long ago. *So long ago.* And there in the green eyes of her nephew she read the meaning of this day. The true meaning, for it stood before her in the recreation of her brother. The past was dead and gone. They had been given a clean slate, she and Morley, a new life. What they made of it was up to them. The past no longer had a purchase on their future.

Jorge's gift wasn't quite a surprise, yet it was. He had whittled her an object, a miniature—

"I'll be damned," Tyler laughed beside her.

She took the little wooden parasol in both hands and examined it from all sides. *"Perfecto,"* she whispered. After a moment of hesitation, she added, *"sobrino."* And he came into her arms. She hugged him hard. Nothing timid about her now.

"Tía," he mumbled when she released him. Then, as grown-up as a boy of fourteen could be, he extended a hand to Tyler. *"Tío."*

Tyler shook the boy's hand while sliding his other arm around Madolyn. Her heart was so full she feared it might burst. Never had she dreamed her life could hold so much love. Never had she dared hope her life would include such a warm and wonderful family. And this was only the beginning.

While Maddie and Carlita opened the rest of the gifts, Tyler drew Goldie aside. "Haven't had a chance to thank you for your part in all this."

"My part? Reckon I did meddle some. Don't know why. You know my views on true and lastin' love."

"You're wrong this time, Goldie."

"I hope to the Lord above I am."

"Don't worry, I'm not about to hurt her."

"For both your sakes," Goldie added. "We'd have a hell've a time puttin' Humpty Dumpty back together if that pretty little suffragette knocked you off the wall."

"There'll be a few rocky roads," Tyler conceded, "but we'll make it. Don't ever doubt that."

"I'll just have to hide and watch." She sobered. "Don't reckon we'll be seein' much of you anymore after tonight. Or of her. But I'll keep up."

"Hell, Goldie, I still have my room up at the house. Besides, we live in the same town—the one you were so dead-set on reunitin'."

"I know. But . . . well, me an' mine, we'll be confined to certain areas again, once the new wears off."

"No way. You'll be welcome . . ."

"Where? In church? At the garden socials? Truth known, I don't want to be. Socializin' with the wives would be downright bad for business."

Tyler laughed. "You have a point." Madolyn glanced around, beckoning him with a smile that showered him with sweet sensual yearnings. "Thanks again, Goldie. I owe you."

"What were you and Goldie hatching up?" Madolyn accused.

"Nothin'. I just thanked her for holdin' onto you until I managed to catch you."

Madolyn laughed. "Men! I should have known you would take credit for all this."

He leaned forward, whispered in her ear. "I'm gettin' danged anxious to take credit for a whole lot more. How much longer before we can go to the hotel?"

"The hotel?"

He rolled his eyes. "Our weddin' night, case you overlooked the most important part of this day."

"I didn't overlook it." She felt her cheeks flush. "But we can't spend it at the hotel. We have to go back to Goldie's."

"To Goldie's? You moved out."

"You still have your room," she reminded him. "The girls are counting on it, Tyler. They've gone to a lot of trouble to prepare us a honeymoon suite."

"I knew bein' married to a suffragette was goin' to be interestin'. Never figured on spendin' my weddin' night in a whorehouse, though."

"Tyler Grant, I'll thank you not to talk about Goldie that way. She's the best friend I've ever had. The most sensible one, too."

"You don't mean to say she's displaced Miss Abigail?"

Madolyn laughed, and once started, she couldn't stop. She laughed from the belly, from deep inside her, from her heart. She threw her arms around her new bridegroom and knew she was happier than she had ever dreamed possible.

Later when he lifted her into the wagon the women had decorated with paper flowers and streamers, Madolyn admonished him. "We have to go through the front door, Tyler. And up the central staircase."

Tyler grinned. Scanning the crowd, he quipped, "Guess I know who wears the pants in this family. Case I'm ever in doubt, though, I'll just ride over to the depot and take a gander at the station sign. Madolyn, Texas! Don't know of another man who lives in a town named after his wife." Stepping up beside her, he kissed her a long smacking kiss, to applause from the gathered well-wishers. "But then you're one of a kind, Maddie Grant."

Moments later he drew up in front of the house and walked her to the front door. There he stopped, turned her to face him, and kissed her, long and wet and deep and wonderful. She had just sighed for the second time, when the gaudy front screen burst open. Goldie's girls rushed out, squealing congratulations. Suddenly a voice called them from the yard.

"Mrs. Grant!"

Madolyn turned toward the sound with Tyler's arm firmly around her waist.

"Hold that pose," Price Donnell hollered. A second later, a flash blinded them.

"You set me up again, Mr. Grant," Madolyn accused,

laughing. "I'll be front-page news, same as before. On the porch of the House of Negotiable Love, surrounded by Goldie's girls."

Tyler kissed her tenderly. "Not the same as before, love. In this picture you'll be kissin' your husband." And with that he scooped her in his arms.

Penny-Ante rushed to hold the door.

"Thank you, Annie," Tyler said, as he carried Madolyn over the threshold of the house.

"Thank you, Annie." Madolyn whispered. She watched the soiled doves flock in behind them. Without breaking stride, Tyler took the stairs.

"Have fun!" Two-Bit called.

"Take off your spurs, big boy!" Dolly advised.

Gaining the second floor, Tyler chuckled. "Sorry we didn't go to the hotel?"

Madolyn snuggled her lips against his neck. "No."

"Don't break Goldie's bed down," Daphne called up.

"If he gets too rough to handle, Miss Maddie, give me a holler," offered Annie.

Tyler stepped onto the third floor. "Sorry we didn't use the back staircase?"

She laughed, so happy she couldn't bear it. "Any way you cut it, it's two flights of stairs. And, frankly, I wouldn't have missed this for the world."

"Neither would I, love." When he opened the door to his bedroom, the cloud of scented candles and perfume nearly knocked him off his feet. "Damnation, Maddie, it looks like a first-class whorehouse."

"Goldie runs an exemplary establishment," she admitted, amused at the red satin that draped the bed and the abundance of lighted candles.

"Wonder how your Miss Abigail would feel about this."

Madolyn couldn't suppress a giggle. "She would be mortified! No doubt about it."

In the end, they used her old bedchamber. The room was

barren, the air a bit stale, but the bed was made. She opened windows, while Tyler blew out the candles in his room.

"I'll take stale air over perfume any day of the week . . ." Returning, he stopped, still as death, in the doorway. "Damn, Maddie, this isn't right. You deserve to spend your weddin' night in the finest hotel."

She stood equally still. Absorbing the essence of him. His beloved presence filled her room and her life, now and forever. A shyness that she hadn't expected crept up her neck. "I wouldn't trade this room and this town and this day for any other place in the world."

When he started to shuck his black jacket, she stopped him. "Wait, let me look at you. I've hardly had time."

He grinned, self-conscious himself now, she could tell, as she perused him from top to bottom.

"Do you want to know my first impression of you? The day I arrived in town?"

"I hope I've changed your mind about all that."

She smiled, savoring his soft drawl. She could hear his love for her, in his tone, in his words. "I thought you looked like a man who belonged in a real suit."

"Time was . . ." His words drifted off. She sensed melancholy. Moving into his arms, she held him fast.

"When I moved over to Horn and thought I would never see you again, I realized that I didn't know anything about you, about your life, your past. It devastated me. Now we have all the time in the world."

He kissed the top of her head.

"But let's save it for another day."

"My thoughts, exactly, Mrs. Grant." He drew her back, ran a hand down the fine needlework on the yoke of her wedding gown.

"I should have bought you a new gown."

"You don't like this one?"

"Hell, Maddie, you'd be beautiful in a flour sack. But Goldie's weddin' dress?"

Beautiful? Her? Probably not. But how utterly wonderful that he thought so. "It's too beautiful a dress to waste. It didn't work for her, so it deserves a second chance." She glanced to the bed where it had all begun, and where now they could start anew. She lifted her arms to him. "The best part is that we have another chance."

And they took it. Shedding clothes, falling into each other's arms, giving and taking, in haste and impatience, in long savoring slowness and mind-boggling tenderness, savoring their limitless passion.

"Say it, Maddie," he encouraged once. "What you were thinking out there at the railroad tracks."

She didn't have to ask what he meant; neither did she hesitate, except to clasp his face in her hands and kiss him tenderly and gaze deeply into his warm brown eyes.

"I love you, Tyler."

"Is it such a horr—?"

She kissed him, deeply like he kissed her; deeply, like he loved her; like she loved him.

"In our case, love is the most wonderful word ever invented." And throughout the long night, she showed him time and time again how wonderful it was—how wonderful he was.

Before drifting off to sleep, she pulled him closer. "No one can ever say this is no place for a lady now."

Nudging her face up, he studied her beloved features, her sensuously tangled hair, her puffy lips and begging green eyes.

"You've proved that, my love." In a fluid motion, he moved himself over her, spraddled her with his legs, and sat back on his heels, studying her by the flickering candlelight. "And I don't mean just the town. You're every inch a lady . . ."

Speaking, his hands left her face and swept at a snail's pace down her body. He lingered on her breasts, at her waist, on her taut belly. She glowed from the touch of his hands, from the fire in his eyes. Then he lowered himself, entering her with the same agonizing slowness as before, and she felt for the hundredth time today that she might burst from all the joy that filled her heart. And her life.

". . . and you damned sure belong here," he whispered, filling her body deeply, joyously. ". . . here in my bed, in my heart, in my life every night and every day for as long as we live."

From the Author's Notebook

adiós   Good-bye

agave   A thorny bush of the amaryllis fam-
                   ily. Once in this plant's lifetime a
                   spike of waxy white blossoms lifts
                   from the center of its cluster of
                   thorny, blade-like leaves; after
                   blooming, the plant dies; by-products
                   are the liquors mescal, pulque, te-
                   quila; fibers for baskets and ropes;
                   and a substance Indians have long
                   used for soap.

agrita   A small thorny bush with holly-like
                   leaves and red berries that make a
                   clear tart jelly.

ahora   Spanish for "now"

aloe vera   A plant whose succulent leaves fur-
                   nish a substance used in medicine
                   and cosmetics

alto   Spanish for "stop"

basque   Fitted bodice on a woman's dress.

bienvenida   Spanish for "welcome"

buenas noches   Spanish for "good night"

cabrito   Spanish for "young goat" (in English,
                   a kid); generally refers to a dish pre-

	pared by roasting, broiling, or boiling the meat
café	Spanish for "coffee"
carne guisado	In Spanish, a thin stew, made with beef
chingaba	Anglicized swear word
cholla	A species of cacti that grows into a small multi-branched tree
cold-cocked	Western colloquial expression meaning "knocked out"
cup towel	Texan's term for dish or tea towel
de nada	Spanish meaning "don't mention it" literally, "for nothing"
dip cattle	A method used to treat diseased cattle by swimming them through a "dipping vat" built usually of rock and filled with disinfectant.
donde está	Spanish for "where is [it]"
duckins	Men's trousers made of a heavy cotton fabric called duck, worn in the West before Mr. Levi invented denim.
dust devil	Small whirlwind
El Capitán	A peak in the Guadalupe Range in the Trans-Pecos region of Texas. At 8,085 feet above the sea, 2,000 of which forms an imposing sheer cliff that can be seen fifty miles away, El Capitán is the eighth highest peak in Texas.
es	Spanish for "[it] is"
fishplate	In railroading, a steel plate joining rails
gracias	Spanish for "thank you"
gyp water	water saturated with gypsum; many creeks and rivers in cow country are full of gypsum or other alkaline salts.

hablas español	Spanish for "[you] speak Spanish"
hermosa	Spanish for "beautiful"
hola	Spanish for "hello"
jefe	Spanish for "chief"
madrone	The Texas madrone tree, found only in the Trans-Pecos region, has a slick trunk, limbs of varying hues of red, glossy green leaves, white blossoms, and edible red berries. An endangered species
mi	Spanish for "my"
muy bien	Spanish for "very well"
no puede pas—	Spanish for "you cannot go"
para ti	Spanish for "for you"
pero	Spanish for "but"
qué pasa	Spanish for "what's happening"
quantos años	Spanish for "how old [are you]"; literally, "how many years"
railroad trap	A pen near a railroad used for holding and loading cattle
rebozo	In Spanish, a woman's shawl made of wool, cotton, or silk, worn about the shoulders, sometimes covering the head
sí	Spanish for "yes"
serape	In Spanish, a man's cloak made by slitting the center of a heavy woolen or cotton shawl to fit over the head
siete	In Spanish, the number seven
sobrino	Spanish for "nephew" (*sobrina* = niece)
sotol	A plant similar to the agave in appearance, sotol belongs to the lily family. The liquor mescal is made from its sugary center, which also makes good cattle feed.
Spanish dagger	A term usually applied to the yucca

plant, sometimes to sotols and agaves, too. Thorns at the tips of yucca leaves are strong enough to be used for needles. With skill one is able to break off a thorn and peel away a long attached strand of fiber, producing a needle and thread in one piece.

tía Spanish for "aunt" (*tío* = uncle)

tu Spanish for "you"

ven Spanish for "come"

wedding-ring collar On a lady's dress, a banded collar that encircles her neck like a wedding band.

wedding-ring quilt A quilt pattern made by repetitively interlocking two rings of colorful patches, symbolizing the unity of marriage.

TODAY'S HOTTEST READS
ARE TOMORROW'S SUPERSTARS

VICTORY'S WOMAN (4484, $4.50)
by Gretchen Genet
Andrew—the carefree soldier who sought glory on the battlefield, and returned a shattered man . . . Niall—the legendary frontiersman and a former Shawnee captive, tormented by his past . . . Roger—the troubled youth, who would rise up to claim a shocking legacy . . . and Clarice—the passionate beauty bound by one man, and hopelessly in love with another. Set against the backdrop of the American revolution, three men fight for their heritage—and one woman is destined to change all their lives forever!

FORBIDDEN (4488, $4.99)
by Jo Beverley
While fleeing from her brothers, who are attempting to sell her into a loveless marriage, Serena Riverton accepts a carriage ride from a stranger—who is the handsomest man she has ever seen. Lord Middlethorpe, himself, is actually contemplating marriage to a dull daughter of the aristocracy, when he encounters the breathtaking Serena. She arouses him as no woman ever has. And after a night of thrilling intimacy—a forbidden liaison—Serena must choose between a lady's place and a woman's passion!

WINDS OF DESTINY (4489, $4.99)
by Victoria Thompson
Becky Tate is a half-breed outcast—branded by her Comanche heritage. Then she meets a rugged stranger who awakens her heart to the magic and mystery of passion. Hiding a desperate past, Texas Ranger Clint Masterson has ridden into cattle country to bring peace to a divided land. But a greater battle rages inside him when he dares to desire the beautiful Becky!

WILDEST HEART (4456, $4.99)
by Virginia Brown
Maggie Malone had come to cattle country to forge her future as a healer. Now she was faced by Devon Conrad, an outlaw wounded body and soul by his shadowy past . . . whose eyes blazed with fury even as his burning caress sent her spiraling with desire. They came together in a Texas town about to explode in sin and scandal. Danger was their destiny—and there was nothing they wouldn't dare for love!